RACHEL L. SCHADE

SILENT KINGDOM SERIES
BOOK 1

RACHEL L. SCHADE

Silent Kingdom

SILENT KINGDOM SERIES
BOOK 1

DRAGON SHADOW
PUBLISHING

Cover design by Chicklen.Doodle and MiblArt

Map by MoorBooks Design

ISBN 978-1-7364856-8-2

www.rachelschadeauthor.com

For my parents, who never stopped giving.
Until we meet again.

OTHER BOOKS BY RACHEL L. SCHADE

Silent Kingdom Series

Silent Kingdom (Book 1)

Forsaken Kingdom (Book 2)

Broken Kingdom (Book 3)

Cursed Empire Series

Empire of Dragons (Book 1)

Empire of Traitors (Book 2)

Empire of Monsters (Book 3)

Empire of Ruins (Book 4)

PRONUNCIATION GUIDE

Characters

Halia (HAY-lee-uh)
Zarev (ZAIR-ev)
Avrik (A-vrik)
Velaire (VUHL-air)
Narek (NAIR-ek)
Kyrin (KIE-rin)
Lyanna (LIE-an-uh)
Elena (ELL-in-uh)

Locations

Misroth (MIZ-roth),
Misrothian (Miz-ROW-thee-un)
Vorvinia (Vor-VIN-yuh),
Vorvinian (Vor-VIN-yun)
Argelon (AR-guh-lawn)

Other

Felwe (FELL-way)
Azlin (A-zlin)
Vehgar (VAY-gar)

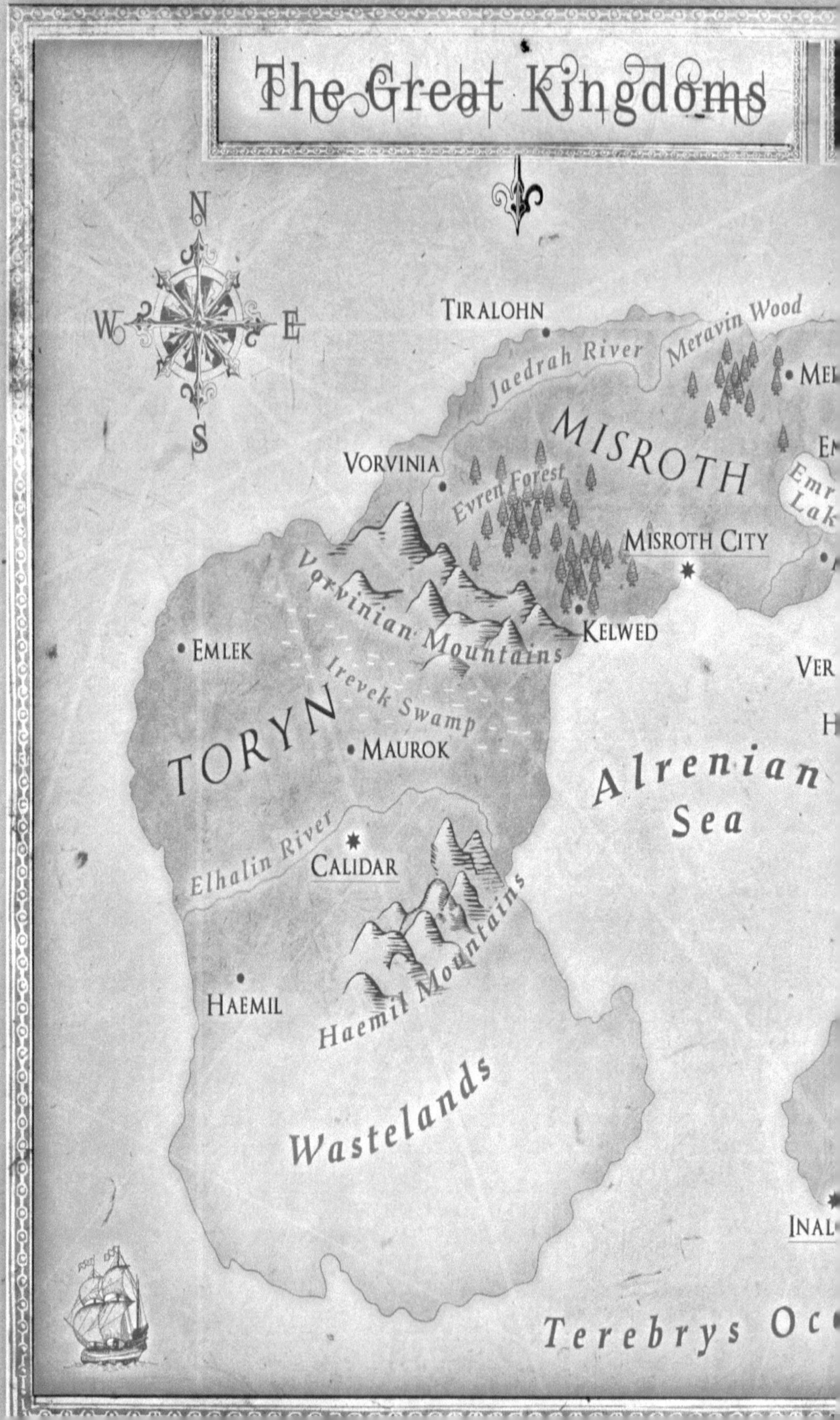

The Great Kingdoms
N
W
E
S
TIRALOHN
Jaedrah River
Meravin Wood
MEL
MISROTH
VORVINIA
Evren Forest
Emr Lak
MISROTH CITY
Vorvinian Mountains
KELWED
EMLEK
VER
Irevek Swamp
TORYN
MAUROK
Alrenian Sea
H
Elhalin River
CALIDAR
Haemit Mountains
HAEMIL
Wastelands
INAL
Terebrys Oc

he Lesser Kingdoms
Hült Mountains
HÜLTEN
Shüldi River
BREVINN
Brevi Mountains
Great Sea
Wild Lands
mrell River
ON
Kyvok River
Brema Wood
ALRENOR
ARAMITH
Brema River
Aramith Mountains
Forest
RHAEDA
Silondrian Mountains
FORWYTH
TERAMYL
VICIDOR
Maelvoc Forest
Xelrios River
Tuiros River

CHAPTER ONE

I WAS THIRTEEN WHEN THE truth first revealed itself to me.

It happened on a day usually set aside for celebration in Misroth, now weighed down by the loss of our king. The air felt heavy and still under the grey afternoon sky as I walked amidst the coronation procession. All around me, councilmen strode silently, their cloaks swirling about their legs, their boots thudding a steady rhythm along the cobblestone streets of the capital. Arrayed in elaborate scarlet and blue, the King's Guard formed a protective barrier around the procession's outer edges, as if they could save my family from the pain that had already taken residence in our hearts. Even in the dim light, the guards' steel armor glinted. I watched them in awe, for I had never seen them in anything other than their everyday chainmail and leather breastplates, and they looked ready for battle.

Before me, my mother and father walked with their heads held high. Mother's long, dark hair was plaited delicately and her emerald green dress was so long it trailed along the street behind her. Father kept his grey eyes focused on the crowds around us, nodding to citizens as we passed. He had warned our family that we should not let this dark time steal our dignity, and had reminded us that tears were for the weak.

To my shame, my vision blurred with tears anyway. *Perhaps I'll always disappoint Father.* I blinked them away hastily and turned to my cousin Gillen, who trudged beside me. His golden, shoulder-length hair tousled in the wind and fell into his face when he hung his head. I knew he was trying to hide his eyes, which were usually bright, but today were swollen and red.

I reached out and gave his arm a reassuring squeeze, wishing I could lend the last shreds of my strength to him.

"Thank you, Lia," he muttered for only me to hear. "This is not a day I feel strong."

But he had to be. One day he would be our new king. I opened my mouth to murmur something comforting but choked on my words. *He is healed now. We will see him again.* What nonsense. The words were all hollow and brittle, crumbling as soon as I thought them. Gillen didn't want to hear them, and neither did I. Frowning at my feet, I clamped my mouth shut.

Drawing a deep breath, I dared to raise my gaze to study the rows of citizens lining the streets. Their faces were solemn and their eyes seemed to reflect my own fears: fear of change, fear of the pain and death we had witnessed. This was no joyous coronation procession, not when it followed a funeral. We had left grieving citizens and my weeping aunt at her husband's graveside to wind our way through the wide streets of Misroth City, past the towering stone buildings and houses. There were no cheers or fists raised to hearts in salute; no ribbons were waved, and no songs were sung. Throughout the city, a heavy silence hung in the air.

We halted in the main square, surrounded by shops closed for business today, and stood, hushed, as my father approached the waiting priest, who stood in the center of the square before a marble statue of King Eldon. Beside the priest, a solitary Royal Guard stood bearing Misroth's banner, adorned with the stars of the dragon constellation, Vehgar. Father's velvet robes, midnight blue and trimmed in silver, trailed along the cobblestones behind him. Dressed all in red, the royal priest stood tall and solemn, his dark face masked by the large hood he wore. His cloak billowed about him, but he was motionless.

"Today is a day of many emotions," the priest announced. In the stillness, his voice was startlingly loud, echoing off the buildings around us. "We grieve the passing of our beloved King Reylon. Together, we mourn the loss his family feels. But we have hope and comfort in this dark time. We know the Giver of Life has carried our king to another, better place, and King Reylon's brave brother, Zarev, stands before us willing to accept the throne until King Reylon's son Gillen is of age. Misroth will not be leaderless."

Lifting his arms, the priest began to sing an ancient blessing over my father. The words were in Alrenian, a language no longer understood in our kingdom, but the meanings of the old songs were still remembered, passed down from generation to generation. This was a traditional coronation blessing, asking the Giver of Strength to equip my father for the task before him.

O bren valt hali,
O bren valt mis.
Mari, O emba l'val.
Thero, yagen sem forith.
Thero, yagen sem mis.
Thero, val re rynnet...

All around me, heads bowed in reverence. It seemed as if others felt comforted by the priest's words, but I felt numb. I didn't want to be the daughter of a king, even a king regent. I didn't want to return to a home bereft of my uncle's kindly smile or his exciting stories shared with Gillen and me by the fireside.

My armband of mourning was constricting, and I wanted to rip it off. Why would the Life-Giver bring us death?

I was startled out of my reverie by my father's voice, repeating a pledge before the Misrothian people and the Giver as he accepted kingship. The priest's and my father's voices trailed on, alternating as the priest spoke and my father recited the words.

"I vow to protect my kingdom with my own blood, to dedicate my service to the Giver of Life and to Misroth..."

"My father was supposed to live a long life," Gillen whispered, his countenance still a picture of shock. "Not leave me to rule as soon as I am eighteen. That's four years from now," he choked out.

Grasping Gillen's cold hand in mine, I bowed my head, knowing nothing I said would help my cousin.

"…and, if circumstances demand it, to give my own life for Misroth."

My father rose, the king's silver crown contrasting with his long dark hair as he faced the crowd. His voice was steady and confident. "…and, if circumstances demand it, to give my own life for Misroth."

As the priest called my mother forth to declare her own pledge as queen, I wished for something to say, anything to ease Gillen's pain.

If only I'd known how dangerous words can be.

The dining hall felt too empty with my uncle gone and my aunt and cousin absent, having retired early for the evening. Shadows curled about the ornately carved wooden pillars lining the sides of the space. I glanced up toward the vaulted ceiling, too high in the dim evening light for me to see. The room was too vast, too empty—a great cavernous expanse being slowly swallowed by the gathering darkness.

I shuddered and remained silent while my parents, seated together at the far end of the table, discussed the day's events. Their eyes flashed from the glow of the fire set in the grand marble hearth behind them.

"Reylon was ill a long time, but his death was still a shock," Mother murmured. "The people…they will take some time to adjust to having you as king regent."

At that moment two servants entered the dining room, bearing trays of food, and my parents' conversation paused. When one of the servants set a plate before me, the scent made me scrunch my nose as nausea danced along my tongue. Normally the aroma of boiled lobster, steamed carrots, and sugared apples would have made my empty stomach growl in anticipation. Instead I sighed, poking at the meat and sliding the vegetables around on my plate. I stared listlessly at my glass, but the sweet, bubbly agma juice, harvested from berries native to our kingdom, held no interest for me tonight. No matter how hungry I was, I knew as soon as any food touched my mouth it would threaten to come back out again.

My sorrow chewed on my insides as relentlessly as my hunger did.

Father cast a curious glance from the servants to his wife. "Two servants tonight?" he asked.

Mother lowered her fork to speak. "I ordered the staff to take the evening off so they can mourn and honor Reylon properly and celebrate your coronation in their own ways."

Father nodded silently, satisfied with her answer.

I stared as wax dripped from the candles and hardened on the table cloth; I gazed out the windows on my left, flung open to welcome the breeze from the Alrenian Sea. I did anything but focus on the food laid before me.

Fortunately, my parents took no notice of my disinterest in the meal. Father rarely took notice of me, anyway, unless it was to reprimand me for conduct unbefitting a member of the royal family; even Mother was too preoccupied these days to spare me much time.

"And Velaire? How is she?" Father inquired.

Mother's hand trembled as she lifted her fork to her mouth. She let the mouthful linger on her tongue before she swallowed and answered. "Velaire is…in shock. He was a strong man and the illness wore him down so…completely." Her soft green eyes, shadowed by dark circles, lifted to meet Father's gaze. Looking at my mother was almost like looking into a mirror, a reflection of what I would look like when I was older. We shared the same green eyes, the same ivory skin, and the same deep brown hair, only mine tumbled past my shoulders in waves while hers was straight and glossy. I wondered if my own face looked as pale, if my own eyes were as dim with grief.

"Gillen is especially at a loss," Mother said, sorrow edging her voice despite her efforts to keep her pain at bay.

"Do you think the Royal Council was wise to name me king regent?" Father's voice was steady, but his expression was uncertain. I couldn't recall him ever looking uncertain in his life. Did he always depend on my mother so, when he had spent my entire life reprimanding me for moments of indecisiveness or displays of weakness?

Mother raised a hand to the gold chain resting on her neck and fingered the single large emerald set in her necklace. It shimmered in the ever-changing light of the candles and the fire in the hearth behind her. A single lock had escaped from her plaited hair and settled gently beside her cheek. She seemed so fragile to me, so worn.

"Gillen is too young to rule; we all know this. There was no one else related by blood to King Reylon and of age," she said. Then her voice grew firmer, more certain. "Your Majesty…the people need you." Her eyes met his and he nodded slowly.

"Perhaps you are right, my dear. Perhaps they do need me. Perhaps this is for the best."

Far below the castle walls, waves tumbled against the rocky shore. I glimpsed their crests when they rose to their full height, flashing like moonlit soldiers in silver armor.

"…and if Gillen should wish it, once he takes his father's place," Mother was saying, "you can remain near him, to train and advise him…"

"Indeed," Father said. He paused to set down his knife and fork and run a hand through his thick brown beard.

That was when visions overwhelmed my mind, unasked for and uncontrollable, as fierce as the waves outside. I hadn't even been thinking of the days before my uncle had died; I'd been trying to block out the memories all day. But now my eyes drifted shut as I saw scraps of my own memories tangled up in events I had never seen before…

I saw Father kneeling at my uncle's bedside, patting his hand, reassuring him. "It will be all right…I can manage in your absence. Focus on recovering. You'll be well before you know it…"

Then I was reliving a moment in the past, standing near my uncle's bed and studying his worn, pale face. A sweat-soaked nightshirt clung to his chest, where his breaths rose and fell in feeble puffs of air. His shaking hand reached for the goblet by his bedside, full of the medicine the latest healer had prescribed. He couldn't reach it; my aunt grasped it for him and sat upon the bed, pressing the goblet to his mouth. My lips moved in a voiceless plea: *Giver of Life, can you hear me? Don't let him die…don't take him now…*

The images snapped to a memory of my older cousin Gillen, standing several inches taller than me, but looking so vulnerable. His eyes were puffy from sleepless nights, his face pale with exhaustion and worry. "What's wrong with him, Lia? Why doesn't he get well? The healers have tried everything… What if he doesn't survive this?"

Then I saw another vision of Father, whispering in the corridor to Mother: "I can do this. I can lead the people in my elder brother's absence, as the council has voted I should do. Do you doubt me? Do you doubt my abilities?"

"Zarev…I don't know what you mean. He will be well in a few days. It's only a mild fever."

"Right. I suppose I'm overreacting. And nervous. I'm nervous, Ryn."

"There's nothing to be nervous about…" Mother began, her voice quavering, her lips a thin, pale line. She stopped when she heard the door down the hallway opening.

Father turned as another servant exited the king's bedchambers. He glanced back at my mother, her brow crinkled with confusion and worry, and shook his head. "Yes. Nothing to be nervous about."

They walked through the doorway and gazed down at my uncle where he slept fitfully in his bed. Sweat dotted his pale forehead. Father set the glass of water he carried on the nightstand and touched Uncle's shoulder. "Get well, brother," he said.

The scene faded away into one last view of my father, huddled over a desk in his private study. His jaw was tight, his eyes focused as he clutched a sprig of pale golden leaves in his hand, turning it over again and again, studying it silently. He rubbed one of the leaves between his thumb and finger, crumbling it slowly.

My mouth went dry, my hands shook, and suddenly, somehow, I *knew*.

With a gasp, I opened my eyes and stared across the table at my parents. Realization crystallized in my mind. I couldn't escape the truth that surged into my brain.

He killed him. He killed him. He killed him. The truth taunted me, laughed at me, all the while swirling around my brain like a vicious storm.

Sometimes truth cannot be silenced. Even when you wish it could be.

"You killed him."

The words were out of my mouth before I could stop them, before I even knew they were dropping off my tongue. I clamped a hand over my lips—too late, too late. My stomach plummeted and a taste as bitter as vinegar filled my mouth.

Where had those visions come from, and why hadn't I been in control of my own words? Nothing like this had ever happened to me before. It seemed like truth had stolen my tongue.

I moved my gaze to the fire; I didn't want to meet their looks now. But I could feel the weight of their eyes on me. A flame sparked, and one of the logs snapped and hissed its surrender.

Sweat condensed along the back of my neck beneath my knot of hair and my gown clung to me, heavy and constricting. The certainty behind my words made my head spin and my body tremble. I couldn't tell if it was horror or fear that brought my tears. The room swam before me until I blinked them away, letting them trickle freely down my burning cheeks.

Cautiously, I lifted my face and matched my father's stare.

"What?" My father's voice was low, barely more than a growl, but his gaze held mine with a threat. He dared me to repeat my words, to determine my fate. The wavering candlelight traced every wrinkle and scar on his face, every part of it that I knew so well. There was no fatherly tenderness in his stern expression or cold, fathomless eyes. In my peripheral vision, I noticed my mother's pale, perplexed look. *She doesn't believe me, does she?*

In my mind, I could still see the waves outside, rolling over each other, spilling out, disintegrating into foam and sea spray on the shore. Irrepressible, my words wouldn't stop either, even though my mouth was dry, even though my throat was so tight my voice cracked. A tear dropped onto my plate. "I know you killed the king."

I bit my lip. *Too late.* The words could not be retrieved. Why couldn't I control my voice? Why couldn't I stop the words?

He exhaled, stirring the candle flame in front of him into a frenzy. "So." His voice was even, quiet. "This is how you insist to behave?"

He searched my face for several long, terrible moments. My heart rammed into my chest, but I couldn't turn away, couldn't lower my eyes.

I didn't want to—tried not to—but I whispered, "Yes."

What's wrong with me?

The smallest trace of anger flared in my father's eyes, making them gleam silver in the candlelight.

How could you? Those words, however, wouldn't move past my tongue; they were lodged in my throat, where I felt like I was suffocating on them. *How could you kill your brother? My uncle?*

Desperate for help, I looked at my mother. Her face registered disbelief. Her horrified eyes turned not to her husband, but to me. *Why? How could you accuse your own father?* her open mouth pled, though she never moved her lips. The shocked words were written plainly all over her face, shouting in my own brain.

But how could he kill his own brother?

Father's deep, callous voice tore through my mind, shattering my hope that this was all a terrible dream. "My own daughter is a traitor," he announced to two of his guards, who had already stepped out from the shadows.

My heart quickened. I hadn't seen them there, hadn't imagined my father would request members of the Royal Guard to be present during a simple family meal.

My father stared at me. "She is willing to spread rumors and lies to tear the kingdom apart and is a threat to us all." He turned to Narek, Captain of the Guard, and gestured with a flick of his wrist. "Take her to her chambers and guard the door."

Would he really convict me of treason and make me a prisoner in my own home?

Arms grasped me and lifted me from my seat before I could react. "Please, please!" I shouted, but I had no argument to make, no pleas to soften a murderer's heart.

My mother stood, her body trembling as her wide eyes fixed on me and then on her husband. "Zarev…Your Highness…what is this? She is only a child…*your* child…"

"She's thirteen, nearly a woman, and old enough to know what she is saying."

"But…she's in shock—grieving…" my mother's voice shook; it was flimsy, uncertain. Her feeble argument faded in my ears while the guards carried me out kicking and screaming. The only replies to my shouts were the sounds of heavy doors slamming and the guards' footsteps echoing in the long, empty hall.

They carried me to my bedchamber and shoved me into an armchair by the fireplace. Despite the warmth from the fire crackling on the hearth and the familiar atmosphere, chills shuddered down my spine. I gasped for air and tried not to think about what could happen to me. Shapes seemed to move in the shadows collecting near the entrance to my dressing chamber, in the darkness settling around my bed.

I stared up at the men, wondering if they felt any hesitation, any misgivings about what they were doing. But their expressions bore no compassion.

They began to file toward the door, leaving me huddled in my chair, when I heard approaching footsteps from the hallway outside. "Wait," a voice called out—the king. I froze.

They swung the door open. As my father strode through, he glanced over at his men. "Leave us." While the guards retreated silently, he stared down at me.

Blood throbbed in my ears and my breath lodged in my throat. I stared down at the floorboards, refusing to meet his gaze.

"Where did you get such a mad idea about me?" His voice was low, full of a threat I'd never heard before. Where was the man I'd called father? Certainly, he had always been stern and withdrawn, someone I longed to please, someone I longed to hear loved me; but he had never treated me poorly. Tears erupted, smearing the floor into a smudgy brown mass. "Look at me."

Slowly, I raised my head, blinking in a feeble attempt to hide my watery eyes, but there was no masking my pain and fear.

"Why would you think I killed my brother?"

I swallowed and stared at the patch of silver hair collecting in his dark beard. When I was a child, I giggled whenever the rough stubble tickled my cheeks as he hugged me goodnight. Those embraces had been too rare.

"Answer me."

His frown deepened the wrinkles around his mouth. Those lips had told me to be strong, to never show signs of fear or doubt. Those lips had given me commands I'd tried to obey in hopes they would one day say that he loved me and was proud of me, his only child.

Manipulator. Liar. Was everything he did a ploy for power? An act to fool people into serving him in some way, even if those people were of his own flesh and blood?

"Did you overhear a rumor? Servant's gossip?" His robes whispered around his legs, brushing the polished wood floor as he stepped closer. "*Who else have you told?*" He dropped his hand on the back of my chair, jostling me in my seat.

I lifted my face. He hovered over me, so close now that I could feel his hot breath on my forehead and smell the lobster from dinner. "*Now* you refuse to speak. Do you retract what you said?"

The word leapt out of my mouth: "No."

A flicker passed over his eyes—anger? Or perhaps more disappointment in me. "Your uncle was weak. I can build a great kingdom, and you, as my daughter, can rise to power with me. Would you turn down this chance due to your own sentiments? Will you side with your uncle or your own father?"

Tears hung in my eyes. *My own father is a monster.* "How could you?" I choked out.

For a long moment, he watched me, his cold eyes sending a chill down my back. "You are a fool," he murmured. Before I could react, he turned on his heel and swept from the room without another word.

As I drew a deep breath to calm myself, I realized I'd been left unsupervised. Racing to my door, I tried the knob to find it locked. Footsteps beat a steady rhythm in the hallway: a guard was pacing before my door, hemming me in. My windows overlooked the beach far below, and I knew the drop was too high and the roof too steep for me to jump or climb to escape. I was a prisoner in my own chambers.

Despairing, I plopped back into my chair and tried to determine a course of action, but my thoughts felt foggy and sluggish. I closed my eyes and prayed I was trapped in a nightmare. When I opened my eyes, none of this would be happening. My uncle would still be alive. My father would order me to continue my horseback riding and archery lessons. My mother would ensure I spent hours learning etiquette, which would someday help me win the heart of a handsome nobleman and secure a royal marriage. My life would be routine and predictable again. Isolated yet important. Uneventful but comfortable.

Footsteps thudded along the hallway outside, snapping me out of my daydreams. I clenched my clammy fists tightly. But no one entered my chambers—not yet. Instead I heard movement outside my door as another set of footsteps walked away. The guard?

My bedchamber disappeared. As suddenly as the first, another vision flooded my brain, showing me one of the king's conference rooms, used for royal meetings.

"What will we do with her?" My father paced back and forth in front of a long table.

I didn't know if my urge to scream came from my sense of betrayal or fear.

"We are not sure if she has, or will, tell anyone," another man, standing at the edge of the room in the shadows, said. It was Narek, Captain of the Guard. He was no longer dressed in heavy metal ceremonial armor, but in his black leather breastplate and greaves, red tunic and pants, and blue cloak that signified his position as a member of the king's Royal Guard. Misroth's insignia, the dragon constellation Vehgar, glittered across his chest nearly as brightly as real stars.

"She must have received her information from someone." My father rubbed his beard angrily. "She saw nothing of what happened."

"Are you sure?"

"I'm certain of nothing at this point, Narek. I thought my wife and daughter were kept ignorant of my plans." He spun on the captain. "Only *you* knew."

There was a pause before Narek replied. Not yet eighteen, he was young for a captain, but his face was as hard and impassive as a more seasoned soldier. His tight lips and black eyes betrayed no fear. "If I wanted to betray you, your daughter would be the last person I'd confide in, Your Majesty. I know you hold my abilities and my intelligence in higher esteem than that."

My father's anger seemed to abate a little. He nodded, glancing down at the floor as he gave himself time to think. His voice came out quiet but steady. "She will have to be disposed of."

Narek frowned slightly. "She isn't much for talking."

"She did not keep silent tonight. Any servants who overheard will have to be removed…any guards whom you do not trust with the truth."

"Allow me to manage it all, sire. But the question remains: how to keep her silent. Disposing of her…she is only a child. And *your* child, the princess of Misroth, no less. There will be questions…" Narek was flustered, and I couldn't remember ever hearing him sound that way. "It could leave a larger mess than the one we already have on our hands."

"I trust you with my kingship and my life, Narek. Her words could make the people question my rule, even if we tried to make her words out to be a wild claim of a half-wit. Let her punishment fit her crime," his firm voice rang out, ricocheting off the walls, settling deep within my mind and my heart.

Let her punishment fit her crime. Let her punishment fit her crime.

The king stopped his pacing and spun to face his captain. If possible, his voice became even firmer, layered with emphasis. "Need I remind you of your allegiance? Or our agreement?"

"No," Narek murmured. He held a fist over his chest. "I will dispose of her."

As he backed out of the room, the vision faded and I found myself still in my bedchamber. I stared up at my ceiling, studying the carved designs of waves set in the wood molding. My own father was going to murder me, like he had murdered my uncle.

Before the visions had appeared to me tonight, I had been content in my ignorance, resigned to the fact that my father would always be distant and stern, but never suspecting he was capable of such cruelty. Knowing the truth was bad enough, but giving it voice was about to kill me. *I'd rather never speak again than have this new curse,* I thought angrily.

My heart jolted when I heard footsteps outside my chamber. I didn't have much time. Narek was already on his way.

Scrambling from my chair, I tiptoed next to my door and pressed myself against the wall, listening to the approaching steps. I told myself not to move, not to breathe. The door swung inward, and the guard stared blankly ahead, scanning the room for a cowering girl.

With a deep breath, I kicked him as hard as I could in the groin. Crying out in pain and surprise, he tried to grab me. But I was already moving, dashing past him, through the doorway, and down the hall.

I swept down the hallway, my footsteps creaking and echoing on the wood floors so loudly I was sure my presence was being announced to every guard in the castle. Stern faces of past kings and queens stared down at me from old paintings and tapestries hanging from the walls and looked as if they were accusing me of treachery as well. Darting down different intersecting hallways, I put as much distance between the royal quarters and myself as I could, doing everything I could to confuse my pursuer. But I knew I was delaying the inevitable. I had to get out. And how would I ever manage to get past the king's guard?

Farther, farther. Turning into the conservatory, I collided with a lone servant, who gasped and began apologizing. "I did not see you, princess…I'm so sorry…"

Her voice trailed off as I ran past her. Lush plants and trees stretched toward the glass ceilings, their flowers and branches upturned to the stars, but I found no peace in the fragrant space that had once been a regular retreat for me. I dove under a leafy branch right before it smacked me in the face and charged through the back exit.

I threw myself into the room beyond—a study reserved for the royal healer's use, but tonight the small space was empty. My steps were soft on the velvety carpet. The only wall not composed of floor-to-ceiling shelves was the far one, which held a window overlooking the castle grounds and the sea far below them. Pushing past the untidy desk resting before it, I wrenched the window open and I poked my head outside. The drop was terrifying. I felt my stomach plummet and my heart rise to my throat. Far below the cliff the castle and its grounds rested upon, sea waves rolled on the beach. The salty breeze brushed against my cheeks, so brisk that tears stung my eyes.

Go. Now, I urged myself.

I swung my leg over the windowsill and leaned out to study the stone wall outside. There was a narrow ledge running the length of the wall a short drop down, and plenty of hand and footholds in the gaps between the stonework, if I could keep my feet sure and my hands strong. Reaching out with a shaking hand, I grasped the top of one of the stones and strained to reach the ledge with my foot. For one terrifying instant I hung halfway out the window and halfway in, struggling to find the courage to let go of the sill and swing out onto the ledge.

Gasping, I let go. I swayed and caught myself, clutching the wall with both hands and regaining my balance. The wind whipped my dress around my legs as I crept sideways along the ledge, and my fingers slipped when I felt for new handholds. I paused, teeth chattering, and carefully wiped one hand at a time on the skirt of my dress.

My head spun and my pulse pounded. Somehow I had to find my way down the wall, when I could barely even hold on now. I dared a look over my shoulder to try to search for another foothold but immediately regretted it. The world tilted around me; my fingers weren't strong enough; I was losing my hold; I was going to fall…

There was a thud beside me, and strong arms grasped me roughly by the arm. Narek. A scream swirled inside me but never made its way past my throat. In a stomach-churning moment, he lifted me over his head and into the arms of another guard waiting at the open window. They wrenched me inside, shoving a sack over my head and tying it in place. I tried to shout, hoping someone in the castle might hear, but a hand pressed over my mouth, pressing the rough sack close to my nose until my whole world was nothing but darkness and a musty scent. Though I tried to kick and struggle, the guards were too strong. Together, they lifted me effortlessly, carrying me on a winding route through the castle.

When I heard doors swing open, chill air snapped at my face and ripped my breath away. The echoes of the waves against the cliff's face sounded like distant thunder in my ears and the stench of salt made me scrunch my nose. I shook with fear and cold as the men dragged me forward and tied my wrists and ankles together. At the edge, blinded and disoriented, I could sense the dizzying drop. Though I couldn't see it, the sight I'd memorized as a child flashed before my mind's eye: a sharp descent beyond the jagged cliff; the grey, windswept clouds above; and the deep, swirling water below.

I knew the usual method for executing criminals all too well. A plunge into the cold water of a small cove cut into the side of the cliff, where the waves were placid and where the sea was deep enough that rocks were scarce. With no weights to pull one down, the struggle was prolonged and violent. I'd read once that drowning was the worst way to die. At the time I'd wondered how the writer could know this for a fact, if he were still living and could not consult with the dead. I had no desire to find out now if he was right.

Without ceremony, they yanked off the sack and dumped me over the edge. For one brief instant the wind tore at my body and muted my scream, and then I plunged into icy darkness.

Panic pulled my body out of shock and into motion. I flailed around in the water, trying to find the surface but unable to tell which way was up. My feet kicked in a failed attempt to force off my shoes; I wriggled my arms and shoulders as I strained against the rope.

Those seconds felt like an eternity before I broke the surface. I spluttered and gasped, struggling to suck in air. Legs kicking in unison, I fought in vain to keep my head up. The waves dragged me forward, onto my face, pushing my mouth and nose under as I bobbed in the water. Salt stung my eyes and burned my throat. I squirmed furiously, but without the help of my arms, tipping myself onto my back was impossible. My dress, full of the sea, entangled my body and dragged me down again.

Another shot of desperation surged through my veins and I pulled fiercely at the ropes around my feet again. To my shock, the binds gave way, cutting deeply into my ankles as they fell away and sank into the water. Blood seeping from my raw skin tinged the foamy waves around me pink. I kicked to propel myself upward, giving me a chance to lift my head out of the water, but I couldn't force my hands free.

I knew my chance at survival was still frail. Over and over, no matter how I kicked and fought, the current pulled me down. Each time it was nearly impossible to fight my way to the surface, and I was too disoriented to know if I was headed toward the shore or not.

My heart felt heavy in my chest and my lungs burned. As I sank deeper into the water than ever before and my body seemed made of lead, black spots danced before my eyes. I tried to kick, to force myself upward one more time, but it seemed impossible. Death's fingers tightened around my chest.

Don't give up. The thought felt powerful, stronger than my panic and confusion. *You can do this.*

With a final effort, I kicked and stretched my bound wrists upward— or in the direction I thought was above water. I rose, so slowly, too slowly, until at last the surface was so near I thought I could see the glitter of starlight on the water. I could imagine air rushing into my lungs, painful and beautiful all at once. Just a few more kicks, and I would break the surface again; I could survive to fight a little longer. I kicked once, twice— reaching, reaching.

When my head rose above the water at last, the night air felt heavy around me, the tumult of the waves strangely dull in my ears. Why was it still so dark? I gasped, sucking in air.

But no…it wasn't air. I was still underwater. My lungs gulped in water, letting it rush into my chest, filling me like a final weight that dragged me down still deeper into the sea. The darkness rushed and spun, and the void far below me yawned ever wider, stretching its arms to receive its next victim. Then the shadows consumed me.

CHAPTER TWO

COUGHING, I JERKED AWAKE AND vomited up seawater. Every inch of my body trembled with cold so intense I wondered if my insides were freezing. My back rested against solid wood, though the world still swayed and I could hear the rush of water around me. I opened my eyes to the night sky, as soft and dark as the velvet robes my father wore for his coronation. The stars burned pale and distant and the moon was gone, buried behind thick black clouds.

A man's face loomed over me, blocking out the sky. Snatching my bound hands into fists, I swung at him, but his strong arms grasped mine. I thrashed, trying to aim my kicks low while I worked to wrench my hands free.

"Don't panic!" the man said. "I'm here to help you. You were drowning and I pulled you from the water. You're safe now. You're safe!"

His words took a moment to register. Pulling back my fists, I blinked and studied his face. He was a man of perhaps thirty, with a thick, brown beard and kind dark eyes. Best of all, his hair was cropped short to signify he was not a noble, and he wore no weapons other than a short knife clutched in one hand.

"To cut your binds," he explained when my eyes landed on his blade.

My heart slowed to a soft thud and I let him slice through the rope. He was my rescuer, not another threat. I winced as I studied my raw wrists, and my body still felt heavy and sodden, but I was safe; I was alive.

As if echoing my thoughts, the man called out, "She's alive!" He glanced over his shoulder, apparently speaking to someone else on the sailboat. The boat was not large, but in my brief glance, I couldn't see anyone else nearby.

Closing my eyes, I drew a deep breath, relishing the feel of the air, even if it hurt my burning lungs. My throat was swollen, my mouth tasted bitter, and every muscle in my body ached. I shook and coughed some more before someone threw a blanket over my body and lifted me. Enveloped in wool yet still shivering, I felt arms carry me across the boat and into a cabin. I turned and saw a woman's face, her long blonde hair shimmering almost white in the starlight.

Once inside, the woman set me on the bed, stripped me out of my soaked clothes, and replaced them with thick, warm ones. She laid me on the single cot and pulled blanket after blanket over me, then climbed in beside me and pulled me close until my shivers subsided. Slowly, gently, warmth crept over my body. I slipped into unconsciousness.

When I opened my eyes, I was fiercely hot, and the cabin was shifting while the world lurched and shuddered beneath me. All around was the roaring of waves: angry, relentless, and deadly. They screamed in my ears until I could feel water closing in. It was beating against my chest, soaking the cot, swallowing me whole.

Thrashing at the sheets, I tried to shout, even though the effort tore at my raw throat. No sound came out. Beads of water coated my forehead and snaked down my temples. My chest was wet, soaking through the nightgown I wore, and the sheets were drenched. *I'm dying.*

The world was dark. Water weighed heavily on my lungs and I could scarcely force air into them anymore. They were burning; my whole body was burning. My muscles were on fire and my throat ached—water was pouring down it. Stinging saltwater dripped into my eyes.

A cold hand reached out and touched my forehead, causing me to shudder. *Don't let me die!* I wanted to cry out the words, to plead for help, but my throat was too constricted. *Why don't you pull me out before I drown?*

The darkness descended upon me, and it was strangely silent. Peaceful.

The next time my eyes opened, the world was steady and quiet. My trembling, sweaty body felt weak and my lungs were heavy. I reached to push back the sheets but a woman's gentle voice stopped me.

"Stay still," she murmured.

All of my muscles hurt enough that it took an effort to turn my head and face her. She sat in a wooden chair beside the bed. With one arm she pulled me to a sitting position, while with the other she pressed a cup to my mouth until I forced down some water. It was refreshing on my tongue, but scratched and hurt like gravel as it slithered down my throat. I grimaced and she lay me back against the pillow.

My eyes fluttered shut. I was so tired. A breeze drifted across my face, a breath of soft air that temporarily chilled the fire beneath my skin, and I sank into sleep once more.

It was a delight to be in my riding clothes again, to wear my light, comfortable leggings and tunic rather than a heavy royal gown. My hair hung loose, free for the breeze to whisper through it. Laughing, I pulled back on my mare Felwe's reins and glanced toward Gillen. His hair was tied back from his face, giving me a clear view of the smile dancing on his lips.

He sighed, leaning back in his saddle as Azlyn, his sleek black stallion, slowed to a walk. "It's good to be away from all of the tiresome lessons."

I spread my arms wide, as if to embrace the empty expanse of the beach and the whole sea beside us. "An entirely free day to do as we please!"

The summer sun, still high in a perfect blue sky, warmed my back. I nodded toward the waves, where the light sparkled and flashed with each crest. The breeze cooled my cheeks and ruffled my hair, but it didn't diminish the heat radiating back at us from the long stretch of pearly sand.

Gillen fired a mischievous grin in my direction. "I'll race you to the water!"

Without waiting for a response, he dug his knees into Azlyn's sides, making the horse lunge forward.

"This is not a fair contest, Gil!" I shouted. I urged Felwe toward the sea as Azlyn kicked sand back toward my face. Even if Gillen hadn't gone first, he rode a royal stallion bred for speed and strength. I leaned low against Felwe's back, dropping the reins to let her run freely until her white mane flew back into my face.

"Victory!" Gillen called as his stallion splashed into the waves.

Laughing, I entered the water just behind him. "An easy victory for someone who started unfairly," I taunted.

We spent the afternoon at the beach, letting our horses roam nearby while we waded, splashed, and swam in the shallow sea and then lay out on the sand to dry. As the sun set, turning the sky fiery shades of orange, gold, and scarlet, we at last mounted our steeds and turned back toward the castle grounds.

When we ascended the last slope of the path leading toward home and rode into one of the side courtyards, guards and servants alike cast us small smiles. We were damp and covered in sand, still full of laughter and joy at our short-lived freedom.

"If only everyday could be like this," I said as one of the stable boys led our horses away.

We trod the old cobblestones toward the heavily boarded double doors. As we passed beneath its shadow, the weatherworn statue of Queen Tamelle, her stone face etched into a stern expression, watched us disapprovingly. We walked on unfazed. The two guards standing watch under the arch of the entryway pushed open the doors and pressed their fists to their hearts in salutes as we passed through.

Gillen squared his shoulders for appearance's sake, even as he turned to whisper to me. "I may be the crown prince, but don't think I won't still shirk my studies and training from time to time to have fun." His eyes sparkled with mischief even as he tried to compose his face into a solemn expression and sink into his role of a confident and thoughtful prince.

But that was our last true moment of freedom. As we swept down the marble hallway, a servant intercepted us, pressing her lips into a firm line to hide her worry.

"Your Highness?" She saluted to Gillen, who nodded in acknowledgment. "Your father has taken ill."

The memory had been such a vivid dream that I was left with a throbbing ache in my chest when I awoke.

Gil. Are you safe? Do you know I am in danger? Are you wondering where I am?

I squeezed my eyes shut, hoping I could force the tears back before they trickled down my cheeks. Though I was not a priest, I dared to beg the Life-Giver for Gillen's protection and then forced thoughts of him away. *I can't change what's happened,* I told myself firmly.

When I sat up, I was dizzy and my head felt too heavy for my neck. But I had at least managed to sit up, proving that my body was stronger than it had been before. I ran my fingers along the warm, dry skin of my arms and realized my fever had passed.

I was clothed in a comfortable nightgown that was too large for me, like a tent, rather than the dress I'd been wearing at the castle. I wondered if my rescuers had recognized my clothes from my uncle's funeral and my father's coronation, or if they had guessed my identity because of the red armband of mourning I had been wearing. *Or maybe it fell off in the water,* I thought hopefully.

Heart jolting with another fear, I lifted a hand to my tangled hair. Had they recognized *me*? I'd made few public appearances outside of balls and dinners spent with Misroth's nobility, but I had my mother's eyes and my father's jaw and nose. Would my own features betray me?

Deep breaths, Halia. You aren't home, or in the dungeons, or dead. If they haven't returned you to the king yet, they must not know.

Indeed, my surroundings were entirely foreign to me, as used to the castle's extravagance as I was. Aside from the bed I occupied in the corner of the cozy room, it contained only a small hearth, a chest of drawers, a hand-woven rug, and a faded armchair. Everything was plain yet inviting, made for function rather than embellishment. Cream-colored curtains were drawn over a window beside me so only faint light trickled in. I pulled them back and gazed out on a small, empty patch of land backed by forest. A few leaves still clung to the trees, but most littered the ground. The moon stared down at me, so large and bright I had to blink to adjust my eyes. How many days had passed since the funeral, since the onset of the visions and truthful words that had nearly killed me?

I turned toward the opposite wall, to a fireplace red and warm with dying embers. Beside it was a closed door with the soft glow of candlelight seeping in through the gap between it and the floor. Voices followed the light, and I strained to hear the words.

"I know I've said it already, but I still can't believe it. Who would do that to a child?" The woman spoke so low that I almost didn't catch her words.

"Perhaps she is awake now. We need to talk to her." I recognized the voice of the man who'd rescued me.

As they approached, I sank back onto my pillow and waited.

They pushed the door open. The woman held a candlestick in one hand, shielding it with the other. "You're awake," she said, her voice soft, her blue eyes gentle. She stepped toward the bed, setting the candle on the nightstand and reaching out a hand to feel my forehead. "Your fever has broken. How do you feel?"

Fine. I opened my mouth to speak the words, but no sound came out. Not even a groan. Instinctively, my hand flew to my neck, clutching at my throat as if I could assess the internal damage.

The woman pulled up the chair sitting against a wall and sat beside the bed. Her husband stood behind her, his hands resting on the back of the chair. "It's all right," she said. "Your throat probably still hurts from nearly drowning. We only want to ensure you are safe and can return home." She looked over her shoulder and patted her husband's hand. "Fetch a pen and paper."

When he returned, he held the pen and paper out to me. I grasped them uncertainly, realizing with growing uneasiness that they would want to know who I was, who my parents were. *What do I tell them? Where can I go now?*

"Could you tell us who you are and what happened?" the man asked.

I swallowed. *I am in danger,* I scrawled across the paper slowly. My hand trembled, making my handwriting shaky and uneven. *I can't tell you more. You can't tell anyone about me, or those who did this will find me.*

Glancing up, I watched concern flicker in the woman's eyes. "I know you are frightened," she said, "but you must have parents who are worried about you. They need to know you're safe, and they can protect you from further danger."

They are the ones who did this to me. I drew a deep breath, trying to quell the pain and fear in my heart.

"I'm sorry…" the woman began, reaching out a gentle hand to grasp mine.

Pounding on the front door interrupted her, echoing throughout the house and matching the throbbing of my heart. The couple exchanged a glance, their eyes alert and their faces wary. I could read the question in their look: *Who would be at the door at this hour?*

As the man left to answer the door, his wife crept to my bedroom doorway and peered out. I closed my eyes, trying to keep my imagination from running wild. The king and his loyal guardsmen believed I'd died in the sea, so why would they be searching for me now?

I tried to focus on the voices, but it was hard to hear over the beating of my heart.

Snatches of the conversation reached my ear: "We are sorry to trouble you… Princess Halia is missing…"

It was Narek's voice. My throat tightened and the air caught in my chest, not letting me breathe. Did they know I'd survived, or was this search for mere show? Was there no escape?

"The king and queen fear she has been kidnapped…"

The world tipped in front of my eyes as fear overtook me. I clutched at the bedsheets, as if they could offer me protection, until my knuckles turned white. *Here is the part where these people give me away and hand me back to my enemies,* I thought. Who would disobey the King's Guard?

Blinking, I realized the woman was standing beside the bed. "Get up," she said.

I opened my mouth, gasping for air like a fish as I struggled to croak out something, anything to let the woman know I was in danger, but nothing came. Desperate, I shook my head and prayed my fear showed on my countenance.

Her eyes flared with something. Realization? Determination? I couldn't tell.

"You are in danger from *them.*" It was a statement, not a question.

I nodded frantically.

Eyes widening, the woman pulled off her hooded cloak and threw it over me.

Her voice was a whisper: "Quick!"

I stood from the bed, the cloak so long it brushed the floor behind me.

She threw aside the curtains and pushed the window open, then turned to me. In the moonlight, her eyes flashed like sapphires and her lips were a grim line. "I'll lift you out and try to distract them. Get as far away as you can. We are outside the city walls, but not far enough from the capital. Find some place safe." Her slender arms hoisted me up over the sill.

I dropped to the earth and spun to face her as she prepared to shut the window. My heart fluttered at the thought of the risk this woman was taking if Narek and his men ever realized what she had done, but her command urged me on: "*Run.*"

I plowed forward, my bare feet pounding against cold grass. Reaching the forest, I raced through without any direction or purpose other than to flee. How long I should run, or how far, I did not know, nor did I have any way to measure.

To my horror, voices echoed somewhere behind me. Were the

guards in pursuit already? Had they seen me flee? Did the woman's husband give me away? I tried to increase my pace, but I was tired, cold, and weak. The world felt distant and yet all too close at the same time. I couldn't catch my breath and sparks of light began to dance before my eyes. Blinking, I tried to make them disappear, but the world only seemed to close in on me further. How long had I been ill? Branches reached toward me, tearing at my hair and clothes and cutting my face. I stubbed my toes and tripped over roots and underbrush, slicing my foot on a sharp rock and nearly crying out in pain.

"This is a fool's errand!" someone behind me said. His words echoed in the forest, bouncing off the trees until it sounded like they were surrounding me.

Stopping and pressing my back against a trunk, I scoured the trees for my pursuers. If I couldn't outrun them, I could make myself quiet and disappear.

"Stop complaining," another man snapped. "There's no danger this close to the forest's edge."

This is Evren Forest, I thought with a shudder, wondering why the obvious thought had not clicked into place sooner. *The forest of myth, the one featured in so many of the frightening fireside tales of Misroth.*

But I had a real, living danger to worry about, because the voices were getting closer. Glancing up at the branch stretching over my head, I felt adrenaline fire through my body, giving me another round of strength. I leapt, catching hold of the branch and swinging my body higher, higher, until my muscles strained, ready to give out under my weight, and I managed to slip one leg over the limb. Beneath the nightgown, my bare legs scraped against the rough bark as I straddled the branch. I clung to a crevice in the trunk and pulled myself to my feet. Stretching on tiptoes, I found I could reach the next branch.

Twigs snagged at my gown and cloak, but I tore the fabric away and kept going. The branches grew thinner until they began to shake beneath my weight, and still I pressed onward. I wasn't satisfied until I found a perch tucked safely against the trunk, secured by three branches that gave me enough support and space to sit with my back against the tree and my feet tucked up beneath me. From here, I could see the tops of the smaller trees surrounding me. Though most of the tree branches were bare, anyone scanning the trees from below would still have trouble finding me in my perch. I pulled my knees to my chest and willed myself to be smaller, pressing close against the branches and letting them shield me. Then I held my breath as I listened to the approaching footsteps. The men were jogging, moving quickly in their pursuit, yet slowly enough to scour the forest.

Giver of Protection, hide me safely in Your arms… The words from the old song the castle priest recited, or at least the closest translation we had of them, flew into my mind and became my prayer.

"There is no way she is here, in these woods," one of the guards panted. "We should head back now."

"I wanted to be sure. That couple seemed to be hiding something, and I was certain I saw a figure in the woods. Besides, if I show my dedication, perhaps the king will retract his decision to name a *boy* Captain of the Guard."

The footsteps were right below me now. I held my breath.

"You probably saw an animal. There's no way she is alive." The first guard stopped and forced authority into his tone. "And you would do well not to speak ill of our captain, who we both know has proven his skill, or I will report you. Let's go back."

"Aren't you a brave member of the guard?" the second man sneered. "Or shall I report *you* as a slovenly coward?"

My foot slipped, dislodging a loose patch of bark. I bit my lip; the noise seemed amplified in the quiet of the nighttime forest.

The second guard's posture changed, his puffed-up chest and swaggering confidence morphing into a shrinking look as he reached for his sword hilt. "Wait…did you hear that?"

"It was probably a squirrel. Come, if you're in such a hurry to report back to Narek and impress him with our search of Evren Forest, then follow me!"

The footsteps retreated and relief eased its way through my limbs. I relaxed out of my cramped huddle and, once I felt the guards were a safe distance away, began my descent. Several times I slipped and my weary, trembling limbs almost couldn't support me anymore. I hit the ground panting and exhausted, but my desire to put space between the guards and me overpowered every other feeling. I burst into a run, forming a meandering trail through the underbrush.

Seconds turned into minutes. My cheeks burned in the cold and my lungs ached. I kicked up dead leaves and twigs and tripped more than once. The cloak grew hot, clinging to my arms and hanging heavy against my body. As it dragged behind, it caught in the branches littering the ground and snagged until it tore and sent me sprawling on my face. My chest heaved; I coughed and gasped for air.

I struggled to my feet and slipped the cloak off, draping it over my shoulder. Shaking and struggling to catch my breath, I stood motionless, straining my ears for any sounds of pursuit. Wind shuddered through the trees and stirred dead leaves across the ground. A squirrel scampered out from between two trunks, stared at me, and then flung itself up the nearest tree in two great bounds.

No one, I thought in relief. *No one's following me.* My head spun and I nearly tripped over my own feet as I tried to keep walking. I wiped the sweat from my forehead and drew in deep, cooling breaths. I must have been ill longer than I'd thought.

At first the breeze caressed my face and refreshed me, but soon it crept through my nightgown. The sweat coating my body made me shiver, so I threw the cloak back on. My legs were numb and even my back and arms ached. I ran my tongue along my dry lips and longed for even one sip of cool, fresh water, but I had no hope of finding any soon. There was a hole in my stomach from hunger, and the further I walked the more it stretched until it felt like I had a gaping chasm growing deep inside me. When *was* the last time I had eaten? It must have been days ago, when I'd forced down a few bites at dinner with my parents. My heart aching with pain and anger at the memory, I pushed the thought away.

The trees towered high and drenched me in shadows while clouds gathered in the sky and enveloped the moon. Unseen animals darted from tree to tree, scurrying through the leaves on the ground and climbing among the branches over my head. Every time something moved nearby, my pulse quickened and I froze, as if standing still would make a hungry animal blind to my presence. I vaguely remembered whispers of terrors, intelligent creatures that lurked in Evren Forest and preyed upon humans, and nervous glances between adults whenever anyone mentioned the topic of traveling through these woods, but I reminded myself that the guards' fear had been misplaced. *The tales are myths. Only stories to scare children,* I reassured myself.

Still, I hated the thought of staying in these dark woods alone, but I was lost and too exhausted to move another step. Sinking to the earth and huddling close to the trunk of an old maple tree, I shut out the night and the sounds by burrowing into the oversized cloak.

Somehow I dozed, my sleep interrupted by nightmares of creaking branches and royal guards chasing me through dark wilderness. At last, sunlight peeked through the treetops, waking me to a frosty morning.

Shivering, I stretched and found that my back and neck ached from my uncomfortable sleeping position. My head throbbed, my legs were sore, and my whole body was weak, but I didn't have time to rest longer. Hunger pangs had set in and I knew if I didn't push my way through this wood soon, I would freeze or starve.

As the day wore on, the sunlight slowly warmed the earth and melted the frost from the remaining leaves on the trees. I decided to follow the sunlight and hope that I could keep a westerly path. Though I knew nothing of traveling through wilderness, I had a fairly clear picture in my head of the world maps I'd been forced to memorize. Evren Forest lay to the west of Misroth City, with a few scattered towns along its opposite borders. If I could just make it through this forest, I could find a haven where someone might help me.

Even in the daylight, I couldn't shake the eerie feeling the forest gave me. Shadows hid beneath the trees and strange noises followed me everywhere. Birds lighted on perches high above me, but their mild presence couldn't chase away the nightmarish thoughts collecting in my mind. *What if the creatures are real?* The longer I traveled through the woods alone, my real fears of becoming lost forever and starving were matched by my irrational fears.

Despite my concerns, the day passed without incident. As another night fell, my hunger making my stomach feel like a great abyss, I collapsed on a soft bed of moss to rest. *Sleep. You'll make it out of this place soon, somehow… Forget the stories about monsters. Forget that you might be lost. You need the rest.* I shut my eyes against the night and tried to block out every sound.

My efforts didn't work.

Overhead, the boughs creaked in the wind and the leaves scattered, drifting onto my cloak. I shivered and stared up at the stars. If I focused on picking out the constellations Mother had shown me as a child, maybe I could dispel my fears and fall asleep. But any memories of my mother shot poison through my veins.

How could you and Father betray me like this?

Unbidden tears splattered down my cheeks and spotted my nightgown, mingling with the twigs and dirt. I leaned my head back against the rough bark of the tree and felt it scratch my scalp. At least my anger and sorrow consumed me, drowning my fear.

A heavy thud jolted me out of my despair and wrenched my eyes wide open. Standing, I pulled the cloak close about me and searched the forest. *It's nothing, you fool,* I thought, but I couldn't dispel my terror this time.

My breath caught in my throat as two large, reptilian eyes appeared in the blackness. Gleaming bright gold, cold and intent, they fastened on me unblinkingly.

Panicking, I stepped backward, my heel slamming into the tree. I suppressed a cry of pain and staggered around the trunk, unable to tear my gaze from the eyes that were still studying me. *Move. Run.* I had to plead with myself while my body struggled to catch up with my mind. Blood pounded through my head. Did I dare turn my back on this creature? *Now,* I commanded myself.

Spinning around, I darted through the trees, winding my way around underbrush, leaping over roots and branches. Leaves flew up around me as my sore muscles found new life. I heard nothing behind me—had it changed its mind? Or was it that quiet?

I didn't dare turn to look. My chest burned; my throat was on fire. Though my body was warm and coated in a layer of sweat, my hands were cold and clammy as they pumped at my sides. *Keep. Going.* I begged my legs to go faster, faster, faster.

Sweat snaked down my brow. I leapt over a fallen tree and my knees almost buckled underneath me as I hit the ground. My breaths came in uneven gasps, so loud that I knew I had to be alerting every beast around me that I was weak and half-starved.

I will not die here, I resolved.

I couldn't hear any sounds over the hammering of my heart, the thudding of my feet, the wheezing of my lungs. In a surreal burst of perceptiveness—perhaps to make up for the fact that I heard nothing, or maybe to appreciate the beauty of the world one last time—I became intensely aware of every sight around me. Ahead, the sky was grey and starless, and I realized it was almost dawn. Around me the forest was thinning: the underbrush was scraggly and sparse, and the trees stood further and further apart.

Then the canopy of branches spread wide and the sky was open above me, swirling with soft clouds. Just beyond the trees stretched rolling, green countryside dotted with farms, fields, and pastures. At that instant light sprang over the horizon: a warm glow piercing through the grey, edging the easternmost clouds in pale gold. The sun followed, peeking over the edge of the earth and flooding my eyes with light. Hope burst inside me.

I sprinted forward, plunging out of the forest into the tall grass, and collapsed. I tumbled sideways, rolling down a soft descent until my momentum died and I slammed onto my face. For several minutes I lay there, too exhausted to move, fearing the creature would pounce.

Seconds inched by. My heart slowed until I could no longer feel it pulsing in my ears. I raised my head from the grass and stared over my shoulder into the forest, but there were no eyes gazing back at me. Sighing with relief, I staggered to my feet. I set my gaze ahead, scanning the farmland. There was a cabin nearby…if I could force my legs forward a little more…

I staggered toward the cabin, nestled against a hill and belching a welcoming curl of smoke from its chimney. As I drew nearer, I noticed a boy close to my age in the yard, stacking wood blocks from a pile into his arms. His clothes were made from simple homespun material, his boots were muddy and worn, and his dark hair was cropped short. When he caught sight of me, he froze, a frown crinkling his brow as he stared. I wanted to run, to beg for help and food, but my body was too faint, and I collapsed.

CHAPTER THREE

THE BOY SHOUTED WORDS I couldn't hear past the ringing in my ears. Coming to the front door, a man paused on the porch and stared me up and down. I lay in the grass trembling, my cloak and gown in a heap around me. The whole world blurred and teetered, and black dots obstructed my vision.

"She needs help, Father," the boy begged. He kneeled at my side and peered down at me, his deep brown eyes filled with concern. He felt my forehead with trembling fingers. "I think she came from the woods; she must be hungry."

Another friend? Shelter? Food? I hoped.

Without a word, the boy's father turned and slammed the front door. After several minutes he appeared again in front of me, shoving a slice of bread and a cup of water in my face. Somehow my senses sharpened at the sight of food and I found strength to snatch at them. I devoured the bread, not caring as crumbs spilled down my front, then gulped down the water, savoring every drop. My empty stomach growled for more; the water seemed to slosh in the vast empty space left inside me. The man lifted me into his arms and carried me, the boy trotting along behind him.

Hating that I was not strong enough to walk myself, I blinked in the sunlight and clung to the stranger's shoulders. My head lolled back against his chest and I closed my eyes. Too tired, too tired.

Eventually I was aware of slightly less movement—the world still spun but the man had stopped walking. I cracked open my eyes and saw we were standing before another cabin, this one surrounded by a homey garden. Though it was dead now, I could tell it had been well-tended before the frosts came.

The man pounded on the door. After a moment, it opened inward to reveal a middle-aged man with short, ruffled hair and brown eyes almost lost behind his spectacles. His skin was a softer tone than that of the others, the color of someone who spent most of his days indoors. He blinked in surprise and raised a hand to run through his locks. "Kyrin, what brings you here?" he inquired. He glanced down at me, then at the boy behind me. "Ah, Avrik. Good day. Who…who is this?"

"I found her; I think she was in the forest, but—" Avrik offered, but his words were cut short by his father's.

"She's ill, Rev," Kyrin said gruffly. "As you know, I'm in no position to nurse a girl back to health. But perhaps you and Lyanna…"

A round-faced woman popped her head over her husband's shoulder at the mention of her name. Her pale face was dusted with flour that matched the white streaks adorning her ash-colored hair. "Oh!" she exclaimed, throwing a hand over her mouth. "The poor girl. Of course we'll take her in, Kyrin." She pushed her way past Rev and clasped me by both hands. "You'll be fine, dear; we'll get you plenty of food and rest." She nodded to Kyrin to bring me in.

Rev blinked and ran his hand through his hair again, though he made no protest. Kyrin carried me through the doorway into a warm living room with a large fire burning in the hearth.

"Take her to the guest room; she looks exhausted," Lyanna urged, and Kyrin followed her to the back of the cabin into a small room containing no more than a bed, a dresser, and a nightstand. He laid me down, and I promptly fell asleep.

Hours passed before I awoke to the tantalizing scent of venison. My head felt better, but I was faint with hunger. Turning my head, I stared out of the sole window in the bedroom, watching the dying sunlight through the bare branches of a tree outside. I glanced around, taking in the blue and white quilt draped over me and the bedframe, hand carved with a simple floral design. The room's walls were bare; the wood floor uncovered. It was strange to see such simple living arrangements compared to the luxury I had grown up in, but the atmosphere felt comfortable and inviting, a welcome change from the great expanses of the castle.

Sitting up, I slipped out of bed and relished the feel of the floorboards, cool and smooth under my bare feet after days of trekking through the woods. Somewhere in the kitchen, Lyanna was humming while she worked. I took a few steps toward the bedroom door and the floor creaked beneath me.

Hearing me stir, Lyanna poked her head in the doorway and gave me a soft smile. "Awake? Dinner is almost ready; I'll have Rev heat some bathwater so you can wash beforehand. I found some of my old clothes that should do for you to wear for now…" She helped me to my feet and led me out by the fireplace to sit and wait.

Lyanna called to me a short while later. As she returned to the kitchen, I shut my bedroom door and stared at the copper tub, full to the brim with steaming water. A towel, bar of soap, comb, and change of clothes rested on my bedcovers.

I wasted no time in stripping the dirty nightgown from my body and easing into the bathwater. The water relaxed my sore muscles until I leaned back and closed my eyes in bliss. I snatched at the bar of soap and began to work it into a lather, scrubbing at the layers of grime coating every inch of my skin and hair. When the water turned lukewarm, I stood resignedly and stepped from the tub.

After I'd dried myself, I turned to the undergarments and dress Lyanna had laid out. I could tell from a glance the dress was too large, but it was clean and warm. The plain brown fabric was faded from use, yet when I slipped it over my head, I found that it was still soft. Once dressed, I combed the knots from my hair before the small looking glass set over the dresser. Though my reflection was pale and dark circles shadowed my eyes, there was a flush to my cheeks and light sparkling in my green eyes. Already I felt infinitely better than I had only hours ago.

When I was finished, I joined Lyanna and Rev at the kitchen table for dinner. Neither pressed me to speak as I consumed a heaping serving of venison stew, potatoes, and bread. Dinner was far simpler than the extravagant castle meals I was accustomed to, but it was delicious, a hearty meal that warmed and reinvigorated me. When I gratefully allowed Lyanna to fill my plate and bowl with second portions, she began to ask questions.

"Where did you come from, my dear?"

I lifted my head from my plate and gulped down another mouthful of stew. Fear knotted in my stomach when I imagined trying to explain what had happened—no, revealing my identity was too dangerous. I shook my head, remembering how I couldn't speak earlier. Maybe I could now, but I didn't want to try yet. It was easier to remain silent and hold my secrets close.

Lyanna pursed her lips and glanced at her husband. Silence settled over the table, and I shoveled another forkful of potatoes into my mouth. Lyanna shrugged, took a sip of water, and started to chat about her plans for her garden.

Thank you, I thought in relief. My appetite returned in full force, and I cleaned my plate for the second time with embarrassing speed. My mother would have been aghast at my horrible manners and lack of etiquette, but Lyanna didn't comment.

Once she and Rev cleared the table, the two of them settled in the living room. Lyanna motioned to invite me over. "Come join us," she offered.

In the corner near a set of bookshelves and a desk, Rev paused while selecting a book to look over his shoulder and nod. "Yes, you should warm yourself by the fire for a bit."

I eased awkwardly into a wooden armchair by the fire and waited for them to ask for more information. It was only natural.

Picking up a piece of knitting, Lyanna studied me. "Do you like to knit?" She gestured to the basket beside her, full of yarn and various sizes of knitting needles.

Knit? I don't know if I like to knit. I like to ride, to shoot, to read, and to pretend I'm on grand adventures with my cousin. Once I liked to swim and listen to my uncle tell stories by the fire. But knitting…that is something I wasn't taught, not as royalty.

Uncomfortable, I glanced down at my hands, folded tightly in my lap.

"It's all right." Lyanna smiled. "I just want you to feel welcome." She hesitated. "What…what can we call you?"

I stared into the fire. Was it safe to speak? *Could* I speak? I cleared my throat, trying to find words to say. *I don't know…* My lips formed the words, but no sound came. *I can't say…*

Wide-eyed, I turned to Lyanna and shook my head.

Maybe this muteness was a mercy. Maybe whatever had cursed me with my visions was gone with my voice. If I never spoke, then my uncontrollable need to tell the truth could never endanger me again.

But Lyanna wasn't finished trying to discover more about me. "Do you have family looking for you? You can stay here as long as you need to, of course, but I really would hate for your loved ones to be worried while you stay here, and we have no idea…"

Again, I shook my head. This time I touched my throat, and Lyanna nodded in understanding.

Rev looked up from the book he'd been engrossed in. "Lyanna, don't pester her. Clearly she has been through a lot. She might be ready to talk in a few days."

Lyanna nodded. "No more questions," she told me. "When you've had time to rest, you can share your story, if you want. I only want to ensure you can return home."

I was standing beside my uncle's bedside as, pale and shaking, he stared up at me. My eyes were full of tears, so I couldn't see him clearly at first and didn't realize he was trying to speak to me. When I blinked, I saw his lips opening, but only a moan escaped him.

"I'm here, Uncle Reylon," I whispered, stretching out my fingers to grasp his hand. His skin was cold and clammy. "You'll be fine; you just need to rest…" But even as I said the words, I knew he wouldn't be fine. He was slipping away. If only he could say the words he was trying to speak…

I leaned in toward him, heard the breath leave his mouth. It brushed my cheek, warm and moist in the cold, dark room. He groaned again, but then it became a new sound—a word.

"*Pleaaasse…*" His voice was barely above a whisper. It cracked as the plea died on his lips.

Pulling back, I searched his face frantically. "Please, what? What is wrong? Uncle? Uncle!"

He collapsed onto the pillow, eyes closed, and the servants around him went wild, rushing forward and pushing me out of the way. One shouted at another to fetch the healer. My aunt, on the other side of his bed, was crying hysterically.

"Give him his medicine! His medicine!" she cried.

I groped for the glass on his nightstand and charged back to the bed. "Help me," I begged of the nearest servant, who helped me lift my uncle. I touched the mug to his lips…

His eyes sprang open and his hand jerked upward, knocking the glass from my fingers. It flew across the room and struck the floor, where it shattered into a thousand shimmering pieces. Deep purple liquid splattered across the floor, onto the rug, and up the wall. The servants were still calling out to one another in worry, but my eyes were locked on my uncle.

His eyes were burning with fury as he grasped my wrist in a steely clutch. But his eyes were all wrong—they were no longer sky blue, but grey. As grey as his brother's. "How dare you!" he shouted, his voice strong, angry. "How can you let me die? Why are you poisoning me? Why are you killing me?"

"No, no!" I screamed, fighting to escape his grip, but he only strengthened the hold. "I didn't do it! I didn't know!" His grasp was becoming unbearable; his eyes alight with the same cruel fire that had burned behind my father's gaze as he'd sentenced me to death.

And then I was in the Alrenian again, plunging down, down…suffocating…my lungs filling with burning liquid…

My rolling and thrashing woke me, and I lurched forward in my bed. The sheets lay in a tangled mass at my feet and I was soaked in sweat.

Cries of alarm erupted from the other room, followed by racing footsteps as Lyanna and Rev rushed into the room. The light from the candle Rev clutched reflected in their pale, worried faces.

"What's wrong, dear?" Lyanna gasped. "A nightmare?" When her gaze fell on me, her soft blue eyes widened even further and she snapped a hand to her mouth.

With a start I realized the taste of blood was thick in my mouth. I raised my fingers to my lips and brought them away red. Trembling, I focused on catching my breath and reminding myself that I'd only had a nightmare.

A nightmare about real life.

"Are you all right?" Rev demanded, his forehead crinkled with concern. Without his glasses, he squinted at me as if he were looking across a great distance.

I nodded.

Tears sprang into Lyanna's eyes. "Oh, honey. Who are you? What has happened to you? Can't you find a way to tell us? Isn't there something we could do to help?" She knelt at my bedside, reaching out a hand to pat mine.

I glanced down at her hand over mine and realized my knuckles were bleeding. Apparently I'd also been punching the headboard in my sleep. No wonder Lyanna and Rev were so concerned.

Drawing a deep breath, I tried to slow my pounding heart. I was half-convinced that if I blinked, I would open my eyes to the chill darkness of the sea pressing in on me once more.

"You're safe here," Rev told me, reading the fear that must have been shimmering in my eyes. "I promise it's safe."

There had to be a way to communicate with these people who had so kindly offered help. But what was safe to share? Slipping out of bed, I dashed to the front room. In the darkness I almost stumbled into one of the chairs until Rev's pool of candlelight enveloped me. I glanced back and smiled at him and Lyanna, who stood watching me curiously. I threaded my way around the furniture toward the corner of the room, where Rev's desk sat. It was strewn with empty paper that might give me a way to communicate, even when I didn't know what to say. Picking up one of his pens, I dipped it in ink and scribbled down a message.

I don't have a home.

Rev and Lyanna crept up behind me and stared down at the words.

Lie…make up a name, I told myself. *Give them something more. They're going to ask.* My hand trembled over the paper, letting ink drip off the pen's tip and blot over my words. *Think of a name.* I concentrated, but my head ached. Only one word forced itself into my brain, repeating over and over as if it were echoing the heartbeat throbbing in my skull. *Halia. Halia. Halia.*

"Who are you? What's your name?" Lyanna whispered.

At a loss, I gaped up at them both. *I can't lie; the words will not come. What's wrong with me?* Finally, I shook my head.

Rev ran a hand through his hair. "What happened to you? Can you…tell us about it?"

I drew a deep breath and stared at the paper. My mind was void of everything but the horrible, terrifying truth. *No, I definitely cannot lie.*

Was the curse still on me somehow, even when I couldn't speak? Would it force me at some point to share the truth again? As much as I hated to lie to these kind people, the truth was too dangerous.

I can't tell you my name, I wrote. That, at least, was true.

"You don't remember?" Lyanna gasped.

I simply frowned up at her. *Let her believe that. Let them both believe I don't remember anything.*

They hesitated, exchanging a glance. Then Rev faced me, clearing his throat. "We know you've been through…a lot, and we won't force you to speak about it. If you do not have a home, you have one here," he offered, and Lyanna nodded, her blue eyes glistening with tears in the candlelight. They were almost the same shade as Gillen's, but deeper. Stinging with grief, I pushed thoughts of my cousin from my mind.

"Our little village of Evren is simple, but it is comfortable and quiet," Rev continued. "Few travelers come into this valley from the sea, and even fewer traverse Evren Forest. Too many still believe in the old tales about the forest. But it's safe here, and we aren't troubled much by the outside world. I hope this is reassuring to you."

I smiled, touched by their generosity and comforted by their words. Quiet and set away from the world—that is what I needed. But could there be any safety for me, condemned to death if the king's men ever found me? Or perhaps the visions would return and endanger me again, even here.

Rev picked up a leather-bound journal from his desk and handed it to me. "Here, take this. It's empty and I think you'll have more use of this than me. Keep it for whenever you need to speak." He winked at me.

"Let's clean you up now and then get you back to bed," Lyanna said. Walking to the kitchen, she gathered a bowl of water and a bar of soap and gently cleaned my lips and knuckles. Rev fetched me a cup of water, and the cool liquid felt refreshing, but I cringed when my mouth burned and the coppery taste of blood lingered.

Walking me back to their guest room, Lyanna and Rev helped me climb back into bed and settle under the quilt.

"Giver of Peace, we ask you to protect this girl with your presence tonight," Rev said. "Remind her that you are near."

I glanced up at him, surprised at the conversational way in which he addressed the Giver of Life. I'd never dared to address him like that until I had faced death. Would he concern himself with my petty fears?

Lyanna smoothed my hair back from my face, letting her hand rest briefly on my forehead. "Goodnight, dear. Get some rest."

Rev set his candle on my nightstand. "If you want, I'll stay with you."

Though I appreciated the gesture, I refused to admit to the weakness and let him coddle me like a child. Trying to offer him a reassuring smile, I shook my head.

"We are nearby if you ever need us," Rev reminded me. "You are not alone."

I grinned at him and slid under my covers. Though he and Lyanna had comforted me, when they returned to their bedroom with their candle and blackness settled around me again, my thoughts kept me awake far too long.

I can't lie even to protect myself? What is wrong with me? Where have the visions gone, and why can't I speak now? Will I ever be forced to speak the truth again?

I tried to close my eyes, but the darkness reminded me of the sea's deathly clutches. The shadows were as thick as its depths rising to meet me as I fell, surrounding me, crushing me. This reminder brought my worst fear to the forefront of my mind: thoughts of my father finding me and accusing me again. Staring at me without a shred of love or mercy in his face. Betraying me. Killing me.

Does my father think I am dead, or will he find me here?

CHAPTER FOUR

THE NEXT DAY WAS A school day for Evren's children, Lyanna told me, but she said I would stay home and rest until I was well enough to go. It was strange to think that I'd attend school with other children who lived normal lives. What was it like to *not* be royalty? What was it like to not bear the weight of the world on your shoulders?

"Stay in bed and get some sleep," Lyanna said, patting my cheek. "You still look so pale and tired. I'll make you a nice, big breakfast." With a grin, she departed.

I lay back, trying to settle comfortably into my pillow. Sunlight danced through my window, drawing my eyes to the world outside. Most of the flowers in the garden beside the house were dead, but I recognized rose bushes and lavender, even in their faded, wilted forms. A young maple tree overshadowed the garden, extending bare boughs up to a pure, cloudless sky. Beyond the tree, the valley stretched into the distance, dotted by distant, rolling fields. To the right, the land swept upward toward mountains dark with pines.

This was vastly different from the castle, with its view of the Alrenian Sea and the castle grounds with both summertime flowers and those that bloomed year-round. I thought about Gillen and our days pretending to fight invisible enemies throughout the castle grounds. *Is he safe? Is my aunt safe too? Do they know what my father did, what he did to me?*

I wiped a tear from my cheek.

Just then Lyanna bustled in and out of my room, bringing me hot porridge, fresh bread with butter, and milk, and stacking a few books at the foot of my bed. "There, dear, if you feel well enough, you can pick a book and I can read to you so you can rest your eyes."

Curious, I lifted each book to study the covers in turn: a book of Misrothian history; a book about its neighboring kingdoms, Alrenor and Toryn, and how we had cut ourselves off from them in order to emancipate ourselves from the old Alrenian Empire; the *Book of Life* that told the stories of the Life-Giver in Alrenian; and even a short volume about the little village of Evren itself. Slowly, I flipped through the pages of the leather-bound *Book of Life*. The gold etching across the cover intrigued me.

Lyanna's brow furrowed. "Surely you've been taught about the Giver of Life? The tales of all he's given and all he does to rescue us, and how some—though it's rare—have even met him personally." A smile lit up her face. "Wouldn't it be exciting to actually speak to him? Do you think he would tell us what it was like to fashion the stars, or why he placed pictures in the sky?"

I nodded thoughtfully. My tutor at the castle, Meeryn, had told me about the Giver of Life, though she had kept the discussions impersonal. Only priests were to speak with the Giver of Good Things, because they were holy men who had dedicated their lives to his work. The royal priest had taught our family about the Giver and the Book of Life, but none of us read from the book ourselves. We couldn't read it anyway, since it was in the ancient language of Alrenor, a language forbidden and forgotten in our kingdom. It surprised me that Lyanna and Rev, simple countryside citizens, would have such a holy book among their possessions.

My heart jolted inside of me as I ran my hand along the cover of the book. It felt wrong to touch it, as if I were desecrating a pure thing. I hadn't dedicated my life to holiness, like the priests of Misroth. I drew my fingers away.

But isn't he the Giver of Answers? Maybe he would know what is wrong with me. The answers are probably in his book, if I could read it.

Lyanna said the book contained stories of how the Life-Giver rescued us, but he hadn't rescued my uncle. He *had* rescued me, but for what? To live exiled from my home and hunted by my own father?

Frustrated, I decided it was time for a different topic. I lifted *Tales of Evren* and passed the book to Lyanna.

With another gentle smile that sparked light in her blue eyes, Lyanna pulled a chair from the corner of the room over to my bedside. "I always wanted a child, to read to and teach," she said, almost as if to herself. She settled her plump form into the seat and smoothed over the skirt of her cream-colored dress. "But..." Her voice quavered slightly. "That never happened." She lifted her face to mine and the right corner of her mouth tilted upward once more. "I'm glad I can help you. I just wish you could tell us more about yourself, and how we can help..." Letting her voice drift off, she snapped her head back down to her lap, where the book rested. "Right. Reading. Well then..." And she pried open the cover, settled back in the chair, and began.

I was in the forest again, staring into those hungry, fathomless eyes of gold. Paralyzed, I felt fear wash over me and waited for the creature to pounce.

Black, scaly skin, nearly impenetrable, even with the strongest, sharpest blades...claws like daggers...thick yellow fangs...

The voice echoed through my head, faint yet so close. My breath was stuck in my throat, and I couldn't breathe, couldn't stumble backwards, couldn't even blink. The eyes were piercingly bright, burning back into mine and imprinting themselves in my mind, so that even when I finally managed to tear my gaze away, I still saw them looking back at me. Everywhere, behind every tree, every log, every bush—merciless golden orbs watched me.

Quiet...almost undetectable in the night but for their bright eyes...

It was going to charge me at any moment; and I couldn't run. This time, I wouldn't escape. I was going to die.

With a fierce shriek, like nothing I'd ever heard before, the eyes sprang forward—the creature was leaping toward me—I was trapped—

it was too late—

My eyes opened to Lyanna and Rev's guest room…my room. Lyanna still sat in her chair. She'd set the book down in her lap and was studying me, worry crinkling her brow.

"I hadn't realized you'd fallen asleep…maybe we should stop. I don't think reading about these beasts is helping your nightmares," she finished firmly, plopping the book down on my nightstand.

Sitting up, I wanted to protest, wanted to tell her I needed to know more. *What was that? I saw it!*

"Maybe if I leave, you will sleep more restfully," Lyanna continued.

I bit my tongue, swallowed back my words. Hesitantly, I tapped the book's leather cover.

Her eyes followed mine, tracing the book's title with trepidation. "Really…I don't think…" Lyanna hesitated. "It's not as if you'll have to worry about the sedwa, as they are called. They are merely creatures of legend, an old tale some still like to share by the fireside to scare children, or perhaps a rumor the people of Evren began years ago to deter travelers from venturing this way. Our village has been safe; I've never even heard of one attacking anyone." She shook her head. "I don't see why you'd want to know more about these nightmarish things."

Despite her words, she reseated herself with a sigh and picked up the book resignedly. Skimming through the pages, she paused midway through and cleared her throat. "There isn't much more about them: *Rarely seen by villagers, few accounts of the sedwa exist to give an accurate description. In fact, some insist that these creatures are purely the result of overactive imaginations. Only a few scattered attacks have been attributed to the sedwa, and then only because no other animals were identified as the predators and the victims' descriptions of their predators matched those above.*

"*These beasts only attack if threatened or first pursued by humans, and they hunt alone. Once one of their kind is attacked or killed, the sedwa do not forget and continue to pursue humans until their bloodlust is quenched…* This is certainly not the type of thing you will be learning about in school, once you're well enough to attend." She peered at me over the book's edge. Returning to scanning the page, she finished, "It looks like that's about all there is to read. I think it's safe to say they don't exist."

I frowned, craning my neck to see the book and then reaching out to turn the page for her. The text continued, so I gave her a pointed look to say, *The chapter continues…see? Why won't you read it to me?*

Lyanna cleared her throat uncomfortably. "Well…this book is old. There isn't much talk of this these days…I am unsure if it's because they are foolish tales founded in myth, or if the royal family has tried to block it all out of Misroth's memory to try to protect us."

My heart leapt with curiosity and anticipation, and I frowned, hoping my eyes looked pleading enough to convince her to continue. *Please read. I need to know. I'm not too frightened.*

She sighed, unable to resist. "If you really wish to hear…I suppose there's no harm." She drew a deep breath: *"Those who do believe in the existence of the sedwa believe they are native animals to the Wastelands south of Toryn. They are said to be remnants of many dangerous creatures that were killed off or expelled from Misroth through the protective spell that continues to ward them off from our land."*

The chair creaked as she stood and set down the book once more. "It's about lunchtime. I'm sure you're starving."

I cross my arms across my chest.

"That is all the book says about that matter," Lyanna explained. "Only a few old books mention any of those myths about the Wastelands and the spell."

As she bustled out of the room, I let my gaze wander around the room, settling on my view out the window again. *The sedwa definitely exist. Did the one I encountered in the forest choose not to attack me because no humans have harmed any of them? Or was it going to attack me? Has someone been hurting them?* Drawing a deep breath to settle my racing heart, I tried to thrust the image of the eyes far from my memory. *Are the myths true? Are there other monsters out there, beyond Misroth?*

A knock at the front door startled me out of my thoughts. I listened curiously as Lyanna answered.

"You're out of school early." Lyanna's voice trailed into my room.

A boy's voice answered. "I wanted to come over on my lunch break to see if she is all right, since I found her." *Avrik?*

Lyanna's voice was low. "She doesn't talk yet. I'm not sure if it's due to trauma or if she was always a mute, but she can't tell us much, not even a name or where she is from, so…don't upset her. But it's good you stopped by; I'm sure she could use a friendly face, especially since you'll be going to school together once she's well. She insists she has no family, so unless circumstances change, she will be staying with us."

My guess was confirmed when Avrik poked his head around the corner to peer into my room. "Hi, feeling any better?" he asked.

Sitting up, I nodded.

He shuffled into the room, sliding the books out of his arms and onto the floor, and dropping an empty lunch pail and a bow and quiver beside them.

I raised my eyebrows at the weapon, and Avrik grinned at my surprise. "I'm going hunting with Father once I return home," he explained, and plopped into the seat Lyanna had left at my bedside. "I don't have a lot of time," he continued. "But in case you didn't already know, my name is Avrik. Lyanna told me you're staying here. Evren's nothing special, but I do have some friends I can introduce you to, once you feel well enough to go to school." He hesitated, studying my face as if he could see every line of fear and pain etched on my forehead, every nightmare traced in the dark circles I knew rested beneath my eyes. "I'm sorry for…whatever happened to you. Maybe I can understand a little, though. My mother died when I was young…I never knew her…" His voice trailed away and he stared at his hands in his lap. Clearing his throat, he added quickly, "I'm sorry, I shouldn't trouble you with that."

I couldn't help but stare at him, wondering if maybe I had found a friend, if there was any way he *could* understand. He looked like he was about my age, built tall and lanky with hands and feet that didn't quite fit the rest of his body yet. His tanned skin, the color of the sandy beaches at home, spoke of long days spent outside, maybe playing with the friends he had mentioned and doing chores for his father. Short chestnut hair swept up from his scalp like waves on the restless Alrenian Sea. When he lifted his head to face me, I found some comfort in the familiar brown eyes that had watched me with such concern when I'd stumbled into Evren yesterday.

I offered a half-smile to reassure him. *Thanks for trying to understand the nightmares,* I thought.

Apparently reading my mind, he said, "You're welcome. I suppose I'd better go back to school now. Hopefully you will be well enough to come to school soon."

I'm well enough now; Lyanna just needs some convincing to let me go.

He sprang to his feet. "I'll stop by tomorrow morning to visit. You're my closest neighbor now, so when you are well, we can walk to the schoolhouse together." And offering me one last grin, he picked up his belongings and left.

It was five full days later, filled mostly with sleep and reading, before Lyanna decided I had recovered enough to go to school. She found an old leather pack to carry my lunch pail and any books the teacher sent home with me. Handing me an old dress of hers and a pair of boots too large for me, she apologized that she didn't have anything new for me yet, but I didn't mind. I was so eager to leave the confines of the house and explore my new hometown that I could hardly wait for Avrik to arrive at the door. When he knocked, I swung it open and nearly leapt out the door.

Lyanna laughed. "Have fun today. Don't overexert yourself!"

As Avrik and I walked to the schoolhouse together, I noticed that he not only had a pack slung over his shoulders, but also his bow and quiver. I blinked. Was it only a habit because he often hunted with his father, or a matter of protection? Did the people of Evren feel safe here, or did they all make a habit of carrying weapons everywhere they went?

Oblivious to my worries, Avrik was rattling on about one of the games he and some of the other boys in the village had been playing after school. Half-interested in what he had to say, and half-occupied with my thoughts, I strolled along at his side and watched the countryside around me. In distant fields, horses and cattle grazed. Brown, harvested cornfields, dotted with wilted leftover stalks, stretched toward the horizon. I inhaled the fresh air gratefully, feeling revived. The open world around me was a relief after the constricting sensations of fear and the nightmares of almost drowning. I didn't feel trapped anymore.

"…and sometimes we wrestle," Avrik chattered on, "but since you are a girl and it would probably be considered improper, we can change that and tap you… You'll have fun anyway though…"

Though I tried to tread carefully, I stumbled in Lyanna's boots. Avrik shook his head and, with a laugh, caught me before I fell. Grasping my arm as if he thought I needed help keeping my balance too, he took in my outfit with a mischievous grin. I rolled my eyes at him and glanced down at my secondhand clothing.

Lyanna's old blue dress was worn and faded to a dull grey color. Though the fabric hung loosely on my tiny frame, I must have been taller than she was when she fit in the dress, because the hem rested above my ankles and left room for the large boots to show. Over it all I wore a long black cloak, which had once been Rev's, so long it dragged a little in the grass behind me.

I stared straight back into his glinting eyes and glared at him. Out of habit, I opened my mouth, only to draw in a deep breath and clamp it shut again. Would I ever be able to speak again, if I really wanted to? *Did* I want to? I pressed my lips together.

"Lyanna will make sure you have new clothes soon," he said, forcing the smirk off his face in response to my frown. "Don't worry. Besides, it's not like we are in a big city where all the girls talk about is fashion and they're always fussing about their hair and dresses… Though I suppose there are a few here who do that." He scrunched his nose in distaste and waved a hand dismissively, like he was ordering those girls out of his presence.

You've been in big cities? I raised an eyebrow at him in surprise. What if in his travels he had learned more about the monsters like the sedwa and the myths about the Wastelands and the kingdoms beyond ours?

Avrik seemed to read my mind. "Yes, I've been to some of Misroth's other towns and cities with my father. He's a hunter and trader, so he does a lot of traveling. He sometimes journeys as far as Argelon, but he's never let me go with him."

My curiosity stirred, but my question was answered. Avrik knew nothing of the myths, or surely he would already be launching into his third or fourth mesmerizing description of the monsters lurking in foreign kingdoms.

He seemed wistful, but then he brightened at another memory. "But I have been to Misroth City before. Have you…?" He hesitated, stopping before he finished the question, as if afraid to ask me about my past.

I finished his question for him in my head. *Have I ever been to Misroth City before? Yes, but this, Avrik, is the farthest I've ever been from home. I always thought I'd travel throughout all of Misroth someday, see my entire kingdom, and even explore the kingdoms and lands beyond ours despite our closed borders. I never thought I'd be hiding in a little village where no one knows me, making friends with a boy I can't talk to. So please, please don't ask any more… Not now.*

Pain welled in my chest, stinging relentlessly in my throat and eyes, but I forced back the tears.

Avrik turned from me with a shake of his head. "I wish you could share your name, or where you are from, but I won't pester you. If something terrible happened to you, it makes sense you'd want to forget." He sighed and quickly changed the subject. "Don't be nervous, though, about your first day of school."

I don't think you'll mind having a quiet friend when you seem comfortable enough with filling the silence, I thought. *Good. We'll get along well.*

"Although, I will warn you, word spreads fast around here," Avrik told me as we trudged up one of a series of hills in our path. "Everyone already knows about you, and Teacher is expecting you. She encourages us to read often, so if you enjoy reading as much as Lyanna told me you do, you should enjoy our schoolwork."

Panting, we reached the crest of the hill and paused to take in the view. Grey and white clouds smothered the sun and sky and swirled together, wrestling with one another to determine which would choose the weather of the day. A cool breeze tugged at my cloak and brushed leaves past us, sending them rolling down the hill. Slashes of brown obscured my vision as locks of my hair, hanging freely about my shoulders, blew across my face. Up ahead, tucked behind a few more hills, rested a one-room building, about the smallest building I'd ever seen. I blinked, wondering what it was like to have to walk somewhere to school every day and share your teacher with a room full of other students.

With mild surprise, I realized Avrik was talking still.

"My mother liked to read a lot too… I think Father is lonely without her. Some of the townspeople like to spread rumors about his hunting habits, say he acts suspicious with his frequent travels and his long days up in the mountains and out in the forest. They do not like that he rarely socializes. Sometimes they tell stories about how he must be traveling across our borders and joining in forbidden deals with Alrenor and Toryn. He likes to keep away from everyone…avoid the talk…" Pain leaked into his dark eyes and I found myself feeling sorry for him.

You have things you want to forget too.

Questions about his mother flitted through my brain, things I'd hesitate to ask even if I could speak.

He whispered, "She became ill when I was only a baby. No one really knew what was wrong. But Father tells me about her, and she left a journal behind." He shrugged, as if tossing his grief aside like an unwelcome weight.

I offered him a half-hearted smile, trying to express my encouragement and sympathy in one look, and he returned it gratefully.

"Anyway, everyone at school will probably be in awe of you, a mysterious outsider." He laughed. "But I'll keep you company." Then his lips quirked in a playful expression and his eyes sparked with fun. "I'll race you the rest of the way there!" he exclaimed, and before his words registered with me, he was gone.

Grinning, I sprinted down the hill after him as gracefully and quickly as my clunky boots would allow. He drew up beside the schoolhouse, standing apart from the clump of children gathered at the door. Gasping, I stumbled after him.

Race me when I'm wearing shoes that fit and then we'll see who wins, I thought, recalling all the times I had bested Gillen in races through the castle grounds and along the beach.

I glanced over Avrik's shoulder, my eyes skimming over a group composed of children from six years old to a few years older than me. Relieved, I noticed that no one else seemed to be armed with any sorts of weapons, but they didn't appear surprised at Avrik's accessories either.

Avrik nodded and wished them all good morning, but most were staring at me with large, curious eyes instead. A girl my age, dressed in a floral print dress, scanned my large, faded outfit and quirked an eyebrow. I shot her a sheepish smile, but she turned away, tossing her blonde braid over her shoulder.

"Don't mind Jayn," Avrik whispered in my ear. "She thinks having a wealthy merchant for a father makes her royalty."

Before he could say more, a young woman waded through the group of students, pushed open the door to the schoolhouse, and urged us all inside. Long black hair draped past her shoulders, and her eyes were pale blue like Lyanna's and full of a kind light.

Following the other students, Avrik stepped through the doorway and leaned his pack, bow, and quiver against the wall. I followed, but the teacher made me pause when she held up her hand.

"I've heard about you," she said. "I'm Ara. We'll have to come up with a name for you I suppose, if you don't remember yours. I heard you can write and that you love to read." Her eyes flitted to Avrik and I nodded eagerly. "Well then I think you will get along in class well. It won't matter that you cannot speak. Talking is often valued more highly than it is worth."

I wasn't sure if it was my imagination or not, but I thought I saw Avrik turn a shade redder out of the corner of my eye.

As I seated myself beside Avrik, I drew far more gazes than I wanted. Self-conscious, my face grew hot, but every time I turned to Ara—or Teacher, as everyone called her—I felt the knots in my stomach lessen. At lunchtime, after several hours of studying history, she told us to put our books away and invited us to join her outside to eat.

I lifted the pail of bread, cheese, and fruit that Lyanna had prepared for me and followed Avrik out into the schoolyard. The older girls had clustered close to one another against the schoolhouse wall to avoid the cold breeze and bent their heads close together as they ate their food and chattered. One of the younger girls looked over her shoulder and caught my gaze, then turned back to whisper to Jayn. Jayn lifted her golden head and met my stare with her perfect blue eyes. She shot me a smile that clearly said: *You are not welcome with us. Find someone else to sit with.*

I shuffled uneasily on my feet. The life of a royal had always been somewhat isolated for me: my world had mostly revolved around time spent with my family, my tutor, and the occasional visits, balls, or feasts with nobility, consisting of the councilmen and their families or the city and town Leaders from throughout the kingdom. I had never had to impress any person other than my father. Gillen had been my best friend, my mother had been nurturing, if demanding, and visitors respected me as a member of the royal family. As long as I strove to follow the rules of conduct for royal blood, my father had been content. Before, my mere presence had been enough to earn respect and admiration from others; now I was being judged as unworthy just as quickly.

A stocky boy, with dark grey eyes and hair red as strawberries, approached Avrik and nudged him. "Are you eating with us?"

"Uhh…" Avrik hesitated and glanced at me. "What about her, Jaren?"

Jaren frowned. "You don't even know her name, and you want to forget about us to spend time with her? What about archery tonight? What about—"

"Jaren," Avrik interjected, "I am still your friend. But she's my neighbor and I want her to feel welcome."

Another boy with golden blond hair joined us. "She can eat with the girls." He paused and wiggled his eyebrows, adding in a taunting voice, "Unless she's your lover."

I bit my lip and felt color flood my cheeks.

Avrik rolled his eyes. "She's a *friend*, Shilam! Why can't she join us?"

Shilam shrugged. "The girls never eat with us. They want to talk about…well, I-don't-know-what."

"Give her a chance." Avrik turned to a boy further back, with sandy hair and soft brown eyes. He was tall yet quiet, observing the conversation thoughtfully. "Bren, help me out here. She wants to join us to shoot bows and swordfight too—"

I cast Avrik a sidelong glance, surprised at his words, but not unpleased. He must have assumed my long silence this morning as he'd described he and his friends' activities together had been assent.

"*What?*" Jaren's eyes went wide. "What kind of girl is she?"

Now my whole body went hot and I stiffened. *What kind of* boy *are you?* I thought fiercely, wishing I could yell at him.

"There's nothing wrong with her," Avrik said. "She simply isn't dull like the ones you know." His grin was bright and made his eyes sparkle, and I couldn't stop the smile that spread across my own face at his words.

Jaren raised up his hands. "I'm sorry…I did not mean it that way…"

"So she is interesting, like you," Shilam said, smirking at Avrik and nudging him on the arm. "I'm surprised she doesn't carry a bow and quiver everywhere also."

"It's a habit of my father's to always be prepared," Avrik said, the sparkle still in his eyes even as he crossed his arms across his chest. "Is that so wrong?"

The other boys chuckled, clearly enjoying their opportunity to poke some lighthearted fun at their friend.

Clearing his throat, Bren finally spoke. "I'm with Avrik on this one. There's no reason she cannot join us." He shot me a welcoming smile and I breathed a sigh of relief.

Jaren shrugged and Shilam nodded at me, saying, "If you don't want to spend time with the girls, you can sit with us."

We settled in the grass with some of the other boys. Sitting cross-legged with Lyanna's dress pooling out around me, I rested my lunch pail on the ground and began to empty its contents.

Avrik leaned over to whisper in my ear. "I'm sorry about all of that. Jaren usually likes to tease and doesn't mean most of what he says." He grinned again. "He tries to accuse me of having a love interest every week, but that is because he is jealous of the attention I get." He winked and shot a glance over at the girls, who immediately noticed his gaze and lost themselves in giggles and bashful smiles as they hid their faces.

Suddenly self-conscious, I nodded and played with the hem of my dress. Taking a bite of bread, I swallowed and tried to pretend nothing about this unusual environment made me feel shy or out of place. How strange to feel familiar in the spacious corridors and vast expanses of the castle, yet uncomfortable here in a cozy, secluded village.

"And I'm sorry they weren't open to you joining us immediately...Shilam and Jaren are not always open to new things," he explained simply. "But Bren is my best friend; he has always supported me, no matter what. I know in the end they will all like you."

I smiled at him to show my thankfulness.

Avrik turned back to his friends. "By the way," he announced, "she does have a name. It's Elena."

My mouthful of bread went down hard and felt like it lodged itself somewhere in my throat. I swallowed again. This was a bold move on Avrik's part, and I wasn't sure if I liked the fact that he had taken it upon himself to give me a name.

"Wasn't that your mother's name?" Shilam asked.

Looking uncharacteristically bashful, Avrik toyed with the slice of cheese in his hands. "Maybe."

Noting his discomfort, I patted his arm and smiled, and Avrik's face brightened. Studying the light dancing in his eyes, I realized how much my silent acknowledgment meant to him. The name was important to him, a clear sign that he was welcoming me into his life. With my parents' betrayal still searing my heart, his token of friendship felt like a healing balm.

Thank you, I thought. *I can be Elena. I can be your friend and live this new life.*

Maybe life in Evren wouldn't be bad. Lyanna and Rev made their house feel like home, and though no one could replace Gillen, I could make new friends. Perhaps someday I could even feel safe here.

Back in the classroom, Ara continued with a general history lesson addressed to all ages, before giving different writing assignments to each group to turn in the next day. Finally, she brought me a small stack of books.

"These are for you to read—history, mathematics, writing lessons, literature. I'll occasionally review what you have learned from them. I do not know what you have or haven't learned before this, so we'll start with basic information and go on from there."

I ran my fingers over the titles of the books, taking them in, certain I already knew most of the lessons they had to offer, but grateful for a distraction from my troubled thoughts. I missed the castle's vast libraries and was eager to read again.

After school, Shilam, Bren, Jaren, and I accompanied Avrik back toward his home. We stopped briefly to tell Lyanna where I would be.

"Elena is coming home with us for a bit, if that is all right with you," he said.

Lyanna brushed flour onto her dress and looked at me in surprise. "Elena…?"

Avrik turned red and glanced down at the floor. "It—it's what I have decided to call her."

Lyanna's face softened into a look of understanding and she said no more on the subject. "Do you plan to be gone long?"

Avrik cracked a smile. "Trust me, none of us would want to be late for dinner! We only plan to shoot for a short while."

She blinked in surprise before sighing and waving us on. "As long as you make sure Elena doesn't overtire herself." She shook her head, but I saw a smile nudge the corner of her mouth. My urge to roll my eyes at her concern melted away at the sight.

As we trudged toward Kyrin and Avrik's cabin on the edge of the forest, my nerves tensed up and knots curled in my stomach and I imagined the sedwa's eyes watching me once more. *It can't reach you here.*

I tried to focus on the boys' conversation and push the images of the sedwa from my mind.

"Let's see if you can hit the target at fifty yards now," Jaren teased, nudging Shilam in the stomach with his elbow.

"You were the one complaining about the 'breeze' last time!" Shilam protested.

"Well, I am glad you've all realized there's no contest with me," Avrik said. His eyes were alight with mischief. "I'll outshoot everyone."

Bren rolled his eyes. "As usual."

Avrik laughed. "As usual!" He flung out his arms with a flourish, then spun around to offer us all a quick salute and bow of his head. "You're welcome in advance for the fine performance you are about to witness," he said with a smirk.

The boys shook their heads, not even deigning to respond.

We stopped before the small shed beside Kyrin's stable. A horse whinnied from within and Avrik glanced at the boys. "I'm going to check on Billa. Set up the targets and I'll be right back."

Despite my attempts at reassuring myself, I watched the woods nervously as the boys retrieved targets out of the shed and set them up. They had stowed their bows and quivers in Avrik's shed, apparently because they most often shot here, so I was the only one without a weapon.

As Avrik returned from the stable, brushing dust off his trousers, he smiled at me. "I have an extra bow for you," he said. He entered the shed and a moment later approached me with a bow and quiver full of arrows and handed it to me. "They are yours to keep."

I studied the bow: it wasn't like the gaudy, ornately carved one I had left behind at the castle, but it was just as well-made, with no unnecessary decorations or frills. It felt lightweight and strong in my hands, familiar yet new. If weapons could have personalities, this one was warmer and homier than the showy pieces at the castle. As much as I had once appreciated my old bow, this one felt…right.

I felt a soft smile play across my lips. Moments of archery practice with Gillen returned to me, happy memories forever etched in my mind. Although many reminders of my past life were painful, it did feel good to be doing something familiar. I held up the bow and tested the string, pulling it to my cheek and taking a practice aim at the nearest target.

That was when I realized the boys were all looking at me. Shilam's eyes were wide. "You've shot a bow before?"

I lowered the bow and smirked. *I'm a girl, not a donkey. Of course I've shot a bow before.*

Bren rolled his eyes at his friend. "You say it like no girl has ever used a weapon before."

"Sorry, I—I don't see—my sister does not care about—I'm sorry," Shilam stammered.

Lifting the bow once more, I shot at the target, my arrow easily finding its mark on the bullseye. I turned back to the boys and quirked an eyebrow expectantly.

Avrik chuckled and turned to Shilam. "Well?"

Shilam crossed his arms. "I'd like to see you compete with her."

Bren and Jaren exchanged looks and nodded. "Yes, let's see the master archer go up against Elena," Bren said with a playful grin.

Avrik lifted his chin and cracked his knuckles. "Very well." He tossed a glance in my direction. "Those three never prove to be much competition. Let's see how you measure up."

Smiling softly, I offered him a casual shrug and watched as he strung an arrow to his bow and tugged on the string in one swift motion. I blinked and his arrow struck the target directly next to mine. Beaming, he turned to me to salute again, and his friends began laughing, cheering, and applauding in delight.

"I'm taking a seat for the performance," Jaren said, plopping down in the grass, and Bren and Shilam joined him.

Without responding to Avrik's impish look, I stepped forward and raised my bow again. *Thud.* My arrow found its mark, leaving three perfectly aligned arrows to fill the small red space painted on the target. I stepped back and coolly gestured toward the spot I had just vacated, watching Avrik expectantly.

"It looks like you have met your match, Avrik!" Bren cried.

Avrik laughed and rose to my silent challenge, this time slicing one of the arrows on the target in half. "I could do this all day!" he said.

My eyes met his and I broke into a smile. *So could I.*

We shot long into the evening, the other boys eventually joining in but leaving most of the competition to Avrik and me, each of us never besting the other for long and continuously seeking new ways to heighten the challenge. Sometimes we shot from a greater distance; other times we aimed at smaller targets or fired at boards Shilam or Bren tossed into the air for us.

At last, Shilam, Bren, and Jaren left for their homes and Avrik escorted me back to Lyanna and Rev's cottage. We paused at the door, my hand on the knob.

"Thank you for the competition," he said, his eyes dancing with a playful light. "As I said, the other boys haven't been much lately, and do not have as much time to devote to practice, so I was in danger of growing bored with our shooting matches. Anyway, I'll see you tomorrow!"

He backed away and I nodded, watching my new friend as he dashed through the grass toward home before I slipped into the welcoming warmth of my own.

CHAPTER FIVE

MY BLUE SILK DRESS FELL in a long, heavy curtain to the floor. I gathered the folds up from about my feet, but still tripped as I walked down the hallway.

"Careful, Halia," my mother murmured, reaching out to steady me. I grasped her arm, her velvet sleeve smooth and cool beneath my fingers.

The guards opened the double doors before my family and me, revealing the great sanctum. Its high ceilings arced above us, their polished wood accents glimmering in the light of the torches lining the walls. Standing like a row of sentinels along each side of the room were wood columns stretching toward the ceiling. As we walked along the marble floor, our footsteps echoed in the vast space. Compared to the rest of the castle, the sanctuary was almost stark. There were no intricate paintings adorning the ceilings or artwork hanging from the walls, no statues depicting past royals, no plush carpets, no gleaming gold or silver chandeliers—not even windows to allow daylight or a view of the wind-tossed Alrenian far below. The high royal priest often explained that beauty was a distraction from worship.

As I walked, head held high despite how uncomfortably close-fitting the waist of my dress was, I wished the priests' belief about beauty extended to clothing. Instead, we were to wear our best attire as a display of respect. *Perhaps breathing also shows disrespect, and that is why my dress discourages it.*

We slipped onto one of the several wood benches set in rows along the far end of the room and looked up at the altar. Its sides were engraved with tangled vines and flowers, the only aesthetic touch in the sanctuary, while its surface was piled high with logs soaked in oil, prepared today only in symbolism, but on holier days for sacrifices of incense and fresh game.

Once we settled into our seats, the visiting Leaders of Argelon and Emrell and their families entered the sanctuary, followed by some of Misroth's nobility, and last of all, the castle staff. Always close, always wary, the Royal Guard stood at attention in the far corners. Narek, my uncle's youthful new Captain of the Guard, remained near the front, closest to King Reylon.

The high royal priest, dressed in the customary red trousers, tunic, and cloak, removed one of the torches from the wall and lit the logs resting on the altar. Flames blazed to life and began a furious dance, sending hot air rushing against my face until sweat gathered along my forehead. My dress was so heavy, so hot, and my necklace, bracelets, and the circlet in my hair weighed me down like anchors cast into the sea.

"Let us offer our service to the Giver of Life," the priest intoned.

As one, everyone in the sanctum rose to their feet and repeated after the priest. Suppressing a groan, I fanned my face with my hand and cast a sidelong glance at my cousin. He forced a smile, as if trying to remind me through his expression that we would be free soon.

Father noticed our exchange and frowned at me, the line of his mouth rigid. His eyes flashed in the firelight, silently bidding me to remain obedient and to follow rules. *Live like a royal. Make your people proud*—his usual refrain played through my mind as clearly as if he were speaking it again.

"Do not forget that the Giver of Life is also the Giver of Death," the priest was saying as we all sank gratefully back into our seats. "To disobey him is to invite death…"

I opened my eyes, and I was back in my bed in Evren, the morning sunlight streaming into my room with a friendly glow. My throbbing heart slowed and my constricting chest relaxed. *It was only a dream, a memory.* I sighed and wiped the sweat on my forehead away. It was strange how memories of my life at the castle were sometimes injected with as much fear as if they were nightmares; they all carried the weight of the truth about my father, always hovering somewhere in my mind, always tugging at my heart. The ominous feeling hanging around me felt as heavy as a physical presence, and I found myself scanning my room for several moments before, finding it unoccupied, I sighed with relief.

"Good morning," Rev's soothing voice drifted toward me. I looked up to see him standing in the doorway. "Did you sleep well?"

Stretching, I grinned back at him. No need for him to know about my troubled sleep. Other than occasional strange dreams, which were already growing less and less frequent in the past couple of days, I slept peacefully under his and Lyanna's roof.

The sunlight sparkled in his brown eyes, making the green flecks in his irises stand out. "We will leave soon."

I rolled out of bed and approached the washbasin to freshen up and prepare for the day. Once I was dressed in a comfortable, loose-fitting brown dress Lyanna had made for me, I stepped into the kitchen to find Lyanna setting the table for breakfast and Rev stoking the fire.

We settled around the table and Rev thanked the Life-Giver for the meal. It was strange enough to hear Rev and Lyanna speak to him as if he were a friend; it was even stranger to prepare to go before him without having to smother myself in layers of heavy, elaborate attire.

Once the meal ended, we cleared the table together and left the dishes for when we returned. Gathering our cloaks, we bundled up against the chilly autumn air and stepped outside. The morning sun was shrouded in pink clouds hanging low on the eastern horizon, and fog swirled in the air and drifted in patches over the rolling fields as far as I could see— which was not far. We waded through cold mist that coated us in water droplets and made bumps sprout along my arms.

Winding through the grass, we turned away from the rising sun and joined the dirt road that led into the heart of Evren. As we walked through farm and pastureland, others joined us out on the road, until we were all clustering together in one large band of townspeople. When I noticed Avrik and Kyrin, I waved to my friend until he trotted toward me.

I shot him a curious look, wishing someone would explain this day to me.

"We celebrate and pay reverence to the Giver of Blessings in the Evren Leader's garden," he whispered.

When my eyes widened with shock, it was Avrik's turn to look surprised.

"Do you…did you not do it that way?" His forehead scrunched in confusion.

I shook my head.

"You'll have to tell me about it later." He shrugged. "I mean, write to me later."

With a smile, I rolled my eyes at him to mock his overreaction to his mistake. *I'm not offended,* I thought, as if he could hear what was in my mind.

We trod into town and down the main road, passing the rows of businesses and homes, now all silent and still, until once again the street began to cut through farm fields and over hills. Soon the ground began to steepen as we approached the largest hill yet. Sprawling across its top lay a large home of faded grey stone, its walls climbing with ivy and its grounds composed of one great, lush garden that took my breath away.

Although I knew there were flowers that grew year-round, even in Misroth's harshest winters, I had never seen so many vibrant flowers blooming at this time of year—or any time of year—in one place. The rich scent of countless flowers and herbs traveled toward us on the wind. Despite the cold, even flowers I had only ever known to grow in spring or summer were blossoming, from blood-red lamirae with spiraling petals extending toward the sky, to sparkling blue embyth sprinkling the earth like fallen stars. Somehow, the grass within the space was lush and green and every tree was covered in leaves. At the far end of the garden, beyond the shrubbery and trees, I could make out a stream splashing along the edge of the grounds, dividing this strange feat of nature with the withered brown grass of the rest of the winter world. The castle grounds could never rival the beauty of this place.

"The stories say that a long time ago, one of our first Leaders dedicated this land to the Life-Giver," Rev whispered to me, "and the Life-Giver sanctified the land in return, as long as the Leader residing here follows him. These grounds are always a beautiful garden, one set aside as holy, so most of the townspeople only enter it on our holiest of days once a week, along with special celebrations recognized in Evren throughout the year."

We stepped into the garden and again I was overcome with wonder. As if we'd passed through an invisible barrier that brought us into a different world, the weather around us immediately changed. The air became warm and soft, the mist melted away, and the clouds above vanished to reveal an orange dawn bursting across the sky. All around, I only saw grass and plants, flowers and trees—the wintery hills and the mist from the world beyond the barrier was hazy, as if only this garden truly existed and all else was an indistinct memory.

Everyone around me began to shed their cloaks, dropping them in a pile beneath a wide, old oak tree and laughing as if they were experiencing this garden for the first time too. I turned to Avrik to see what he would say, but surprisingly, he was silent. Instead, he threw himself onto the grass and began to roll in it like a child. Grinning, I dropped down and joined him, relishing the way the warm earth felt beneath me. It was as soft as a feather mattress and smelled sweet, like the world always did after a warm, springtime rain.

It took me a minute to realize that even the adults around us were frolicking like children, dancing and twirling under the trees or rolling in the grass as well. Drawing a deep breath, I lay still on the earth and stared up at the sky as the sun climbed higher.

It felt like I could have been in that beautiful place for mere moments or an entire age of the earth when an elderly man from somewhere deeper in the garden approached us. His long, white hair and beard were streaked with silver-grey and his soft brown eyes shone in the early morning light.

"The Leader," Avrik murmured to me, scrambling to his feet and pressing his fist over his heart in a respectful greeting. I quickly followed his example.

"Welcome back, my friends," the Evren Leader said. His eyes seemed to pick me out immediately from the crowd. "Who is this? A guest or a newcomer?"

I felt my face turning red as others glanced toward me. Although not every resident of Evren was present, most were, and their attention made me uncomfortable. Even during royal events, I had never been the focus of much attention, since Gillen had always been the one meant for the throne. I shuffled my feet uncomfortably and studied my boots.

"A newcomer, Corin," Rev said. "She—well, she was ill and traumatized by unknown events she doesn't seem to quite remember. She cannot speak and has no family left, so we have taken her in as part of our family." He smiled down at me like he was proud to present me. "She goes by Elena."

Corin smiled at me, the wrinkles in his tanned face creasing even deeper. "Welcome to Evren, Elena."

Without a spoken cue, everyone began to sit on the grass in a circle, with Corin joining as if he were merely another member of the town and not its Leader. I sat between Rev and Avrik as a woman somewhere further along the circle began to sing softly. Her dark hair shimmered in the dawn, catching the orange, pink, and yellow hues of the sky, while her voice rose stronger and sweeter.

I recognized the sounds of her words, although I could not translate them. She was singing in Alrenian, the past language of Misroth before the New Language had been formed to separate us as a people from Alrenor. No one in Misroth studied Alrenian or understood the words to the old songs, but we remembered many of the songs' meanings.

The breeze swayed the tree branches and the flowers around us as the woman sang of walking alongside the Life-Giver and speaking to him like he was a friend. Then her tone changed, dipping low and soft, and her song compared the Giver to a father, comforting and gentle, and appearing to his people in order to offer love and guidance. The song described him as he healed his sick and broken children. Finally, the woman's voice swelled with power—and when I didn't think she could sing out louder or hit a sweeter note, she sang about him giving life and ending death.

When her song ended, I was left breathless, as if I'd been the one singing. No one had walked with the Life-Giver on Earth in hundreds of years. Yet this citizen of Evren had sung with audacity in her voice, like she herself had met with him, and not like she was simply singing the words to an old song.

And…this woman was not dressed in the attire of a priest. How was she allowed to sing to the Life-Giver if she had not committed her life to service?

This is no morning in the royal sanctum, I thought. These people lived so differently, yet their ways were already endearing to me, and somehow I could not think of these actions as sacrilege, despite all I'd been taught growing up.

Together, the citizens' voices rose in another song. I listened in awe. *Everyone here is permitted to speak with the Giver of Blessings.*

If he'd cared enough to listen to my prayers when my father had nearly killed me, maybe he could tell me what had happened to me— where my visions and knowledge of the truth had come from and why they'd disappeared. Why I had suddenly become mute. Maybe he would forgive me for being a coward and abandoning my cousin and aunt, and protect them from the king.

I could hope.

The months passed and I adjusted to my new life, growing more confident with each day that the danger was gone. The king didn't know I was still alive, or didn't know where I was. And he wasn't searching here.

Lyanna purchased clothes for me to wear at a local dress shop, as well as material to fashion clothes for me herself, though she always requested my help in an attempt to sharpen my almost nonexistent skills. Even with my new clothes, the girls at school all but ignored me, the strange, silent girl, but with Avrik and the other boys to call friends, I didn't mind.

I fell into an easy schedule of schoolwork and reading, helping Lyanna with chores around the house, and spending time with Avrik and his friends, Shilam and Jaren and Bren. When Rev returned home from his work keeping the books at the bank, he would sit by the fire and tell Lyanna and me all the news he'd gathered, either from clients or from local merchants after they returned from trips to nearby cities.

One evening, as I sat beside the fire, struggling to knit as Lyanna had taught me, Rev pulled up a chair and said, "Kyrin's behavior sure has been starting a lot of rumors lately."

Lyanna, knitting in the armchair by the fire, frowned at him. "I don't think we should partake in the town gossip."

Rev shrugged, straightening his glasses. "No, you are right. I can't deny it's fascinating though, the things people dream up. Poor man, I think he only wants to be left alone. You can tell Avrik would like to socialize more. I'm glad you and he are such good friends." He smiled at me.

I poked myself with one of the knitting needles and started in surprise. *Oh. Knitting.* I dropped my head back down to focus on the task.

Lyanna glanced over at me. "Tired, Elena? You can set that aside and we'll work on it some more tomorrow."

Gratefully, I set my unfinished blanket and needles in Lyanna's basket by the fire. Suppressing a yawn, I strolled back toward my bedroom.

Lyanna lowered her voice as I shut my door, but I left it ajar so I could catch her words. "I can't believe no one ever taught her…thirteen years old and no clue how to knit or cook… What kind of mother did she have?"

I almost smiled. *A noble lady for a mother, who had servants do the cooking and cleaning and knitting while a private tutor taught me how to sing and ride and dance and play music...* But memories flashed through my head, and with a jolt of pain I saw my mother again in my mind's eye, watching me as she had on that horrifying night I had accused my father.

Her face was white; her eyes wide with shock. But she did not run to me. She didn't save me.

She let the king sentence me to death.

Once I closed my eyes, I was at home again, the walls on either side of me covered in old paintings of Misroth's history. Racing down the hallway, I tried not to laugh or tread too loudly. My cousin Gillen was at my side, stifling his own laughter. Ahead was the familiar staircase we sought so often in the summertime: twisting and narrow, it wound a path up one of the old towers to an open rooftop. My foot landed wrong and I nearly tripped, but Gillen caught my arm.

"Wait," he whispered, and we both hesitated, waiting for the sound of our tutors' footsteps behind us. When nothing but our own ragged breathing filled our ears, he burst into a chuckle. "They'll be discussing and arguing that old philosophical stuff for hours. Let's go!"

Dashing forward once more, we scaled the steps and reached the tower door. Gillen shoved it open and let me pass through first. The warm night air greeted me with its gentle embrace, full of the sound of a tame sea, its waves lapping gently on the shore far below. I gasped when I saw the sky: a rich, silky black spotted with millions of gems that traced patterns in the heavens. The moon hung soft and low in the sky, a sliver almost outshone by all of the stars' combined light. I couldn't remember ever seeing the stars look this vivid, not any of the times Gillen and I had snuck away to stay awake long into the night.

"Gil, look!" I whispered, pointing to one of the constellations. "Vehgar: the Dragon." We both stared in awe at the cluster of stars that also adorned our kingdom's flag, a symbol that reminded us of what the constellation represented: strength, beauty, and light.

He beamed. "I told you tonight would be perfect. Eryk and Meeryn should let us out to appreciate nature more." Puffing out his chest proudly and trying to deepen his fourteen-year-old's voice, he said, "When I am king, that will change immediately. Every student will be free to study the stars." His voice cracked on *stars*, and I dissolved into giggles.

Gillen glared at me as I snorted, making him burst into laughter with me. Catching our breath and wiping the tears from our eyes, we lay back on the cool stone roof to better view the sky.

"Do you think they will be mad at us?" I asked after several silent minutes. "For encouraging their debate on theology and stealing off to do what they asked us *not* to do?"

Gillen smirked. "That's the joy of being royalty: they can be frustrated, but they can hardly be angry at their future sovereign or his favorite cousin, can they?"

I laughed and shook my head, feeling that Gillen was possibly taking the privileges of his status a bit far and most definitely exaggerating his power. We both knew that as soon as we were caught, we would be reprimanded, but the reward of a late night under the constellations was worth any potential punishment.

"It's strange to think you will someday be ruling Misroth," I said.

Gillen grew solemn. Storm clouds seemed to pass over his blue eyes and his mouth tilted in the half-frown he made whenever he was meditative or troubled. "You know I do not like to think of it seriously. I wish I could remain a prince forever. I would rather not bear that responsibility, and I certainly don't want to think of my father…" He didn't finish the thought.

Uncle Reylon was strong and healthy, so I knew it would be a long time before we needed to worry about losing him. Still, I imagined myself in Gillen's place for an instant and felt the anxiety that likely weighed him down every day. The older he became, the more Reylon included him in meetings with the royal councilmen, proceedings before the throne, and dinners with the Leaders of Misroth's cities that the rest of the royal family did not always attend. Every day Eryk seemed to add more books to the unending pile Gillen had to read and more lessons in conduct and law. It was overwhelming even for me to watch, especially when I was compelled to wait hours each day before Gillen finished his lessons and we could enjoy free time together horseback riding, exploring, swimming, or pretending to be adventurers roaming throughout the castle gardens and grounds.

Footsteps creaked on the stairs and Gillen and I sat up quickly, expecting our tutors. The door swung open and a tall, slender form stepped onto the rooftop. I didn't immediately recognize the face beneath the hood.

"Mother?" I asked in surprise.

"Eryk and Meeryn said you both were missing, but I knew where to look." Her voice sounded soft when I expected it to be stern. "You should both be in bed."

"Yes, Mother," I said, bowing my head. It was a small inconvenience for me to disappoint and frustrate Meeryn, but now my father would be firm with me tomorrow and that was far more difficult to abide. His disapproving gaze always pierced me to my soul until I was fiercely disappointed I had let him down. He and Mother expected perfect obedience from me as they and Meeryn worked to mold me into a perfect lady. They were proud of their royal heritage and wanted me to honor it in all of my actions. I groaned inwardly. "I'm s—" I began.

"It is quite beautiful out here tonight, isn't it?" As she lifted her face to the sky, her hood fell back. The starlight sparkled in her deep brown hair as if hundreds of tiny gems had been set in her tresses. Her face relaxed into a smile and she closed her eyes, like she could soak up the beauty of the night and keep it forever. As breathtakingly lovely as she was standing there, wrapped up in her brief moment of joy, I half-believed that she really was absorbing it into herself. It was in that moment that I realized how little I ever saw her smile or lose herself in simple pleasures.

Then the moment was gone and she opened her eyes. Turning to Gillen and me, she drew a deep breath and settled her face back into a regal, impassive gaze. "Goodnight," she said, bestowing this one word upon us less like a blessing and more like a command.

Wordlessly, we crept back down the steps and toward our bedrooms. But that vision of my mother played in my head long afterward, making me wonder which royal responsibilities had weighed her down and stolen that enraptured look from her face.

With a deep breath, I sat up in my bed in Evren, suddenly awake, and the castle faded away from me. It had all been so vivid, another memory I had revisited in my dreams. Moonlight spilled through my window and onto my bed covers. Everything was quiet and dark, and the house was still.

How is Gil now? Is he safe, or is my father going to attempt to kill him too? I'd left him and my aunt Velaire to an uncertain fate. What if they were already dead? I shivered, although it wasn't cold beneath my blankets.

How could I have left them? I closed my eyes, as if I could block out the anxiety and guilt washing over me. *But how could I save them? My father would have me killed as soon as he saw me. I can't ever go back. I'm powerless against him and his guards.*

But these thoughts didn't change how I felt, or how much the aching longing for my cousin and aunt gnawed at my heart. It didn't change how much my parents' betrayal filled me with sorrow and anger. And it didn't change the fact that I was still terrified of being hunted down by my father's men, even here in Evren.

Catching my breath, I lay back down on my pillow and realized my cheeks were wet. Lifting a hand to my face, I brushed away the tears.

The next day after school, I accompanied Avrik back to his and Kyrin's cabin. When we arrived, he gathered some wood from the chopped pile in his yard, and before I could reach his front door to open it for him, he elbowed the knob and kicked the door open.

"Father won't be back for a few days," he panted as he deposited the wood on the hearth. Kneeling down, he piled the logs into the fireplace and set to work starting a fire. "In the past, I've stayed with Lyanna and Rev when he was gone on long trips I did not accompany him on, but I'm old enough now to care for myself." He paused, pressing his lips into a firm line. "Ever since my mother died, my father has spent more time away hunting and traveling." He glanced up and noticed my raised eyebrow. "I'll be fine, Elena."

Sitting down in the worn armchair near the fireplace, I pulled my journal and pencil from my backpack and scratched out a message. I knelt beside Avrik and held the paper out in front of him. *You can come over for dinner tonight, at least.*

He smiled at me in response, lifting his face so that the firelight sparkled in his warm brown eyes. I dropped my gaze back down to my paper and fiddled with its edges.

"I'm glad you are my friend," he said softly. A frown crept over his face. "I have friends, but sometimes I think that their parents limit the amount of time they can spend with me." He shrugged. "No one likes to keep company with sorrow. I feel like you are the only person who truly understands, somehow. You don't shrink away like some others do, and you don't pity me."

I bit my lip, studying his face while he stared into the fire. In the six months I'd known him, Avrik had not often talked about the deeper feelings brewing beneath his cheerful exterior, and I was glad he trusted me, even if his words made me ache with sympathy. I reached for my journal, grasping for words to share with him, but stopped myself. No words would ever be more powerful than the presence of a friend. I lay my hand over his and watched the fire with him as dusk fell and the shadows in the house lengthened.

At last, I nudged his arm and he stirred suddenly, like he had been dozing. I glanced at him and he offered me a sheepish smile. "I was thinking," he said. I wanted to smirk, because I'd never heard Avrik stay silent that long, but I caught myself when I noticed the serious expression still on his countenance. I had learned to recognize that look, even if it rarely flitted across his face. He'd been thinking of his mother all this time.

Avrik pushed to his feet and helped pull me to mine. Shrugging my backpack over his shoulders, he doused the fire and headed for the door. The icy wind felt as sharp as a cold knife cutting into my cheeks when we stepped outside.

Avrik stared at his feet for a minute before he spoke. "Mother was a good listener, like you." He paused and laughed, looking self-conscious. "I mean, I know you sort of *have* to listen since you can't speak. But you don't have to keep my company, or give me attention when I talk endlessly…" He cleared his throat and stared off over the hills, toward the Vorvinian Mountains. "I think everyone in Evren loved her," he said softly. "I wish Father were around more."

You will always have Rev and Lyanna and me, I wanted to say, but even if I could have spoken, I was not sure if I would have said the words. Who could tell what the future would bring?

CHAPTER SIX

THE FIRST SNOWFLAKES OF THE season were beginning to fall as Avrik, Bren, and I trudged down the main street of Evren one evening. Most of the citizens were indoors where it was warm, tucked away in one of the houses with windows flickering from firelight and smoke curling from their chimneys. A few businessmen and farmers strode briskly along the street, huffing great steaming breaths in the winter air and rubbing their arms as they went.

Despite my cloak, hood, and mittens, the brisk air made me shiver as well. I tucked my hands inside my pockets and glanced at my friends. Bren was heavily bundled too, but Avrik had his hood pushed back and only his fingerless shooting gloves on his hands. As usual, his bow and quiver were strapped to his back, as if he were preparing to go on the hunt for his dinner, not order a meal at the local inn.

The old inn, constructed from dark, weatherworn logs with a sign reading *Wanderer's Rest*, waited for us across the street. In the dim evening light, it looked ominous—or perhaps I only found it that way because of what Lyanna had said. I glanced at the swirling, snowy sky and wondered how late it was and if she was expecting me home for dinner yet.

Avrik noted my restless mood and shot me a carefree grin. "It'll be fun, Elena. Lyanna worries about travelers because she thinks the outsiders are gruff, but she knows nothing about them. Father and I have made plenty of trips; there is nothing to worry about. Besides, we rarely have any visitors anyway. To most, we are not worth the journey, and as close to the border as we are, there are few travelers ever passing through."

"Come on," Bren urged, pushing past us to cross the street.

I glanced at Avrik, who smiled reassuringly at me and took my arm to walk with me.

My mouth opened with the thought: *I don't need to be escorted!* But when I tried to speak, no words came out. Frowning, I pried my arm from his grip. He shrugged and scuffed his foot in the dirt before dashing ahead to catch up with Bren, and I followed.

Bren yanked open the heavy inn door and light spilled out from inside. The scents of the fire and hot food—especially baking bread—mingled together in the air and tempted our noses. My stomach growled.

Avrik leaned in to whisper to me. "Like I said, they have some amazing food." His warm breath tickled my ear.

We sat at a small round table near the corner closest to the door and waited for Selna, the innkeeper, to take our orders. I glanced around at the warm, busy atmosphere of the inn. The main dining area in which we sat had a low ceiling of rough-hewn wood beams. A few support columns were spaced out across the creaking, mud-stained floor. To our right, in the center of the room, a roaring fire blazed in a huge fireplace. Nearly every wall was lined with shelves stocked with canned goods, dried herbs, sacks of flour, and other baking ingredients, as if Selna felt the best way to create a homey feel was to surround her patrons with components of the food they were about to eat.

The room was flooded mostly with local farmers, dressed in faded shirts, patched trousers, and mud-crusted boots. One group was seated in armchairs near the hearth, smoking pipes and chatting about crops. Here and there, at the various round tables scattered across the floor, businessmen ate and talked both business and leisure. One or two families were seated in corners of the room, but for the most part, all of the inn's customers were men at this time of day. The majority of Evren's women were at home preparing dinner, and most children went home after school to eat. This place was radically different from the royal dining hall of my upbringing, or even Lyanna and Rev's cozy kitchen table, and I loved it.

I pulled my journal, pencil, and the little pouch of spending money Rev had given me from my cloak pocket and jiggled it, listening to the coins inside. The concept of paying for anything was foreign to me; the castle had provided me with everything I could have imagined, and servants had attended to my every need or desire often before I even realized the needs and wants were there.

Scrawling "tea" across one of my journal pages, I pushed it toward Avrik.

"Not going to try the food?" he said.

Lyanna will want me to eat dinner with them, I wrote. I gave him a pointed look.

He nodded. When Selna bustled over to our table, he and Bren put in our orders. It only took her a few moments to return, plopping a large mug of steaming tea in front of me.

As the chatter of the crowd enveloped us, Bren and Avrik pointed out various Evren men and women, telling me who they were and what they did. For the most part, I tried to listen, but my mind was restless. I tapped my boot softly on the floor and doodled on my slip of paper. *It's getting late, and Lyanna expects me home soon,* I thought.

Finally, Selna arrived with two heaping bowls of venison stew and a plate full of fresh bread coated in butter for the boys. For a few minutes, they were too consumed in their food to pay much attention to anyone else in the inn. I inhaled the aroma of mint tea rising from my mug and tried to relax.

Then something caught Bren's attention. He paused with his spoon halfway to his mouth and nudged Avrik. "Over there," I heard Bren whisper. He nodded his sandy blond head toward the opposite end of the room, where a staircase led to the second floor and most of the inn's guestrooms.

Descending the steps were two men in travel-stained scarlet and blue cloaks: the colors of the King's Royal Guard. One of the men was unfamiliar, but the other I recognized, though I did not know his name. He was one of the men from the dining hall, one who had helped drag me away from my parents when my father accused me of treason. I was sure he would know me immediately.

My mouth ran dry. A jangling noise jolted me back to my table, where Bren and Avrik were studying me curiously. I glanced down and realized I'd dropped my coin pouch on the floor. With a trembling hand, I reached down and clutched it tightly.

The guards must not have seen me yet. Do I leave now? What will Avrik and Bren think? How can I tell them I need to leave? They'll ask questions, want answers…

I swallowed and stared at the table, determined not to meet the boys' gazes and give away my fear.

Why would royal guards travel to Evren? Are they looking for me? Have they asked around—will they talk to Lyanna and Rev? Panic screamed in my head; the questions were coming so quickly they were tumbling over each other, swirling in a confused mass in my brain.

Avrik's voice pierced through my thoughts. "Are you all right?" His dark eyes glinted in the firelight.

If Avrik and Bren realized the reason why I was upset…well, I didn't want to think about the trouble it could cause.

Grabbing my pencil, I scribbled frantically. *I don't feel well.*

Avrik's brow knotted. "Bren, we have to take Elena home."

Bren's face fell, but he forced a smile and nodded. He dropped a few coins on the table to pay for his meal, and Avrik did the same.

Without a word, the boys stood and yanked on their cloaks. I fumbled with mine, realizing my fingers were quivering too violently to fasten it under my chin properly. The world seemed to be pulling away from me and swaying like a ship's deck all at once. Inwardly hating myself for my fear, I grasped for the table to catch my balance, but my hand landed clumsily in my mug of tea instead. Recoiling, I knocked the mug over, splashing its contents across the table. The mug rolled over the edge of the table and shattered on the floor, its broken shards mixing with the widening puddle of tea.

I was sure every eye on the inn was on me.

Wide-eyed, Avrik was at my side in an instant, trying to steady my trembling body with a reassuring hand on my back. I thanked the Life-Giver that the guards were behind me and could not see my face.

"What is this?" Selna strode to our table and studied our faces. "Is something wrong?"

"She's ill," Bren said, nodding to me.

"Oh, Elena, your face is as pale as the snow outside," Selna gasped. "Boys, go fetch Lyanna and Rev and I'll set her up in a cozy room where she can relax."

No, don't leave me here! I wanted to cry out, to beg them not to leave me here, but Avrik and Bren bolted out the door instantly and Selna tugged gently on my arm.

"Come, I'll make you comfortable and send for the Healer."

Shaking my head, I tried to fight against her grip, tried to pull away and chase after the boys before the guards saw me, tried to—

It was too late.

The guard's boots thudded dully on the floorboards as he approached. I recognized the shock of brown, curly hair and the deep blue eyes: it was the guard from the castle. "What seems to be the problem?" he inquired. He glanced at Selna before dropping his gaze to my face. I refused to meet his look, staring hard at the fireplace on the far wall, as if I could find sanctuary somewhere amidst the flames.

I tensed, waiting for the inevitable. Would he reveal my identity to Selna and pretend the king and queen missed my presence, or would he accuse me like a wanted criminal and drag me away?

"The girl is ill, sir," Selna said, bowing her head in respect. "I appreciate your concern, but there is no danger in my humble inn."

She pulled me away, leading me past the second guard, who gave me an uninterested glance. There was no glint of recognition in his expression, but that wasn't comforting to me, not when I knew his companion remembered me.

At the top of the stairs was a hallway lined with flickering candles set in sconces and several closed doors, leading to guest rooms. Selna opened one of the doors on the right and ushered me into a small bedroom. There was a small window set in the far wall, its pale green curtains tightly drawn against the night. On the left was a small bed and nightstand, and on the right was a fireplace.

Selna removed my boots and cloak and ensured I was settled in the bed before she turned to start a fire in the hearth. "We'll find the Healer for you, as soon as possible," she murmured as she exited the room. She closed the door softly behind her.

I sat up in bed, throwing the covers off and springing onto the floor. The floorboards were cold under my bare feet as I fumbled for my stockings and boots. Pulling them on, I snatched my cloak from where Selna had tossed it over the foot of the bed and wrapped it around my shoulders. My fingers still trembled slightly as I tied it around my neck, but this time determination fired through my veins and helped keep my hands steady.

Stumbling toward the window, I tore open the curtains. The view from the second story offered a glimpse of a dark alleyway behind the inn. Moonlight glistened off the dusting of snow coating the earth while more snowflakes drifted down from the fluffy grey clouds concealing the stars. I shoved open the window and leaned out, watching my breath being carried away on the cold breeze.

Don't hesitate out of fear now, I prodded myself. *There's no time to waste. The castle guard recognized you. This room is your prison cell; he will find you here.*

Memories of climbing down the castle's stone walls flitted through my mind as I swung my leg over the windowsill, and I prayed this venture would not end as badly as my last. I peered down to search the bricks for hand and footholds. The air nipped at my fingers and made them numb, but I didn't dare fish the mittens from my pockets and try to climb in those. I grasped at a chipped brick with my left hand and shoved my boot into a gap in the wall before drawing a deep breath and swinging out the window. My arms shook and I nearly slipped as I struggled to grasp the wall with my right hand and plant my right foot. Once I was safely out, I scrambled wildly down the wall, sliding on patches of ice and missing most of my intended holds until I fell the last several feet and landed on my back in the snow.

My breath knocked from my lungs, I lay staring up at the sky for several moments while my heart throbbed in my ears. The world spun and flecks of snow pelted my face and melted in my eyes, blurring my vision. *Get up, get up. Run.* With a shuddering gasp, I finally inhaled some air and leapt to my feet.

"So it *is* you, Princess Halia." The grating voice slammed into my ears and made me spin on my heel. The king's guard, the one who had recognized me, was standing behind me in the alleyway, his cloak rustling around his heavy boots. Snowflakes melted on the scarlet and blue hood pulled so low that only his dark beard and sneering lips were visible. "At first I thought you must be a ghost, to be alive after my captain executed you. And yet…here you are, trapped again. Did you truly think you could evade His Majesty this easily?" Silver light glinted off the sword hilt at his side.

I turned and bolted, my boots slipping on ice and my heart feeling like it was ten feet ahead of the rest of my body. But I was no match for the speed and strength of a seasoned guard. In a few swift strides he was upon me, grasping my arm and wrenching me back. He slammed me down to the earth, pinning me down with his arms and knees as I flailed and pulled against him.

When I stared up at him, his piercing blue eyes met mine. "Who have you told about the king?" he snarled.

Gasping, I shook my head, my hair tumbling about my face. Cold snow bit into my back and melted against my neck until it slithered beneath my cloak.

He slammed me back down into the snow and dug his knee into my chest. *"Who?"*

I ground my teeth together and struggled for air. Moving my lips, I mouthed the words "no one."

In one smooth motion, the guard pressed a dagger against my throat. "I'll give you a final chance to speak, you vile traitor," he hissed. "Child or not, you are old enough to face the consequences of your treasonous actions."

The dagger's edge nicked my skin and warm blood trickled from the wound, but I couldn't fight back, couldn't flee, and couldn't speak.

No one, no one, no one! I cannot speak! I wanted to scream, but I knew the words wouldn't change my fate. He would kill me anyway, regardless of what I said. He might kill me faster if I had a confession for him, rather than drawing out the kill in a painful interrogation process.

From somewhere in the night came more running footsteps. Probably the other guard, realizing his companion had exited the inn and joining to help. But as the guard turned away from me, glaring over his shoulder, I heard a cry of rage, and the voice was familiar. Avrik.

The guard sprang to his feet to face Avrik and gave me a clear view of my friend, his bow and quiver still strapped to his back. His hands moved so fast they were a blur in the darkness. One second he was shouting, the next his bow was notched and pointed at the guard. Before the man could speak or reach for his sword, Avrik fired.

Sprawled out on the ground, I did not even have time to sit up. With a dull thud and a sickening spray of crimson blood in the snow, Avrik's arrow sliced through the guard's throat and dropped him to the ground, where he lay motionless, a corpse in a cramped, dim alley.

Avrik threw down his bow and dashed toward me. His whole body shook and his face was pale as he kneeled beside me, taking in my rumpled clothes and bloody neck. "Are you all right?"

I nodded, still blinking at the prostrate form behind my friend. Avrik had slain a guard. A member of the *King's Royal Guard.*

His voice quavered. "I didn't…I wasn't trying to k-kill him. I saw the man was hurting you and…" He turned and gaped at the body, then glanced back up at the inn, its lit windows casting small pools of light down on us. "We have to find my father. He'll know what to do, before someone sees…" He stood, grasping my hand and yanking me up with him.

Still clutching my hand in his, he raced down the alleyway and through the side streets and alleys of Evren until we were back out on the rolling hills of the countryside. The wind whipped around us, snapping our cloaks behind us and stealing away my breath as I followed Avrik's footprints in the snow. It only took us a few minutes to reach Avrik's home.

"Father!" Avrik cried, bursting through the door in a swirl of snowflakes and wind.

Kyrin, lounging before his fireplace on his settee and sharpening a hunting dagger by the flickering light, glanced up sharply. His brow crinkled and concern flared in his eyes at his son's frantic tone.

"A man was trying to—to hurt Elena," Avrik panted, "but I…I shot him. He's dead. In the alley behind the inn…I don't want people to… What if they accuse me? Or you?"

Kyrin threw his cloak on and was out the door before Avrik had finished speaking. "Lead the way."

We dashed through the night, Avrik holding my hand like it was his lifeline in the blackness. As soon as we reached the alley, Kyrin surveyed the scene and turned back to his son. "Go inside. Leave this to me."

Without a word, Avrik nodded. He sprinted toward the street and dragged me after him. Once we arrived at the inn's front door, he finally released me and breathed deeply. "Why would you leave the inn?" he demanded. "Was that man going to…?" He bit his lip, his face going red.

I blinked back at him. *Was he going to rape me? No, he was going to slaughter me, when it* should *have been his mission to* protect *me!*

Avrik shook his head, pressing a hand to his face like he was warding off a dizzy spell. "Never mind. Does your cut hurt?"

When I shook my head, he lifted his hand to wipe away the blood.

"The blood has clotted now. It's so slight I doubt anyone will notice. Just a small cut we could explain away." His hands still trembled.

I threw him a curious frown, wishing I understood his fear.

"Most of Evren all but hates my father, now that he keeps to himself," he sighed. "I would rather no one has to know that I…that I…"

With a soft smile I hoped was comforting, I laid my fingers on his arm and squeezed. *You did nothing wrong, Avrik. You saved my life.*

Avrik massaged his left temple. "Let's go inside. Bren went to Lyanna and Rev to bring them to you, but I turned back, realizing someone should stay with you. I was worried about you…I guess it was good that I did…" He let his voice trail off.

I squeezed my hand tighter on his arm when he moved toward the door. There was still another guard. Though I hadn't recognized him, that did not mean he hadn't discovered who I was, especially when his comrade could have told him before going in search of me.

"It's fine, Elena. I'm sure Lyanna and Rev are here by now," Avrik said, not looking at me and therefore not seeing the panic on my face. With a deep breath, he threw open the door and we stepped back into Wanderer's Rest.

The air felt trapped in my lungs as I scanned the main room for any sign of the second guard, but he was nowhere to be found. Instead, Bren, Lyanna, and Rev stood near the door, calling to Selna to ask where I was.

"She's here," Avrik said.

The three turned startled faces toward us. Avrik tugged me further into the inn and shut the door behind us.

"Why did you leave the inn?" Lyanna cried, racing toward me to yank me into a fierce embrace. Rev was directly behind her.

Selna marched toward us, her hands on her hips. "I've sent for the Healer. Why did you leave your room?" she cried when she saw me.

"She needed fresh air," Avrik cut in. "I found her going for a walk and brought her back inside. She'll be fine; she only wants to go home."

Selna threw a suspicious glance at both of us, but Avrik offered her one of his charming smiles and she relented. "I can tell the Healer to visit your house," she suggested.

I shook my head. All I needed was to have a Healer studying the cut on my neck and asking questions.

Lyanna searched my face before she turned back to Selna. "If she doesn't want the Healer to visit, I will care for her. We will send for him if she shows any more signs of illness." She smiled proudly. "I nursed her back to health when she first came to us, and I'm sure I can help her now."

"Well then, get out of here before you upset my customers with your carryings-on!" Selna shooed us back toward the door.

I breathed easily when we stepped back out into the night. However, my spinning head and hammering heart did not abate. I knew I couldn't rest until the second guard left Evren. Was he searching for me even now? Would he reveal who I was?

Avrik kept a hand on my left shoulder and Lyanna stayed close to my right side, while Bren and Rev followed behind. The five of us treaded through the snow silently, following the road until it became the winding countryside path that led toward home. We passed several cabins and stone houses before we stopped in front of Lyanna and Rev's house. My house.

"I'm sorry all of this made Elena late to dinner and had you worrying," Avrik said to Lyanna, then glanced at me. "I hope you feel better."

I struggled to smile at him. Despite the cold, I still felt sweat lining my forehead, and I knew he was still affected too. I could see the familiar glimmer disappearing from his eyes, like clouds slithering over the sun.

"Goodnight," Bren said.

He and Avrik set off into the darkness, each going their separate ways, and Rev, Lyanna, and I turned back to the house. Stepping eagerly inside, I plucked off my boots and hung my cloak on one of the hooks by the door.

"Are you hungry?" Lyanna asked as she pulled her mittens off.

Even though my encounter with the guard had stolen my appetite, I shrugged, not wanting her to worry about me. Lyanna took my noncommittal response as a yes and steered me toward the dinner table, already set and laden with food.

As we ate, I tried to pretend to enjoy the beef and potatoes, even though I could scarcely choke the food down.

"You are *certain* that you are fine?" Lyanna asked, turning to me and brushing her hand gently over my forehead, pushing strands of brown hair out of my eyes. She stared at me so intently that I dropped my gaze to my plate to hide the cut on my neck and the fear on my face.

At last Lyanna appeared satisfied and the conversation turned toward normal topics. Rev told Lyanna about his day at work, and then mentioned the latest village news: the arrival of the guards.

"Everyone was a bit surprised the king sent two royal guards rather than simple messengers, but maybe he did not trust anyone else to make the journey," Rev said while adjusting his glasses on his nose.

Lyanna raised her eyebrow. "You mean, because of the stories?"

"Yes, I do believe word of our mysterious sedwa lurking in the Vorvinian Mountains and Evren Forest has spread." Rev shot us an amused smile. "They took the old route through Evren Forest, since it is faster than the route by sea. Anyway, they came to bring us news. Old news, they said."

"News of what?"

My stomach clenched. What if they had come to search for me? What if my father suspected I'd survived Narek's attempt to drown me? I waited for the words that would send my world spiraling out of control again.

"News of King Reylon's death. He passed away from his illness—a type of fever, they said—and because his son, Gillen, is too young to take the throne, his brother Zarev has taken his place."

I hesitated, staring into my cup and waiting for the next sentence.

"King Zarev and Queen Ryn announced that their daughter disappeared not long after, and they fear she was kidnapped."

Lyanna gasped and I shifted uncomfortably in my seat. What would happen if everyone guessed my secret and tried to return me to the castle? I held my breath.

"That is terrible," Lyanna said. "I can only imagine the grief that family is enduring." She frowned in thought. "I don't remember much about their daughter. All the news was always about Crown Prince Gillen."

Rev took a sip of water. "I believe she was young—only a small child of five or so. The king and queen have lost hope of finding her alive, for she has been gone for weeks. In fact, the guards only came to spread the news about our new king—the search for his daughter has turned up no leads. A memorial service in the poor girl's honor will be held in the capital soon."

I thanked the Giver of Blessings for how little I had been a point of interest as a child. Few people in Misroth knew enough about me to suspect my secret.

"The guards will be leaving tomorrow," Rev was saying, but I knew I wasn't out of danger. The second guard was probably looking for me. Now that he knew I was in Evren, there was no way he would depart without me—or my body.

Shivering, I lay in my bed, staring into the darkness. Outside, the snow continued to fall and the wind howled against my window. Somewhere out there, a royal guard was hunting for me while another was dead, slain by my friend's hands. How was it that even the death of a guilty man continued to haunt me? The moment played itself over and over in my head: the arrow slicing through the air, hitting its mark, and bringing a man to his death. His blood spilling onto the snow.

I rolled over onto my side, but I couldn't shake the feeling that footsteps were coming for me again. Another guard would peer into my face and threaten me with death. It would be my blood staining the snow.

But where could I run? Who could I tell? Should I steal out into the night and travel until I found a new haven? Tears stabbed at my eyes at the thought of leaving Lyanna, Rev, and Avrik behind.

You did the same to your aunt and cousin. My jaw clenched as I tried to shove my guilt and sorrow back down inside myself, where I'd been trying to hide it for weeks. Unbidden memories leaked into my mind: Gillen's laughter as he and I rode our horses along the beach, chasing seagulls; Gillen's bright smile when he first defeated his trainer in a swordfight while I watched from the sidelines; Gillen's boisterous spirit, kind blue eyes, and gentle nature. Gillen with his golden hair that stuck up from his head like a small mountain when he woke in the morning and pushed away his personal attendants until after he ate breakfast. Gillen with all his uncertainty and fear about taking the throne, his great desire to please his father coupled with his desperate wish for a life of freedom from the heavy responsibility of the crown. Gillen with his heart to help, to heal, to protect, whether his attentions were concentrated on an injured gull outside his chamber window or his people.

I shut my eyes tightly against the shadows creeping about my room. Gillen wouldn't have abandoned me, if he were in my shoes. He would never have left Misroth City until he had found me and helped me escape with him. My cousin was as brave as any of the heroes he pretended to be when we'd played as children in the castle. He wouldn't have left me to an uncertain fate, as I had done to him.

I bit my lip. *I cannot return; I'd die. Even if I did find him and convince him to escape with me, that would only endanger him more. As long as he doesn't know who my father is…what he has done…* I inhaled deeply, trying to convince myself my hopes were true. *As long as he is ignorant, he is safe.*

A dark shadow flitted across my mind before I could banish it completely. *But will my father abandon the power he killed for and let Gil rule once he is of age?*

Before that thought could drag me down into further fear and guilt, someone pounded on our front door. My heart jolted and I sprang from my bed.

Run. Get out of here. I pulled my stockings and boots on before I even allowed myself to consider what exactly I should do or where I should go.

Rev left his and Lyanna's bedroom, his bare feet pattering on the wood floor as he approached the front door with a candle in hand. Heart pulsing madly, I stepped to my doorway and peered around to watch. Rev yanked open the door and snow poured inside. The dark figure standing outside our home was difficult to make out, even as Rev lifted his candle higher to illuminate the stranger's face.

"Kyrin?" Rev asked.

Kyrin—not the royal guard? Did I dare let relief flood me?

"There was an…attack in the forest tonight," Kyrin said gruffly. "I wanted to warn those closest to the forest's edge."

Rev stepped back to let Kyrin in and shut the door. "What happened?" he asked as Kyrin brushed the snow out of his dark brown beard.

"I was out hunting this evening when I came across the body of one of the king's royal guard."

Rev frowned. Lyanna strode out of the bedroom in her robe and crept to her husband's side. "What was he doing in Evren Forest alone?" she asked.

Kyrin shook his head. "I do not know what folly led him there without his companion. His body was…" He shook his head. "I brought the remains back for his comrade to dispose of, and helped him bury the man."

"Will he travel back through the forest now?"

"He was as shocked as I was and unwilling to risk the danger. He said he will depart in the morning for the Alrenian and take a ship out of Kelwed." Kyrin shifted on his feet.

"What do you think it was?" Rev murmured.

"Some will say the sedwa …" he sighed. "But I doubt it was anything other than a bear. No sedwa attacks have been reported for many years. Even if it was a sedwa, they have never been known to leave the forest or mountains. But I decided not to take any risks and warn the people of Evren, in case the sedwa choose to ignore the legends surrounding them and take up a new habit of attacking our village."

"I am sure it was merely a bear, as you said," Lyanna replied, unable to keep the tremor from her voice. "Not a creature of myth."

Kyrin's eyes looked so dark they were almost black. His gaze flicked toward me briefly—though Lyanna and Rev hadn't noticed me, I couldn't conceal myself from a hunter—and settled back on Lyanna. "Let us hope we are right."

When I flung the door open the next morning to walk to school, Avrik was waiting for me. His face was devoid of his usual grin; he had dark circles under his eyes and his complexion was paler than usual. Before Lyanna could come to the door and grow concerned over Avrik's appearance, I waved to her and stepped outside.

For a while, Avrik said nothing, staring down at his feet while he walked. Then he sighed. "I couldn't sleep last night," he said softly. "I kept seeing that man—the man I killed…" He fidgeted with the quiver on his back and glanced at his hands, as if he could see blood staining them.

I opened my mouth before I remembered no sound would come out. *Curse this silence.* I wanted to shout to make him understand he wasn't a killer. He had saved my life.

Stopping in the snow, I turned to him as he stopped with me and studied his face, wished he could read my thoughts.

"He was going to hurt you," Avrik whispered, staring back at me.

I nodded vigorously.

"Do you know why?"

My mouth went dry and I averted my gaze. Hopefully he would take that as a no, since I couldn't lie directly and couldn't risk sharing the truth.

When I dared to turn back to Avrik, a shadow passed over his face. "You don't know why." It was a statement, not a question. "Father…he says some people like to harm without purpose, to hurt simply because they can."

And some harm with an evil purpose, destroying everything they touch. I returned his gaze without flinching, hoping my expression wouldn't give anything away and he would accept my silence as an affirmation. No matter how grateful I was to Avrik, no matter how much I disliked withholding information from someone who was fast becoming a close friend, I had to leave my past behind. If I wanted to survive, I had to live like Halia had died months ago in the depths of the Alrenian.

Swallowing, Avrik stared toward the schoolhouse in the distance, blinking like he was trying to prevent tears from flowing. "I won't regret what I did," he said at last.

By the time school ended, Avrik's mood had improved considerably. We left the schoolhouse in a companionable silence. The day had warmed and yesterday's snow was beginning to melt into muddy puddles. Where there had been a mass of foreboding clouds last night, there was only bright blue sky, and though the breeze was cool, the sun was putting up a valiant fight against the onset of winter. I breathed in the fresh air and let relief and peace soak deep into my heart.

The other guard is not looking for me. He's gone. Somehow, he must have never even known I was here.

I turned my face to the sun and let its warmth envelope me. I noticed a sparrow flying overhead and realized I felt a lot like it must feel: happy, free…safe.

The king won't find me here.

"I have something for you," Avrik said, snapping me from my thoughts.

I turned away from the brilliant sky, where I'd been following the sparrow's path as it chased the sun. My eyes met his and I cocked an eyebrow at him. His smile brightened his whole face as he continued, "It's a surprise. Do you like surprises?"

Frowning thoughtfully, I shrugged. *None of the surprises I've had recently.*

With a smile, he added, "Well, you'll like this one. But you'll have to race me home first!"

As he burst into a sprint, I raced after him. Soon I was hurtling over the grassy hillsides and sliding in the snow and mud, coating my new boots and dress in grime that would make Lyanna cringe. But my heart felt as weightless as the sparrow had looked. The sun glared on my back and sweat lined my flushed face. Flying past Avrik, I stopped at his house and leaned back against it, arms crossed. I wiped my forehead, smearing mud from my hands across my face.

"All right, you're fast when you're not tripping over your own shoes," Avrik exclaimed, panting as he reached me a couple moments later.

I responded with an upward tilt of my chin and a sly smile.

"*Next* time, I will leave *you* behind," Avrik said, but he grinned, letting his loss fall away with an easy shrug of his shoulders. "Your surprise is inside, but you'll have to take those shoes off." He nodded at my mud-encrusted boots. "Father gets really grumpy if I track dirt inside, because he hates to clean. Usually he makes me do it, but I hate it too, so…I always take off my shoes."

We yanked off our boots and left them in a row by the front door before we slipped inside.

"Sit down." He gestured to one of the armchairs by the fireplace and started to build up the fire. I tugged at my shirt sleeves and scratched my forehead where the mud was beginning to dry and itch. Avrik didn't even turn as he grumbled, "You're getting mud all over that chair, aren't you?"

I smirked at his back.

As the fire roared to life, he rose to his feet and reached for the mantel. That was when I noticed the long piece of wood lying there. He spun and held it with both hands palm-up like he was presenting me with an elegant sword. That's when I realized it *was* a sword: a practice sword hewn from some of the dark Evren Forest wood. The blade was wide and long, carefully balanced.

Standing, I reached out carefully and found that the hilt was matched perfectly to my hand. I glanced up at him in astonishment.

He shrugged, appearing almost shy. "It took me a while to get it right, and I had to guess a lot, but…it wasn't too difficult to decide on measurements. I figured maybe you would let me teach you? That is…if you don't already know how to sword fight." Half teasing me about my mysterious past and half enamored by it, he grinned.

Then his smile faltered for a moment. "I was already working on this, before…before… Well, after last night, I decided now was the time for you to learn. And we'll hope you never actually need to use a real sword, but just to be safe…" He shuffled his feet uncomfortably.

I gave him a reassuring glance and nudged his shoulder. *Thank you for caring enough to worry about me.*

Avrik forced another smile. "Let's take it outside and try it out. I have a few of my own; I'll go fetch one now." He left the living room and strode down the hall leading back toward his and Kyrin's bedrooms. After a few seconds, he returned with a worn-looking practice sword.

Slipping our feet back into our boots, we exited the cabin. "I'm not an expert, of course, but Father has been teaching me since I was six. He expects I'll be quite skilled by the time I am eighteen," Avrik explained proudly. He gestured to my practice sword. "Try giving your practice sword a few swings to see how it feels in your hand."

In the shade of the forest, Avrik watched me as I tested out my sword. Feeling self-conscious under my friend's gaze, I grasped the hilt with both hands and imagined I was swinging at an enemy: Captain Narek himself. The stick felt awkward and heavy in my hand; my father had never encouraged me to learn sword fighting. He and Mother always told me it was a man's skill. It felt good to be doing something they had disapproved of.

When I dared to turn to Avrik, a mischievous glint sparked in his eyes. "Well…it looks like I am the first person to teach you."

I shot him a playful glare.

"Your first problem is that you should grasp this type of sword with only one hand. The next is that you aren't standing properly," Avrik explained. He stood across from me and demonstrated a sword fighting stance, standing with his feet shoulder width apart and his right foot forward.

I attempted to imitate him, but he shook his head. "You're too rigid. Bend your knees."

I relaxed, and he nodded when he was satisfied with my stance.

As the afternoon wore on, Avrik taught me how to grasp a sword hilt, and then how to swing and jab, parry and defend.

"Your opponents will underestimate you," Avrik said as we sparred. "They might be stronger, but you are fast. Use that to your advantage.

Move a lot. Come in close for an attack and then leap away before they can counterattack."

At last, panting and laughing, he stepped back from me and glanced up at the sun, hovering over the woods. "It's getting late. I'll walk you back to your house, but I have one more surprise."

He led me back inside, through the living room and down the hall, past closed doors toward one final open doorway at the end of the hall. The evening sunlight streamed from a window within and played along the hallway floor and walls, chasing away shadows.

At the doorway, he paused and turned to me. "Are you ready?" He was beaming. Stepping backward into the room, he made way for me and swept out his arm in a grand gesture as I looked around.

It wasn't a large room, and, if anything, it was dusty, but it *was* a good surprise. Rows upon rows of shelves full of leather-bound books covered the walls. A small writing desk rested before the window, while in a corner, a small armchair created the perfect retreat for reading. My heart quickened in my chest as I approached the shelves and traced several books' spines, reading their titles and soaking in the possibilities of knowledge and wonder this room held.

Avrik was studying my face in triumph. "I *knew* you would like it!" he said. Then his expression grew serious, and he lowered his voice. "This was my mother's library."

I shot him a quick glance. *You want me to read these books?*

"When you're reading…that's the only time…well, one of the only times you really look happy…" His voice trailed off. "I come here a lot to sit and read or think. I wanted you to know that you can come here any time you want, and you can borrow any book you'd like. I know Lyanna and Rev don't have as many books. He's more interested in numbers, and she in gardening and cooking."

I crossed the room and ran my fingers along several book spines, relishing the smooth leather beneath my fingertips, the scent of crisp old pages hanging thickly in the air like a familiar perfume. There were fiction books, history books, and informative books…the largest collection I had ever seen outside of the castle libraries. The possibility of reading every one of those books brought a sense of excitement to my being like nothing else could. More than anything, I craved answers to the questions plaguing my days, solutions to the problems haunting my nightmares.

Could one of these books hold answers to my questions? Could they tell me what is wrong with me…why I can't lie, why I couldn't stop myself from speaking the truth? How I knew the truth in the first place? The questions pounded through my head. *Are there others like me, people who see visions and know truth? If I stay silent, are the words gone forever?*

But the answers did not come in the way I hoped they would.

FOUR YEARS LATER

CHAPTER SEVEN

A RE YOU PREPARED TO LOSE?" Bren teased, nudging Avrik's shoulder and sinking into a fighting stance.

"Are *you*?" Avrik fired back, lifting his practice sword to meet his friend's.

The firelight from the living room hearth flashed across their faces as they smirked at one another for a half second before plunging into their third skirmish of the evening. I closed the book lying on my lap and settled back into my armchair to fully appreciate their performance. Lifting my hand to my mouth, I tried to conceal my amusement, but the boys were too intent on their mock battle to mind my reactions.

"Two out of three!" Bren cried, the point of his sword pressed to Avrik's throat.

Avrik dove back, the wood floorboards creaking beneath him as he landed, and aimed a kick at Bren's knee. With a grunt, Bren lost his footing as Avrik leapt to his feet and pressed his own sword to Bren's chest.

"You were too cocky," he said with a shrug. Grinning, he stepped back and swept his arm wide in a flourish.

Bren scoffed, muttering something unintelligible. Tossing aside his practice sword, he tramped toward the settee and plopped down. Leaning forward, he carefully lifted his jiadro from its case and ran his fingers along its polished wood surface and taut strings. Settling into an upbeat turn, he glanced toward me and then back at Avrik. "Are we going to let Elena practice her dancing now, or continue to train her in weapons until she awes every man she meets?"

If you only knew the balls I've already attended, the hours of practice I've endured, I thought, but I had already agreed to this earlier. I could imagine the questions I would be asked if I didn't pretend to still be perfecting my graceful steps and twirls like the rest of the Evren youth. Every night for weeks, Rev and I had been dancing partners, twisting and twirling through the living room, the garden, or beside Lyanna in the kitchen, much to her frustration.

Avrik raised his brows and a playful light danced in his eyes. "I haven't finished training *you* in weapons yet."

Bren rolled his eyes.

"All right," Avrik sighed. "If she wants, you may practice for the Great Feast."

Bren handed his instrument to Avrik, who began plucking at the strings absentmindedly.

I stood and smoothed my skirt as Bren extended a hand to me. He was tall and sturdy, already losing the lanky build of a youth and looking more like his father, a farmer near the outskirts of Evren, each day. "I've practiced with my three sisters for months," he said, leading me toward the center of the room. "There are so few times in Evren that we dance, so naturally most of the girls are beside themselves."

He grasped my hand and waist while I reached for his shoulder, and Avrik began to play, his rhythm occasionally sounding off before he sank into a steady pace. I was surprised with how graceful Bren was as he swept me across the floor, his feet never once faltering, his steps all landing exactly where they were supposed to.

"You're doing well," he said after several minutes. He glanced over his shoulder at his friend. "I think she should teach *you* now. How else do you expect to keep the interest of a pretty girl?" he teased. "Do you want them to gaze longingly at you the way they did today ever again?"

Gritting my teeth, I unconsciously tightened my grasp on Bren, digging my fingers into his shoulder. He cringed. "Ow!"

Sheepishly, I smiled an apology and glanced down at the floor.

"Do you mean the way they look at me every day?" Avrik asked slyly.

Bren and I both rolled our eyes.

"All right," Bren said. "Let me play and you may dance now. It's time for you to participate in something you do *not* have a talent for."

I stepped back, letting Bren walk back to the setee and pry the jiadro from Avrik's hands. Standing, Avrik crossed his arms. He was not as broad-shouldered as Bren, but taller than both him and me by several inches. His eyes sparked with mischief and his smile still lit up his face in the familiar, boyish way the schoolgirls had admired for years.

"I only tease you because you are so envious, as if you think the girls never look at you," Avrik told Bren. "Perhaps if you only talked to Dienn already…"

Cheeks flushed, Bren stared down at his jiadro, intent on strumming the strings to warm up for his song.

Avrik turned to me and held out his hand. "May I torment you with this dance?" he asked, smiling sweetly.

I bit my lip to repress a smile.

"Take her hand already!" Bren ordered as he lifted the jiadro.

Avrik reached out and grasped my hand, gently pulling me closer, and my heart quickened. As I set my hand on his shoulder, I refused to meet his gaze and stared down at my feet instead, pretending that I needed to concentrate on my steps.

"Injuries are inevitable, so I hope you don't plan on being able to use your feet again for the next week," Avrik continued.

Bren started to mutter something, but seemed to think better of it and began to play instead.

At that instant, the door opened and Kyrin stepped in, his tall form filling the entryway.

Immediately, Avrik released my hand and pulled away. He strode over to greet his father, who dropped a travel-stained pack by the door and rubbed his temples wearily. Before Avrik could say anything, Kyrin muttered, "I stopped at Wanderer's Rest on my way home, and Corin has returned from the castle. He is calling for an assembly at the inn tonight to share what he has learned, and he seemed troubled. We need to go."

Bren, Avrik, and I exchanged glances. "I should find my family,"

Bren said, placing his jiadro in its case and reaching for his cloak, where he had strewn it across the setee.

Kyrin turned to me. "Rev is already there, if you wish to accompany us."

I nodded, grasping my cloak as Avrik donned his, gathered his bow and quiver, and put out the fire. We set off into the evening, a bitter wind rustling through our hair and cloaks as we turned our faces toward the dying light in the west to walk into town. Bren waved and dashed ahead of us, moving north toward his family's farm. As Avrik, Kyrin, and I passed my home, a tendril of smoke curled from the chimney and I imagined Lyanna standing beside the hearth, stirring a pot and waiting for Rev and me to return.

As we entered town, we joined growing crowds in the streets composed of men, women, and children gathering to hear Corin's news. The assembly grew thicker the nearer we drew to Wanderer's Rest, until the street was so full of people that we could barely move forward. No matter which way I turned my head, there were far too many townspeople for me to find Rev in their midst. It took some jostling through the group clustered outside the inn before we could see the Evren Leader standing at its doorstep and waving a hand to quiet the townspeople's murmuring. A member of the King's Guard, dressed in full uniform, stood beside him.

I drew a deep breath. *Why is a guard in Evren? Will he recognize me too?*

Hearing my gasp, Avrik gave me a sympathetic glance and reached out to squeeze my hand. He leaned in close to whisper, "I would hope not all of the king's men are scoundrels."

When he pulled away, I tried to make my smile look convincing, and he seemed satisfied. He released my hand and turned back toward Corin, who had finally quieted most of the people.

"I trust most are here now," he said, scanning the people as if to count them all and raising his voice so that it rang out clearly in the street, even above the occasional whisper or whimper from the children. "As you know, I recently joined the other Leaders of Misroth at the king's castle in Misroth City. I want to share some grave news with you: the kingdom of Alrenor is attempting to expand its borders once more and reestablish its old empire. Our kingdoms are now at war, and King Zarev is already gathering troops in Argelon to train. The Royal Council has been temporarily disbanded, in order to expedite the king's ability to make vital decisions while we are at war, and it is likely that soon Misroth will need even Evren's resources and young men."

Kyrin shifted on his feet. "Will they demand every young man's service?" he called out over the crowd.

Corin nodded gravely. "Yes." He gestured to the guard beside him. "One of the king's Royal Guard, Paol, is here to share more information of His Highness's plans to protect our kingdom. You may speak to him if you wish to learn more."

"I will," Kyrin muttered, clenching his fists and turning away from the crowd.

Avrik grasped his father's arm. "Father, you needn't worry…"

"No, you need not worry," Kyrin said. "Believe me, you will *not* be going to war. I will see to it."

One week later, on the morning of the Great Feast, everyone was still fretting about the news Corin had brought from Misroth City. As we waited for our teacher to arrive at the schoolhouse, the other students settled into their chairs or gathered into groups near the fire to engage in conversation, but I kept to my seat, poring over maps of the Great Kingdoms.

"The guard left for Kelwed this morning," Shilam told Jaren as he and Bren shuffled toward their seats. "Did your father ever have the chance to speak with him?"

Jaren shook his head. "He's been busy with his shop, and everyone else in town was eager to speak with the guard as well. He never had the chance." He shrugged as he settled into his seat. "I don't see what difference it makes. If the king needs our services, he will call on us and we will go. That is how it has always worked."

"Except that we have been at peace for two hundred years, since we broke free of the Alrenian Empire," Dienn cut in. The boys looked up, surprised to see her turn away from the group of girls she had been hovering near the fire with and approach them. Her dark eyes were wide and her voice trembled. "We haven't seen war in generations, haven't had anything but peace and prosperity. And now, as we finish school…" Her eyes drifted to Bren before she glanced down quickly.

As Bren turned red and started to stammer, I shot a glance at Avrik, who was watching the exchange with a smile playing about his lips and didn't notice my look. I stared back down at the map before me, tracing my finger from the point I knew Evren, too small to be included in this map, should be, past the capital and Emrell and toward Argelon. I studied the curve of the Layvok River that separated Misroth from Alrenor, that kingdom we had severed ties with long ago, and a familiar longing to explore lands I had never seen overcame me.

I felt Avrik's eyes on me and looked up. "Are you worrying like everyone else?" he asked, but the smile hadn't left his face. He leaned out of his chair to peer over my shoulder at the map I was studying before turning back to me. "Or are you daydreaming again about all the places we will one day explore?" Leaning closer, he lifted his hand and swept a strand of hair back from my cheek. My breath caught in my throat.

Stop, I ordered myself, and turned my head away. I felt more than saw Avrik sink back into his chair, but I knew he was still watching me. With a sigh, I shut the book and flipped open my journal. *Both,* I wrote to him. Then, collecting myself with a grin, I added, *Who will I put to shame in shooting matches if you are called to Argelon?*

Avrik laughed, but I could see other emotions stirring in the depths of his eyes and robbing him of his carefree expression.

The schoolhouse door swung inward and Ara stepped inside, offering us all a friendly greeting and putting an end to our conversations.

"Open your history books first," she began, but as I flipped my copy open and stared at the text, I could not stop thinking about all that my father was doing in Misroth City and the war he had started, a war affecting the people I loved.

First Gillen, now Avrik. Could I ever truly escape the king's influence?

The sun was casting its setting glow all the way across the sky, stretching so far it was making even the bare branches of Evren Forest look like they were alight with orange fire. I brushed the flour from my hands onto my apron and peered eagerly out the window.

"It's still too early for Rev to arrive home from the bank," Lyanna laughed when she caught me looking. "It's time we cleaned ourselves up!"

I nearly skipped toward my bedroom and my washbasin. Relieved to clean the flour and dough from my hands and face, I sighed and tossed my apron into a corner.

"Elena!" Lyanna scolded as she walked through the doorway.

I grinned back at her, and she simply shook her head.

"I have your dress and cloak ready," she continued, taking the clothes she had draped over her arm and laying them on my bedspread. She'd kept the new outfit a secret for weeks, insisting that now, as I was a young woman, it was time I had finer attire to wear to special events.

Standing beside her, I reached down to feel the fabric. The dress was made from purple satin the same shade as the lavender Lyanna grew in her garden, but the bodice and sleeves were covered in a layer of lace. Lying beside it was a deep blue cloak lined in wool. I stared in awe: bright dye was rare in Evren, since not many citizens grew the necessary plants or found them useful to our simple lifestyle, and merchants rarely traded for such a luxury. Lyanna must have paid a small fortune for the fabric to make these clothes. Throwing my arms around her, I gave her a hug to express my gratitude.

"You're welcome." She stroked my hair and beamed down at me. "You deserve something special, and with the Great Feast happening and your education nearly at an end…well, you're nearly a woman now and you needed something for the occasion."

I slipped into the dress and accompanying black slippers, and paused to admire Lyanna's handiwork in the mirror. The dress felt light and comfortable, with its skirt cascading in longer folds in the back but reaching only to my ankles in the front so I could walk easily. This was nothing like the stifling attire I'd been compelled to wear at the castle. I sighed in relief.

Lyanna returned to comb my hair and tie some of its waves back with a purple ribbon. She let the rest fall about my shoulders. "You look beautiful. But wait!" She dashed from the room and returned with a silver necklace adorned with a single diamond. "Rev gave this to me when we were married." Her blue eyes twinkled. "I think you should wear it tonight." She clasped the necklace around my neck and turned me to face the mirror once more.

The diamond rested right beneath the hollow of my neck and sparkled in the evening light like a tiny star. It was strange to see myself in fine clothes and jewelry again. I twirled like a little girl and laughed, making Lyanna laugh too.

Just then the front door opened and Rev stepped into the living room. "For tonight, I have a coach to escort you to the feast!" he announced proudly.

Lyanna and I entered the room and Rev paused to give me an appraising look. "Elena, you look …you look like a young woman." He smiled, but I noticed the slight tremor in his voice. With surprise, I realized how many wrinkles the last few years had added; I noticed how starkly the grey streaks through his hair contrasted with its natural brown.

It wasn't long before Lyanna and Rev were dressed in their fine clothes too. We slipped on our cloaks, Lyanna gathered the bread we had made for the feast, and we departed. Rev eagerly opened the door to a small carriage, painted blue, and helped Lyanna and I climb into the cushioned seat in the back. It felt strange, since we usually walked everywhere. Very rarely did Rev need the mare he kept boarded at a stable in town, and I only rode on horseback for pleasure when I wanted to traverse the fields and hills alone. The last time I had ridden in a carriage was four years ago, on a drive through the capital streets with my mother and father. The reminder stung a little, but I shook the feeling away. That was another life. Another me. Halia, not Elena.

Rev drove over the familiar dirt road, winding through fields and over hills, through the town, and back into the countryside. I peered out the carriage window at the sunset and the fields, now bare and brown in the wintertime. The orange sky faded slowly as the sun slipped past the horizon and the first stars began to twinkle overhead. The closer we drew to the garden, the more carriages I saw joining us along the road, pulling in ahead or behind us from connecting paths.

Then the hill rose before us with the Leader's home shining like a beacon on top. Each window glittered with the lights of dozens of candles set all about the house. But far more breathtaking was the landscape stretching below it. Its flowers gently nodded on the breeze as their sweet aroma drifted toward me, and every tree and shrub was alight with hundreds of sparkling orbs, like small stars that had descended to earth for an evening. As we drew closer, I realized they were fireflies, blinking as they rested on the plants or danced in the air.

Although I'd been to the garden many times in daylight over the years, I had never seen it in its full glory at night before. Every year, Evren celebrated and remembered the town's dedication to serve the Giver of Life with the Great Feast, but only once every five years did Evren hold the feast in the garden. This was the only time, other than one day a week, when it appeared in its full glory for all the citizens to enjoy.

Rev stopped outside the garden to let us out before he took the horse and carriage to the stables.

As Lyanna and I entered the garden, the chill winter air dissipated and mellow warmth greeted us. Fireflies twinkled all around and a few even landed in Lyanna's hair, making us both smile like giddy children. We pulled off our cloaks and draped them over a tree branch before joining a gathering around tables set beneath a cluster of trees. Torches flickered all around the garden to brighten the night, although the stars overhead flared with such intensity and the fireflies were so numerous that they hardly seemed necessary.

I stared around at the beauty surrounding me and wondered if I should try speaking to the Giver again. I hoped he listened to my pleas to protect my aunt and cousin, though he didn't seem to listen to me whenever I asked for answers about my past. Here in the garden dedicated to him, I always hoped that he would be more likely to hear me and that I would be more likely to hear from him.

Or maybe answers don't matter anymore, and I'll never have another incident like I did when I was thirteen. Maybe it's time to forget. It's part of the past.

"Elena!" Avrik's voice rang out behind me, and my worries were forgotten.

I turned to see him approaching with his father. Both were dressed in black pants and boots and pressed white shirts, and I was relieved to see that Avrik had substituted a hunting knife for his bow and quiver. Avrik's short chestnut hair was almost neat, except for the few strands standing on end that the wind had probably tousled on the ride here. His eyes widened when he saw me. "Lyanna did good work, didn't she?" he asked with a grin.

My heart hammered against my chest as I nodded.

Avrik offered me his arm. "Walk with me?"

We strolled away from the cluster of people, following a dirt path that wound through clusters of tall bushes and flowers of vibrant red, blue, and gold. The garden's perfume was heavy here, offering a peaceful atmosphere that eased the cares and worries of the world.

Nearby, a group of men and women seated beneath a large tree with low overhanging boughs began to play their instruments. The notes of harps, jiadros, violins, and wymets arose and blended into a sweet, soft melody until one woman raised her voice in an old Alrenian song addressed to the Giver of Good Things.

"Val re shem thyre…"

Her song wound through the garden, a gentle rhythm on the breeze. I recognized the tune and knew she sang of beauty and life, of happiness and love. I was thankful for the dim, flickering glow about us, because I could feel my cheeks turning pink.

What is wrong with me? It's only Avrik.

He spoke and pulled me from my thoughts. "This is my favorite celebration in Evren," he said, staring up at the sky. The constellations seemed so close here in the garden, even closer than they had up on the castle tower with Gillen when I was a girl. "It's when I'm in the garden that everything seems…clearer to me. If I could come here every day, I would, but I know it'd be frowned upon to set foot in this sacred place so often, unless I became Leader. I suppose the peacefulness of this place clears my thoughts."

The song ended. Avrik paused, but whatever he was about to say was interrupted by a loud, powerful voice echoing through the garden. I peered through the trees ahead and caught a glimpse of the Evren Leader standing near more tables laden with food.

"Welcome, citizens of Evren!" Corin cried. "I am pleased to celebrate another Great Feast with you here in Evren's garden and commemorate the day Evren was committed to our Giver of Blessings. Please, eat and take your fill, sing and rejoice, and enjoy this evening spent with friends and loved ones. Give thanks to the Life-Giver and rejoice with me!"

Citizens all around us cheered and applauded, but Avrik was silent and thoughtful beside me. When the excitement faded and the singing resumed, he was still gazing out over the grounds, his fingers toying with the hunting knife strapped to his belt. Rousing himself, he smiled at me. "Should we eat?"

Should you tell me what's on your mind? I responded in my head, but I nodded.

We returned to the tables and loaded plates with heaping piles of the different foods the citizens had contributed: roasted chicken, venison, turkey, and sugared ham; fresh bread and butter and cheeses; baked apples and berries gathered from the garden and teeming with flavor; pastries and cakes smothered in frosting; and countless other dishes stretching endlessly across the tables. Joining a group seated at one of the tables near a patch of delicate blue embyth, Avrik muttered something about drinks and dashed off to fetch us some.

Impatient, my stomach growling in anticipation, I began picking at my food until Jayn approached the table with her friend Emalet. Their golden hair shimmered in the light as they leaned toward each other, murmuring and giggling together. Jewelry inlaid with gleaming sapphires, emeralds, and diamonds hung from their necks and arms, and their deep blue and green skirts swayed around their hips while they walked. Their fathers were frequently away on travels, but they were wealthy merchants who provided only the best for their families.

"I *cannot* wait to finish school," Jayn said, pausing within earshot of my seat. "Mother can concentrate on training me to run a home properly and be a good wife." A dreamy smile played about her lips.

"Do you think we will attract many suitors?" Emalet asked breathlessly, her violet eyes wide with eagerness and apprehension.

"I have my eye on someone." Jayn's voice took on a sly tone. "I wouldn't need many suitors, as long as I captured the affections of one good man." She toyed with the braid tumbling down her back.

Emalet beamed. "Oh! I know who." She covered her mouth to stifle a giggle. "But what about…" Her voice drifted away.

My jaw clenched, because I already knew who they were talking about. I glanced back down at my food, staring hard at a slice of Lyanna's bread and a piece of cheese and trying hard to pretend I wasn't listening, that I hadn't heard a thing. *Ignore them,* I told myself.

"She can't even speak," Jayn said, not even trying to lower her voice. "Who would want a mute woman?" She laughed cruelly.

I swallowed hard. *Suitors? Men? Is that all they think about? If I could speak, I would have so much more to say.*

Quickly, I tried to shake away my anger. *It does not matter. What they say doesn't matter, and I don't care about suitors. I'm only seventeen.*

But then why did my stomach tighten? When had Jayn's idle speech ever cut me like this?

Avrik returned to the table bearing two cups of golden agma juice, and Jayn spun quickly to meet his gaze. "Hi, Avrik. It's nice to see you here tonight," she said sweetly.

Emalet blushed and looked down at her feet, giggling idiotically. I wondered how she would fare with my practice sword pointed at her perfect nose.

"Hi, Jayn, Emalet." Avrik returned Jayn's smile and set our cups down at the table.

"You look handsome." Jayn batted her long eyelashes at Avrik, who returned the gesture by blinking and averting his gaze. "Perhaps after dinner, when the dancing starts, you will be my partner?"

He smiled. "Thank you. I look forward to it."

My fist tightened around my fork so tightly I half expected to break it in two. Clearing his throat, Avrik sat beside me and tossed back a long draught of his agma. I didn't release my grip on my fork until the girls walked away, whispering eagerly to one another.

Trying to ignore the trembling in my hands, I forced myself to eat a few bites of food. I didn't even notice what I was eating or how it tasted; everything melded into dry clumps in my mouth and lodged in my throat.

Avrik turned to me. "I'm sorry." He spoke in a low voice that rose just above the music.

I glanced at him, trying to keep my expression light.

"Can you imagine Jayn's great shame when she dances with me?" He winked and chuckled. "Clearly she thinks I have improved since the last town celebration."

The tension in my chest released and I smiled back.

His face turned solemn. "But earlier...I was thinking about the future, and how everything will change once we finish school. Remember how we always talked about traveling together to see Toryn, and Alrenor...even the lands and kingdoms across the Great Sea, like Teramyl and Brevinn?" He reached out and rested his hand on mine, but I yanked my hand away in surprise and embarrassment.

Frowning, he pulled back in his chair until the distance between us felt like miles. "What is wrong?" he asked.

I shook my head, pressing my lips together and cursing my stupidity. *He's your friend. Don't be a fool.*

"Are you all right?" he pressed.

I nodded, hoping he would let the matter go. Dissatisfied but realizing I wasn't going to share my troubles, he gave in. Our silence extended as men and women walked past us or joined us at our table, nodding in our direction or exchanging greetings and pleasantries with Avrik.

Finally, Avrik shifted in his chair uncomfortably and fidgeted with his cup. "What I wanted to say, was that..." He hesitated. "Do you want the life that Lyanna wants for you?" His gaze was intent, searching my face. "Do you want to spend time, three years perhaps, continuing to learn about cooking and knitting and…" He waved his hand vaguely into the distance. "Whatever else women are supposed to know."

I smirked at that, and he took my amusement as encouragement.

"Or…do you want the life we dreamed about? I'll be a hunter and trader like my father—he's been training me all my life—and you can travel with me to all those distant lands we want to see. You're my closest friend, Elena, and you don't want to…I mean," he stammered, "I don't want you to…"

A woman's cry erupted from somewhere nearby, causing all talk and music in the garden to cease. Eerie and uncomfortable, the quiet enveloped us. Everyone looked around, trying to find the source of the sound. Avrik leapt to his feet, reaching for his dagger.

"Help!" A form came into view, staggering and panting beneath the shade of a thicket of trees at the far side of the garden. The moonlight fell upon her face and I recognized Selna. She looked pale and her black hair tumbled down in ragged tangles, as if she had run the entire length of the town to us. Blood stained the front and sleeves of her dress. Gasps and murmurs broke out.

"A man has been attacked. I need the healer!"

Velnik, Evren's healer, rushed forward. "What happened?" he asked.

"One of the sedwa attacked," Selna choked out. "My husband found a man in the woods. He's at the inn."

Velnik dashed out of the garden with Selna behind him. Everyone else began talking at once. The peace of the evening was shattered, with anxious mothers grasping for their children and people everywhere asking questions that couldn't be answered by anyone.

Fear made the warm, sweet air of the garden feel icy against my skin. Closing my eyes, I could see a flash of gold staring at me from the darkness. I was thirteen years old, trapped in Evren Forest as I faced down one of the sedwa… My eyes snapped open to reality, but I didn't feel much better.

"Will we be safe in our own homes?" a woman cried fearfully. "The sedwa were supposed to be a myth!"

"It's Kyrin's fault," a man standing close to our table said, his gruff voice rising over the tumult around us. He pointed toward Kyrin, where he stood with a cup still in his hand. "We would still be safe, if it weren't for him. He travels deeper into Evren Forest and further into the mountains than any of our other hunters. His activities are provoking the sedwa!"

Avrik grabbed my hand tightly. I lifted my gaze to his and met his silent appeal: *Don't let them blame my father for this.* His face was taut; his lips a thin line. He pulled me with him as he dashed toward his father, who was meeting the accusatory looks of the citizens surrounding him with stony silence.

I found Lyanna and Rev sitting at the table behind Kyrin. Relieved to see Avrik and me, they scrambled to their feet.

"Let's leave," Avrik said. He cast the people around us a dark look. "I have no desire to celebrate with people who wish to turn on their own."

As we trudged behind Lyanna, Rev, and Kyrin toward Rev's carriage, Avrik maintained an angry silence. We donned our cloaks and exited the garden to enter the cold night once more. I watched Avrik's dark eyes study the sky and imagined what he was thinking, what he was feeling. Part of me thought I could sympathize. Almost. After all, any cruel rumors or talk about *my* father would be well-founded. But I could imagine how I'd feel if anyone spoke badly about Rev.

Biting my lip, I tugged my cloak closer to block the chill wind. I wanted to say something, but after years of silence I finally felt resigned to the fact that, for whatever reason, I might never be able to speak again.

I contented myself with reaching out and touching Avrik's shoulder. His step faltered, and he paused and turned toward me. The wind whipped around us, brushing long strands of hair into my eyes and billowing my skirts and cloak around me. His brow was furrowed and his expression pleading when he searched my gaze. It was then that I noticed the stubble shadowing his cheeks and chin. In that instant, with the weight of his worries hovering over him, he looked older, more mature yet more conflicted: gone was the lighthearted friend of my childhood and in his place was a troubled young man.

"You don't believe all of those rumors about my father, do you?" His voice was low.

My face involuntarily matched his frown. I blinked and shook my head, trying to cheer him with a smile.

"Good," he whispered, and pulled me into a hug. His embrace brought welcome warmth to my shivering frame. Since I couldn't say anything to reassure him, I clung to him tightly instead, hoping this gesture would mean more than words. As he pulled away, a strange emptiness settled in my stomach.

"I'll see you tomorrow," Avrik said when we reached the stables.

Rev paused before our carriage and turned back to Kyrin. "Would you like a ride home?"

Kyrin shook his head. "We'll be fine walking."

Opening the door for Lyanna and me, Rev gave Kyrin a friendly nod. "Goodnight."

"Goodnight to you all," Kyrin responded. Without another word, he and Avrik set off into the night. I sighed and watched Avrik's form shrink away into the distance, until he was swallowed up by the blackness.

CHAPTER EIGHT

THE NEXT DAY, I WOKE with a heavy heart. I rolled over with a sigh, and then I remembered: *Gil.* His eighteenth birthday was next month. My heart ached.

Someday soon, Misroth City would be filled with celebrating citizens as Gillen, finally of age, accepted the throne. The streets would be decorated with banners, singers would lift their voices in celebration, and children would wave ribbons at the royal procession.

Tears stabbed my eyes. What I would give to be there to see Gillen crowned, to congratulate him and let him know how proud I was of him.

Please let him be safe, I begged the Life-Giver. *Let him be the strong king I know he can be.*

I stared out at the Vorvinian Mountains through my window, knowing it couldn't be that simple. Anxiety tugged at my heart. *My father won't give up power easily.* Would he poison my cousin like he had his father? Or would he try to manipulate Gillen once he began his rule?

With a sigh, I pulled myself out of bed. Entering Misroth City would mean death for me if I was recognized. What could I do against my father? Who would believe me if I tried to spread the truth, even if I *could* speak? Returning to the capital would be suicide.

I wiped my tears from my cheeks and prepared for school. As I walked toward the front door, passing Lyanna where she was seated by the fireplace, she glanced up from her sewing. "You look upset, dear. Is everything all right?"

Nodding, I pulled my journal and pencil from my pack and wrote, *Only nightmares.*

Lyanna's brow crinkled with sadness. "I'm sorry," she murmured. "I hope you have a good day at school."

With a smile, I walked outside to meet Avrik.

At school, the rumors about last night's sedwa attack continued to circulate, much to Avrik's frustration.

"The man is an outsider," Bren shared with us eagerly at lunch. "I heard he comes from Misroth City itself."

My stomach jolted at the mention of my old home.

"Does it matter?" Avrik mumbled.

Bren's face was firm. "Just because we are interested in the stranger, or even the attack itself, does not mean we are accusing your father."

Avrik stared down at his sandwich and did not respond.

"Will he live?" Shilam asked.

Bren shrugged. "Who can say? We can only hope."

Jaren bit into a slice of cheese. "He will have an interesting story to share, if he does."

Lyanna greeted me cheerfully at the door when I returned from school, darting inside quickly to escape the blustery weather. "How was your day?" she asked.

I nodded and shot her a half-hearted smile, but Lyanna didn't seem to notice that I was still troubled.

"I'm glad, dear. When you've warmed yourself, could you help me with dinner? And I have a few chores for you…"

My heart sank. It wasn't that I had a problem helping Lyanna; it was simply that Lyanna's version of chores for seventeen-year-old girls usually involved domestic responsibilities I wasn't overly fond of. If I ever attempted to spend time with my friends, or stay after school, Lyanna would generally scold me and tell me that a young woman had no place spending so much time playing childish games with boys. Her verbal lists of reasons why a young woman needed to be at home were only matched by her long lists of tedious chores and sewing projects.

I wonder if there's any way I could convince her to let me slip away to Wanderer's Rest to speak with the stranger. Curiosity tickled my brain. *But what kind of excuse could I make to Lyanna to go to the inn?* I frowned at the fire and rubbed my hands more vigorously. Rev might come home with news tonight, but I knew that wouldn't satisfy me. I needed to see this man face-to-face and hear from his own mouth about his encounter with the sedwa. And, in the furthest crannies of my mind, another need resided: where had this man come from, anyway, and where was he going? My paranoia would not let me rest until I had a chance to find out for myself.

"Elena!" Lyanna called from across the cabin, where she was kneading dough for bread.

Resigned, I stood and started on my work for the evening. I rushed absent-mindedly through most of the tasks Lyanna asked me to do, poking myself more than once with my needle as I sewed a patch on a pair of Rev's pants and nearly burning the soup by forgetting to stir it. At last, with the table set and dinner prepared, I was able to retreat to a corner by the fire and try to think of an excuse for leaving after the meal. I was still at a loss when Rev entered and Lyanna called us to the table to thank our Giver of Life for the food.

My opportunity came unexpectedly when Rev began sharing the day's news as we ate. "There's news that the stranger at Wanderer's Rest does indeed have…an interesting story," he began. "Perhaps about the sedwa, as suspected."

Lyanna looked up inquiringly and I felt my heart beat faster.

"How is he?" she asked.

"He will live," Rev reassured her. "He's recovering at the inn. They've had to keep a number of visitors away. Everyone wants to hear his story and know about the sedwa…"

Lyanna shuddered. "They are myths, stories. If the sedwa were real, why haven't we heard more of them? Seen more attacks on Evren and its people?"

Rev frowned thoughtfully at his soup. "The stories all said they were elusive and that few people survived their attacks. But…" He shook his head and said no more.

"The stories also say they only attack if provoked. What was the traveler…?"

"That is what everyone has been saying, but the traveler was on a peaceful trip. He had plenty of supplies with him and money for along the way. He wasn't hunting. He brought a bow with him for self-defense, but he bears all the signs of a man coming to trade goods."

Lyanna swirled her spoon around in her soup silently.

"Tomorrow evening I am going to Wanderer's Rest to hear the man's story for myself," Rev announced. "If danger lurks near our home, I want to know more about it."

"But, Rev, you said they were trying to keep people away…"

"That doesn't mean I cannot have a moment with him. The men of the village are saying we should prepare for grave danger. I want to see if there is any credence to the panic. To see the man, see if he is believable, see his wounds… I want to know what, if anything, we should prepare for, in case the worst is true."

"Does everyone think there will be more attacks, even outside of the forest?"

"Some of the old stories spoke of the monsters leaving the Vorvinian Mountains and forest and attacking the outskirts of the village at night, though most say the sedwa do not leave the cover of trees. But if they are attacking this close to the forest's edge now …well, the woods are Evren's hunting grounds, and we live almost under the forest's shadow. We cannot be too careful."

I cast Rev an eager glance, hoping he could read the question in my eyes without me having to fetch a piece of paper. For the most part, Lyanna and even Rev had become quite adept at reading my thoughts and emotions, but Rev had a tendency to get lost in his own thoughts and become oblivious to the world around him. This time, though, he answered my look immediately.

"You may come with me, Elena," he said with a smile.

"Rev…" Lyanna began in her scolding tone, but stopped.

"There is no danger at the inn, love," he told Lyanna. "And I won't keep her out late. You can't completely tame that sense of adventure in her." Rev shot me a wink and I beamed back at him.

The wind had grown stronger since my walk home that afternoon, and stormy dark clouds were riding in on its current. As Rev and I made our way through the hilly countryside toward Evren's town center, I watched the clouds slither across the sky, revealing patches of stars far above and casting rolling shadows along the waving grass. The air was cold and ominous—or maybe that was my imagination as I thought of the sedwa creeping through the nearby forest, seeking cover in the same shadowy night that embraced me.

As we entered town and traversed its main road, I noticed that Evren was bustling with far more people than were normally out this late on dark winter's evenings. Every shop and business was closed except for the inn, whose fires sent a radiant glow through the street, attracting a growing crowd like a swarm of insects to light. I studied the dim faces staring up at the inn: some of the citizens I knew by name; others I only knew by sight.

"No more gawkers!" Selna shouted, standing in her doorway and shooing townspeople away. "If you are not here for the food or a place to stay the night, carry on with your business!"

Several people gave up and departed with shrugs or sighs, but still more pressed even closer to the front door.

"Selna," Rev called as we approached.

Selna broke into a smile when she saw us. "Rev and Elena! I suppose you are not here for the food or drinks either," she said, quirking an eyebrow at us.

Rev and I squeezed past a few more people until we stood in front of Selna, close enough to see past her into the empty inn. "Is no one here for the food?"

Selna crossed her arms across her broad chest, but her lips curved in a half-smile. "I haven't trusted anyone who said they were."

"I confess we are as curious as the rest of Evren," Rev said, keeping his voice low, "but I hoped that for faithful friends and longtime patrons—especially ones who live so near to Evren Forest and desperately want answers—you would make an exception."

Selna sighed and tossed a glance over her shoulder into the inn, as if she could see up the stairs and into the stranger's room from her position. "All right," she relented quietly. "But you two are my last 'exception' for the day!"

Thanking her as she backed up to make way for us, we entered the warm inn and Selna hurriedly closed and bolted the door, shutting out the disgruntled crowd behind us. She set a hand on her hip and turned to me, as if I would understand her frustrations better than Rev. "Ever since our mysterious traveler showed up, the whole town's been trying to barge through our doors to pester him. Forget food and drinks!" She rolled her eyes in frustration. Seeming to anticipate a reprimand that would never come from me, she added quickly, "No, no, it's not that bad," with a wave of her hand. "It really could be good for business, but we can't have everyone upsetting the man when he is recovering. Of course, we can't keep the crowd out forever, either. Now why don't the two of you find yourselves a seat and have a drink first?" she asked hopefully, gesturing to the empty tables. Without waiting for a response, she grasped a broom from where it leaned against the wall and began to sweep the room in firm, quick strokes. She looked like she was wielding a sword against an invisible enemy, rather than cleaning a room.

Frowning up at Rev, I reached into my cloak pocket for my journal and pencil and scrawled a message on one of the empty pages. *I want to see the traveler.*

Rev walked over to Selna, who was continuing to face her unseen foes in combat, and cleared his throat. "We would rather not wait. Elena is especially eager to see the man."

Selna studied me carefully and shook her head. "Are you sure, child?" she asked with a sigh. "His story is…troubling."

I fought the urge to frown at her. *I'm seventeen—not a child.* But I merely nodded.

Leading the way, Selna strode across the floor to the staircase, its steps wide and rough, hewn from aged oak. At the top, she turned and knocked at the first door on the left before gently pushing it open.

"You have some visitors, if you are up to it," Selna said. I waited at the top of the steps with Rev as a muffled voice replied to her from the room's interior. Flickering candlelight danced along the hall behind Selna as she stepped back from the doorway and nodded at me. Head spinning in anticipation, I squeezed past her swishing skirts and into the room.

The long, narrow bed took up most of the small space. A candle sat on the nightstand beside it; its flame sent shadows flickering along the walls and across the face of the man buried beneath the bed covers. He appeared to be in his late twenties or thirties, his black hair beginning to thin and recede from his broad forehead, his skin was coated in sweat, and deep lines furrowed his brow. His dark eyes were glassy yet intent on me as I crept forward. My fingers trembled when I saw the pain etched in the shadows under his eyes and the taut line of his lips, but the sheets covered any other signs of injuries.

When I blinked I could see the yellow eyes of a sedwa watching me from the shadows. What horrors had this man faced?

His head stirred ever so slightly on his pillow and I glanced back at Rev, who stood in the doorway behind me, a silhouette casting a long shadow into the bedroom. A floorboard creaked beneath my boot and I hesitated, wondering how to begin. Grasping my journal and pencil in my hands, I sank into the chair beside the man's bed and scribbled out a message for Rev to read. With a sigh he drew near, and, one hand adjusting his glasses, the other holding my journal toward the candlelight to see, studied my words before turning to the man. "I am Rev, and this is my daughter, Elena."

Even though this wasn't the first time he'd introduced me as such, my heart never ceased to warm at the word. *Daughter.* I shook my head to focus my thoughts as Rev continued.

"She is mute, but she wanted to ask you some questions, if you are well enough…" He hesitated, studying the man's face.

"I'll tell you what I can," came the man's raspy voice. "I suppose you want to know who I am and what I was doing traveling this way, and…about that…animal."

His eyes were focused on mine, so I nodded. Averting his head to stare up at the ceiling, he let out a soft sigh.

"My name is Marke and I'm a merchant from Misroth City. Lately, business has been…less than ideal, due to the war. I have two daughters and a wife to provide for…you know, the story of a desperate man." He shifted to look at Rev. "So I decided to take matters into my own hands and bring my business to another city, before we reached the heart of winter and traveling would be even slower and more dangerous. I gathered some of my wares and set off for Vorvinia. Evren Forest is not a prime travelers' route, but with a wagon loaded full of goods, little money, and even less time, it was the best choice for me. Sailing was out of the question and every other route is either as dangerous or too time-consuming."

I shuddered when I thought about the forest and what it would be like to venture into the shadows and face the sedwa again.

"It's not a long journey from Misroth to Evren—if you manage to stay straight and true," Marke continued, "but the old pathways are becoming overgrown, and trekking through the thick forest with a wagon is no easy task. In some cases I had to make my own trail by beating back undergrowth, and so a journey I'd hoped to accomplish in less than two days began to look like it would take double that time. By the second night, I was sure something was wrong in the forest: the animals were too quiet; the night felt…ominous."

Marke hesitated, and I brushed at my arms, trying to chase the cold chills away.

"I'd heard the rumors about the sedwa stalking the woods and mountains, and knew why the forest path was rarely used, but since recent rumors have not spread…" He paused to catch his breath, and his eyes drifted briefly toward Rev, but then locked on me.

A queasy feeling formed in the pit of my stomach. *Does he recognize me? What are the chances? The people of Misroth City rarely saw me, and I was a child then. Surely the likelihood of him recognizing me now is almost impossible…though I know I resemble my mother…*

He broke into my thoughts. "Well, that last statement wasn't entirely true. There have been a few tales in Misroth City and surrounding towns. I didn't believe they held a lot of credence when I first heard them; to be honest, I thought there were other dangers and difficulties that kept travelers from using the path through Evren Forest other than the sedwa…"

Rev was frowning intently at Marke. "What form do these tales take in the capital? Are they similar to ours?"

"The tales speak of attacks from strange monsters. Dark creatures, with scales like dragons, sleek bodies toned with muscles like great cats, teeth like bears, and claws like…well, like no other creature known to man." Marke shook his head. "Even more unbelievable to me were the myths whispered among some foolhardy citizens in Misroth City: that King Eldon did not simply close our borders to the Alrenian Empire to promote our independence, but that he found a way to cast a barrier around our kingdom that forcefully blocked our borders from intruders. The stories say that he did so to keep monsters like the sedwa out of our lands, and that he and his men hunted down the remainder still living in Misroth until all were extinct, all but the few that went into hiding. These rumors claim the sedwa are some of the creatures from the Wastelands."

There were those stories about the kingdoms beyond Misroth again. A longing to travel beyond my small world, to see new lands and explore these mysteries, burned in my heart. *Concentrate,* I reprimanded myself. I shifted in my chair and looked back at Marke.

"What was I to make of this nonsense?" Marke said, glancing at both Rev and me. "If these animals existed, why were they the stuff of legend? Why were they not regularly seen, hunted…or at least why weren't the people living near the forest and Vorvinian Mountains plagued by regular attacks?"

He stared at us for a long moment, as if assessing something. At last, he spoke. "I have a gift for discernment, so I suppose I can trust you."

Rev shot me a look, his eyebrows raised and his eyes wide with skepticism. I could almost see the thought flitting through his mind:

Perhaps this man is delusional.

"In Misroth City," Marke continued, "word is going round that there is a conspiracy involving the sedwa…that they only started making systematic attacks on citizens throughout Misroth once they are provoked by hunters. And not provoked by just any hunters, but by specific men appointed by the king to anger the sedwa and spread terror among the people so he could promise us protection and hold greater sway over us. Now, I am not one to question the oppressive state of his regime or his clear desire to tighten his hold over us, but…this all seemed…farfetched."

Rev was running his hand through his hair again. "We have heard news of oppression from the king, but mostly scattered tales told by travelers and the occasional whispers of merchants. Could you tell us more?"

My heart hammered against my chest. There wasn't an ounce of doubt in my mind: what Marke was saying was not myth. I knew what lengths the king would go to establish his power; I'd tasted them myself. And few in Evren were questioning the sedwas' existence now. The tension in my head grew. Conditions throughout the rest of Misroth must be worse than I'd ever imagined or feared.

"Of course, I had forgotten how Evren mostly keeps to itself." Marke sighed, letting his head sink further back into his pillow. "Many are discontent with King Zarev's rule, but few will speak out against it and fewer still have chosen to oppose it outright. But…as I said…I see I can trust you."

Rev and I exchanged another glance, and I realized my fingers were clenched together in my lap.

Marke drew a deep breath. "The king is ruthless in his efforts to control—citizens' lives mean nothing if taking them means he can tighten his clutch on us all. Priests are forbidden to teach about the Giver of Life because the king is bent on spreading death; citizens are forbidden to gather together without express permission; guards patrol the streets everywhere and inflict terror and punishment through the torture and execution of any who speak out against the king. The slightest word can be twisted, called treachery, and used against you. There are no trials; there is no justice for us. Even the King's Council has been disbanded under the premise that the action is only temporary and only a necessary evil during wartime. Yet despite this clear injustice, so many believe in King Regent Zarev's goodness; they trust his lies and think he is protecting us all. Only a few of us dare to meet in secret within the capital, to share news and plan ways to oppose the king. And none of this is the worst news…" He closed his eyes, drawing a deep breath once more.

Glancing down, I realized my fingers were curling into fists. I relaxed them and lay my hands in my lap, but I couldn't stop from fidgeting as Marke went on.

"The war's expenses are taking its toll on us all. Our taxes are high, and our young men are being sent to Argelon where they can be trained as soldiers or guards. Evren is one of the fortunate towns too distant to feel the effects yet. And Gillen, our rightful heir to the throne, is nearly of age, but I fear he will never rule. Instead, word has it that Gillen himself led a regiment into battle."

My stomach clenched; my head was spinning again. *No.* The room felt like it was closing in on me and I thought I would fall from the chair. I pressed my hands to my temples and forced myself to focus, to push the panic back. I needed to hear everything Marke had to share.

Steadying my breathing, I sat up and dared to look in Rev's direction. Thankfully, he was too engrossed in Marke's news to notice my pain. I turned back to Marke, fearful of what he would share next, but desperate to know more.

"He has been gone at the front for months now with no word. We have little hope…" Marke gasped and ran a weary hand over his brow. "We have little hope he will return any time soon, if ever. Few even remember to call Zarev king regent anymore."

I swallowed, wishing the chill gripping my heart would melt away, that I could convince myself the worst had not happened to my cousin.

Marke didn't stop. "So, as I said, things are…not going well in Misroth. You're fortunate to be cut off from it all, but I doubt it will last long. Zarev's greedy eyes will roam toward the smaller, more distant towns and he will not be satisfied with leaving them untouched. He will take supplies for his army and force his laws upon you as well. If it is true that he is endangering you by angering the sedwa, then he is simply waiting for you to begin clamoring to him for protection."

Rev stirred uncomfortably in his chair. "So…the sedwa…"

"As I said, that second night of my travels I started to have my doubts. The forest was ominously quiet and I knew something was wrong; something was hushing nature into an unnatural silence. My horse knew this too, and was restless and agitated all night. I hardly slept, but I neither heard nor saw anything of the sedwa. The arrival of daylight rallied my courage and I shrugged off my nighttime fears. I told myself my imagination was running wild and that perhaps stormy weather was on the way, or some other predator, perhaps a bear, had been roaming the woods.

"However, as soon as twilight descended, the quiet did again too; and my steed was even more unnerved than before. As soon as I tied him to a tree for the night, something spooked him and he began to rear and kick. My efforts to calm him were to no avail." He looked at me. "That's when I saw it.

"First I noticed the eyes: brilliant gold shimmering in the moonlight as they watched me. The pupils were such thin slits they were almost lost in the wide glow of its irises. The way they stared at me, unblinking, chilled me and kept me frozen to the ground. I had never seen eyes like that in any creature. My thoughts were going wild and I could not keep my wits about me to determine what to do next: flee on the horse without my wares, or stand and defend?

"I was desperate, hoping to save my supplies, to make money for my family, so I suppose I took the fool's choice. I dashed back to my wagon where I kept my bow… Yes, I'd been so overconfident in my belief that the sedwa weren't real that I hadn't even kept a weapon on my person." He sighed. "Maybe movement is what attracts them and entices them to strike. All I know is that it took mere moments for it to spring. It was so swift it was merely a mass of darkness, great golden eyes, and fangs and claws diving toward me. It leapt and snapped at my neck, but I managed to jump back. Its fangs grazed my chest instead." He tapped the sheets gingerly to indicate the hidden wound. "I did have a dagger in my belt and had the foresight to draw that. I buried it deep into one of those eyes."

He shuddered. "The rest of the fight is a blur in my mind. I slashed when I could, but the sedwa overpowered me. It was impossibly fast and powerful and unnaturally intelligent, studying my every move. At some point, by some miracle, it left me bleeding on the ground. What kind of animal leaves its prey to die, I do not know. It was Selna's husband who found me as he was returning from a hunt. If not for him, his wife, and your healer, I would have died there alone, unable to even attempt to find help, for my horse had long since fled."

He glanced at me again. I bit my lip, but still he said nothing.

"We are sorry if we troubled or upset you," Rev responded, his brow furrowed.

Slowly, Marke shook his head. "No, I am glad I could tell you about the sedwa and what is going on beyond your town's borders." He closed his eyes, drawing a deep breath. "Call me a traitor now, if you will, but I promise you that no good has come of the war or King Zarev's reign. You will see all too soon for yourselves."

"I fear you may be correct," Rev said, his face whiter than I had ever seen it. "Thank you for your information. We will let you rest now."

Marke nodded, his head moving against the pillow, and Rev and I stood. Tiptoeing through the doorway, we met Selna in the hall.

"Will he be all right?" Rev whispered.

Selna's forehead pinched with concern. "I hope so."

My head ached from all of Marke's news; my thoughts and fears were consuming me. Heart pounding, I followed Rev through the backdoor and out into the cold night air. The wind rustled around us and snowflakes fluttered into my face and melted in my hair.

Rev reached out to offer me his arm, so I humored him and leaned against his shoulder as we trudged back through a light dusting of snow. The townspeople's voices carried to us on the wind as we wound our way from the inn, avoiding the crowds still lining the street and hoping for news of the stranger. Icy air fingered its way past my cloak, but I knew it wasn't the cold that was leaving me breathless and numb. The knowledge of what was happening to the kingdom of Misroth as I hid away sent a chill through my veins. Old memories flitted through my mind but the hurt was distant—they were only well-remembered nightmares that held no power over me in my waking hours. Not for now. Not when I kept my heart hard against them.

There is nothing I can do, I told myself. *Knowing the truth does not mean I can change what is happening.* I shoved the guilt away and pressed closer to Rev's warmth, tucking my arm tighter in his.

But Gil. Gil… I sent up a silent plea that the Life-Giver would bring him back safely to Misroth.

The sound of crashing waves roared in my ears and the wind tore through my hair, swirling my skirts around me and wrenching my breath away. Tears from the cold air stung my eyes and traced down my cheeks, but I was too numb to feel the cold on my skin. Instead, the icy fingers crept into my lungs, stifling me, forcing my words down inside of me. I could not speak, could not protest, though Marke was condemning me. He stared me down with an accusatory glare as I stood frozen on a precipice overlooking the sea, Misroth's Royal Guard holding me over the edge. My back was to the sea, but I was all too aware of the vast drop between me and the tumultuous water.

"You let them die," Marke was saying. There were men, women, and children standing behind him, crying and wailing and wearing red armbands of mourning. Blood was running through the streets of Misroth, staining the castle, the shops, the houses, and the ramparts crimson.

No, no… Horror and guilt shot through my veins and clenched at my heart. My lips were frozen and would not move. The wind howled in my ears, but I could still hear the low laughter of the guards beside me.

"You did nothing even though you knew what your father was doing—what he was capable of! How could you?" Marke was furious.

I couldn't do anything…no one would have believed me… How could I stop him?

"For that you have been sentenced to death!"

Already the guards were shoving me over the edge. My scream tore from my throat and was stolen by the wind as I tumbled, suspended in the air for a few terrible seconds, and then plunged into darkness. The water was icy cold and suffocating. My hands were tied again. The sea pressed in heavily on all sides, threatening to crush me slowly…

With a start I awoke, trembling from head to foot in my bed. Outside the wind was shrieking. Slipping from beneath the covers, I approached the window and shoved aside the curtains. Snow swirled in blankets of white past the house, almost masking my view of the tree outside my room. I shivered, not sure if it was more from the cold or my nightmare, and turned to tumble back into bed when I saw flickering candlelight outside my bedroom. Lyanna paused in the doorway, her long nightgown nearly covering her bare feet.

"Are you all right?" she whispered. "You were tossing and kicking in your sleep again."

I blinked, and to my surprise I felt a tear snake down my cheek. Touching my hand to my face, I tried to brush it away as I nodded, but Lyanna broke the distance between us in a few easy strides. She set the candle on my nightstand and pulled me into an embrace. With a sigh I rested my forehead on her shoulder and inhaled the familiar, comforting scent of lavender soap. But Lyanna's embrace couldn't erase the guilt and fear weighing heavily on my heart.

How many more people had died at the king's hand? The question persisted no matter how many times I tried to banish it. But still worse was another question, growing louder in my head with every passing hour:

What if Gillen was dead?

CHAPTER NINE

T HE ICY WIND BIT AT my face and tore straight through my cloak no matter how closely I tried to wrap it around my body. I shivered miserably as I walked beside Avrik, trying to listen as he eagerly related Marke's tale, not knowing that I already knew it all.

"I can hardly believe it," he said. "Selna didn't want word to get out about the king supposedly encouraging men to provoke them because of the controversy it would create." He glanced over at me and I frowned in confusion. "She couldn't keep people out forever when there were men who wanted to learn about the sedwa and decide if they are a threat to Evren. But I agree with her…none of the hunters in our village would be committing such a crime against the town. After all, they'd be endangering themselves. It's not as if the king's guards are here to protect us. I'm sure the sedwa attack whenever they are hungry like any other predator does. No one is *doing* this to us." There was a firmness in his tone that I was not used to; an edge that cut through the air like a dagger and snapped my attention toward him.

Biting my lip, I rested my hand on his arm in what I hoped was a comforting gesture. He paused, his boots sinking into the snow as he turned to look at me. I stopped too, gazing up into his dark, troubled eyes.

"Everyone will be accusing my father…" he said.

In response, I patted his arm feebly until he moved away. For one moment I was hurt and glanced down in embarrassment. Then his arms were around me, pulling me into an embrace. I forgot about the cold as I basked in his warmth; forgot even what we'd been talking about while we stood there, silent. He held me long enough for me to wonder if he could feel my heart pounding against his chest. "Thank you for believing that he is innocent," he murmured in my ear. "Sometimes it seems like no one else does."

He released me as abruptly as he had hugged me, leaving my head spinning. *Get a grip, you fool.*

We continued to trudge through the snow toward the schoolhouse. It still seemed distant in the vast white landscape, tucked snugly among the hills. The wind stung my cheeks as I thought about how quickly my trips here were drawing to a close. Then Lyanna would have me helping her at home full time, expecting suitors to show up at her door over the next few years and whisk me away to a new life. I frowned at the thought and promptly dismissed it, as I always did. Somehow I couldn't see the village boys finding a mute wife particularly appealing when it came to practical tasks, such as raising children.

And maybe those practical tasks don't appeal to me *anyway.* Having a family someday was not something I was against—but being trapped in a life revolving around baking and sewing sounded like a nightmare.

"Elena?"

I snapped my head back to Avrik, who was walking slowly by my side, studying my face with a bemused expression.

"You didn't hear a word I said, did you?"

Smiling sheepishly, I admitted my mind had been wandering with a reluctant shake of my head.

"I was saying after school, Bren and Shilam wanted to do some target practice. Do you think Lyanna will miss you if you aren't home right away for your sewing or baking lessons?"

I rolled my eyes at his mocking tone, but my smile gave away what he already knew: I agreed with him. Even after several years of attempts, no amount of patience, prodding, or stern lectures could prompt my interest in the chores Lyanna offered. My stitches were passable; my food at least edible, but polishing them beyond minimally functional skills taught by necessity would never excite me. More than once I'd watched

Lyanna throw up her hands, sigh, and dramatically proclaim that I was hopeless as Avrik or Bren arrived at the door to rescue me from domestic responsibilities. She would have been a little more convincing if a smile didn't tug at her lips every time.

I considered Avrik's invitation with mixed emotions. Ever since I'd listened to Marke's story, my memory of the sedwa, with its glowing eyes fixed on me, had prowled through my head. The thought of being even closer to the woods made my pulse quicken. On the other hand, I'd never heard of the sedwa attacking anyone outside of the forest, and the idea of escaping Lyanna's endless chores even for an extra hour or two was always tempting.

Shrugging, I let Avrik arrive at the answer I couldn't vocalize for him. "She'll mind…but not that much…if you're not *too* late." He broke into a boyish grin. "No worries; no one in the village will want us out too late near the forest now with those rumors." A slight shadow passed over his face again, but he fought it off this time. "Bren's and Shilam's mothers will panic and I'm sure Lyanna would too if we stayed out very long. We can walk back to my house after school and we won't go far."

I sighed, wishing I could tell him that the threat *was* real. It wouldn't be long before he and his father spent another long day within the woods to track and hunt, and though I could not stop them, I wanted them to use caution. Once we reached the schoolhouse, I would have to write down a message, something that would warn him and his father. But if he refused to believe what he'd heard about Marke's tale from others, would he even believe me?

We reached the schoolhouse as Teacher was opening the door and trudged in line behind the other students. I slid into my seat beside Avrik and pulled my journal and pencil from my pack. Quickly, I scrawled words across an empty page: *Rev and I visited Marke last night, and I think his story is true. You probably would have believed it too if you had heard it from his own mouth. I only want you to be careful.*

When I brushed my journal onto Avrik's desk, I watched his eyes scan the page and a frown crease his forehead. He glanced over at me and carefully mouthed, "You believe too?"

I scrambled to take my journal back and write: *There's surely a reason why this rumor came about and why Marke was attacked. It doesn't make your father guilty, or anyone else in Evren. Perhaps the hunters are men from other towns near the forest and mountains. Maybe they are even from Vorvinia.*

He caught my eyes again; his expression difficult to read. Was that fear? Did he trust me or was he concerned that I might give credence to the rumors about his father? I could not tell.

Stretching back the bowstring, I held it to my cheek and gazed down the length of my strung arrow toward the wooden target Avrik had set up in his yard. In my mind, I imagined setting the arrow free and watching it soar across the yard, arcing in its path, and slamming into the target. *A little to the right, because of the wind*, I thought. I shifted my bow slightly to compensate for the steady easterly breeze and then let it fly. I held my breath as it zipped through the air and buried itself in the red bull's-eye Avrik had painted on the target.

I glanced toward Avrik, who smirked back at me in a silent challenge. "Good luck, Bren," he said as Bren stepped forward to take my place.

"Splendid," Bren said with a sigh. "Could we hold a harvesting competition next? Come out to our fields next autumn and we will see who gathers the most crops the fastest."

Shilam and Avrik chuckled.

"On with it!" Avrik said.

"Don't take all day," Shilam added.

Almost without thinking, I glanced toward the woods as Bren strung an arrow to his bow and took aim. A cold breeze stirred through the bare branches and made me shiver. Shadows were beginning to stretch across the snow and I knew I couldn't stay out much longer. Who knew what could happen at night, at the edge of the forest? I blinked and tried to focus on Bren's shot. His struck further from the bull's eye than mine.

"Too bad," Shilam teased. "Maybe next time."

Bren shrugged and smiled at me sheepishly. "Defeated again."

Avrik shuffled forward to take his place.

"Maybe we should remove the arrows so you don't strike any," Shilam said, but Avrik waved him away. Everyone knew he would hit the target dead on. I could count on one hand the number of times I had seen him miss: three, exactly the number of times I had bested him in our shooting competitions, and one more time than he'd ever defeated me. I smiled at the thought.

The breeze strengthened, tugging wavy strands of hair in front of my face. With an impatient move I brushed them back. Was it my imagination, or had I heard something? My eyes darted back toward the trees. *Of course it is your imagination. Even if a sedwa was there, you would not hear it.* I squeezed my eyes shut, then looked back at Avrik as he yanked the bowstring back and released his arrow. It soared easily toward its mark, splitting my arrow to take its place.

Bren and Shilam clapped and cheered.

Again, I was too preoccupied to partake in the excitement. An uneasy sense that we were being watched flooded over me, and I turned to search the woods again. My heart throbbed against my chest but I saw nothing— no eyes stared back at me. Yet. I knew it was time to leave; it was too late to be this close to the forest and not expect trouble.

"Looks like a draw between Avrik and Elena," Bren said. "Again."

"I haven't shot yet!" Shilam protested.

I strode over to Avrik and grasped his arm. Frowning, he glanced down at me, reading my expression as only he could do. "Already?" he sighed. Then his countenance hardened. "You really are afraid, aren't you? How can you believe—?"

Bren cut him off. "Avrik, do not be angry with her. There's no harm in being careful. She's not accusing your father of anything by believing Marke's story."

Avrik cringed and spun toward him. "Do *you* believe it?"

"Don't be ridiculous. I think there could be something to it—but you know I trust your father. Those who truly know him do not place their faith in the town gossip about him."

"Not many people like my father, and you know it," Avrik said. I could hear a slight tremor to his voice.

Shilam broke in. "That is only because he has kept to himself. People will spread their gossip—let them. Those who matter don't believe it. You needn't be so defensive."

Avrik's eyes were fiery. "How would *you* behave if it was *your* father being accused of…of *murder*?" he spat.

"We're not the ones—" Bren began, but a dark form launched from the woods and cut his words short.

Somehow Avrik saw the sedwa a second before it leapt on him. He stumbled backward, avoiding the sedwa's pounce and collapsing in the snow with the creature snarling down at him. Stringing an arrow to my bow, I inhaled deeply to steady my aim and shot for one of the sedwa's golden eyes. As I released the arrow, the creature sprang again and I pierced one of its paws instead. Avrik kicked, his booted leg driving into the sedwa's midsection and working its momentum against it so that it flew backward. It rolled in the snow, snarling and leaving a trail of slick black blood behind it.

My mouth was dry and my limbs were shaking. On either side of me, Shilam and Bren were fumbling for arrows, still grasping what was happening. Only Avrik, his years of hunting honing him for moments such as these, seemed to be fully in control of mind and body as he jumped smoothly to his feet and drew another arrow, his eyes never leaving the sedwa. Growling, it staggered to a crouch and began slinking backward toward the shadows of the forest. In the growing darkness, all I could see was a mass of black fur and scales and shimmering golden eyes trained on Avrik.

There was a breathless minute in which Shilam, Bren, and I were motionless, unable to react as the sedwa and Avrik stared each other down. Then, with an angry cry, Avrik charged.

My throat constricted and I longed to be able to shout out. My brain screamed instead: *Avrik, you fool! It's still dangerous!*

He pounded through the snow, chasing the sedwa as it slunk back, eying him with hatred and preparing for another strike. Shilam and Bren were firing now, but the beast darted past the tree line and their arrows fell useless. Avrik disappeared into the forest after the sedwa.

"Avrik! What are you doing?" Shilam shouted. He strung another arrow to his bow and chased after his friend.

Bren and I scrambled after them, my pulse pounding so loudly as I sprinted into the woods that I could hardly hear anything else. Somewhere ahead, the sedwa's snarls echoed off the trees. Then another cry rang through the night: a sound that sent shudders through my body. It was a voice almost more familiar than my own, so long had it been since I had been able to speak. *Avrik.*

It's too late; it's too late. The thought pounded through my head viciously with every pump of my legs, every gasp for air. Bare twigs reached for my face and scratched my cheeks. I stumbled through snow and mud and over roots jutting up in my path. I wasn't sure which way I was running or if I was still going in the direction from which Avrik's cry had come, but I didn't dare slow. My bow weighed heavily in my hand yet my grip remained firm. Somewhere beside me Bren was charging through the trees, but I was only vaguely aware of his presence. Panic had overtaken my every thought. My friend was gone, or soon would be.

I plunged through a tangle of underbrush and stumbled into a clearing to see a form ahead. He was huddled at the edge of the clearing, and I couldn't make out his face in the darkness. I wished I could say his name, say anything, but I stood there gasping for breath and half-afraid to step nearer. Where was the sedwa? I glanced up at the sound of rustling and saw Bren dash around from the opposite end of the clearing, closer to the still figure.

"Elena? Bren?" It was Shilam's voice quavering in the darkness.

My emotions unleashed in a strange mixture of relief and fear. Shilam was alive, but where was Avrik?

"What happened?" Bren asked, kneeling before Shilam. He scanned the trees warily before laying his bow at his feet and reaching out to his friend.

"I don't think I am badly wounded, but Avrik...he's still out there with that...that monster..."

"Let me see it. I think you will be all right, but we need to staunch the blood flow..."

My own thoughts drowned out Bren's voice. I felt my fingers

fastening around my bow as courage mixed with fear and adrenaline coursed through my being. I broke into another sprint, tearing through the forest, away from the sound of Shilam's and Bren's voices.

The pleas in my head sounded eerily like the ones I'd once offered up for my uncle. *Life-Giver, if you've ever listened to me, listen now and spare Avrik.* A dozen awful thoughts flitted through my head as I imagined Avrik trying to fight off the sedwa. *I will do anything you want, but do not take my friend.*

Some of the snow drifts were so huge that I sank waist-deep into them and crawled out wet and shivering. I slipped and stumbled over patches of ice, sometimes snatching at a tree branch to catch myself. The twigs clawed at my face as the forest closed in around me, the sky all but disappearing under a patchwork of gnarled branches. Darkness deepened and clouds gathered over the moon, hiding all but a few lone stars. My breath was loud and ragged in my ears; snapping twigs echoed in the quiet, but I heard no other sounds, no sign that either the sedwa or Avrik was near. In the shadows, the forest was silent.

At last my lungs screamed for air and a persistent stitch in my side forced me to a walk. Sweat snaked down the back of my neck but the chill breeze rattling through the branches quickly made me shiver. Gradually the trees thinned out again and I found myself in another clearing, this one even larger than the last. I stopped and tried to search the blackness, but it was impossible to see far into the night. My fingers trembled as I brought them close to my face, yanked off my shooting gloves, and blew warm air over them.

Then, without the warning of approaching footsteps, I heard a man's voice ahead of me. "Who is there?"

I started, my heart leaping in fear, until I realized the voice was familiar. Kyrin. Had he found his son? Hope flooded through me. I rushed forward, but paused in the middle of the clearing when I saw the figure standing amongst the trees. The man was alone, armed with his bow, and as he plodded toward me under the open sky, a patch of starlight fell on his face.

Although it had been four full years since the last incident, it happened again: a revelation came to me, hitting me with the force and suddenness of an unseen blow:

In my vision, Kyrin was in a small side room set apart from the main dining room at the inn, sitting at a table across from a member of the Royal Guard. Firelight from the hearth beside them flickered off their faces as Kyrin leaned forward.

"I have lost enough in this life. I'll do anything to keep my son safe, to ensure he is never called to war."

The guard pulled an envelope, marked with the royal seal, the dragon Vehgar, from his cloak pocket. "Then I have a mission for you from the king. He is willing to pay handsomely for it and will never call on Avrik to join his army, in exchange for your silence. One word about this to anyone else—including your son—and you will die."

The scene shifted. Deep in the forest, Kyrin crouched in one of the trees, his dark cloak pulled closely about him to help him blend into the shadows. He tugged on his bowstring and released an arrow—letting it fly toward the golden eyes gleaming back at him from the blackness.

My eyes jerked open. *My visions have returned!* And just as before, I could not hold back the truth once it came to me. My voice squirmed up my throat and slithered across my tongue, coming out in a raspy whisper. "You *are* hunting the sedwa for the king."

The words cut through the air, sharper than the edges of the icicles clinging to the trees. I blinked and bit my lip, dumbfounded at the sound of my own voice.

Kyrin stopped midstride. Snow dusted the scruff on his chin and melted in his hair, brown mingled with grey. A sneer twisted his lips. "So, you're not a mute after all. Look who else has been keeping secrets."

Mouth dry, I groped for the arrows in my quiver, but to my horror I found I was down to one. I hadn't thought to pause to fill my quiver before chasing after Avrik.

Kyrin strung an arrow to his bow, and my shaking fingers responded by notching my last arrow to mine. "The sedwa haven't bested me; do you think you can?" he demanded.

Before I could react, he released his arrow and pierced my right arm. Pain screamed through it. Jerking back, I lost my grip on my bowstring.

My arrow soared high and landed harmlessly behind Kyrin.

Groaning, I dropped my bow and staggered backward. I resisted the urge to claw at the arrow in my arm as searing pain roared all the way up to my shoulder and down to my fingertips. My pulse crashed against my ears.

Kyrin lowered his bow with a gloating smile. "Out of options?"

My mind felt paralyzed with fear and pain, but one thought echoed through my head with piercing clarity: *Run.*

CHAPTER TEN

SPINNING AROUND, I SPRINTED BACK into the forest, snapping twigs and skidding on ice. He was all but silent behind me, possessing the sure-footed, swift pursuit of a hunter. I felt strong arms grasp mine and jerk me backward. One of his hands caught at the arrow in my arm, breaking the shaft and making blood ooze from the wound. Screaming, I squirmed, yanked myself free, and tumbled into the snow.

Kyrin snatched my hair in his fist and dragged me through the snowdrifts. I cried out and clawed at his arm, but he didn't let go until we were back in the clearing. My scalp burned, my head ached, and my arm throbbed and left a bloody trail in the snow. I stared up at sky, tracing the sharp edges of the tree limbs clawing at it, as if desperate for escape from this world. I cringed as Kyrin bent over me, a coil of rope in his hands.

"It's unfortunate you chose to run into the forest at night. Lyanna and Rev will be worried sick about you, and Avrik will miss you, but sadly, by the time I find you deep in the forest where you lost yourself, it will be too late. I will discover your mangled body, just as I found that guard's years ago."

I struggled, punched, kicked; I even spit in his face, but he was twice my weight and his work was effortless. He bound my arms behind me, tying one end of the rope around my wrists and the other around the trunk of the nearest tree.

After years of being mysteriously mute, I wasn't sure if my voice would still be there now. Perhaps it had only returned to deliver this last fatal message. To my surprise, when I tried, the words fell easily from my lips. "How can you do this?" I shouted, my voice cracking in the frigid air. I yanked futilely against the rope. The trunk trembled, shaking the branches and dusting me with snow. "You're endangering your own son! He is out here somewhere, being attacked by one of the sedwa, because of *you*."

"You should know that I, of all people, know how to find and protect my own son. He will return home safely tonight. I am giving him food and shelter and ensuring us protection from the king and his guard; he will never be called upon to enter the war. As for the lives I endanger…I hold no allegiance to the hateful people of Evren." His steamy breath followed his words, ghostly in the silver light glancing off the snow. "And no matter what you mean to Avrik, I will let you die before I see his own life in danger." For a moment, his gaze seemed almost to soften. "It is a shame he will have to lose you. But think of it as an honor, Elena, to die to save the life of a friend."

Then he was gone, winding his way through the trees, leaving me breathless, without a single retort on my lips. *Of course. Of course he would do this for Avrik. He would do anything for Avrik.*

Exhaling slowly, trying to still the racing of my heart, I watched my breath escape, rising in the dim light. The snow under my cloak dissolved into icy water that seeped all the way to my skin. I tugged and strained against the rope until my left arm ached almost as much as my right, and my wrists were raw and bleeding nearly as much as my wound. Minutes stretched into hours and the night deepened. Trying to shut out the eerie silence and the memories of the sedwa, I collapsed in the snow. Not an owl, not a squirrel, not a single animal showed itself or made a sound. It was too quiet, even for a night in the dead of winter. *Never a good sign.*

I imagined something lurking among the trees nearby, something with claws and fangs. *This is not how I want to die.*

Abruptly, my fear and despair erupted into anger and I screamed at the sky. *All those years of silence, all those years without visions or a need to share the truth…they did nothing to save me. Why did I suddenly have to speak now?*

Where did my voice go, and why did it return?

The waiting was the worst. My half-hearted hope that Shilam and Bren were safe and would come searching for me faded. *Even if they are looking, what are the chances they'll find me in time? And what if they are hurt or...*

Or worse?

I lay shaking in the snow, wet, freezing, and terrified. As the dark clouds swirled overhead, they covered what little starlight I'd had and deepened the night from charcoal to black.

A noise shattered the silence and my head snapped up. I scanned the trees ahead fruitlessly. Though I could not see anything, I knew I wasn't alone. Something was breathing, its slow, heavy exhalations nearly matching my own, nearly fading into the night without a trace and leaving my mind wondering if I was imagining the sound. But I was not. The sound of its breaths continued, rising and falling, and the sounds were coming closer.

My teeth chattered. I scrambled to my feet and yanked against the rope again. More snow. More of the rope digging into my raw, bleeding skin.

Then I saw it: a huge, four-legged shadow lurking at the edge of the trees. No sound escaped my mouth. I was weaponless, bound, defenseless; there was nothing I could do to save myself. I bowed my head and squeezed my eyes shut in a pathetic attempt to block out the paralyzing fear. *It's not real, it's not...*

But I knew pretending could not stop the attack.

A heavy, scaly mass collided with my chest and shoved me back into the snow. I heard a scream spear the air before I realized it was coming from my own mouth. In seconds, my brain registered several facts, as adrenaline heightened all my senses. Hot breath tickled my cheek, sending chills rolling down my back. Pain from several points—the sedwa's claws—digging deeply into my chest began to radiate outward, and the weight of its body was so great I thought my lungs were being crushed, my breath coming in shallow gasps, my head spinning. The snow beneath me was so cold it burned my skin. Sweat trickled across my temple, toward my ear. I'd landed on my hands, bound and pinned beneath me, but the rope tying me to the tree had snapped. My eyes sprang open to the sight that had haunted my nightmares: golden orbs, with pupils like wide slits into a bottomless abyss, glared back. Dark fur bristled along its neck. The sedwa's scaly black jaw opened to reveal its yellow fangs, dripping with warm, rancid saliva that dribbled onto my cheek.

With a grunt, I kneed the creature in its stomach. The sedwa only responded with a snarl and swiped one of its paws at my face. I turned my head in time and its claws brushed air.

I refused to accept my fate. I would not die. Not now. Not here.

As suddenly as the sedwa landed on me, the weight lifted from my chest. I opened my eyes to see it hunched several yards away. It snarled but kept its body low, fur bristling and scales flashing in the moonlight. As I watched, it slowly backed up, like a terrified animal that knew it had met its match. I blinked in confusion. Was it retreating?

Then I realized that it was not even looking at me, but glaring at something behind me. My blood ran cold. I scanned the ground, searching for a rock, a branch—anything I could attempt to grasp with my bound hands and use to defend myself. If I had to die, I would die fighting as a daughter of kings, heir of the great Eldon, and not as a child, whimpering and wounded in the snow.

With a cry I wrenched myself into a sitting position and glanced over my shoulder. The dark form of a man stood motionless behind me. As I squinted in the darkness, I could not make out any weapons strapped to his belt or back, and his hands, clenched into fists at his sides, held no blades; but all manner of daggers and knives could easily be concealed within his cloak or boots. A hood hung low over his face, shrouding his features in shadow and making his expression inscrutable. All I could discern was the strong line of his jaw, his head held high as he stared in the direction of the sedwa—or me. Though his clothing was tattered and weatherworn and he wielded no visible weapons, his mere presence radiated something mysterious and powerful; something that made my tongue cleave to my mouth and my breath catch in my chest, something that made the moments slow and the very air about me seem to still.

I heard another growl and dared to turn back toward the sedwa as it slunk away into the woods. Had the man done that with a mere look? I wanted to look brave, to mask my fear, but my body trembled. What sort of man could wield power this fearsome, that a mere look could send monsters fleeing before him?

"Halia!" a voice cried.

I jerked in shock. *My name, my* real *name. How...?*

Striding forward, the stranger knelt beside me. He threw back his hood to reveal short brown curls sweeping over a brow crinkled with concern. Several days' worth of stubble dotted his face. His complexion was deep brown, and the scent of the forest was strong on him: it was a pleasant aroma, comforting rather than repelling.

"One instant more and the sedwa would have killed you." He touched my forehead, brushed the hair back from my face. Though my heart thudded against my chest and I studied him warily, his touch was gentle. My fear dissipated and relief washed over me; his manner told me he meant no harm. I was safe.

He reached down to the wound in my arm and without warning, plucked the remains of the arrow from it. I opened my mouth to protest, but as I did, the pain melted away. Where the wound had been, only a tear in my sleeve and a small white scar remained.

Questions tumbled through my brain. *Who are you? How did you do this? Where did you come from?* But somehow I felt I should know the answers already and did not dare ask them. If I could think hard enough, maybe I would remember, but every answer that flitted through my brain seemed more impossible than the last: a sorcerer? I had never heard of such power, not outside tales. Someone who had unusual powers such as I did?

Instead, I whispered, "You saved my life."

"It was not yours to lose," the man responded. A smile spread across his lips, lit up his face, and crinkled his eyes. "Your time isn't over yet. There is much left for you to do."

And the answers came to me: as naturally and easily as if I'd known them all along. Perhaps I had. Somehow, impossibly, this man was the Life-Giver, and he meant for me to use the visions and knowledge I had been given. "But my words are dangerous," I protested. "And—and my visions. I cannot control them, or stop myself from speaking the truth when I shouldn't. I do not even know how they came to me...I hoped you would explain…"

The man smiled again, his dark eyes shining in the starlight. "You will learn about it all in time; it is something for you to discover and master on your own."

Sighing, I frowned back up at him, dissatisfied with his answer, but he merely shook his head and continued gently. "Your words are a gift, though few want to listen to them," he said. "The real danger comes from the words they *are* listening to."

The king's lies. This was a revelation I felt no urge to vocalize, and there was peace in that.

He nodded his assent, as if he had heard my thought. "Truth has been silent in your kingdom far too long."

Instead of feeling relief in knowing I had received my gift for a purpose, in having a few answers at last, I was only frustrated. "Why has my knowledge of the truth been gone for so long? And why couldn't I speak for years? I was mute!"

The man's eyes seemed dimmer with sadness. "Sometimes we think we are held back by an obstacle, when our fear is what created the obstacle."

I frowned, letting the meaning of his words sink in. "It was my own fault I was mute. But if I could not control my gift before, how could I hold it in and choose not to speak?"

"You may not yet know how to control your gift, but you can refuse it. And in your fear, you did."

My mind flitted back to that night long ago, when in fear and anger I'd cried out to the Life-Giver, pleading, wishing not to speak again. "But more and more, I have longed to speak again," I said thoughtfully. Perhaps I had warmed to the idea of my gift more as I'd wished for answers that until now had never come. "But even when I can speak, I don't know how to share the things I know. If I go home and share them, I will die and nothing will change."

The man shook his head. "Don't be afraid, Halia. You will not be alone."

I sat up as anger flared in my chest. I'd gone years without answers and with little comfort, and this is what he had to say? "Alone?" I snapped. "I'm always alone! I never have words to speak the thoughts trapped in my head. Or I have all the right words at the wrong time!"

Then as quickly as the anger appeared, it vanished and shame crept in to replace it. This man was the Giver of Life himself, and he had saved mine. What was I doing? I opened my mouth to blurt out an apology, but he stopped me.

"It's forgotten. Now it's your turn to forget: your fear, your doubt." He studied my face. "Is it really the fear of death that you struggle against, or fear of the burdens and pain you carry? Fear that you are insufficient? Are you ready to face your past?"

I avoided his gaze, staring off into the shadowy forest. I swallowed. "I—I don't know. I have no wish to die. Everyone struggles to face death."

"Some struggle to face life most of all." Standing, he reached out a hand and helped me to my feet. "But possessing the courage to live brings its own rewards. If you wish to truly help the ones you care for, overcome your fear and use your gift of knowledge."

As I let go of his hand, the world tipped and my vision blurred, but everything quickly righted itself. I scanned my surroundings in wonder. To the east, the sky was brightening and the stars were fading, melting in the gathering light of a swiftly approaching day. Though the air had been frigid earlier, I felt warm.

Then I remembered the man's words. How was I supposed to use my gift? How exactly could I save Gillen, Velaire, and my people? I turned back, but he had vanished.

In the moments before dawn, the earth lay still and silent.

CHAPTER ELEVEN

I GATHERED MY BOW AND empty quiver, still lying where I'd dropped it as I fled from Kyrin, and set off, eager to leave the woods behind. With the grey light of morning brightening the forest and an unnatural warmth and vigor coursing through my body, the journey toward home felt like it took only a few minutes.

As I stood at the edge of Evren Forest, staring at the distant log cabin I had looked upon as my home for four years, my mind reeled with a thousand thoughts.

How could I slip past Kyrin's cabin without him seeing me? And what about Avrik? *Is he safe?* I wondered. *Are Shilam and Bren all right?*

Had the past night really happened? Or had it been another one of my wild nightmares? If I didn't bear scars on my arm and collarbones, I might have convinced myself I'd imagined everything.

I even dreaded returning to Rev and Lyanna, knowing how terrified they must have been and wondering what I would even say to them. All of these years I had been mute—what would they say if I spoke now? How could I explain? The man in the woods—the Giver himself—had told me that my words were a gift, but they did not feel like one.

Worst of all, I had an idea of what he wanted me to do. *How can I go back to Misroth and accuse the king of treason? Face my mother and father again...*Tears sprang into my eyes. *How will anything I have to say be better received this time? Why would anyone even believe me over the lies they have heard for* *so long?*

My mind flitted to Marke and his group of men who met in secret. But they were just a few. And who was to say I would even survive in the capital long enough to compel enough people to believe me?

"Elena?" a familiar voice called my name and made my heart leap. I glanced up and saw Rev and two other men rushing through the trees. As he neared me, Rev dropped his bow to stretch his arms wide for a hug. I ran into his embrace, my tears falling freely now. "Thank the Giver of Blessings! You are alive!" He was so warm and safe—how could I ever let go?

Rev was the first to pull back and looked down to study me, reassuring himself that it was truly me and I was unharmed. Behind his glasses, his eyes were shadowed with dark circles, and his hair stood all on end, tousled in every direction. He noted the tears in my clothes and his forehead creased with worry. "Are you all right?"

I nodded. Glancing over his shoulder, I noticed Bren's and Shilam's fathers, each looking similarly ragged and weary. I turned back to Rev, hoping my question was clear.

"Yes, Bren and Shilam are all right. They are home. Once we ensured that Shilam's wounds were not serious, we left to search for you and Avrik. Kyrin came forward to say that he found his son, and he has been out looking for you all night as well. What a relief that you are all right! We must hurry home—Lyanna has been so worried…"

At the mention of home, weariness descended on me. Rev reached out to lift me into his arms. I wanted to protest, but it seemed useless. In his mind, I was still his child, a child he had nearly lost last night. He didn't know the burdens I carried.

"It's all right," he said as he carried me out into the open.

The first rays of sunlight sprang over the horizon and bathed the snow in a golden light. I glanced up at the sky, soaking in the red, pink, and orange hues of a morning I'd thought I would never see. The last of the energy and warmth from my encounter with the man in Evren Forest slipped away and I longed for bed.

But no matter my relief and exhaustion, one thought refused to stop replaying through my head, haunting me with the possible answers attached to it: *What am I going to do now?*

I knew the instant my dreams transformed into a vision. Everything I saw became clearer and more vivid, feeling all too real compared to the muddled dreams. I was outside, standing amongst a group of shadowy figures I at first did not recognize under a starless night. On either side of us, two lone trees stretched bare limbs toward the sky, their branches bending and swaying like writhing ghouls in the chill breeze. An eerie silence hung in the air, so palpable I could feel dread clawing its way up my throat.

"Did you hear that?" one of the men muttered, pointing a nocked bow toward the sky.

The men cast anxious glances all around them, but I could see nothing in the blackness beyond the trees until the clouds moved, and, under a brief flash of moonlight, I discerned the mud and murk—we were standing before a vast swamp under an open sky. The silence gave way to the sound of wind whispering through the tall grass behind us, grass that stretched endlessly over the flatlands behind us.

"There is nowhere to hide," another man hissed. "Crouch low! Get down!" He stretched out his arm and shoved the man beside him to the earth. Another cloud shifted and starlight glinted off the prostrate man's golden hair. My breath caught in my throat. *Gil.* Then the breeze wafted the clouds back over the stars and we were immersed in darkness once again.

Another sound emerged, a sound that turned my heart to lead in my chest and made me wonder if it was even still beating. The very air around us seemed to shudder with the slow, heavy throbs of great wings approaching us. I scoured the sky, but in vain. The sound could have been coming from any direction and I couldn't even make out a shadow in the night.

All around me, men dove to the earth in a panic, raising their weapons in various directions and stifling their breaths in a desperate attempt to melt into the darkness. An instant of quiet swept over us again, and then the screaming started.

"Over there!" a man in front of me cried, pointing to our right, where a great shadow seemed to consume one of his comrades.

Chaos erupted as arrows sang and men cowered in terror. More shouts pierced the night and then, as someone dove atop Gillen to shield him, something warm and wet splashed against my cheek and dripped into my open mouth. I gagged on the coppery taste of blood.

I woke with a gasp, my mouth full of blood from biting my lip in my sleep. Trembling, I stared out my window at the familiar tree standing against the backdrop of the snowy mountain in the distance. The day was overcast, with fluffy grey clouds swathing the world in cold light. It seemed too bright, too kind compared to the dark world I'd emerged from. Outside my bedroom, I heard Lyanna and Rev muttering, discussing what had happened and worrying over the fact that the boys and I had run off into the forest at night.

Gil is in danger. I wanted to wrench the sheets from my bed and fly out into the snow in a mad dash to save him. But where would I go? Marke had said he was in Alrenor fighting my father's war, while that shadowy land I'd seen him in seemed vastly different from the descriptions I'd heard of Alrenor.

I clenched my hands into fists. *My father and his war.*

All of Misroth was suffering because of the war and executions done in the king's name. Unless I stopped my father, I was as guilty as he was. And if I did nothing to save him, if I sat by and he were harmed, Gillen's blood would be on my hands.

I had to return home and stop my father. I had to end the war so Gillen could come home.

I didn't know how I would convince my people of the truth, but I did know there was a group of people who already didn't believe in the king. If I could find Marke's shop, perhaps I could join members of the rebellion and stand with them against the king. Maybe I would even find an opportunity to share the truth with them, and together, the rebels and I could spread it amongst the people. No more hiding in fear, relishing my own safety while my kingdom deteriorated and Gillen suffered. I would finally be *doing* something.

If a guard didn't recognize and kill me first.

Though my heart raced with urgency and my brain felt muddled with panic, I attempted to reason through my plan.

Lyanna and Rev would not let me go of their own accord, even if I did speak to them and explain who I was and what had happened. Unless I wanted our last moments together to be filled with arguments, I would have to slip out unnoticed and alone, and break their hearts by disappearing, maybe to never return.

If I was careful tonight, I could slip out of my bedroom and collect only the food and items necessary for the short journey to Misroth City. I did not want to take too much from the people who had given so much to me.

Slowly, I pushed myself out of bed, splashed some water from my basin onto my face to force myself to appear calm, and stepped into the living room to see Lyanna and Rev.

Lyanna was leaning against the mantel, stirring the fire. She glanced up at me when I walked into the room, then back down at the hearth. "We were so worried last night." She raised her head again to give me a stern look, but I saw the fear and sadness written across her face.

Hesitating, I blinked back the tears threatening to gather in my eyes and approached her. After the years of care and love she had lavished on a stranger, I had nothing to give her. In one night it seemed the wrinkles on her face had deepened and the light in her eyes had faded, leaving them pale and cold. I leaned in and embraced her, burying my face in her shoulder and inhaling the smell of smoke and lavender. They were familiar scents now, things that reminded me both of her meals and her love of gardening and drying flowers to adorn the cabin throughout the winter months. *This is home.* Something inside me broke. I pulled back, blinking as tears threatened my vision.

It felt impossible to leave, but it was more impossible to stay.

I tried to apologize with my expression, but I knew nothing I could say would ease the pain of the loss she would bear. *You've been more like a mother to me than my real one ever was.* The thought tore at my heart. My eyes flitted over to Rev, where he sat at his desk, his hair still disheveled and his own gaze clouded with tears. I darted over and embraced him as well, relishing the feelings of safety and love. Maybe for the last time.

"I know you didn't mean for any of that to happen," he said to me.

"It is not safe to stay out after dark anymore," Lyanna said.

My throat burned, but I nodded vigorously and tried to ignore the urge to cry.

Lyanna's gaze softened as she watched me. "I'm about to start dinner. Would you like to help?"

With a deep breath, I nodded again. There would be one last dinner with my family before I faced the unknown.

Shortly after dinner, someone knocked softly at the front door. At first my stomach lurched in fear, and I wondered if it could be Kyrin, eschewing the risks and coming to kill me even with Lyanna and Rev present.

No, I thought. *He would never be so forthright; if any of the townspeople knew, if there was ever the possibility rumor could spread and Avrik would believe it... He would wait; ensure my death appeared to be an accident. I'll have departed long before he has another chance.*

The door pushed inward, and Avrik stepped inside.

"Avrik!" Lyanna greeted as she scrubbed the dishes. Rev glanced up from his position by the hearth, where he tended the fire. I set the towel and dish I'd been drying on the counter and ran to him, pulling him into an embrace.

"You're safe," he murmured against my ear. He smelled of fresh soap and smoke, comforting and familiar, and I realized that this was my goodbye to him too.

I pulled back to study him again and reassure myself that he was healthy and whole, that nothing had happened between his father and him last night. His eyes, though shadowed in dark circles, still sparkled with his usual warmth, and there was not a hint of concern or pain in his expression. There were scratches on his face and he had a bandage wrapped around his left arm, but otherwise, he looked fine. Gently, I reached toward the bandage.

Avrik shrugged. "It's nothing, only a scratch." He grinned at me. "You look tired. But you are all right?"

I nodded. Though I longed to speak, I bit my lip and held the urge back. There were too many truths I was not yet prepared to share with Lyanna, Rev, and Avrik, as long as my gift didn't force me to.

Pulling Avrik toward a seat by the fire, I sat down next to him. Even Lyanna put aside the dishes to join us all.

"Shilam and Bren have minor wounds and will be fine," Avrik said. "After you've rested tonight, I'll take you to visit them tomorrow."

I tried to smile, but felt my lips falter. Turning, I stared into the fire instead.

I won't be here tomorrow, Avrik. I'm leaving and I might never be able to return, and you will not understand. Please, please forgive me.

The next morning, I lay in bed until the last possible second, shivering under the covers as I gazed out my window and wondered what the day would hold for me, alone in the woods. I had drifted off to sleep the night before, half-expecting to be woken to Kyrin attempting to slip into my room and steal me away to a place where he could kill me and leave me never to be found again, but the night was uneventful. That fact still didn't ease the fear twisting in my stomach.

On my nightstand rested two carefully folded notes I had written last night. One more time, I lifted the first paper, opening it up to read it.

Rev and Lyanna,

You have done so much for me over the years and I cannot thank you enough. You have truly been my parents, for I know you have loved me as much as you would your own daughter. You have shown me more love than anyone else ever has.

The night I was in the woods, I tried to find Avrik, afraid he was hurt. Instead, I encountered his father. Marke was right: the king has hired men to hunt and provoke the sedwa to attack innocent people, and Kyrin is one of those men. He bound me and left me to die, and, as he had hoped, one of the sedwa attacked me.

I know this seems unbelievable, since few have ever seen him, but a man—whom I believe was the Life-Giver himself—saved my life. He said that there is something I have to do. It is something that I've known for a long time; I've only pretended, even to myself, that I did not know.

I wish I did not have to leave you. I'm sorry I can't give you more answers or even promise that I will be able to return. I miss you already.

Please give the second note to Avrik.

Elena

I sighed, my heart too heavy for tears. My note to Avrik said much of the same, thanking him for being a true friend, and, as gently as possible, explaining the agreement his father had made with the king. I could only hope all of my loved ones would forgive me. Folding my note once more, I laid it back down and hoped I would be miles away before Lyanna or Rev discovered it in my bedroom.

I eased myself out of bed and lifted my pack off the chair resting by the window. It was heavier than usual as I lifted it and checked my stock one last time: a small supply of food, extra clothes for warmth, and a carefully bundled tent that Rev kept for travel and almost never used. I opened the drawer to my nightstand and pulled out the sheathed dagger Avrik had given to me for my fifteenth birthday. Satisfied, I dressed in some of my warmest clothes, shoving the dagger into my right boot, and stepped out of my bedroom, pack in hand, to pull on my cloak, scarf, and mittens.

Lyanna was seated by the fire, sewing a patch in a pair of Rev's trousers. She glanced up when I entered the living room, her face somewhat pale. "Please come straight home tonight."

I offered her a small smile, inwardly hating myself for the deception.

She would know soon enough.

As I pulled on the mittens she had so carefully knit for me, I set my jaw and told myself I had cried my last tears. Once I reached the forest, I would need all of my focus and strength to keep myself alive.

"Have a good day, dear," Lyanna called as I stepped out of the house.

I raced through the snow, around the house, and into the shed, where I had carefully rested my bow and quiver the day before. Drawing a deep breath, I slung the quiver over my shoulder, grasped the bow in my hand, and plowed through the drifts toward the forest. I all but ran, fearing Lyanna would step into my room and see the note or somehow suspect something was wrong; fearing that Kyrin would pursue me; fearing that that though I'd left earlier than usual, Avrik would meet me before I could disappear into the forest.

The day was still, with nothing but my trudging feet breaking the silence. High overhead the wind chased clouds across the sky and welcome sunlight poured to the earth, bathing it in a white, cheerful glow, even if it was too distant to provide warmth. I drew my hood closer around my face and pulled my scarf up higher over my mouth. The sweeping hills lay pure white before me, stretching almost entirely unbroken by footprints except for a trail heading toward Kyrin's home.

My heart pounded at the thought of encountering Kyrin again. I angled myself closer to the woods and prayed I would not encounter him a second time in the forest.

But I was too late to escape unnoticed. A form crested the slope ahead: Avrik was approaching, intersecting my path. I circled wide in a hopeless attempt to push past him, though I knew he had seen me.

"Elena!" Avrik broke into a run. "Wait!"

Cringing, I stopped and waited. What would he say?

He shook his head, glancing at my bow and quiver. "Where are you going? Why didn't you wait for me?"

There is no gentle way to say, *Your father is a murderer.* There is also no way to ease someone toward the fact that a mute friend can actually speak. I swallowed. This time, the words came out easier than they had when I'd first spoken to his father.

"I…" I swallowed, inhaling deeply. "I am…I am not going to school today."

In all the years I had known him, Avrik had rarely been left speechless. This, however, was one of those times. He gaped at me. "What…? How…?"

Gesturing for him to keep walking with me, I glanced over my shoulder toward home. I proceeded and Avrik followed, still dumbstruck. I clutched my bow still tighter in my hand, steeling myself for the inevitable protests and confusion. "I'm going home," I offered by way of explanation.

"Home? What home?" Here came the questions. "Who…who *are* you? How are you able to speak now, after all these years? Or could you speak all this time? Where did you come from? How did you get here? Why didn't you say…anything?" His tone was angry, as if I had betrayed him. In a way, as I'd prepared to leave him behind with hardly a goodbye, without any answers, I supposed I had. Even if it had all been to keep him safe.

I cringed. "I *couldn't* speak. At least, I did not think I could. It's a long story…"

As we approached the woods, I tried to explain everything as quickly as possible, all except my encounter with his father before the sedwa's attack. I could not tell him that—yet.

"I am…Princess Halia, daughter of King Zarev," I began. My voice still sounded raspy and my tongue stumbled over the words. "I am the princess that went missing four years ago."

Avrik blinked, studying me like he had never seen me before. "Why…what happened?"

I raised my eyebrows at him. *I'm still your friend,* I thought, before catching myself and remembering I could speak. "I'm hardly a princess now. My father would not claim me as his own. In fact, he sentenced me to death for treason."

I explained what had happened the night of my father's coronation, how visions, a strange gift giving me knowledge of the truth, had come to me though I'd never had any before. Then I told him how my father had condemned me and the Royal Guard had thrown me into the sea to drown, how I had been rescued and had fled the city and come to Evren, unable to speak. At last, I described the sedwa in the forest the night I'd tried to save him and my conversation with the man in the woods.

At the edge of the forest, I paused, breathless.

"How do you know that *he* is trustworthy? Where is he now?" Avrik studied me skeptically.

I hesitated. Despite the people of Evren's faith, they spoke of meetings with the Life-Giver as a thing of the past, something lost to Misrothians now. "He was the Giver of Life, Avrik."

Avrik stared and I let my words drift away. Of course he wouldn't believe me. I sounded mad, even to myself.

"And you are returning to Misroth City, even though if *anyone* recognizes you, you will be dead." He shook his head. "Do you really think, if so many people have believed the king's lies for this long, they will believe you now? And even if they do, how do you expect to stop the king before he kills you?" The questions would not stop, concern shining in his eyes and the taut lines of his mouth. "Why join a band of rebels now? Why leave Evren when it's the safest place you can be? Leaving means death. Elena, you *cannot* go." He was desperate, all but pleading.

Avoiding his gaze, I shook my head. I didn't need to be reminded that I was leaving safety behind, so I ignored his questions and plunged into the woods. His footsteps followed me again.

"Elena!"

I spun around to face him. "My people—they need me. My *cousin* needs me. He's almost of age, and if he ever returns from battle, I know my father will never let him take the throne. He's in danger." My voice broke. "I left him behind. I left my people behind…"

Avrik shook his head. "You would have died. There was nothing you could have done. You were *thirteen*, Elena."

I stood taller and set my jaw. "I'm not thirteen anymore."

Avrik ran a hand through his hair. "If you won't change your mind, I'm coming with you."

If Avrik came with me, he would be facing the dangers of the forest again, and the threats that waited for me and anyone associated with the rebels or me in Misroth City. I shook my head before remembering my voice. "No. I can't let you risk your life."

Avrik raised an eyebrow. "You risked your life to try to save me when the sedwa attacked. Would you have listened to *me* if I'd had the chance to tell you not to?"

"No, but this is different. This is my burden, Avrik, and…"

"And you are my friend. You can't stop me from coming with you."

Frustrated, I opened my mouth to speak, but my protests faded. *No, it is better this way. Then there's no way anyone can accuse him of working with his father. He won't have to be there when the townspeople throw him into prison. And maybe I can find the words to tell him…so that he can hear it from a friend. Not from a letter.*

I frowned, but I was relieved to have his company, despite my concerns for his safety. "If anything happens to you, I'll never forgive myself," I said.

"My choice. How do you think I would have felt if you hadn't made it back yesterday morning?" His eyes searched mine until I looked away, unsure why I felt uncomfortable and shy suddenly.

"You don't have any supplies," I pointed out, still staring at a distant tree.

Avrik smirked, pulling his pack from his shoulders and dropping it to the ground. "You mean my schoolbooks will not be enough?" He patted his quiver and bow. "I think I can manage. Besides, you do not want delays if you don't want Lyanna and Rev to know, and if I returned home, my father would suspect something. If we leave now, we may not be missed until after school."

"All right," I relented with a sigh.

"Let me take the pack," Avrik said.

Rolling my eyes, I grasped the strap harder. "I can manage—"

"I know," he interrupted, a smile playing about his lips. "But now that I know I am in the company of a princess, it hardly seems dignified for you to lug this about." He gently pulled the pack off my back, swinging it over his, and winked at me as we set off through the forest.

Struggling to hold back a smile, I looked away and tried to concentrate on the nature of what we were setting out to do. If I could focus, I could keep the blush from staining my cheeks.

Despite the light-hearted tone he had adopted, I could see the uncertainty in Avrik's eyes, the way he studied me every time his gaze met mine, as if he was not sure how to behave, as if he wasn't sure he truly knew me.

"Do not treat me differently now. I'm still the same person."

Avrik cast a sidelong glance at me as he ducked beneath a low-hanging branch. "It'll…take me some time to adjust."

As night fell, we huddled close to the fire we built and prayed it would not snow any more. I'd let Avrik do most of the talking all day, as usual, but tonight he'd fallen quiet. When we both finished dinner, we set to work putting up the tent and loading our supplies inside. Once we finished, he perched on a rock by the fire and watched the flames gnaw on the wood.

I felt too restless to sit. Now that darkness had fallen on Evren Forest, I imagined I saw forms or glowing eyes wherever I looked. How would I ever sleep while trapped in these woods? My nightmares, old and new, lurked in the shadows.

At last, Avrik spoke, tugging me away from my fears. "Everyone back home is probably spreading more rumors about my father after the attack. Yet here we are, leaving him behind when I could be back there, defending him, telling them all it's a lie." He shifted uncomfortably. "I wish I could be with him and with you at the same time."

I swallowed, saying nothing. What could I say? What kind of friend was I to keep the truth from him? But what kind of friend would I be to reveal it to him?

"I was attacked, and my father found me and rescued me." Avrik's eyes met mine. "Before or after you met…the Giver of Life…did you see him out there? Could you be a witness with me to prove his innocence?"

"No." I shook my head, slowly.

"You didn't see him at all that night?"

I bit my lip, longing to formulate a lie: *No.* My mouth opened but the words died before I could make a sound. *Of course…I cannot lie!* Bursting into bitter laughter, I spoke the words in my frustration, before I could stop myself. "I *cannot* lie!"

Avrik stared at me, his lips a firm line, his dark eyes inscrutable. He looked much like his father in that instant. "Then tell me the truth."

There was no holding back the words now. There was no way to phrase it gently; the facts leapt out and smacked Avrik headlong, leaving him motionless, speechless.

"The night you were attacked by the sedwa, I chased after you. But I didn't find you…I found your father. He *is* hunting sedwa for the king— I saw so in a vision, and he did not deny it. He…he wanted me to die for knowing the truth, Avrik. He bound me to a tree and left me for the sedwa. That is when the Life-Giver saved me. I…I'm sorry."

Clenching his fists, Avrik gazed down at his feet. From what I could see of his face in the firelight, his brow was furrowed and every other muscle in his face was taut. I waited for him to speak, but he said nothing. He was so silent it was like we had reversed roles and he was now mute. I grimaced, wishing my words back and knowing there was no way I could unsay them.

He hates me. He doesn't believe me. The thoughts carved through my being like knives.

"Please…" I murmured. Gingerly, I stepped toward him and reached out, longing to touch him on the shoulder, to hold him and tell him it would be all right.

But that would be a lie I could not speak: it wasn't all right. For years, his father had been all he'd had, and I had just aligned myself with the townspeople who had made Avrik and Kyrin feel isolated. Even if he believed the truth of my words, I understood why Avrik could not look me in the eye.

"Don't talk to me," he muttered, turning away. "I liked it better when you were mute. When you were not royalty."

Choking back my pleas, I blinked when I found my eyes were burning. I climbed into the tent and burrowed deep into the blankets.

Keeping the dagger strapped to my belt, I lay my bow and quiver nearby.

Sleep was all but impossible. I spent most of the night listening, fearing what might be lurking in the woods, agonizing over what I had told Avrik. I listened to him pacing outside as the hours dragged on and I tossed and turned. Anxious thoughts flitted through my brain so persistently I found no rest, even in the little sleep I had.

Avrik had been my first true friend since I had stumbled into Evren—could he forget all of that now?

Of course he could, because he felt like I had betrayed him. And as I'd thought before, I thought again: Perhaps I had.

Early rays of sunshine stabbed through the tent's canvas and wrenched me out of a doze. I rolled out to find Avrik propped up against a tree trunk, asleep, but he opened his eyes when he heard me stirring. The sight of him sent my emotions spiraling—I felt a mixture of hurt and panic, guilt and rejection, all at once. Opening my mouth, I tried to say something, anything. But words that could help wouldn't even come to mind. Perhaps because there were none.

Alone, I tore down the tent and repacked my belongings, then kicked snow over the fire's embers to put them out. The thought of breakfast made my stomach churn, so I hoisted my pack and quiver onto my shoulders, grasped my bow, and started walking. Gradually, Avrik pulled himself to his feet and followed. He did not offer to help carry the supplies like he had yesterday. He did not say anything. He did not need to—I could feel his accusations and anger cutting deep into my heart already; the air was laced with tension and pain so heavy I could hardly breathe.

As the light grew and the silence stretched on, I struggled to find a way to break it. To try to mend things. If he hadn't left yet, perhaps he did not hate me.

It was then that my thoughts were interrupted by new ones. Though unaccompanied by visions this time, the flash of clarity that always preceded my untimely words surged through my mind and turned my sense of foreboding into certainty. Avrik's feelings played through my head as clearly as if they were my own: anger, skepticism, hurt, doubt.

I stopped and spun to him, my stomach taut, my fists clenched in a sudden onset of anger. It was easier to be angry than sorrowful. As always, the truth escaped my lips, even when I did not want it to. "You're going to turn back."

Avrik's face twisted into a frown and he stepped back, staring off into the forest. He refused to look at me. "My father would never put anyone in harm. He wouldn't do that to Evren—to me."

I can't lie, Avrik! I thought. *Why would I ever want to lie to you? To hurt you?* But my lips would not move; my tongue was frozen in place. *Why am I speechless* now? I thought, frustrated.

Avoiding my gaze, Avrik continued to watch the trees ahead of us. "I *want* to believe you would never lie to me. But…" He sighed. "I can't. You don't say a word for four years and then when you start to speak, you share a mad, impossible story about my father?" He turned to look at me at last. "My *father*, Elena."

His eyes shone with something. With more anger? With tears? My mind flipped through memories: had I ever seen Avrik cry?

My anger melted away, giving place to desperation that he would believe I never wanted to hurt him, never wanted this for him. I opened my mouth, but my protests remained voiceless; my emotions drowned out all words. *Speak, speak…*

"I've heard enough of the rumors throughout Evren." His words sliced through my thoughts as he stepped nearer, so close I could feel his breath on my face. How could we be so close yet feel so far apart? "I don't need to hear more from someone who is supposed to be there, to be my friend."

My world was crumbling around me and I couldn't do anything about it. "Avrik, I *am* your friend," I whispered, forcing the tears back even as my throat burned and my voice came out tight and raspy.

Biting his lip, he stared back at me, his dark eyes searching my face, lingering. For one heartbeat, I thought he would change his mind, that he would wrap his arms around me and whisper that he was sorry for doubting me. But he pulled back, pain etched across his face in the lines on his brow and in his frown. His eyes no longer shone with either tears or longing; they were unfathomable, masking his thoughts again. He was lost to me.

"I don't know why you would lie," he said, "but I know my own father, and I know he would not kill. He has protected me all of my life."

Where was the boy who had always been by my side and defended me all these years? He refused to believe the truth when it was staring him in the face, because he did not want to believe it.

Avrik's voice rose, ringing out in the still, snowy forest, and I noticed anger biting into his tone. "Yet you want me to listen as you call him a murderer? As you claim he tried to kill you? I'm supposed to believe *that*?"

My hands shook. Tears blurred my vision and tightened my throat but I refused to let them win. "You're supposed to believe your *friend*." It was all I could do to keep the tears from spilling down my cheeks. But I wouldn't cry, not now.

"And I'm supposed to believe my *father*," he said, his voice almost breaking on the word. "I didn't think you'd ever make me choose between the two of you. It wasn't supposed to be this way. We were supposed to… I wanted…" He lifted a trembling hand to brush back the hair from my cheek, his fingers tracing the curve of my jaw. I reached for his hand, but too late; as if recalling himself, he jerked his hand away and clenched his fists. "I've already lost my mother," he whispered, taking a step back, "I'm not going to lose my father also."

"Avrik…"

"I'm going back. Father needs me; he has no one else."

He spun around, plowing through the snow drifts we'd already trudged through. For a long moment I stood motionless, my mind reeling and my heart torn with too many emotions to sort through. Then, once he disappeared, clarity returned to me.

"Avrik!" I shouted, stumbling after him. "There are sedwa in this forest; don't leave to face them alone!" A tree branch scratched across my cheek and another snagged itself in my hair. Wrenching myself free, I thrust the branches out of my way and dashed forward. I opened my mouth again, but his name died on my lips. He was gone, his form lost amidst the tangle of dead underbrush and towering trees.

Running in the direction I'd last seen him, I chased him desperately. I plowed my way uphill through a snow drift and my foot struck an unseen root, shoving me off balance. The snow swallowed me, seeping through my cloak as I fought to rise to my feet. Coldness soaked into my bones; I shivered with the chill and my anger and shock.

"Avrik!" My voice sounded broken and I hated it. It echoed through the dead forest and taunted me with its emptiness.

He would be safer in Evren, if he ever made it back home. I had to hope for the best for him now. He was gone.

Drawing a deep breath, I yanked myself up with the help of a nearby branch and let my anger fuel me. I turned my face back toward Misroth City—away from Evren, away from Avrik. Charging forward in my wet clothes, I let my exertion and raw emotion warm me until I couldn't feel the pain or the burning in my eyes anymore.

As the sun began to dip toward the west, I stopped and set up my tent. I failed to start a fire, so I retreated to the tent to change into the only dry clothes I had and bundle up in blankets. Now that the anger was fading into biting sorrow, I felt cold inside and out, and my body would not stop trembling. Tears streaked down my face.

What am I doing? The question plagued me. *What can I do, alone?* I thought of the king and the powerful hold he had on my people—of the powerful hold he'd once had on me. He had deceived so many. *How can I stop him?* Doubts circled around in my head like vultures.

I stared up at the cloudy sky and spoke into the cold air. I wasn't sure if I hoped to see the man from the woods again, or if I was simply angry. "Giver of Life, you gave me this…burden." My voice broke, but anger gave it new strength. "Why? *Why* won't you tell me what to do? Who will listen? What good has ever come from speaking the words you give me?" I bowed my head and inhaled deeply. "I need help."

The woods were silent.

I was alone.

My eyes shot open in the middle of the night, darkness still embracing me as I lay curled in the tent. Reaching forward, I felt the reassuring solidness of my bow beneath my fingertips, where I'd laid it next to me before drifting off to sleep. Still, the weapon could only bring so much comfort. I was in the same woods where I'd been both stalked and attacked by monsters that had haunted my nightmares for years. And I was on my own.

I tried to calm my ragged breathing so I could hear whatever stirred in the woods outside my tent. *Something woke me.* Then the realization hit:

It was too quiet.

Not again. My heart raced and my palms were slick as I clutched the bow and sat up. The stabbing knife in my stomach deepened; something inside me felt ready to snap. A giant fist was buried in my gut, squeezing, squeezing. I struggled to force air into my lungs, though panic felt like it was constricting my throat and every breath heightened the stabbing sensation inside me.

Slowly, I pulled myself from my layers of blankets and rose to a crouch. With trembling fingers, I reached for the quiver and pulled out a single arrow. Moonlight spilled onto the earth and drifted through the tent's fabric, casting long shadows from the trees across the sides of the tent. I tried to breathe quietly and steadily as I turned my head cautiously to study each side, to search for any moving shadows, to listen for any approaching sounds. Nothing.

Where are you? I didn't dare move, didn't dare push my way out of my tent only to stumble out blindly to the sedwa as it stalked me. But I hated to sit there in the tent, a blind target.

I drew a shaky breath. *Giver of Life, you gave me my life, and you saved it for a reason. You gave me my gift for a reason. Don't leave me now. If I die tonight…it will all be for nothing.*

I nocked the arrow to my bow and creeped toward the front of the tent. Pulling one of the flaps back a sliver, I peered into the night. The forest was drenched in shadow, a wispy layer of clouds shrouding the stars and moon. Even the snow looked grey and dull. The bare branches of the trees looked like waiting claws; my breath in the chill air was a ghostly fog. Nothing moved and no golden eyes glared at me from the blackness, but I could feel the sedwa's presence as surely as if it were standing right in front of me.

It's there. It's waiting.

The thought sent my heart hammering even harder. I could picture its eyes glaring at the tent, preparing to leap. Flashbacks from when I'd last encountered one of these monsters shot through my head. I saw the eyes watching me, saw the leaping form, saw the fangs. I felt the sharp pain of the claws digging into me.

Not this time.

I tightened my grip on the bow and steeled myself. The monster would leap without warning, without a sound. I would only have one shot before it was upon me. I slipped from the tent, crouching low to peer around in every direction, searching for any sign of the creature.

Any moment.

The silence was nearly unbearable. As I strained to hear any sound, any movement, even just a breath of wind, my ears started to ring. I clenched my jaw and prayed for them to stop so I could concentrate on the outside world, but the ringing persisted.

My dry throat and mouth refused to let me swallow when I tried. A trickle of sweat escaped from my hairline and dripped down into my eye.

And then I saw it.

The sedwa's glowing eyes stared down at me from the branches overhead, poised to strike. I released my arrow, but it glanced harmlessly off the scales covering the sedwa's chest. Snarling, it launched toward me and I leapt backward, my fingers clawing for another arrow.

In the night, the creature was a part of the shadows, soundless as it charged. My second arrow pierced its left eye, extinguishing its glow as quickly as the snuffing of a candle. But the sedwa did not hesitate, did not slow. It sprung again, a blur of claws and fangs too swift for me to stop. I threw myself backward, tumbling down a hard-packed snowdrift and desperately clinging to my bow.

The sedwa landed two yards from me, its open maw dripping saliva and revealing even more fangs, these ones smaller than those protruding from its mouth but still as sharp as daggers. I leapt to my feet and nocked a third arrow to my bow, my body shaking with cold and adrenaline as the sedwa and I stared one another down. Exhaling, I concentrated on stilling my arms so my shot would fly true.

Find its weakness. I inhaled, watching hundreds of pounds of muscle and impenetrable scales prepare to attack again. This time it would not miss. It was too near, too angry. I was close enough to see the creature's chest rise and fall as it breathed, to see the line of black fur bristling around its neck like a mane, to see its pupils dilate before the leap.

I crouched low, firing as soon as the sedwa soared into the air, its powerful legs propelling it high above me in an arc. At the height of the sedwa's jump, my arrow struck its mark, piercing through the soft folds of skin on the creature's underbelly. It roared—like a great cat, like a bear, like no other beast I'd ever heard before—and I rolled to the side to avoid its teeth as it crashed into me.

The impact jarred my bones, my left side taking the brunt of it. I kicked at the sedwa's head as it went down, still snarling and snapping and leaving a trail of black blood in the snow. It swung a heavy paw for me, but I ducked.

Jumping to my feet, I backed up to put distance between the sedwa and myself as it rolled and stood, its head low to the ground, its body shuddering in agony. Still, it wasn't finished. It circled me, its one good eye glaring as it assessed its next move and mine. I aimed an arrow at its eye, but when I drew back the bowstring, it charged straight toward me, snapping the shaft in half with one bite before I could shoot. One swipe of its paw at my left hand and my bow flew from my grasp. Pain sparked in my wrist and the blow threw me sideways.

I fell and the sedwa bore down on me, spilling its warm blood down my front. Even as the light began to leave its eye, as its body spasmed and it panted out its last breaths, it was still trying to take me with it. In one swift movement I drew the dagger from my belt and shoved it upward into the soft skin near where I assumed the sedwa's heart would be.

Another roar. Another snap of its fangs as it breathed hot air, saliva, and blood onto my neck and stretched to bite into my veins. I drove the dagger deeper, deeper, fighting with all my strength to push the sedwa back far enough to prevent its killing strike. Blood flowed down the dagger hilt and over my hand, making the blade feel hot and slick in my hand, but still I held on, still I fought.

It heaved out another breath, another snarl. More blood and spittle splattered across my cheek and stung my eye. I blinked, clearing my vision, and the sedwa slumped against me. The glow in its eye faded; its jaw fell slack.

Slowly, painfully, I dragged myself out from the creature's crushing weight and tumbled out into fresh snow. I welcomed its cold, cleansing power, letting it wash away some of the black blood staining my cloak and dress and coating my skin. The sedwa lay sprawled before me, a gruesome mixture of reptile and mammal, lethal power and stealth.

Panting, I sank onto my back, using the snow as a cushion as I stared up at the sky. It looked greyer, brighter.

Then I heard the soft twitter of first one bird, and then another. They chattered to each other from the trees circling me, until the sound grew into all-out song.

My tense muscles unknotted themselves. I drew a deep breath and felt my heart slow.

I had survived the night.

CHAPTER TWELVE

A T LAST, I STOOD AND reentered my tent. After packing up my belongings, I nibbled on a few pieces of jerky and some dried fruit and set off toward Misroth City. Toward my old home and whatever awaited me there.

Without the darkness surrounding me, the woods were not as ominous. Squirrels raced each other through the trees and reminded me that in the daylight, all was safe. If my uneasy heart truly felt any peace in those hours, it was lighter then.

The day grew colder and clouds began to gather. By the time I stumbled toward the capital late that afternoon, snowflakes were brushing past my cheeks and adding to the piles of snow around me. Pausing, I stared at the great ramparts encircling the city, the gradual incline of streets and grey stone buildings stretching toward the sky, toward the cliff with the castle perched on its crest, rising against the backdrop of sky and distant sea.

I was sick of the blackness shrouding this land, of the shadows that had plagued it for years. I wanted to run from this accursed city and never look back. But I wouldn't abandon my people again.

I braced myself, ensuring I was prepared. If anyone were to recognize me, it would be because my features so closely resembled those of my mother, so I pulled my hood low over my eyes and held my head high. I would walk gracefully, bravely; I would not slink into the city I had been raised in, the capital of my kingdom. Even if he could not see me now, I would not give my father that power over me.

The wrought iron gates were flung open wide for midday traffic flowing in from a broad dirt path bordering the winding, bubbling Emrell and tracing its way through the countryside. It was easy to join the crowd on the path and blend in, keeping my head low to ensure none of the king's men caught a glimpse of my face. Guards stood at attention on either side of the gates while others peered down from the ramparts, all dressed in Misroth's royal colors with Vehgar across their chests and all armed with heavy bows across their backs and swords at their sides. Misroth's colors flashed with resplendent light from banners lifted high over the ramparts, flags all fluttering and snapping in the breeze. Pushing my way through the crowds, I stepped through the gates and entered the capital once more.

Ahead, the stone buildings lining the cobblestone streets seemed even taller than I remembered them; the streets seemed noisier and fuller of smoke curling from the chimneys and hanging in the air over the city like a persistent cloud. And there were people—people everywhere. Even when I'd lived in the city, I had rarely been permitted to venture out into the streets, and then only with escorts. I never had the opportunity to view the capital as citizens did.

Now, everywhere I looked there were people traveling to the capital from the surrounding countryside, some on horseback or in wagons, some on foot. There were farmers in coarse, worn clothes and merchants in finer attire. There were women and families out for a stroll or shopping, carrying bundles and bags in their arms. Brightly painted and intricately carved carriages pulled by teams of horses with braided manes and tails rumbled by, usually with the windows tightly closed but occasionally with a finely dressed nobleman or lady peering out at the crowds. Various guards stood tall and motionless at their posts along street corners, carefully assessing the crowds or patrolling their rounds, walking the streets in careful patterns at regular intervals.

All along the way, even in the cold, vendors with wagons full of wares called out to the passerby, while shops full of enticing jewelry, clothing, or furniture tempted with their elaborate window displays. The scent of fresh bread and roasting meat from nearby inns and butchers and bakeries floated through the air, making my stomach growl in hunger even when the aroma mixed with the foul stench of horse manure lining the streets. Somewhere in the distance I could hear a blacksmith pounding a piece of metal into shape, while closer at hand the bells atop a city sanctuary chimed out, signaling that it was now the seventeenth hour of the day.

I squinted against the falling snow to see the cliff towering over the city. There, sprawled atop the jagged rocks, sat the king's castle, a dark stain against a blinding white sky. While I wound my way through the bustling city, the streets all rising in a gentle ascent that pulled everyone upward toward the cliff, the castle seemed to always be in front of me, taunting me with its presence.

My heart beat out a steady rhythm, matching the pace of my strides, but I swept the doubts and fear to the back of my mind. First, I had to find the rebels, and then everything else would fall into place. *How do I find Marke's shop?*

Lost in thought, I collided with a man and stumbled back. "Sorry," I muttered.

The man eyed me with a frown. "Watch where you're going, girl." He ran a hand through his grey beard and stepped around me.

"Wait…could you point me in the direction of Marke's shop?"

He grunted. "I don't know what you're speaking of." Without another word, he shuffled off, leaving me alone and frustrated amidst the crowds.

Setting my jaw, I pulled my hood low and began asking every citizen I passed. After dozens of suspicious glances toward my concealed face and negative responses, a middle-aged woman pointed me in the right direction.

I thanked her and hurried down the main street, turning at the next corner. Marke's shop was a small brick building tucked between two larger stores. It looked like it had been there for a long while, perhaps generations. A weatherworn sign, labeled simply *Marke's*, hung over the doorway and lace curtains hung in a second story window, reminding me that the family lived above their shop. Stepping inside, my eyes skimmed over the grocery's shelves, lined with countless goods—great bags of flour and sugar and salt, coils of rope, collections of tools, pots and pans, measuring cups, boxes of matches, and much more that my eyes could not take in all at once—and toward the table in the back. Behind it stood a woman somewhere in her early twenties, with golden brown skin, a strong jaw, and frizzy curls pulled into a knot at the back of her head. Her brown eyes lit with curiosity when she took in my bedraggled appearance.

"Good evening. Is there anything I can help you find?"

I shuffled my feet and debated how to phrase my request. If only there had been time to consult Marke before I left Evren, to learn more about the rebellion and how to gain trust so I could join their cause. I approached the table slowly and glanced around, but there was no one else in the shop to overhear.

"Can I—could I speak with someone? I have news of Marke." The words sounded clumsy rolling off my tongue. *My words are definitely a gift*, I thought wryly.

The woman squinted in suspicion. "Who are you?"

"A friend of Marke's." I stood up straighter, trying to make myself appear tall and important, rather than like the scared girl I probably appeared to be. I took a risk and dared to push back my hood, letting the light fall on my face.

She shifted and ran a hand through her hair, but no light of recognition flashed in her eyes, no confused furrow of her brow to indicate she had any idea who I was. "Marke has many friends," she said vaguely.

I met her stare without wavering and forced my voice to remain even, calm. "I'm from Evren. Marke traveled to my village not long ago."

The woman's eyes went wide. "Is he safe? Why hasn't he returned? Why are you here…?"

"He was attacked by one of the sedwa in Evren Forest. He is recovering, but it's too soon for him to make the journey home."

The woman—I assumed Marke's wife—looked pale. "He will be all right?"

I nodded.

She offered me a timid smile and reached out to clasp my hand. "My name is Jennah, Marke's wife. And you are…?"

I hesitated. "A friend. I go by Elena. I wanted to share my news of

Marke and…" I scanned the shop, ensuring there were no other patrons inside. Lowering my voice, I added, "And offer my help to the rebels. Marke told me about your meetings."

Jennah's face scrunched in surprise. Then she set a finger to her lips and shook her head. "Not here. Come with me."

She motioned for me to step around the table and led me to the back room. I waded through piles of crates full of wares, some open and in the process of being unpacked and others untouched.

She turned to me. "Marke asked you to join the rebellion?"

I shuffled my feet. "No…but he told me about it. I thought—I wanted…" Uncomfortable, I bit my lip. "I'm prepared to do whatever it takes to prove myself to you." I lifted my chin and met her gaze unflinchingly.

A light sparked in her eyes and a gentle smile quirked her lips. "If Marke trusts you, I trust you," she murmured.

I tried to mask my surprise. Could it really be that easy? Jennah already believed me?

I shoved my thoughts away as Jennah opened another door, paused to remove and light a candle from a nearby shelf, and swept down a narrow flight of stairs. Cautiously, I followed her, the steps creaking beneath my feet. The steps led to a cramped cellar, its space mostly filled with a square, roughly hewn table and several chairs clustered about it.

She gestured to it. "Once the shop closes, this is where we meet. We don't have much and our numbers are few, but we do what we can and believe that any defiance against the king must count for something." Jennah glanced back at the staircase. "I'll need to return to the shop. We will be closing soon. Once I'm able to lock up, we'll have dinner and you can tell me more. The others will arrive tonight for a meeting."

Following her back upstairs, I watched Jennah straighten shelves, sweep the floor, and glance at the clock resting at her table in the back. No other shoppers arrived in those last few minutes, a fact that seemed to leave Jennah more at ease.

"I always prefer quiet evenings before our meetings," she said as she locked the door.

I followed her upstairs to the family living quarters, where we entered a small, warm kitchen with a pot bubbling over the hearth. An older woman was stooping over it, her dark hair streaked with silver and hanging in humid ringlets about her face. She glanced up at us as she entered, beaming at Jennah and then pausing in surprise when she saw me.

"This is Elena; she will be our guest tonight, Mother," Jennah explained. "Elena, this is my mother, Kam."

"She looks exhausted!" Kam exclaimed. "Supper is ready, so we will eat soon. Elena, you must be starving."

My stomach reacted to the smell of food instantly and I remembered how little I'd eaten all day.

Kam looked pointedly at her daughter. "The girls are ready, so hurry and wash up."

Jennah blinked and then turned to me. "Right. We will clean up. Come with me. You can have the girls' room, and they will stay with me tonight."

After Jennah showed me to the bedroom, she left me to settle in, resting my belongings beside the bed, and returned with a basin of fresh water, soap, and a cloth. "I'm sorry it isn't a full bath; I will draw you one after dinner."

I stepped to the table where the basin waited and studied my face in the mirror on the wall. My hair fell past my shoulders in disheveled waves and a layer of grime had collected on my face. It was a relief to scrub my hands and face clean and run my comb through the tangles in my hair.

When I was finished, I paused, caught off guard once again by my reflection. As I had many times in my youth, I could see my mother's face gazing back at me. I'd seen both of my parents' features in mine before, but tonight they seemed all the more obvious. My mother's eyes flashed beneath my brows; her dark hair, the same shade as chocolate shipped from Teramyl, swept past my shoulders.

A familiar ache reverberated in my heart until it felt numb. Setting my jaw, I pulled my hair back and tied it tightly with a ribbon. *I will not be like her. I won't be like either of them.* There was firmness in the line of my jaw, even if it resembled my father's, and a steely ferocity in my eyes to match his intensity. Where my mother had been weak, I vowed to be strong. Though my father had betrayed and deceived many, I would try to undo his evils.

Stepping out of the bedroom, I joined Kam, Jennah, and two small girls for dinner.

As I sat down, Jennah gestured to the girls. "Elena, these are my daughters, Laydin and Avalee. Girls, Elena is our guest tonight."

The oldest girl was about five years old with curly hair like her mother's and bright, curious eyes. She stared at me, and at first I supposed it was because my quick face wash hadn't removed all the grime from traveling. Then she spoke. "Mama said you saw my Papa. Do you have news about him?" she asked.

"Laydin," Jennah said softly. "She must be hungry. Let her eat first."

She passed a plate of salmon to me while Kam sliced bread and cheese. It felt good to eat a hot meal after two days of chewing crusty bread, dried venison, and fruit.

After we all had a few minutes to eat, Jennah turned to me. "Why did you come to the capital? Certainly you didn't travel all this way only to deliver news about Marke."

I hesitated, poking my fish with my fork before I lifted my eyes to hers. "I came to join your cause."

"But when will Papa be home?" Avalee, whom I guessed to be three, turned pleading eyes toward me.

"I cannot say. But I know our healer in Evren will ensure your father is fully recovered before he travels again."

Jennah studied me curiously. "Surely you didn't come all the way from Evren and its safety to concern yourself with our troubles here."

I chewed my bread slowly, thoughtfully. At last, I swallowed. "The capital's troubles are everyone's troubles. Besides, a sedwa attacked Marke. I believe the tales are true: the king has found men to disturb the sedwa and threaten Evren's safety. My people are in danger."

Jennah nodded slowly. "You speak with conviction, which comforts me. What about your family? Don't you have anyone who misses you back home, who would balk at the risks you are taking?"

Drawing a deep breath, I said, "I...I have no blood relatives in Evren. Some may miss me, but it's worth it to keep the people of Evren safe."

"I'm sorry," Jennah whispered. "You have to understand that I am particular about whom I permit to attend our meetings."

I offered her a small smile. "I understand."

After the meal, Kam took the girls to bed, and I helped Jennah clear the table and wash the dishes.

"You'll want to get some sleep," Jennah said as she handed me a final plate to dry. "We hold our meetings in the middle of the night. I'll draw water for a bath so you can wash before bed."

"Thank you," I murmured, already imagining the hot water massaging my tired legs and feet.

After bathing and changing into the clean nightgown Jennah had left for me, I tried my best to curl up under the blankets in her daughters' narrow bed, but found myself staring at the ceiling. After two restless nights in a tent, I was sure a comfortable mattress would afford me rest, but my thoughts and worries would not.

Giver of Gifts, how can my words be a gift...? What am I supposed to do? You saved my life; you gave me these words and visions...but what am I supposed to do with them?

I wondered if Jennah fully trusted me, what she thought of a teenager traveling through Evren Forest to Misroth City on her own. Several times I considered abandoning my plan of anonymity and revealing who I was to the rebellion during the meeting. But why would they believe me, unless they recognized me, and why would they trust me more as their princess, the daughter of their enemy, than as an ordinary girl? Besides, despite my faith in Marke and my hopes for the rebellion, I couldn't fully trust any of the rebels any more than they could trust me. No, I would keep my original plan and conceal my identity, at least a while longer.

At last I drifted off, but it seemed only a few minutes later there were soft knocks on my door. Jennah peered in, and seeing me sitting up in bed, whispered, "It's time. Come join us."

Out of habit, I grasped my bow and slung my quiver on my back before following her downstairs, through the shadowy shop, and through the back room. Standing at the head of the stairway, she turned to me, the light of the candle dancing on her face and illuminating dark circles under her eyes, ones I hadn't noticed in the daylight. She glanced down at my bow, but made no comment about it. "I don't know what someone as young as you has to do with the movement against the king, but for now, I'd advise you to stay quiet."

I nodded. *That is what I am good at.*

Jennah turned and led me down the steps, a faint scent of mildew mixed with the rich aroma of dirt enveloping us as we descended. In the crammed cellar, dim light from a single candle illuminating their faces, four men huddled around the table. "Here she is," Jennah announced. "Her name is Elena."

Standing beside Jennah before the table, I held my breath, but none of the men showed any signs of knowing who I was. Sighing, I almost allowed myself to relax.

For my benefit, Jennah gestured to each man as she introduced him.

"This is Gare." She pointed to a man with dark skin, a short brown beard, and shaggy hair brushing his broad shoulders. He grunted a greeting to me, barely interested in my presence. "He is a former soldier who trained during our years of peace, but do not underestimate his abilities. Even a peacetime soldier is skilled, and Gare is as strong and fierce as they come." She flashed him a smile.

"Here is Benor, a merchant from Argelon. He resides here in the city for most of each winter and helps spread word of the king's actions and our plans to those loyal to our cause outside of the capital." Jennah nodded to a thin middle-aged man, his face as white as porcelain and his head nearly bald.

"And why is she here?" a voice interrupted. A young man of eighteen, with sharp features and piercing blue eyes, studied me with a frown furrowing his brow.

"That is Layk," Jennah muttered to me. "Don't let him trouble you. He serves as a patrol guard for the city, and since he has also served as our eyes and ears amongst the king's loyal men, he tends to be the most suspicious of us all." She glared at Layk, who leaned back with a sigh but held his tongue.

Jennah turned to the last member of the group, an elderly, clean-shaven man with snow white hair and a friendly smile. "This is Ellok. He is a grocer, with a shop near the main square, and being at the heart of the city, he sees and hears much."

Layk scowled at me. "I think my question warrants an answer. This meeting is no tea party. Why would you share all of this information with a strange girl?"

I met his gaze without wavering. "I live in Evren, the town Marke is staying in as he recovers. On his way to trade with us, he was attacked by one of the sedwa in Evren Forest. I came bringing this news and seeking to join your cause."

Layk's face was grave. "How did you hear about us?"

I relaxed my hands when I realized they were balled into fists at my sides. "Marke told me about your meetings. He wanted the people of Evren to know why the sedwa are attacking them."

The men turned to each other, sharing doubtful looks. Gare and Layk leaned in close, muttering under their breath to one another and shooting me dark glances.

"Why would he trust you?" Gare said.

"Perhaps she is lying about meeting Marke," Ellok suggested. "Maybe she was sent by the enemy."

Layk set his jaw. "If the king's men already know about us, they wouldn't have sent a girl to gather information. They'd be torturing us in dungeons or beheading us by now."

"I'm sure she's no threat," Benor intervened, waving off the other men's concerns.

Jennah lifted her chin defiantly and ignored Benor's comment. "Marke has a gift for discernment. If he trusted Elena with information about us, then I trust her as well."

"You truly believe those old tales about an Alrenian god granting us gifts?" Layk cocked an eyebrow at her.

My heart pounded. If Marke had a gift from the Life-Giver, perhaps Jennah would know more about my own gift. I bit back my questions, knowing now was not the time to satiate my curiosity.

Jennah crossed her arms, her eyes flashing at Layk. "Does my heritage trouble you?" She drew in a sharp breath. "Yes, I believe the stories. Some of you have even witnessed how his gift works."

"Discerning as he may be, I still think he could make a mistake," Gare said, and glanced around the table. "Who here trusts all of his comrades, beyond a shadow of a doubt?"

Layk shifted in his seat. "If I did not trust everyone here, I would be more reserved in sharing the information I acquire while on duty."

"It has taken time for us to build trust, and we still are cautious amongst one another, and especially other members of the rebellion, meeting in other locations," Jennah said. "The only way we can truly know she is trustworthy is to see her in action, to watch her carefully. She already knew of our meetings and where to search for us. Would you have had me send her away? Whether you trust her or not, you have to agree it's safer to keep her near, where we can watch her."

The men sank back into their seats, glancing at one another with milder expressions before looking back at Jennah and nodding slowly, thoughtfully.

"Well put," Benor said, rubbing his beard. "But why would Marke share news with a child in the first place? What can she do for our movement?"

"Don't be so quick to scoff at help when it is offered," Jennah intervened.

"Help?" Layk's eyes took in my slender frame almost with disgust. "How can she offer us help?" His gaze paused on my bow. I could almost see him trying to decide whether I knew how to wield it or not.

Ellok raised his eyebrows. "She made the journey through Evren Forest alone...and lived to tell the tale. Marke himself was gravely injured in his attempt, if her news is true. She seems to be more than she appears."

I stood taller, keeping my expression confident.

Gare gestured to my bow. "Well...if you want to help, prove to us that you can. Let me see you use that bow."

"Really, Gare..." Jennah began, but Layk raised his hand and she stopped.

"Yes, let's see," Layk agreed. He pointed. "Aim for that dent in the beam above us…do you see it?"

In the darkness, I could just make out the flaw in the wood he was talking about. Nodding, I strung an arrow to the bow and aimed for the beam. My hands trembled slightly, so I gulped in some air and released it slowly to steady them, and fired. The arrow struck the dent, embedding itself deep into the wood.

"That was a good shot," Ellok said. "A strong one." He glanced around at his companions.

"Not bad," Layk conceded. "Your aim is accurate, though the distance here wasn't that great. But what else can you do for us? There are hundreds of others who can fire an arrow."

I wanted to protest. *Isn't it enough that you have another person on your side? Isn't that what you want, more numbers?* But I realized that they couldn't accept anyone. I had yet to earn their trust, let alone their confidence and respect. They had to ensure I was worth the risk of bringing into their activities against the king, that I wouldn't weaken their efforts and put their lives in danger.

My heart pounded. *Do I share who I am to convince them?* No…I couldn't risk it. But what could I say instead? I couldn't lie, and they wouldn't believe the truth.

Perhaps part of the truth would do.

"I grew up in the castle, and I'm familiar with its layout," I said. "I believe I could offer you valuable input in your plans for rebellion."

A heavy silence fell. The candles on the table spluttered in their own wax and cast eerie shadows across the men's faces. I tried to read their faces, but their expressions were inscrutable.

If they say no, I'm on my own.

I squeezed my hands into fists again as I awaited their decision.

"You seem to have proven your mettle in your travels from Evren to Misroth already." To my surprise, it was Gare who interrupted my thoughts. He scanned his comrades' faces, then turned back to me. "If you are committed to this cause, you must realize you're responsible for your own fate."

"You must also realize you are not the only one in our numbers with knowledge of the castle," Ellok said, tugging at his beard. "We have others already on the inside, though we could always use more. And the risk is great."

Layk drew a rolled parchment from a sack hanging from the back of his chair. "We have a more pressing matter at the moment. There isn't much time, but we do have a plan you can play a part in—if, as Gare said, you are truly committed to this cause." Hard and unyielding, his eyes met mine.

Once again, I refused to look away. "I will die for it."

The men exchanged looks again.

"In that case…" Benor cracked his knuckles. "Let's explain. In case the laws have not affected those outside Misroth City much, you should know…the king's decrees have grown increasingly restrictive of priests. After all, they teach against hate, cruelty, greed, and lust for power—many have actively spoken against the new laws restricting the people's freedoms and ability to worship; others have cried out for the bloodshed to end, perhaps not convinced that everyone the king has executed is as guilty as he claims. Many have already died. Recently, another of our priests has been condemned to death, and he is to be publicly beheaded at sunset, three days from now. We plan to stop it."

"That's an ambitious mission," I blurted out. "King Zarev has an impressive array of guards at his disposal."

"It's a fool's mission," Benor said. "It will end in executions for all of us."

"We *cannot* sit by as innocent men die!" Gare slammed his fist on the table, knocking over the candle. The light snuffed out and the room became even dimmer than before, lit only by the candle Jennah still held aloft.

"Gare is right," Jennah said softly. "We need to find a public way to stand up to the king's tyranny."

"If we plan carefully enough, there is a possibility we can escape before we are arrested. It's bold, but it's possible," Layk added. "Besides, a public showing of rebellion might be the push the people need to align with the rebellion. It'll give them courage—a cause to stand behind."

"Is it courage the people of Misroth lack, or the truth?" Benor asked. "So many believe the king's lies. Few believe the truth."

Layk shifted in his seat. "Maybe Misroth needs to see a few rebels take risks to wake up to the need for a rebellion. If they know we are willing to risk our lives…"

"Arguing is a waste of time," Gare said. "If Benor doubts, he can stay behind. But we need to plan. Enough hiding in cellars and cowering in shadows. It's time for action!"

Jennah extended her hand to offer me a seat at the table as she sank into another empty chair. "Then let's plan our actions. We haven't much time."

I seated myself beside her, my heart pulsing with anticipation even as I bit back my fear. There would be no more cowering, no more hiding. From now on, I would live—or die—for Misroth.

CHAPTER THIRTEEN

MUFFLED VOICES FROM THE SHOP below snatched me from my sleep. I stared at the ceiling, listening to Jennah attempt to appease a disgruntled man.

"My deliveryman brings a fresh supply this evening. If you return tomorrow, we will have more…"

Tomorrow. Tomorrow we would attempt the rescue mission we had painstakingly worked out in the early morning hours of careful meetings, in casual trips to the main square in daylight hours, in moments of staring out of Ellok's shop windows at the surrounding shops, at the patrol guards' movements, at the vacant executioner's stand waiting for the next scheduled death. The days had passed slowly, and yet, the day I anticipated and dreaded was already almost here and I wasn't sure I was prepared.

If I die tomorrow, will anyone miss me? I let my mind wander to memories of Lyanna, Rev, and my friends in Evren. Did Avrik miss me at all? *Stop thinking,* I ordered myself, before I became overwhelmed with the grief of missing them.

Rolling out of bed, I went to the dresser and poured water into the basin. As I washed my face, I refused to look at my reflection and see my mother's eyes staring back at me. Instead, I concentrated on how refreshing the water felt against my skin and braced myself for the day ahead. While I repacked my belongings, my hand touched the dagger Avrik had given me and I closed my eyes to block out memories of him.

Over and over, I told myself not to miss the loved ones I'd left behind in Evren, or the ones I'd abandoned long ago here in Misroth.

But no matter how hard I tried, guilt settled over me like a weight. It seeped through my entire being, making it hard to move and even harder to smile as I joined Kam and the girls for a late lunch. Even when I tried to distract myself while I helped Jennah in the shop that afternoon, my thoughts wandered.

In my exhaustion, I dropped a sack of flour as I hauled it from the storeroom to restock the front. Sighing, I paused to wipe my brow. *I should have come back long ago. Why did I abandon my people like this? My family? If I'd returned sooner, maybe I could have prevented this war and kept Gil safe.* As I lifted the sack, my trembling fingers nearly slipped and dropped it again.

The bell attached to the shop's front door rang out and a stocky middle-aged man stepped inside, glancing about at the shelves. I lowered my head immediately, my heart thudding against my chest.

Don't recognize me, I prayed.

"Good afternoon," Jennah greeted him.

I fumbled with the sack, slinging it over my shoulder and shuffling quietly toward the shelves. As soon as I set it in its place, I slipped toward the storeroom. I sat on an unopened crate, relishing the safety of the shadows enveloping me even as I hated myself for retreating when customers entered Jennah's store.

Why was I being a coward? The answer came easily: *Because I feel powerless. Even with a group of rebels at my side, I can't even trust them with the truth.*

That night, I tossed in my bed. Doubt, fear, and worry consumed me. Was I leading these rebels in a suicide mission? Was it right for me to encourage them to attempt to save the priest, or to associate with me before or after I entered the castle?

I pulled my old journal from my pack to read the words I'd written during my mute years. It was filled with messages to the people in my life—fragments of another place and time in which I'd felt secure. The pages afforded glimpses into my soul where I'd hidden it, behind masks of paper and ink.

I fell asleep to dreams of Gillen surrounded by enemies in battle. Storm clouds raged overhead and blood soaked the ground. Then the dream shifted to the king's guard slaughtering citizens at the execution, and finally turning to my band of rebels to finish them off too.

When morning light spilled into the room, I squirmed awake. I felt as drained as if I had spent the entire night in battle at Gillen's side. My body was heavy and anxiety clustered in my throat until it became difficult to swallow. *It's your fault he is in danger. You could have prevented this war. You could have prevented everything, and your family and your people would be safe.*

Where was Gillen now? Was he in the middle of battle right at this moment? I squeezed my eyes shut and tried to block out the feelings raging inside.

Disentangling myself from my sheets and nightmares, I stumbled to the window to gaze out at my city. The streets basked in the cold white light of a snowy winter day. Fluffy clouds loomed on the horizon, promising more snow to come, while a lazy sun eased its way into the sky overhead. Everywhere there were people bustling along on business and guards making their rounds through the streets. Anger flared inside me as I watched the men that should be protecting my people glare at passersby. Children stumbled past them in fear and awe while adults averted their gazes.

Turning away from the window, I sighed. Knowing what the rebels and I had planned, Kam and the girls were somber at breakfast. I ate what I could manage to force down of the eggs and bread before me, and joined Jennah in the shop.

The hours slipped by too quickly. I ate about as much for lunch as I did for breakfast, forcing the food down only because I knew I needed my strength. Before long, I watched the shadows outside grow longer, the afternoon light begin to fade, and the sun sink low behind the buildings across from the shop.

The men filed in one at a time, as if they were last-minute customers eager to make purchases before Jennah closed her doors. My stomach churned at the sight of them: only Gare and Layk looked fit to undertake a life-threatening mission. Benor, though not the oldest, had surely seen healthier days in his prime, and Ellok looked like he should be sitting by a fire telling stories to his grandchildren.

Jennah locked the door, and we all looked to Gare.

"Earlier we asked Elena how committed she was to our cause," Gare said, glancing around at them all. "Now I ask each of you the same: are you willing to die?"

Layk raised his eyebrows. "Do you think any of us would be here if we were not?"

The others nodded a silent assent.

"Then that is settled. Whether you live or die, your fate is in your hands." Gare glanced pointedly at me, and I squared my shoulders in response. "Let's prepare to leave."

Jennah pulled her apron over her head. "I can be ready in five minutes."

"I still think you should stay with your daughters," Ellok said, scratching at his beard like it made him uncomfortable. "They are young and afraid, and their father isn't here. They need you."

"And I told you, I will not," Jennah replied. "I would rather die fighting for them to have a safe future, than sit back doing nothing. If I die, I die fighting for them. If I stay here and live, I live allowing them to grow up in oppression." Her eyes sparked. "I'm not afraid."

None of the men had a response. Gare cleared his throat, Benor shuffled awkwardly on his feet, and Layk bit his lip to hide a smile.

"Now that that's settled, let's stop wasting time," Jennah said, crossing her arms. "We already made our plans. Elena and I will be back in a few minutes."

She and I went upstairs to retrieve our weapons. I swung my quiver over my shoulder and attached my bow to its sling on my back. Sliding my dagger into my belt, I pulled on my cloak and set my shoulders. I couldn't hide my bow, but I had managed to slip into the city without any guards stopping me. The king had not yet outlawed weapons in the hands of his people, but Layk had shared that guards often stopped armed citizens for questioning.

I imagined a guard forcing me to a halt to ask questions and catching a glimpse of my face beneath my hood, recognizing who I was and possibly putting my comrades in even greater danger as even more guards swarmed the area. If that happened, I would pray the distraction of my arrest would work in their favor, and not against them. I lowered my gaze, hoping they didn't see the fear in my eyes.

Jennah met me in the hallway, armed with her husband's sword and a traveling cloak to help conceal it. Sharing a quick smile, we dashed downstairs to meet the men.

"I still don't like this," Benor growled.

Gare set a hand on Benor's shoulder. "But at least we are *doing* something!"

One by one, we slipped out into the evening. We followed Layk's lead as he struck out on a winding path through quiet side streets and alleys. Away from the crowd and the patrol guards' posts, we were inconspicuous, but not invisible. I kept my eyes low and my strides short in hopes that no one would give a girl armed with a bow extra attention.

As we approached the heart of the capital, I noticed the crowd thickening along the main street. The road fairly buzzed with excitement as the people chattered and jostled one another in their attempts to travel faster.

Sooner than I expected, we reached an old brick building bordering the main square.

"Here we are," Layk whispered. He turned to me. "As we said, you'll have good visibility here, and most of the guards will have trouble seeing you. Only a few are posted on the other rooftops, and they will be focused on the execution stand until you fire. If you move fast enough..."

I cut him off. "No need to worry. We've gone over this plan many times. I'll be all right."

"She's right," Gare said. "We don't have time to waste." He shot one last glance at me. "Our hopes rest on you. Don't let us down." He turned to the others. "Let's get into our positions."

With a nod, Layk turned away to lead the rest of the rebels to their positions, all set at random points throughout the square. Armed with a bow and sword, Gare would be in the corner closest to me in order to act as my defense. Layk and Ellok had positions nearer the stand in case my shot went awry, and Benor and Jennah, armed with weapons only suitable for hand-to-hand combat, would remain at the edges of the square in the hope that they could hinder the guards' pursuit once I fired my bow and began my escape. I rolled my shoulders as I prepared to climb. It was a desperate plan, formed by a small band with few resources and grand hopes, but it was a plan and I had agreed to follow it.

My arms trembled as I pulled myself up along the crumbling wall, finding cracks in the mortar and gaps from missing bricks to use as hand and footholds. According to Layk, the rooftop was caving in, which meant no guards would be posted on this building and few, if any, would suspect anyone to climb it. But that was because their anticipated suspects were men, large and muscular. I was a girl, shorter and smaller than any of the other rebels, light enough for even the collapsing building to carry my weight if I was cautious. Gare was right: though Layk was also armed with a bow, I had the best position to make the shot swiftly and accurately.

When I reached the top, I peered over the edge. The rooftop was flat and square, which would make it easy to scale, and it was indeed clear of guards; but there was a hole near the middle where the entire roof had begun collapsing inward. Steeling my nerves, I pulled myself up and crept along the edge to give the hole a wide berth, testing my weight on each tile before I fully trusted it. Though the air was chilly, the setting sun was warm on my back and my palms were already growing clammy within my shooting gloves.

I chose a perch on a few solid tiles on the opposite end of the roof and drew an arrow. Kneeling, I rolled my shoulders to ease the tension in my neck and studied my surroundings. Overhead the sky was clear, the eastern horizon tinged purple with the first stars springing into view, while behind me, the dying sun spilled its last rays of light, washing the world in a blood-red hue. Though the nearby shops were closed and the booths shut up or rolled away, the scents of baking bread and roasting meat were still heavy in the air. Every inch of the square below me was packed full of citizens gathering around the stand, set close to the statue of King Eldon, who watched the proceedings with a stern expression on his chiseled face.

As I scanned the people, I could pick out Gare's large from in the corner of the square closest to me. He stood in the shadows, his eyes alert while he watched every movement of the guards stationed near him. The sight was a comforting reminder that I was not alone; in their various positions throughout the main square, my friends were watching and waiting too.

I turned my attention to my task: the execution stand. Several of the king's guards stood on and around it to keep the flood of people a safe distance from the prisoner. At the far corner, the executioner rested his double-bladed axe on his shoulder and awaited his signal. He was cloaked and hooded in black to hide his features from all but the man he was about to kill. Nearby, the condemned priest, bound and held by two guards, bowed his head as if in prayer.

Shrouded in his captain's cloak, Narek stood near the edge of the platform. My heart jolted at the sight and fear and rage curled in my stomach. I bit my lip and forced myself to control my ragged breathing. *Focus.* I wiped a sweaty palm on the skirt of my dress. *Stop the execution. Let Narek taste defeat.*

His voice echoed through the square as he finished a speech to the people. "…to witness the execution this man"—he gestured toward the prisoner— "for his treasonous actions against the king."

The two guards on either side of the priest shoved him to his knees and forced his neck onto the chopping block. They stepped back and a hush fell over the crowd. My stomach churned. What was worse: being thrown to the sea to drown or being publicly beheaded before family and friends?

Time was short. Familiar fear rattled my heart; I had to move swiftly, and I could not fail. But something else touched it too: the memory of the Life-Giver and the purpose that had urged me forward. Reaching back, I drew an arrow from my quiver and notched it to my bow. I drew a deep breath as I pulled the string and focused on keeping my arm steady. An urge to let the arrow soar straight into Narek's heart gnawed at my mind, but I nudged the thought away. I had time for one shot, one chance to save an innocent man. Narek could taste justice another day.

I closed one eye and stared at my target as he lumbered toward the chopping block. Years of archery lessons and practice flashed through my brain, but it wasn't Avrik's voice I heard in my head, but Gillen's. *Stay calm and you will remain steady so that your arrow can fly true. Take deep, slow breaths and release your arrow as you exhale.*

My arrow glided over the crowd and struck the executioner in the chest. With a grunt, he fell backward onto the platform, his axe thudding beside him. Screams and shouts erupted throughout the square, but I was already moving. Before I could look to see if the priest took advantage of those precious seconds to leap from the platform and let the masses swallow him, I dashed back across the rooftop.

I could scarcely breathe as I scrambled down the side of the building. My boots scraped against the bricks when I missed a foothold and began to slip.

My head throbbed and my throat constricted. All of those inner conversations with myself about how the man I had killed was evil, about how he deserved death so an innocent man could live, and guilt still stained my conscience. I imagined my sweaty palm clutching my bow was slick with blood.

"Jump!" It was Gare's voice behind me. "Hurry!"

Glancing over my shoulder, I saw him waiting for me at the bottom. I bit my lip and let go, pushing off the wall and plunging down into his outstretched arms. Wordlessly, he dropped me to my feet and together we raced down the alleyway.

Shouts erupted all around, the sounds of citizens running and our pursuers nearing us, as Gare led me through cramped alleyways littered with reeking trash.

Two guards darted down a street before us and Gare reached to grasp my arm and force me to a halt. My boots skidded on gravel and I nearly fell. He shot me a glare and shoved me back against the stone wall behind us. I listened as the guards' footsteps paused and a momentary quiet sank around us. Clapping a hand over my mouth to muffle my gasps for air, I prayed the men would keep moving forward.

Then there were more footsteps, approaching us. I drew a trembling breath and groped for my quiver, seeing in my peripheral that Gare was tugging on the hilt of his sword. The blade hissed from its sheath and our tense faces stared back at us in its reflection.

When the men veered around the corner, swords drawn and at the ready, Gare launched himself toward them without hesitation. He swung his blade at the first man's legs, forcing him to leap back in defense. The second guard pinned his eyes on me as I drew back my bowstring, my fingers trembling. Memories flashed through my mind: blood in the snow and Avrik's pale face as a man collapsed at his hand; an executioner stumbling backward in front of a stunned crowd. My tongue fastened to the roof of my mouth.

I let the arrow fly a moment too late. It skittered off the wall where the guard had been. He charged me, swinging his blade toward my neck, and I barely had time to drop my bow, dive to the ground, and roll, sharp stones biting into my arms and back. I yanked my dagger from the sheath at my side and plunged it into his boot, slicing through leather and skin and bone. He yelped and swung again, but I was already moving, rolling back to my bow and leaping to my feet. I had my bow lifted and loaded with another arrow before he could lunge at me; I released the string before I could stare into his rage-filled eyes a moment longer and waver once more. My arrow lodged in his neck, and with a gurgle and roll of his eyes, the guard dropped his sword and collapsed in a heap.

I glanced to Gare just in time to watch him wipe his bloodied sword on the other fallen man's uniform. Slowly I lowered my bow and released a ragged breath. Hearing my movements, Gare turned on me.

"I saw you falter. Never hesitate in battle," he snarled. His left leg was bleeding and he walked with a slight limp, but otherwise he seemed unfazed by the encounter, as if he had been a wartime soldier used to daily bloodshed and death.

My protests died before they reached my lips.

His eyes glinted in the twilight. "Hesitation will be the death of you or your comrades."

Before I could even nod, more cries rang out as citizens spilled into the streets surrounding us, tumbling over one another, screaming in fear even as guards called to them: "Halt! Everyone remain calm!"

"Join the fray," Gare grunted, sheathing his sword. I slung my bow across my back and willed myself to be small, to be invisible amidst the chaos.

Limping forward, Gare darted into the crowds and allowed himself to blend in with the panicked, fleeing people. I followed, my heart pulsing, the shouts and screams all but drowning out the guards' commands. Somewhere in the sea of people, a child wailed for his mother; someone's hand smacked my face; a dozen feet stepped on mine. I lost sight of Gare, but continued to push my way through, praying I could make it back to Marke's shop and the other rebels would already be there, safe from danger. Dizzy, I squeezed past frantic women crying out for their children and men grasping at sword hilts and scanning the surrounding people warily. Though the crowd protected me for now, I felt as if I had been swallowed whole. What a pity it would be to succeed in our mission only to be trampled to death in our escape.

Slowly, the crowds began to thin until I could run freely through the streets without being jostled. Already the city was drenched in shadow, the dusk melting into a cold, still night. The noise faded behind me until my own footsteps echoed loudly on the cobblestones and I slowed to a walk. A few others swept their way along the streets beside me, their movements quick and anxious, their eyes constantly roving as they studied their surroundings and cast looks over their shoulders. Lights flickered from windows in the homes lining the way; smoke curled from chimneys. One woman stood framed by light in her doorway, leaning out to peer into the shadows as she waited for a loved one's safe return.

I recognized some of the buildings around me: there was the baker's where Jennah and I had gone two mornings ago to fetch pastries for breakfast. I was almost there.

Hands snatched at my back, yanking me to a sharp stop and throwing my hood back. I grit my teeth and spun to face a guard glowering down at me, suspicion lurking in his face, but thankfully, not recognition.

"What is a girl doing roaming the streets at night with a bow strapped to her back?" he demanded gruffly.

My breath caught in my throat. I let my eyes grow wide and fearful and let tremors fill my voice. "Please…the crowds… I am only trying to get safely home."

"You went to the execution tonight, *armed?*"

I imagined what Emalet would do, her face paling and her eyes fluttering in terror and helplessness. "Oh, please, sir. The city is not *safe*." My eyes darted about, as if I could sense rebels prowling in the dark alleys and lurking on the rooftops around us.

A slow smile quirked the corner of his mouth and amusement danced in his dark eyes. "No, it is not. If I catch you out at night with a weapon again, I'll disarm you and take you to Ugomath for questioning. Or worse. You'd better run home to your Mama and Papa." He chuckled cruelly, shoving me away from him.

I caught myself and spun away from him, clenching my jaw and refusing to run, refusing to tremble. My stomach churned at the thought of visiting the infamous prison, even for questioning, but even that seemed better than being dragged to the castle dungeons. I walked with my head held high, studying the night and keeping my breathing even to hide my fear and anger and distract my thoughts.

The sky was dark with stars flashing overhead and a bulging moon hanging so low I felt I could reach up and touch it. *Almost there,* I thought. *Almost there.*

I rounded the final corner and there was Marke's shop waiting for me. My body nearly sagged in relief. Breathless and aching, I circled to the back entrance and tapped softly. The door swung silently inward and Jennah's face peered out at me.

"You made it," she whispered. Her hair, pulled back as usual, was a frizzy halo on her head and her eyes were alight with relief.

I stepped inside and Jennah locked the door behind me. Layk, Ellok, and Benor sat on nearby crates or lay sprawled on the storeroom floor, their weapons lying beside them.

"That was close," Benor breathed. "We were debating how much longer we would give before setting out to search for you."

Without responding, my eyes swept the room a second time. "Where is Gare?" I asked, concern edging my tone.

"Upstairs. Mother is tending to his wound," Jennah said quietly. "I think it's time the rest of you return home, before it grows too late. Gare will stay here for the night."

Layk nodded and glanced at Benor and Ellok. "Thirty minutes until curfew." His face was grim. "You will be arrested on sight, no questions asked."

As Benor, Ellok, and Layk left, I followed Jennah out of the room and up the steps to her living quarters.

My mind flitted back to the men I'd killed, and I had to quash a wave of nausea. I wondered if I would ever grow accustomed to a life of fighting and bloodshed. I clenched my jaw and tightened my hands into fists at my sides. *Yes, if that's what I must do,* I resolved. *Far better to have the blood of my father's men on my hands than the blood of my people.*

The next morning, Gare departed for home as soon as the first rays of sun peered over the horizon. Jennah closed the shop for a day of housework and rest and immediately set to work preparing breakfast. When she refused my help, I retreated to the bedroom and began formulating possible plans for infiltrating the castle and ways I could spread the truth about the king.

Pose as a servant. Spread rumors amongst the servants, whispers that could reach the ears of the Royal Guard. Set doubts in their minds and make them question their loyalties.

At last I sighed and hung my head, scratching out line after line of ideas in the pages of my journal. Chewing on my lip, I again considered revealing my identity to my comrades, now that our successful mission had built some trust between us. We could spread the news amongst the rebels that Princess Halia was alive and fighting against her father, news that could reach the Misrothian people and set fire to the rebellion's cause. Or put them in graver danger than ever. My father would stop at nothing to find me if he knew I was still alive.

Exasperated, I joined Jennah and her family for the meal. Once we'd finished, Kam took Avalee to the market to purchase food for dinner. While Jennah and Laydin washed and dried the dishes, I set to work wiping down the table, sweeping the stone floor, and dusting the mantelpiece.

As I brushed flour and soot into an ever-growing pile, I couldn't help but watch Jennah in mild fascination as she scrubbed at the plates and hummed a soft tune. Though her hands were calloused, she had the beauty and gentility of a noblewoman. Her skin was dark, with a gold tone that made it shimmer in the light and gave her a warm aura, as if she had captured a piece of the sun to keep for herself. When she turned to pass a dish to her daughter, her brown eyes sparkled with flecks of gold. They were all features that revealed her Alrenian heritage.

Her humming transformed into singing, her rich voice filling the kitchen with alto notes from an Alrenian song, but not one of the traditional tunes the Misrothian people memorized before the language was forbidden. My breath caught in my throat.

"Do you know Alrenian?" I blurted out.

Jennah grinned at me, her eyes dancing with light. "Does it surprise you that a rebel with Alrenian heritage can speak a forbidden language?"

I matched her smile, shaking my head.

"My family has passed knowledge of the language down for generations. Unfortunately, we've forgotten most of the other stories…the tales of the land, its history, its people…" Her voice drifted off.

My heart pulsed with anticipation. I'd been waiting for days for a moment to ask about Marke's gift. "But you remember stories about gifts the Life-Giver bestows? Such as Marke's discernment?"

Jennah sighed softly and stared down at the dishwater. "I remember a few things that the Book of Life told about them. There are many, given to all sorts of people and revealed to them at any time in their lives…but I know little about the other gifts. Marke and I realized his discernment must be from the Life-Giver." She lifted a spoon and stared at the suds collected on it. "All copies of the Book of Life were destroyed in Misroth City, so we haven't been able to study much about it. I wish I could learn more, because…" Shaking her head, she stopped herself and sighed, saying nothing more.

Disappointment clung to me like a cloak. If only I could show her Lyanna and Rev's copy and have her read from that… I shook the wistful thoughts away, resigning myself to the fact that, for now, I only had what information the Life-Giver had shared.

I leaned against the broom and my thoughts drifted to the stories I'd heard about Alrenor. "Do you ever…think of going there, to the Land of the Sun? Leaving Misroth behind for a new life?"

Jennah shook her head, her eyes flashing. "The people of Misroth are my people, and this is my home. I don't want to escape. I want to save my kingdom so my daughters can have a better life…*here*, if they so choose." She dipped her hands into the sudsy water again and grasped another dish. "Have you ever thought of leaving?"

I hesitated. "As you said…this is my home, where my people live. I won't leave them."

Jennah nodded slowly.

Dropping my gaze to avoid hers, I began to sweep again. "What were you singing about?" I asked, desperate to change the subject.

"It was a love song, asking the Life-Giver to keep the singer's beloved and bring him safely home to her again." A soft smile played about her lips, but it didn't quite mask the pain in her eyes.

"I'm sure he will be home soon," I said, pressing my lips together and trying to mask the heaviness that descended on me like a weight.

Jennah studied me, as if by reading the lines of my face she could discern the contents of my heart. "You said you had no family in Evren, but surely you had ties. You left someone…didn't you?"

I stared at the pile of filth at my feet and tried to keep my face smooth, emotionless. "It hardly matters."

With childlike innocence, Laydin stared at her mother and then me, letting her questions pour out like a flood as she tried to understand our conversation. "Is she in love, Mama? Do you miss him, Elena? Why didn't he come with you?"

Jennah shot her daughter a look. "Do not pry, darling."

I lifted my chin and answered Laydin's last question. "He chose a different path."

Laydin stared down at her towel, fidgeting with it uncomfortably. She dared a glance at her mother. "I'm sorry," she gulped.

Forcing my expression to look carefree, I waved my hand. "I told you, it hardly matters. It was only a vague wish. We were not…we were only friends."

Without another word, I swept the dirt pile into the pan and left to dump it outside.

Days slithered by, full of helping Jennah with work in her shop and home and nights of meeting with rebels in various locations. Most often we met in Jennah's cellar, but occasionally she would wake me to lead me out to the shadowy, quiet streets, where we would dodge ever-increasing numbers of patrol guards to meet in another business or home. The rebels usually kept their meetings to a handful of men and women at a time to reduce chances of being discovered, yet this made communication slow and difficult. It also meant that most efforts, like our rescue of the priest, were done with small groups of rebels, in numbers that could be stealthy and swift to avoid capture.

As we met with more and more rebels, I felt my hope grow. Perhaps we could end my father's tyranny. Maybe there were more Misrothians than I'd believed who were ready to end King Zarev's reign.

Most nights, we discussed the plan for me to infiltrate the castle for information that could aid our movement. Layk insisted on introducing me to as many of the rebels as possible before sending me away, in order to ensure that other members and I would be able to recognize one another. The time it was taking to get me into the castle was beginning to wear on me. Already, nearly two weeks had passed since I'd first entered the capital.

Impatience was foolish—deadly, even. But each night my sleep was filled with nightmares of death: the deaths of my people, my cousin, and everyone I cared about.

And I knew I could prevent them.

One afternoon, as we waited in Jennah's cellar to move out and attempt to prevent another execution, I broached the subject. "When do we proceed with the plan to send me into the castle?"

Gare crossed his arms across his chest and leaned back in his chair.

"There is much left to discuss."

I bit back my impatience. "Then let us discuss it."

Jennah shifted in her seat across from me. Her eyes glittered in the candlelight, but there was no amusement in them. "I have waited this long, wondering if you would share more and quelling my suspicion because of your assistance. But I can't ignore the matter any longer." She set a hand on her hip while she scanned my face. It was a simple enough gesture for the slender woman, but something about her mannerisms stirred my memory, reminding me of childhood tales about Alrenian warriors from bygone days. "You do not have the bearing of a servant, yet you said you grew up in the castle. Who *are* you?"

All eyes turned toward me and silence fell.

I swallowed and stared at my hands, folded in my lap so tightly they were white. If I told them who I was, would they trust me? I may have aided them once, but I'd also concealed my identity this long and Gare had watched me hesitate to kill some of the king's men. Besides, I couldn't trust *them*. There was no telling that they would not use my identity to spur their movement forward, that they would not spread word that the princess had returned and was part of the rebellion.

The last thing I needed was for the king to hear about a rebel princess. He wouldn't hesitate to shed more innocent blood to find me; he would find our hideout and raze Marke's shop in an instant. I couldn't take that risk, not when it endangered so many.

The truth has been silent in this kingdom for years. Let it be silent a little longer.

I raised my eyes to meet Jennah's narrowed stare, and chose my words carefully. "I was a child in the castle. Not a servant."

The tension remained heavy in the room.

"You did not learn any of your parent's ways?" Layk's voice was sharp; his bright eyes burned into me.

If only I could lie. A thousand contrived stories swirled through my brain, but my tongue refused to give voice to any of them. Instead, I simply shook my head.

"I understand that your past must be painful, since you said you have no family in Evren." Jennah's voice was gentle, her face warm. "But you have to understand how important it is that we don't withhold information from one another…"

A distant bell began to toll, signaling the seventeenth hour. Layk rose from his chair and lifted his bow from the table. "We need to move now."

The others were on their feet in an instant. As one, we silently mounted the steps to the storeroom and began to filter one by one out the door and into the evening. Clouds muffled the sunlight and a fresh layer of snow crunched beneath my boots as I traced a path through the city's maze of alleys. My bow weighed heavily on my back and I remembered the patrol guard's threat after my first skirmish as a rebel. Layk could pass as an armed guard if he chose, but the streets were growing increasingly unfriendly toward armed citizens. I'd watched countless people questioned outside Marke's shop over the days, and even now, as crowds wound through the streets to behold another execution, I noticed a few wary glances shot my direction.

Jennah was ahead of me, her tall, slender form striding confidently from an alleyway onto the main street to join the crowds. She never shirked from the attention she drew, her gold-tinted complexion shining, her eyes flashing, her steps poised and her smile sure. Her Alrenian heritage was clear and she was unashamed. She welcomed the looks from Misrothians, attempting to draw attention from me while I slunk several yards behind her, doing my best to be lost in her wake.

The change of the crowd's mood was perceptible in the very air around us: the breeze faltered, leaving the world heavy and still, and the people's murmurings became troubled. Ahead of us, Layk froze with the crowd gathering just outside the square. Benor, Gare, and Ellok drew up close behind him and Jennah and I followed, pushing around women covering their children's eyes, men muttering in disgust and anger.

Standing on my tiptoes, I managed to see over the people's heads into the square and my blood ran cold. The stand was soaked in blood, the executioner still hovering over the chopping block with his dripping axe, and guards tossing corpses into a pile at the foot of Eldon's statue. They had started the beheadings early, but that was not what horrified the people.

Standing in rows before their bodies, a dozen heads were speared atop pikes, their wide-eyed stares matching ours. My stomach clenched and I choked on bile rising in my throat. I recognized one of the faces: Murvek, one of the rebels I had met with just the night before.

"They knew our plans," Layk said, his voice low yet sharp as steel. "We've been discovered—or betrayed."

CHAPTER FOURTEEN

JENNAH STIFLED A CRY, RAISING a hand to her mouth. "If they know about the meetings, they could be at the shop now."

I could see the horror transforming to anger and resolve as she thought of her girls in possible danger. Her eyes flashed and she set her jaw, the concerned mother becoming a powerful Alrenian in an instant.

"Wait, we don't know…" Gare began, reaching out to grasp her arm, but she was already shoving past the people, forcing her way back down the street.

"It's a trap," Benor muttered.

Despite his warnings, despite the own sense of danger flaring in my own brain, horror clawed at my chest as the dead faces continued to stare us down. I imagined Jennah's family there in their places and my pulse raged. I pressed through the crowd after Jennah. There was a ringing in my ears, muting the voices around me. The pale, shocked faces of the Misrothians looked distant, as if they were staring at me from a vast distance. My footsteps pounded the cobblestones like war drums and cold air bit at my face, tore at my cloak, and brushed my hair into my eyes. Even as the crowd thinned and I was able to increase my pace, the streets seemed endless—I couldn't run quickly enough, couldn't swallow the distance in time. What if it was already too late?

I rounded the corner onto Jennah's street and it felt like a knife pierced my chest. Shouts and the clang of steel on steel pierced the night: Jennah was surrounded by guards swarming outside the shop, holding her ground with her sword raised high as several mounted an attack against her.

The breeze whispered in my ears, making the hairs on my arms bristle. I yanked my bow from my back and drew an arrow. Panting, Benor drew up beside me. "Wait—" he began.

I let my arrow fly, piercing one of the guards in the chest before he could slice his blade toward Jennah's neck. He tumbled to the cobblestones in a pool of blood, and his comrades raised angry eyes toward Benor and me. Before I could release another arrow, three guards were upon us both.

One smashed the pommel of his sword on my head, knocking me backward. Sparks of light splattered across my vision and warm blood spilled down my temple. The men heaved me roughly to my feet, their fingers digging so hard into my skin I cried out. A third man lifted my bow from the ground and slung it over his own back, sneering at me.

Dizzy, I surveyed the street to see Benor had already been overpowered and disarmed as well. The men dragged us toward the building, where they were disarming and restraining Jennah. Light from the guards' torches glared in my eyes, but I could see more guards approaching from down the street, pulling Gare, Ellok, and Layk toward us.

Then another man rounded the corner, his cloak fluttering around him like a shadow clinging to his presence. Narek. I stood frozen, staring at him as he studied his men's handiwork in one smooth glance: an entire band of rebels captured in moments. I remembered the way it had felt when Narek had carried me away screaming and dumped me over the side of a cliff. Without remorse. My stomach tightened and I found it hard to breathe.

"Burn the place to ashes," Narek ordered. "Let it be a message to all who seek to defy the king."

I swallowed. Where were Kam and the girls? Were they still hiding in the living quarters over the shop? Had they managed to escape?

Thrashing and kicking, Jennah screamed. "No, no! There are children—my children are inside!"

Two men punched through the building's glass windows and began dumping oil inside. When they stepped back, several of their comrades tossed torches through the yawning voids and leapt back. Light flared in a brilliant burst and smoke billowed through the windows. Despair shredded my heart, making my body feel numb and empty. They were murdering Jennah's family, destroying her whole life, and we were helpless to stop them.

Jennah's shrieks of horror ripped at the night. "You *monsters!* They're my *children!*" She tried to wrench herself away from the guards, thrashing and kicking and screaming, but to no avail.

The two guards restraining Ellok released his arms and stepped back. He pulled his arms across his chest and surveyed the destruction dispassionately while Narek approached him. "Thank you for the tip," the captain said, plucking a bag jingling with coins from his cloak pocket and tossing it to Ellok.

I gaped at the old man, at a loss for words.

"*You,*" Jennah snarled, sounding more feral than human. She was on her knees now, fighting with all she had against the men who held her back. Smoke surrounded her like a swirling extension of her cloak and the golden flecks in her eyes shimmered like miniature fires of her own. She flung a series of filthy curses at Ellok, her voice raw with fury and desperation.

Ellok's countenance was unmoved as he stared back at her, his beard so white in the surrounding darkness it hurt my eyes. His face was lit from the raging flames, revealing his wrinkled countenance scrunched up in distaste. "I am an old man, ready to rest in peace. I am not about to endanger my own or my family's wellbeing for a foolhardy cause," he spat. "One way or another, against a king who wields an entire army, against a kingdom that has done next to nothing to protest his rule, you and the rest of the idiot rebels will die."

With Jennah still flinging insults at his back, he shoved the bag into his cloak and turned to slink into the night, his form melting into the blackness.

As Narek turned, his eyes fell on me. A crease settled between his brows and he strode toward me, pausing to stare into my face. He had been a young captain four years ago, and he still looked young now, but even the oldest of his guards gazed at him with deference. He was near enough that I could see the stubble lining his jaw and the recognition that sparked in his eyes. "Princess Halia. You're alive," he breathed, smiling slowly until the hair on my arms prickled. "How nice to see that the princess has returned to her family. What a reunion *this* shall be."

Cringing, I turned away, avoiding his gaze. None of the guards or the rebels betrayed any emotion, and I realized Narek had spoken too softly for anyone else to hear. I was ashamed to find I was relieved. If they realized who I was now, my rebel friends would probably hate me for holding onto my secret this long.

Narek looked at the guards restraining us all. "Take them to the castle dungeons."

The guards wrenched us forward, guiding us through the shadowy streets even as crowds gathered at windows to peer out in fear. One of the men slammed his sword hilt into Jennah's temple to stop her resistance. Her screams died on her lips as she fell unconscious, and the guard slung her unceremoniously across his shoulder. The rest of us remained mute and shuffled along without fighting. We were hopelessly outnumbered.

Slowly, the buildings around us fell away and the cliff loomed near, until, far too soon, we were standing at its base. The guards yanked us onto a winding path that zigzagged to the top of the peak, where the castle sprawled in all its stark glory. Soon snow began falling so thickly that the world turned blindingly white and I could only see a few feet in front of me. The men shoved me forward if I slipped or if my strides failed to match theirs. At first I shivered in the wind, but as we climbed higher, sweat broke out on my forehead.

At last we reached the top and the castle stood before us. A lump formed in my throat at the familiar sight, the focal point of so many nightmares, of so much longing and pain. We swept through the grounds, now mostly barren beneath snow and ice, past guards opening the main gate to us, and into the courtyard. Grim statues stared back at me and made my heart ache with their familiarity. There was no returning home without the bitter pang of childhood memories. Everything that was once dear was now a reminder of horrors, past and future. I tore my eyes away and stared at the ground.

Two men threw open the castle doors for us. The guards led me through the great halls where I'd once lived, played, and laughed. Now I passed through as a prisoner, a criminal, a stranger. The same paintings and banners decorated the walls; the same rugs softened the floor beneath my feet; the same wide windows afforded views of the grounds stretching out beneath the darkening sky. If not for the men at my sides I could have almost imagined myself a child again, wandering the halls in search of my cousin. Everything was the same, yet different—wrong, cold.

My heart throbbed, pounding in my ears so that even my thoughts seemed muffled as I prayed for help.

The guards dragged us through the heavy wooden door and down a stone staircase, into the deep recesses of the castle, a place I had never been allowed to go. The air grew cold and heavy; it felt like the weight of the upper floors pressed down on us. When we paused before a second door, leading to the dungeon corridors, my hands were clammy and my mouth was dry. The guards positioned on either side of it checked us for any remaining weapons, stripping my companions of knives and daggers. Then they shoved open the door and stood aside for us to pass.

The dungeon corridors were long and narrow, with only flickering torchlight to guide our way. Damp and cold, the air reeked of years of foulness. Most of the cells we passed were open and empty, but a few of the heavy wooden doors were shut and padlocked. I was thankful that the grates were set high in the doors, high enough that I could easily look away; I did not want to see the hopeless faces of the prisoners we passed. I did not want to ponder my fate or the long hours and days that stretched before me until I received my sentence. Until I was brought before the king. My heart pounded in my chest as if it were a prisoner too, screaming to be set free.

After a few twists and turns through the dimness, my eyes began to adjust to the light. A guard halted beside one of the open cells, secluded from the occupied ones we had passed earlier, and gestured to the men clutching my arms. Without further ceremony, they shoved me inside and slammed the door. I heard the lock click into place and the retreating footsteps of the guards and my comrades as they were led off to their own distant cells.

The quiet settled around me so thickly I could scarcely breathe. The space was so narrow that I could cross the width of my cell in three steps before my fingers brushed against cold rock. It was only a little deeper. The torchlight from the corridor outside sputtered and my heart skipped a beat. Soon it would go out, and when would another patrolling guard bother to replace it? I would be left in complete darkness.

I had never been afraid of the dark, but the thought of having nothing but blackness, of emptiness, to stare into for hours—even days— made me panic. My mouth went dry. *Please, please don't let it last long…* I'd hardly thought the words before the torch sizzled out and darkness settled around me. Closing my eyes, I forced myself to draw a deep breath and exhale slowly. Once, twice. *It's fine. It is only darkness. It is nothing.*

My head throbbed. I touched the wound near my temple to find that the blood had stopped running, but the cut stung. I winced and drew my fingers away. Disregarding how filthy and cold the rough stones were, I collapsed to the floor and curled up in a corner of the cell.

Maybe this was a blessing in disguise. After all, I was inside the castle like I had wanted to be.

But what can I do as a prisoner? I thought bitterly. *Speak the truth so they can execute me properly this time?*

My stomach dropped. The words the Life-Giver had spoken to me seemed so distant and unclear now. Had he really meant for me to return home and join the rebellion? What was I doing? The sense of purpose that the encounter had granted me was fading too. Avrik was right: I was mad. And now I was going to die.

I thought of my friends, somewhere in the royal dungeons also, awaiting their own death sentences. My strong, courageous friends willing to risk their lives to ensure their families and their people, could someday be free of my father's oppression. They had remained in the city and built a rebellion when I had fled. Yet despite their nobility, they would suffer the same fate as me.

Closing my eyes, I could still see Marke's shop burning, the smoke blotting out the stars. Jennah's screams still echoed in my ears. The king and his men were monsters, and I felt powerless to stop them.

I realized my hands were shaking, so I pulled my knees up to my chest and wrapped my arms around them, clasping my fingers together tightly. Where was the Giver of Life now, when I'd agreed to use the gift he'd given me? *You gave me my life and a purpose. So give me my mission. Now what?*

My only answer was silence.

CHAPTER FIFTEEN

I SLIPPED IN AND OUT of consciousness for hours, praying and thinking with no further clarity. Often I closed my eyes in an attempt to shut out the dark. The cold air kept me shivering even as I pulled my cloak close about me, pulling up the hood and shoving my hands in my pockets. Over the sounds of my heartbeat and breathing, I occasionally heard water drip and distant skittering—probably rats. I cringed at the sound.

Eventually I heard another noise: first, approaching footsteps echoing along the corridors, and then voices. As they drew nearer, I realized that one belonged to a woman. Light pierced the blackness, casting shadows on the wall opposite my cell door. The voices were coming toward me.

To give me food rations? My stomach growled at the thought, reminding me that it had been a long time since my last meal. But anxiety, fear, and sadness still wrestled within me too, pressing down on my heart and twisting in my stomach until I felt sick. I wasn't sure if I was interested in food, but I needed it.

"Here we are, Your Highness," came a guard's voice outside my prison door.

I almost gasped aloud. *Your Highness?*

"Visitor!" the guard shouted gruffly, and he went about unlocking the door as noisily as possible. He swung open my door and stepped aside.

Scrambling to my feet, I blinked against the light streaming in through the open doorway. At first she was just a dark form standing there, still and solemn. Slowly my eyes adjusted so I could see her face, shrouded in shadows. For a few breathless seconds the queen's expression was void of any signs of recognition.

Why had she come?

Then her stern face softened and her eyebrows lifted: she knew me. With a deep breath, I dared to span the distance between us until I stood directly in front of her. Neither of us spoke as we studied each other in the dim light.

I was startled to find that after years of having to stretch my neck to look up at my mother, I was now gazing down at her. Everything about her frame looked fragile and small. I was dismayed to see what changes four years had wrought upon her: her face was creased with wrinkles, her dark hair streaked with grey, and her eyes dim and sad. Even her posture was less powerful and poised. She looked stern and hard, yet fragile, like the smallest shove could loosen her grip on herself and she would finally give up and shatter.

Without warning, my throat burned with tears, but I held them back. I saw the queen glance over her shoulder, toward the guard.

"Leave us," she ordered him.

He walked down the corridor to give us space, his heavy boots thudding dully on the stone floor.

The queen turned to me. "So the news I hear from the guards is true. You came back." Her voice was soft and low. Was she relieved? Accusatory? Prepared to watch me be sentenced to death a second time?

Her eyes. They are so dark. At first I could not respond for fear of crying and my mouth trembled. Angry, I bit my lip to keep it steady. *How can you stand there and do nothing when your daughter is in prison?* I swallowed and managed to speak. "Yes." My voice was surprisingly firm.

She lifted her hand…slowly, slowly…and reached out toward me, as if to touch my cheek. At the last moment her hand wavered and her fingers brushed at my hood, sliding it back. Her eyes weren't as bright as they used to be; they were a faded green that reminded me of seaweed when it washed ashore and began to lose its color. She let her hand fall back to her side.

Our silence stretched on for minutes…hours…years.

Something inside me snapped and I dared to open my mouth, if only to whisper. "Mother." The word tasted foreign on my lips, sliding around on my tongue like a bittersweet flavor. I stopped, not knowing what to say next.

Her body stiffened and she stepped backward. "How dare you use that term to address *me*?" Tears sparkled in her eyes and her lips quivered as they twisted into a scowl. "My daughter, the princess, was banished four years ago when she chose to slander the king's name." The last word came out in a fierce whisper. No matter how angry she had been with me when I was a girl, I had never heard this much fury packed into her voice. "You are not my daughter. *She* would not betray her own father or plot with a band of rebels to murder him. You are nothing but a criminal."

My mind was numb, my mouth dry. I dropped my eyes to the floor, unable to meet her hard gaze any longer. The familiar pain of betrayal returned, coursing through every vein in my body, squeezing through every organ, threatening to consume me. I could not speak or think or even breathe; I could only feel.

Vaguely I was aware of my hands trembling at my sides while my mother spun on her heel and marched from the room. I forced my lungs to work—sucking air in, out, in, out—as I listened to the departing footsteps, as the light slowly drifted down the corridor. Leaving me in darkness again.

I sank to the floor, leaning my back against the stone wall and becoming increasingly aware of the emptiness surrounding me. A thousand thoughts and emotions whirled through me, the most prominent being anger. *She doesn't believe the king is a murderer.* My mind reeled. *She does not* know. *She does not know the king tried to execute me.*

But she had still betrayed me. She stood by the king when he "banished" me, and she didn't even question my imprisonment or execution now. She would let me die. *No mother should treat her daughter this way.* I squeezed my eyes shut against the blackness. *This isn't right.* The emotion grew—a raging fire towering higher, higher, higher—until it overwhelmed me and erupted in a scream.

My own voice sounded strange in my ears, piercing and wild and desperate as it echoed off the walls. My lungs gasped for air and my raw throat begged for relief before I finally let my cries fade into nothingness. After all my years of silence, my wordless shriek expressed more than an entire book could have. Yet at the same time, it said nothing. It did nothing. I was alone and helpless, without an escape. Still, the sound continued to ring in my ears, pierce my heart, and keep me company long after the quiet settled around me.

Exhausted, I pulled my knees to my chest and wrapped my arms around them. Whether I did it to try to shrink until I disappeared into the emptiness, or to pretend to hold myself together, I was not sure. Slowly I gave into tears. I let the sobs rack my body until I couldn't breathe and thought I would be ill. After what felt like hours, I curled up in the corner of my cell and managed to sink into a restless sleep.

It was impossible to tell how much time passed. In and out of nightmares, I opened and closed my eyes to the same unending blackness and stillness. Sometimes my dreams taunted me with visions of my mother returning to my cell and having compassion on me, as mothers were supposed to. Other times Avrik was my rescuer, regretting his decision and rushing to my aid like the heroes in books. But no matter what sleep brought, my greatest nightmares were my waking thoughts.

The pain of loss and abandonment was quickly driving away my fears until my worst fear was not to be executed, but to live. Where was the Giver of Life in this living death? Had he healed me in the woods just to lead me here, into isolation and despair? What good was I doing locked in a cell?

As time dragged on and the tears came and went, I began to hate myself, too. Despite the truth I carried, I had held it in all these years. When I could have spoken and perhaps spared others pain, I'd been silent. *What good are words if no one believes them?* I argued with myself, but I knew I was still to blame. *What good is a voice if I do not speak?*

In my prison cell I saw myself for what I was: selfish and cowardly. Maybe I deserved to suffer, like my people had. Maybe I deserved to be abandoned, just as I had abandoned my family and my kingdom. Maybe I deserved to die.

At great intervals, a guard would break the silence with his distant footsteps. I watched flickering torchlight dance along the walls outside my cell to herald his arrival. Without ceremony he would shove a tray through the gap beneath my cell door and stride away, leaving my ears ringing from the unusual noise.

I left the first few trays of food untouched. I felt sick to my stomach, not hungry. Burrowing my head into my cloak, I squeezed my eyes shut and tried to escape into unconsciousness again.

At some point I drifted off into a dream that was half-nightmare, half-memory. The details were as vivid as they had been the day the events happened, but some were wrong.

In my dream, I walked with my father along the beach, far below the castle, and listened to his stern voice rise over the sound of crashing waves. It was a day not long before my uncle's death, when whispers had begun to echo through the castle corridors about the possibility of a new king.

"There is a chance that you and I both will soon be holding a more prominent position in the public eye," the man before me was saying.

My breath caught in my throat and I stopped in my tracks. It was one thing to hear servants gossip together; it was another to hear my father say the words. Overhead, the gulls' cries sounded mournful, like notes to a tragic song. Even the sea and the wind spoke of loss. A thousand questions spun through my mind and slipped away just as quickly, vanishing into nothingness. There were no words.

I couldn't find my voice.

"It will be imperative that you obey me as both your father and sovereign, Halia," he went on. "I will be ensuring you learn proper behavior for someone of royal blood, someone who might take the throne someday."

I frowned as my father looked down at me. "Your cousin will be king when he comes of age," he explained, "as long as disaster or sickness does not strike him as well." His brow crinkled and he reached out to pat my shoulder. "These circumstances are not pleasant to consider, of course, but they are necessary to prepare for. One can never be too careful."

Aware of trembles running through my frame, I hugged myself in an attempt to keep warm until I realized I wasn't cold. A solitary tear crept down my cheek but I swiped it away. Father was not one to give way to expressions of weakness, and I knew he would think crying during a discussion about matters of state would be inappropriate for one of "royal blood." I hated to disappoint him.

I closed my eyes. In a few moments, I would be fine. *Don't think about it. Your uncle will be fine. Everything will be fine.*

But when I opened my eyes, the dream shifted and the memory transformed into a nightmare. The king was still looking down at me, but his expression was wrong. Instead of his usual firm gaze, he wore an accusatory one. His countenance was hard and unwavering, like the day I realized he was a murderer.

"How dare you betray me," he said. "How dare you speak words of treason against your father and sovereign! Who do you think you are, that anyone would ever listen to your wild ideas? You are no one. You're disowned, an outcast—you're less than a beggar on the streets. Your accusations are nothing but the imagination of a child, the words of a young brat against those of a king."

I tried to protest, but my throat filled with seawater. It burned my throat, my mouth, my lungs. I was mute; I was dying. When I opened my mouth to scream in anger and fear, nothing but water poured past my lips.

I woke gasping and coughing. Instinctively my fingers flew to my lips, but my mouth was parched and my throat felt like sandpaper. How long had I gone without drinking?

Slowly I settled back against the cold wall and tried to curl into a comfortable position. Rats skittered across my cell, exploring the tray of old food. Was it the third tray I'd ignored, or the fourth? I shivered, but the sounds of rats gnawing at my rations in the overwhelming quiet were impossible to ignore. There would be no more sleeping again for a long time.

Instead I lay motionless, staring into the darkness and hoping the rats wouldn't decide to gnaw on me next. *Giver of Life, do you also give death if someone asks for it?*

Memories came and went: moments with my father as he scolded me for behavior unsuited for a princess, hours with my mother as we read by the fireside or discussed my future. The memories were so far removed from me now they felt like they belonged to someone else. They'd occurred lifetimes ago, during a time when I'd known security. When I'd looked to the future, I looked to it with hope and purpose, knowing that as part of the royal family, I would be able to play a role in Misroth's welfare and maybe make my parents proud of me. Maybe even earn their love. There was no anticipation of the nightmare I was living.

Where was that important royal woman now, when I was on the floor of a prison cell, waiting to die?

Another age passed until I heard the guard's distant footsteps returning. As the torchlight flickered outside, the rats scattered.

"Push me your tray," a gruff voice demanded.

I lay there several moments, wondering if I cared enough to move. I could lie here and never move again. I could refuse to give my father the pleasure of executing me; I could stay here until death carried me away and I could stop feeling pain.

But the anger I'd felt in my nightmare still burned inside. How dare my father steal my life from me? How could I give up now, when speaking the truth was my only chance to give my short life some purpose before it ended?

I used my anger to strengthen me and push myself to my knees. Crawling across the rough stone, I shoved the tray through the gap beneath my door and received a new one. In a way it was good that my chunk of bread was hard and chewy, because it forced me to eat slowly. Even so, the beggar's meal disappeared all too quickly. My stomach felt emptier now than before I'd forced myself to eat.

But the weight of my despair had eased. Before my inevitable execution, I would make the world hear my voice. I didn't know how, but I was sure that somehow the Giver would offer me one last gift: an opportunity to speak.

I was sure days had passed when I finally heard two sets of footsteps approaching once again. Had they come to lead me away? Would they bring me before the king, or march me off to be executed immediately?

My heart pounded as I scrambled to my feet and waited for the torchlight to announce my visitors' arrival. When the steps stopped outside my door, I had to blink and squint to adjust to the light and make out the forms before me. One was a castle guard I did not recognize, holding a torch aloft. The other was the Captain of the Guard.

The guard opened my cell door and he and Narek entered. I remained at the back of the cell, pressed against the wall, refusing to move. I wanted to punch Narek's face, to force the smirk from his face, but I knew I would be no match for him in a physical fight, so I glowered instead.

"Come," Narek said. "The king desires to see you."

An icy feeling coursed through my veins as he and the other man shackled me and led me out of my prison cell. Our boots thudded dully on the slick stone and the torchlight cast eerie shadows along the walls.

I kept my posture straight and tall, walking like a true royal, as my father had always wanted me to. No matter what, I would never let the people who wanted me to break see how much damage they had inflicted.

Narek kept a heavy hand on my right shoulder as he guided me forward. I glanced toward him. "You have been slack with your interrogation responsibilities lately."

His face remained impassive, but his eyes were sharp. "Your father has not ordered for you to be interrogated. Yet."

As we wound through the corridors, uneasy thoughts coursed through my mind. Though I wasn't sure if I wanted to see my imprisoned friends or not, I didn't hear a sound or see a sign of occupants in any of the cells we passed. Fear scratched my throat, my heart. *No, they can't be dead. They can't...*

Anger fired through my veins. "How does it feel to have so much innocent blood on your hands?"

Narek clenched his fists, but didn't deign to answer. Still, that slight response was enough to make me smile in victory. In some small way, I had unsettled him.

We ascended the steps and the guard threw open the door, letting daylight pour into the stairwell and sting my eyes. I squinted and blinked against it while the men guided me through the castle, toward the Great Hall.

Guards stationed outside the Great Hall's double doors swung them wide and we swept in. My throat constricted as I took in the huge space. The marble floors sparkled beneath multiple chandeliers, and the ceilings were covered in dozens of hand painted murals depicting Misrothian history. Against the far wall, the king's and queen's thrones of elaborately carved dark wood gleamed in the blinding light. Adorned with the dragon Vehgar, set on a blue backdrop with a scarlet border, Misroth's flag hung behind the thrones. The right wall was one large window overlooking the castle gardens, full of only a few living plants layered in snow and ice.

Standing in a row before the thrones were the rebels, their wrists shackled and guards flanking each of them on either side. I could scarcely embrace the relief I felt, knowing it would be short-lived.

Narek brought me forward to join the row and face the thrones. The queen's was unoccupied, but my father lounged in his. His grey eyes were as piercing as I remembered them; his face, if more wrinkled, still held his typical strong, unwavering expression. He raised a shaggy eyebrow at me when I halted next to Jennah, the chains at my wrists clinking together.

"The prisoners, Your Highness," Narek announced, pressing his fist to his heart and bowing his head.

King Zarev nodded, studying us each thoughtfully. I dared to wrench my eyes from his face and turn toward my companions.

My heart froze as I took in their ragged appearances. Their faces were gaunt, with dark circles under their eyes and pain ravaging their expressions. A jagged, bloody line traced its way from Jennah's left temple to her chin. Gare's hands were fists, but he was missing two fingers from his right one. Benor had a bloody bandage wrapped about his head to cover his left eye, and tears in Layk's shirt revealed burns marring his skin.

Bile tingled along my tongue, but I choked it back, refusing to let the king see my reaction.

My father's lips, usually set firm and unyielding, twisted into something that almost resembled a smirk. "The motley rebel band, prepared to risk their lives to stand against the king. How bravely you withstand interrogations and refuse to compromise your fellow rebels' locations." He scratched his chin, where his black and grey beard shadowed his face.

His stare flicked to me. "And the long-lost princess, returned home at last, as a rebel."

I could feel the eyes of my companions boring into me. Drawing a deep breath, I clenched my jaw and tightened my fists in order to keep my body from trembling.

"I suppose we can't hope to glean any information from you, if you have withstood our attempts this long," Zarev mused. He turned to Narek and waved his hand dismissively. "Schedule a public execution. Make them an example to the people."

The guards began dragging the rebels from the Great Hall. Narek grasped my arm, pulling me back toward the doors with them, but I continued to stare at my father. "You *monster*," I growled. "How dare you, how dare—"

Narek backhanded me across the cheek, making black spots dance before my eyes. I stumbled backward, with only the captain to hold me up on my feet.

"Silence," he hissed, and dragged me from the room.

My cheek smarted and my eyes watered as he led me back through the halls and down into the dungeons. When we arrived at my cell, he removed my chains and shoved me in so roughly I fell onto the stone floor. Pulling myself up, I grunted in pain and glared at him over my shoulder, but he slammed the door. The keys jangled as he locked me in and stormed down the corridor.

The cold, dank space enveloped me once more. Away from the king's and captain's prying eyes, I allowed myself to release the tears that burned my throat.

More footsteps jerked me from a shallow sleep. A night could have passed, or days, for all I could tell. I shielded my eyes against the torchlight as a guard unlocked my door and swung it open, letting Narek enter.

"The executions are scheduled for tomorrow morning," he said, without greeting or ceremony. His face was as stony as ever.

I swallowed, trying to fight the rising panic. The silence settled heavily in the small space until he spoke again.

"You should prepare yourself."

He took a step back, and his movement returned me to reality.

I raised my head and met his stare again. "So it will not be drowning?" My voice was low, full of all the anger that fueled my strength. "Like the way you and my *father* tried to murder me when I was thirteen?"

Although his face remained a mask, he blinked and hesitated before his eyes narrowed. "No. These days we publicly execute our criminals, but you already know that, since you and your comrades were so eager to stop our executions of late. As the king said, you will be an example to the people."

I looked away, staring off into the shadows of my cell.

Narek withdrew and his man shut the door with a clang. Without another word, they left, abandoning me to darkness.

The emotions rose up to greet me, my only companions in the blackness. Sadness. Anger. Fear. They pressed in from all sides, and I shut my eyes tightly, as if that could block them out.

Giver of Life, give me words. Don't let me die without speaking.

If I had to die, I would die sharing the truth.

CHAPTER SIXTEEN

I WAITED FOR DEATH. IT felt surreal, pacing the cell floor, thinking a million thoughts. What would life have been like, if Truth had never come to me? If I had remained ignorant of the king's crimes all these years? Would I be married through a royal arrangement by now? I shuddered at the thought. Would I have discovered what the king had done…and would I have kept that dark secret to myself without a curse that forced me to speak?

My mind drifted to the new path my life had taken. What if I had stayed in Evren, never to return? Once I'd believed I would live there the rest of my life, nestled in a lonely valley far from the king's reaches. I found joy in the freedom of wandering the hills alone or with Avrik, unaccompanied by guards and unrestricted by the rules of royal conduct. I had responsibilities, but there was something wholesome about a hard day's work of cooking, cleaning, or planting. There was the possibility of peace at home and adventure in traveling, because I'd dared to dream of someday helping Avrik trade goods in other cities.

I wondered what it would feel like to die. Would it hurt much? Would the stranger, the Giver, come for me again and lead me to the mysterious world that lay beyond death? My head pounded and my hands grew clammy as I rolled these questions around in my head, inspecting them from every angle.

In the long hours that passed, I prayed and feared. I walked in circles; I paced; I huddled in a corner. I let anger consume me, followed closely by anger's shadowy cousin: despair.

The people I left behind didn't even know who I was, and now I would never have the chance to explain. I longed to be able to tell Lyanna and Rev goodbye, to see friends like Bren and Shilam one more time. I ached for the familiar places of Evren that I would never see again.

When the guard finally brought my next meal, he announced it was my last. I rolled the bread between the palms of my hands as I considered this would be the last food I would ever taste. Cringing, I pushed back the fear that tugged at my stomach and forced myself to chew a couple bites until I realized there was no point in choking it down. I wouldn't need food where I was going.

Exhausted, with no more energy left to feel or think, I huddled against the wall and waited.

It seemed like moments later when footsteps stopped outside my cell again. Keys jangled as a guard unlocked my door and swung it open. I squinted as torchlight flooded the tiny space.

"Up, prisoner. It's time," a gruff voice announced.

I had no reason to resist. Brushing strands of hair from my face, I stood. Two guards stepped into my cell to grasp my arms, chain my wrists before me again, and lead me out. I frowned at their unfamiliar faces. Where was Narek when I wanted to punch him in the face before I died?

They guided me through the dungeon passageways and up the steps toward the main floor of the castle. When we reached the top and they shoved the door open, the daylight was almost blinding. My eyes watered as we traced our way through numerous hallways, toward the castle grounds. We passed servants who averted their gaze or stopped and stared, and I wondered if they had any idea who I was. Each time I stared openly at them, studying their features to see if I could find any familiar faces among them, but I knew no one. Whenever they met my searching look, they quickly lowered their heads and my vague hopes disappeared. Had my father hired an entirely new staff in the past four years? My stomach plummeted when I imagined what had happened to the previous servants.

As we drew near the main doors, one of the servants stepped out in front of us to block our path. He hesitated and cleared his throat, forcing the men behind me to stop. "Her Majesty requests to speak with the prisoner."

The guards' grip on my arms tightened. "This is highly unusual," one muttered.

"Do you wish to disobey your queen?"

Grunting, the guards followed the servant's lead, pushing me through a doorway to the right. I knew the room immediately: one of the dozens of small studies open to anyone in the castle, unlike the king's large personal library. There before me were the floor-to-ceiling windows overlooking the sea that gave the illusion one was standing directly over the water, the view that had made me giddy as a child. Near the back of the room, by the windows, was the door that led to further rooms deeper in the castle: sitting rooms, conference rooms, endless rooms and hallways. On my left and right, the walls were covered in shelves, filled with books I'd spent hours browsing through, to my cousin Gillen's ultimate boredom. Here before me was the old desk I'd hidden under more than once in our games of hide-and-seek. And right beside me was the old statue of Berye, one of the past kings of Misroth, that Gillen and I pretended was a villain with his sword extended to attack us.

As the guards paused, still clutching me tightly, I turned back toward the windows and the silhouette gazing out at the tranquil sea, its waves awash with the pale light of dawn.

I blinked against the light as the servant stepped forward, bowed, and announced, "The prisoner, Your Highness."

"Leave us alone," the queen ordered without turning. Her rich blue dress fell in silky folds about her feet, glittering with hundreds of silver stars embroidered into the skirt and bodice. As always, her hair was pulled back in elegant plaits and her head was lifted high. Yet for all her usual poise, the dress appeared to swallow her small form and, almost imperceptibly, her shoulders stooped.

My heart beat heavily in my chest, making the men's footsteps and the clang of the door dull in my ears. I waited until the queen turned to me and then I forced my legs to move forward. It wasn't until then that I realized I'd been holding my breath; I exhaled slowly, releasing some of the tension inside.

Once again, the silence was oppressive. The queen's face was pale and her eyes—dare I believe it?—seemed softer than before. There was a light in them that I remembered from years ago, a light that had sparked in her gaze whenever she looked at me. Was my mother still in there, somewhere?

This time I had to speak.

"How can you stay here?" My voice broke with the tension of a hundred unshed tears tightening my throat. "The king is a tyrant. Do you not believe your own daughter? You have to *do* something and save the kingdom…save *me*."

The pain on her face transformed into anger, and then confusion. She searched my expression like she could find answers there, and it seemed that the wrinkles on her face multiplied. She shook her head, slowly at first, then more insistently. "You are wrong. You still spread treacherous rumors." Tears sparkled in her eyes.

I could have thrown myself at her feet. *How can you believe his lies? Why don't you see?* I wanted to scream my questions, but I could not cause a scene for fear of the guards overhearing, and I couldn't anger her for fear of losing all chance of reasoning with her. All I could do was repeat the truth, feeding it to her in small doses. "You are not content," I insisted. "The king is using his power to oppress our people, and he is publicly executing innocent citizens in the streets. He has begun a war to extend his kingdom and his power, and Gillen is risking his life because of his greed. All of this suffering is unnecessary, wrong! We need to stop this. *You* can stop him."

Her arms hung limply at her sides and her face was empty. As she took another step toward me, her brow furrowed and her eyes glistened. I watched her mouth move soundlessly, and she reached her hand out to touch my arm. This time, she would not hold back from me. Would she?

Her hand hung in the air, fingers shaking as indecision overtook her once more.

"Even if you believe the king's lies—that I hate you and have joined criminals in order to murder you both—remember Gillen's goodness," I pleaded. "No one has accused him of betrayal, yet look at the price he is paying. He is serving in a needless war, when he should be here, claiming his throne."

The queen's face was pale, her eyes wild with conflicting emotions. "He is fighting to protect us! He is serving his kingdom."

"Please…" My voice was almost a whimper, and I hated how it sounded in my ears. "I am your daughter. Does that mean nothing to you?"

Her lips trembled. No—her whole body was shaking. "You ask me to choose between my husband and my daughter?"

Anger blazed in my heart. "No," I said, my voice firm. "Your husband already forced that choice on you when he sentenced me to death! I ask you to choose between his lies and the truth!"

My mother's eyes widened, flickering with pain and confusion. "Sentence you to death? No, he would not kill you, no matter what you did." She shook her head as if trying to convince herself. "H-he told me you are being escorted out of the kingdom, to be banished. Exiled as you were before…" She gulped and her voice began to tremble as her confidence wavered. "He would not…lie to me?"

I stared at her. He had been feeding her lies all this time, lies she still believed. How many long years had he used and manipulated her? If I could encourage the doubt I had instilled in her a bit more…

A sound jerked her away and snapped my eyes to the back of the room, to the entrance near the window. With a rustle of robe and a stride that beat out a perfect rhythm on the wood floorboards, the king appeared.

My heart dropped. *He heard.*

"Halia," he greeted. A grin spread across his face—a grin that said, *Here you are, at last.* "It has been so long…" He stopped behind the queen and reached with his left hand to grasp her shoulder. "Ryn, my dear, after your support and faith in me all these years, how can you summon this traitor to listen to her counsel? Now she will be late to her own *execution.*"

She turned to him, a protest forming on her lips, but her eyes widened and her body stiffened. A small gasp escaped her lips as blood seeped through the front of her dress, drowning the silver stars in red. The king wrenched his right arm back and I saw the curved dagger he clutched, long and dripping with blood. With a careless toss, he let it clatter to the floor while the queen toppled forward.

Chains clanking around my wrists, I caught her in my arms. Trembling, I kneeled and cradled the woman who had once cradled me. Her body was as light as it looked, a limp form bleeding out onto my clothes. As she stared up into my face I felt tears collecting, blurring my vision until one splashed onto her cheek.

A gurgling sound rose from her throat; her lips could hardly form whatever words she was trying to say. "I…I…" Her voice faded and her mouth moved soundlessly in a message I could not translate.

My breath caught in my lungs, and I couldn't speak. There was nothing I could do but watch the life slip from her eyes. With one final spasm, her mouth ceased fighting to move and her gaze became unfocused, looking through me to somewhere far beyond. I couldn't rip my eyes from her, even when more tears blinded me, even when the sight made me want to vomit and scream all at once. Her form was pitiful, limp and faded where once she had been beautiful and regal, like a wilted flower abandoned and trampled.

I laid the queen down on the cold floor. The blood pooling beneath her made my stomach churn, but I brushed her eyelids closed and stood, drawing in a deep breath and bracing myself. I felt my fingertips, warm and sticky with my mother's blood, tremble at my sides, ready to strike. Ready to fight back.

A shadow moved between the white light streaming through the window and the queen's form. I lifted my face to stare back at the king, the man I'd once longed to make proud, the man I'd wanted to love me.

"It's a shame to have to kill her; she believed everything I ever told her." His gaze rested indifferently on the queen's face before settling on me. "But once you are dead, the rumors of your return will spread beyond the castle walls and the entire kingdom will hear of the hapless rebel princess. Do you think perhaps your mother loved you enough to consider defying me, once she realized I'd killed you?"

With a shrug, the king kicked the dagger with the toe of his boot, sending the blade skidding beneath the desk.

I snapped.

Snarling, I lunged like an animal, colliding with him squarely and forcing him off his feet. We toppled to the floor with my knees lodged in his chest. Even with a chain dangling between my wrists, restricting my movements, I still felt stronger than the aged man beneath me. He opened his mouth to choke for air and I pressed my knees in harder. *Let him know what it's like to suffocate*, a voice inside me prompted. As I gazed into his wide eyes, I imagined that if I only pressed my weight down harder, I could crush his body. I could break him. My fury was so hot and thick I could taste the sweetness of revenge on my tongue, and it was intoxicating.

With one deep gasp, he caught his breath and gained his voice. "Help! Murder!"

Guards threw open the doors and dashed toward me. One of the men wrenched me from the king while two more restrained me.

Others rushed to the king's side to help him up. He gasped, brushing off his robes and glaring at me. His voice feigned fury. "This wretch has murdered the queen!" he announced to his men, stabbing a finger toward the body. "She stole my dagger and, like the animal she is, she slew my wife. Take this prisoner to her execution, immediately!" He flung the words at me like he could pierce me with them. As if he could destroy me again.

"No!" I screamed with all the rage of betrayal, with all the fear of imminent death, with all the horror and sadness of loss. Tears streamed freely down my face and loose strands of my hair clung to my wet cheeks. "How dare you...how..." My words were lost in sobs while I broke down, my whole body shaking as I collapsed to my knees again.

"She's a lunatic," the king said, his eyes turning cold and his voice becoming low and even once more. "Take her away."

This was not how I was supposed to die. I was supposed to stand up against the king and speak the truth. I was not supposed to let him win. But my mind was consumed with emotion, and all I could do was try to wrench myself free of the guards.

I looked up and met the king's eyes: they were ice, silently daring me to say more. I hung my head, biting my lip; this was not the audience I wanted.

The guards led me from the room and stormed down the hall, pausing at the front to wait for two men to open them. We pounded through the main courtyard, through the gate, and into the grounds. The sun was creeping over the horizon, glaring down at me and sparkling on a fresh blanket of snow. The cold air snapped me back to my senses and stopped my tears.

The guards' grasp on my arms dug into my skin a we wound our way past empty flowerbeds and the skeletons of leafless trees, by stone statues weatherworn and solemn, by a few brave flowers pushing through the snow and stretching toward the sun. The descent into the city was a blur.

Time was running through my fingers, out of my grasp. No matter how empty I felt, no matter how much I had longed for death in prison, I did not truly want to die. Not yet. The longing to survive and the fear of death pulsed through my veins with every step I took. Feverishly, I begged the Giver to hear me once more. *I suppose it's too much to ask for another miracle, but if you could give me my life…*

The walk through Misroth was eerily quiet. There was no recognition on the faces of the citizens lined along the streets when we marched through the city. They were cold and silent, watching me with eyes almost as lifeless as my mother's had been. I shuddered and shoved the thought away, closing my eyes to block out the memory. If the people hated the king's sentence on my life, no one was protesting. If they agreed, no one was celebrating. There was a calm familiarity with the proceedings. I was merely one more execution in a long string of public deaths. If the king had his way, I would be forgotten by sunset.

We rounded the last turn and the execution stage, resting in the shadow of Eldon's statue, came into view. Near the edge lay the chopping block where I would soon be resting my neck. The executioner himself stood nearby, leaning on his axe and gazing at the eastern sky, alight with brilliant shades of orange and pink. As the first rays of sunlight leapt past the horizon and glanced off the rooftops, I was nearly blinded.

I averted my gaze and concentrated on my boots as I took each step: *one, two, one, two…* I tried to forget what I was walking toward.

"Move aside!" the guards shouted, their voices ringing harshly in my ears and echoing in the stillness. We began wading through the gathering crowd, the people moving to give us a wide berth.

As we pressed closer to the stand, I noticed a row of prisoners, bound and despondent, lined beside it: my rebel friends from Marke's shop. Jennah caught my eye and shook her head as if to say, "I'm sorry we failed you."

The crowd murmured around me, hundreds of Misrothians whispering about the rebels' upcoming deaths. I glanced up and saw an elderly man nudge the woman at his side and point to something behind me. When I tried to look over my shoulder, the guards slammed their hands into my back to knock me forward.

"Mother, Mother, is the king coming?" a boy to my left asked.

"King Zarev himself at the execution? Is this girl someone important?" a man asked. "Are these five important leaders of the rebellion?"

So that was what had captured their interest. The king had come to watch me die.

I tightened my hands into fists. With a deep breath I lifted my chin and stared straight ahead, refusing to flinch at the sight of the chopping block. The king would not see me cower at the thought of death. I was not the timid little girl he remembered.

The talk around me continued as the crowd parted, staring back at the king and then at me, but I refused to remove my gaze from the stand. With each step I took, the executioner eyed me with an intensity I couldn't read: was he eager to slay the rebel traitors? Did he enjoy his work? I met his gaze without wavering, holding my jaw firm.

I knew there were tracks running down my cheeks from where my tears had mingled with smudges of dirt. I knew my hair fell in tangles past my shoulders and my dress was covered in prison filth and dried blood. I knew my form was thin, my face pale, and my eyes shadowed by dark circles. I knew I probably looked wild and unintimidating, but I refused to look weak.

The wooden steps creaked as I climbed my way to the top of the platform. My heart throbbed in my ears and my legs trembled when I stopped and the guards spun me around to face the crowd filling the city square. Far in the back, the king's procession approached. First came his escort on royal stallions, led by Captain Narek, followed by the king himself and several more guards bringing up the rear. They pressed through the people and paused near the back of the crowd, overlooking the whole scene.

The king needs a royal seat for the show. The thought made my anger flare into rage, but I would not lose control now.

All around, the voices stopped and a breathless quiet descended like mist upon the square. I scanned the people's expressions in vain for a sign of sympathy: there was only curiosity and fear. The only sounds I heard were the horses stomping and snorting impatiently and the wooden planks groaning as one of the king's guard, a heavy-set man, ascended the steps and faced the people.

"Good citizens of Misroth!" His voice was piercing in the stillness as it echoed off the surrounding buildings. "We are here today to witness the execution of a highly dangerous criminal and enemy of the state."

Highly dangerous. Maybe my fear was turning into hysteria, but the idea of being highly dangerous amused me. With layers of dirt and sweat on my cheeks, it took an effort to smile and felt like my skin was cracking.

The man's voice droned on. Were they truly planning to behead me, or was my punishment this long, dull speech? I smiled to myself until my gaze fell upon the king. He stared back at me, his eyes silver and merciless, and my stomach dropped.

I cannot let him win. Even if I must die today, I can't let my father win.

But my time was growing short.

Hands on my shoulders jerked me back into the present. The guards shoved me across the platform, toward the chopping block. I wanted to shout that I was innocent and the king was evil, but I felt like my breath had been stolen from my lungs.

All of my stubborn thoughts of dying with dignity melted away. Dignity was for the weak—I was full of fury. Even though I knew I wasn't strong enough to resist the men, I froze and planted my feet, digging my heels in. They squeezed my arms tighter and dragged me forward.

Leaning on his axe, the executioner's face was impassive. Even though I didn't want to look, morbid curiosity pulled my eyes away from his expression and to the blade he was using as a cane. It seemed smaller than I expected it to be. *What if it doesn't cut through the first time? Will he have to…chop again?* Bile rose to my mouth.

Behind me, the guards kicked my legs, forcing me to my knees. The boards groaned under my weight, a weary sigh. Maybe they were tired of the king's tyranny too.

I wondered how just a short period of time could feel like an eternity. The crowd was motionless, as if every person in the city was holding his or her breath with me. *Are there any rebels left willing to intercede? Doesn't anyone know this is wrong?*

But the people before me were strangers, bystanders refusing to stand up to the king the way the rebels and I had. No one was here to save my friends and me. We were alone.

Wind rushed against my face and blew wisps of hair into my eyes, and the guards shoved my head down until I was sprawled out uncomfortably on the chopping block. It was cold against my cheek.

I closed my eyes, trying to imagine away this place. In my mind, I was back in Evren with my real family, the ones who loved me. I was gardening with Lyanna or preparing dinner with her as I waited eagerly for Rev to come home for the evening. I was practicing archery with Avrik, trading competitive quips as we fought to outdo each other. I was…

My thoughts shattered when I heard the executioner's heavy trod; listened to the guards step back; waited as my heart crashed against my chest. It thudded out the seconds I had left to live.

Fight, Halia. It wasn't a voice; it was a thought. But was it my own, or was the Life-Giver speaking to me again at last? I couldn't tell.

If I tried to escape, I would never make it far. I knew the armed guards stood directly behind me. And I imagined that the execution would be less painful than what the guards' wrath could inflict if I defied them.

I tried to block out the sound of the executioner shifting his weight as he prepared to lift his weapon.

Now would be a good time for the man from the woods to return, I thought.

In my mind's eye I could see my father's smug face, his growing sense of victory as he snuffed out another threat to his throne. *Do not let him win.*

Anger throbbed through my veins. Did I come all this way to die?

The executioner grunted as he lifted his axe.

Say something, Halia. Speak!

The scream building inside me escaped. It was a cry of defiance, fear, and anger. It was a plea for life and a second chance from the One who had already saved me once. It was a shout for justice in the face of my pointless death. But it only came out in one feeble, desperate protest: "No!"

The word tore at my throat and sounded pathetic, like a whimper. But the sound of my own voice gave me strength. I tried again. "No!" This time the sound rang out in the stillness and echoed off the buildings.

I was aware of the executioner's swinging motion above me, how he faltered. Caught in the momentum of his swing, his axe plummeted downward in a jerk. The blade slammed into the wood inches from my left ear.

"Idiot!" the speaker bellowed. The words sounded distant through the ringing in my ears. "Don't let her trick you into pitying her. Give this criminal what she deserves!"

I was already moving, rolling myself off the chopping block and away from the executioner.

A guard was behind me, snagging my elbow and dragging me back toward the block. "How far did you think you would get?" he jeered in my ear, his hot breath brushing my neck and sending a shiver of disgust through my body.

Wrenching away, I kicked at his knee. His leg buckled beneath him and his fingers slipped from my arm. I jumped backward as a second guard pounded across the platform. Despite every instinct screaming at me to run and try to survive, I stood my ground.

"The king is the true traitor!" I cried. My throat was raw, my voice hoarse.

"Blasphemy!" the speaker barked, jabbing a finger toward me.

As I spun around to face the crowd, I saw shock register on their faces. The people went silent to hear my words. "He's a murderer!"

The guards were on either side of me now, dragging me to the chopping block and forcing me down on my knees. *This is it.* The realization struck me like an actual blow.

Words failed me. My gaze settled on the king, staring me down, daring me to speak again before the axe fell. The dream I'd had in my prison cell mocked me and the king's taunting voice rang inside my head: *Who do you think you are, that anyone would listen to you?*

"No." The quiet voice snapped me to the present. Above me, the executioner was shaking his head; the axe remained buried in the chopping block. The word was calm, but firm and powerful. "No," he repeated.

"You dare defy the king?" the speaker shrieked.

"I have never hesitated to kill traitors and rebels posing threats to our kingdom," the executioner said, "but I will not slay a girl. What threat could she possibly hold over the king?"

The people's voices rose like a storm building on the sea.

Hope nestled in my chest. I could survive. I could speak the truth to this crowd, and—

Raging pain bit into my back, all the way through my abdomen, and I lowered my head to see the tip of a sword protruding from my stomach. My scream died in my throat. A patch of blood spread across my chest and ran down the front of my dress. It covered my mother's dried blood; it covered everything with an overwhelming shade of red. Blood—my own blood was everywhere.

I heard a blade clatter to the floor and one of the guards stomp toward me. He leaned in close. "Let's hear you scream out your blasphemies against the king now, you worthless traitor."

The ringing in my ears was loud…loud…louder…so that I could barely make out his words. His face swam as he retreated. My head spun and my hands shook. I felt like I was falling, descending into a bottomless chasm, but I was still kneeling on the platform, unable to move. A shimmering mist quivered before my vision and an icy sensation washed over me. Darkness crowded at the edges of my vision, slowly but surely devouring me within its endless blackness. The fact pierced through my shock and screamed itself at me:

I'm dying.

CHAPTER SEVENTEEN

COUGHING, I GASPED AGAIN FOR air but choked on my own blood. I felt it trickle down my mouth and tasted it on my lips. My heartbeat slowed, thudding heavily against my chest as it pumped my lifeblood into a pool beneath me.

Numbness spread through my body and steadily dulled my feelings—my body's way of coping with the pain. Numbness preparing me for death.

In the distance, the king's voice shouted at me: "How dare you betray me! This is what you deserve. You are *nothing*!"

Or was his voice only in my head? The wrathful words didn't sound like the cold, calculating man I'd once called father, though they chilled me all the same. I closed my eyes; I felt myself fading—falling, falling... By some miracle, I found the strength to catch myself.

But it wasn't my own strength. I became aware of warmth embracing me, overtaking the cold. The warmth was coming from a pair of arms wrapped gently around me, catching my fall and holding me close.

The sound of a man weeping rose above the ringing in my ears, and I opened my eyes to see the man from the woods. Tears leaked down his cheeks and his mouth curved in such deep agony that I was overwhelmed.

But why now, when it was too late? Why hadn't he come sooner and saved me like he had before?

I waited for the crowds to shout in surprise. I waited for him to leap to his feet and defend himself from the attacks that would surely come against anyone who would dare comfort the traitor as she died. He had appeared beside me so suddenly, without any resistance from the king's men. How…? And then I knew: he was here only for me to see. In my final, fading seconds, he had arrived to lead me into the next life.

But I hadn't accomplished what I set out to do, and I was not ready to leave. Although I couldn't hear the king anymore, I knew he was gloating; my defeat was his victory.

I am his daughter. This is all wrong. Speak!

I coughed; I gasped; I struggled to force the words from my mouth.

"This is wrong." It was a croak, barely audible even to me. I tried to draw breath again, and this time I was surprised to find it easier. Air rushed into my lungs, and without thinking, I shouted, "No matter what he tells you, the king is a liar and a murderer!"

It felt like I was looking through a scope, staring at a distant scene of Misrothians gazing back at me. No one moved, and the air seemed impossibly still.

Though I couldn't see him clearly, I addressed my father. "How dare you, the king, execute an innocent citizen?" My trembling voice gained strength. Strength and a feeling brazenly close to hope pulsed through my veins. It was as if my body, while it drained of blood, was being filled with fire instead. "How dare *you*—my father—kill your own wife and your *brother*? Or your own *daughter*?"

Gasps rose from the people, but I didn't care about their reaction. All I wanted to do was tell them the truth and stop the king from snuffing out any more innocent lives.

I found the king, still at the back of the crowd, and settled my gaze on him. With a deep breath, I unleashed my torrent of words, the words I had held back for far too long. "Yes, I am Halia, princess and daughter of King Zarev and Queen Ryn, and niece of the former King Reylon. My uncle did not die a natural death." My heart thudded steadily against my chest and I felt renewed. Perhaps I was somehow borrowing strength from the man holding me up. "King Zarev forfeited his brother's trust and slipped poison into his drinks. He murdered King Reylon to take the throne. When I discovered this, my father sentenced me to death to cover his crime, but I escaped."

I drew another deep breath and found I was no longer choking on blood. How was my voice so strong? I pressed onward, desperate to share the truth before it was too late, before the king's men stopped me forever.

"All of these years you have believed the king's lies and let him tyrannize you. You've been ensnared by a false king, and you've accepted his greed and cruelty."

My firm gaze swept the crowd, scanning faces and reading emotions. Confused and awestruck, the citizens stared back at me in silence. In that moment it seemed as if the whole world had stopped to hear me.

Would they accept my message? Did they believe my words?

Giver of Truth, let them see.

The numbness that had enveloped my body was fading and I felt pain stabbing through me again. I couldn't give up now. I pushed through the pain; I pushed through the fear.

The silent princess would never be silent again.

"How can you listen to this madness?" screamed the speaker. "Kill her!"

The dumbfounded guards drew their weapons as one, but a few of them looked hesitant. Would they execute their princess? Which royal leader would they defy?

My voice was still strong. "How can you live enslaved to lies now that you know the truth?"

As I stared at the guards, I realized my vision had cleared and the darkness was retreating. The world spun and I was thankful again that the man's strong arms were keeping me from falling. Then the dizziness passed.

People were gasping and pointing. Fear jolted through me. Could they see the Life-Giver now? Would the guards attack him? No—they were not looking in his direction. They were looking…at me?

I glanced down at my stomach. My wound was gone. In its place, beneath my tattered clothes, ran a long, white scar. My heartbeat was a solid, heavy rhythm pounding in my head, and there was no more pain, no more numbness. I would have even questioned the fact that mere moments ago I had been dying—or dead—if not for my scar and the blood still pooled on the platform beneath me.

How…?

Shocked, I turned to look at the man beside me, but he was gone.

With a deep breath, I slowly pushed to my feet. Renewed strength and energy charged through my being.

The citizens were shouting, crying out in awe and fear and anger.

I dared to look at the king again. For the first time, uncertainty leaked into his eyes.

"You were dying!" the speaker was shouting in a mixture of fury and disbelief. "You—you should be dead!"

My eyes never left my father's. Around him, his mounted guard drew their own weapons and turned to him, awaiting orders.

He pointed with his blade. "Kill her! Kill all of the prisoners!"

Despite all I had been through, despite the fact that I was weaponless, I felt stronger than I had ever felt in my life.

The executioner yanked a set of keys from a nearby guard, who didn't even speak in protest. He unlocked the chains on my wrists and handed me the keys. Turning, I lifted the sword lying behind me, the one still covered in my blood, and faced the guards lined up behind me.

I sank into a fighting stance while they stormed toward me, but the executioner swung his axe in response, blocking their path. "Go!" he cried to me.

As the king's mounted men charged the stand, forcing the frenzied crowd into turmoil, I raced down the steps toward my rebel friends.

Before I could even aid him, Gare took one of the guards by surprise, swinging his chained arms around the man's neck and pulling the chain taut against his throat until the man began to turn purple. He strained against Gare's hold, but he was no match for Gare's strength and his arms soon fell slack at his sides.

Another guard swung his blade in an arc toward my head, stopping my progress toward my friends as I spun and parried. With a cry, he began an onslaught of strikes, slashing and stabbing with all the grace and strength a member of the Royal Guard possessed. But I was ready. I dodged and blocked, ducked and leapt, matching each of his attacks with my own swift defensive moves until I saw my opening and, with a flick of my wrist, twisted my blade after another block and sliced his hand. It was a small cut, but it was first blood, and the guard's wide eyes and red cheeks proved he was startled and furious.

I wasted no time taking pleasure in my small victory. Before he could tighten his grip on his sword or lift his eyes from his wound, I launched my attack. Gripping the hilt and letting the adrenaline in my veins take over, I stabbed him in his chest. Blood burst from the wound even with the blade still embedded in his heart. He gasped, but the noise died in his throat in a strangling sound and he crumpled forward. I yanked my blade back just in time to leap away and clear space for his body.

My heart was somewhere in my throat and my breath came in rapid bursts; my blood was fire and ice at the same time. There was no time to feel horror or remorse as I clutched the sword hilt, my hand slick with sweat, and dashed toward the other rebels, who were holding their own in the fight even in their bonds.

Gare had stolen a set of keys from one of the guards and undone his and Layk's cuffs. Nearby with her hands still bound, Jennah kicked a guard in the crotch before he could unsheathe his own weapon, and he crumpled in pain just long enough for her to grasp the hilt instead. Snarling, the guard swung a fist at her face, but Jennah ducked and Gare was there to kick at the guard again, smashing his heavy boot into the man's knee. There was a sickening pop and the guard fell with a scream, clutching at his leg. Gare drew the fallen guard's sword and ended his cries with a swift slice of the blade.

Wielding a stolen blade, Layk was locked in a fight with another guard. Gare and I made quick work of Benor's and Jennah's cuffs while two of the guards, their loyalties wavering, dropped their weapons and vanished into the running crowds. Scrambling, Benor and Jennah armed themselves with the forsaken swords and turned to face the charging king and his men.

The square was almost empty of citizens, who had fled to avoid being trampled underfoot or caught in the midst of the growing battle. The king and his loyal guards formed a semicircle around our rebel group while we retreated to the execution stand to gain higher ground. With their swords raised high, I realized that they were prepared to take their time in killing us all and enjoy stifling this last great attempt of the rebellion. The king probably assumed that once he massacred us, the rebels would be too discouraged and frightened to form another grand resistance.

We are beaten, I thought. *Life-Giver, you saved me only for me to watch my kingdom fall.*

A lone arrow soared through the air, striking a mounted guard in the chest and knocking him from his beast. I peered over my shoulder to see another guard crouched on a nearby rooftop, taking aim against the onslaught of the king's men. Around the square, more guards, armed citizens, and men and women I recognized as rebels raised their swords and bows and pointed their weapons toward the advancing men.

"To the princess!" someone cried, and more voices took up the call.

With a great cry, guards and citizens and rebels all clashed together.

Some of the guards encircled the stand on their horses and swung from their saddles, while others leapt from their steeds to face us on the platform. A mounted guard swung at me, only to be stopped by another arrow. I glanced around—the rebels were gathering around me, driving back enemies before they could approach me. They were protecting *me.*

"Enough!" I shouted. At first, my voice was lost in the tumult of battle. "*Enough!*" My cry echoed off the buildings around me, making the king pull back on his reins and glance up at me with a vicious smile, perhaps assuming I was prepared to surrender. I stared him down unflinchingly, hoping the fire showed in my eyes. "This is the king's fight with *me.* If he truly wants to prove himself, he will tell his men to stand down and he will face me alone."

Every horse froze at commands from their masters, and all around us, a heavy silence fell. I could almost feel the tension, confusion, and fear emanating from both sides. The king's men glanced at their sovereign for an order. At the king's side, Narek raised his eyebrows in mild surprise and shifted in his saddle. His blade was drawn yet clean, still gleaming in the early light, and I had to clamp down my anger. *You sit back with the king and watch your men kill for you.*

The king sat motionless on his steed and stared at me with an inscrutable expression. The wind ruffled his hair about his shoulders as he swiped a hand through his dark beard and curved his lips into a leisurely smile.

Slowly, he dismounted and walked to the center of the square, behind the execution stand and under the shadow of King Eldon's statue, staring unmoved at the scene before him. "I do not fear a ragged band of rebels." His voice boomed in the square until his presence seemed to take up half of the space; his aura still spoke of power and his loyal members of the guard still watched him with deference. He flicked his eyes to me and his face blazed with intensity. "Much less one frail girl."

"I know you do not fear me," I whispered. "But you *do* fear the one who saved my life, because it means you do not have his blessing. And that means something to the people of Misroth."

His eyes narrowed, but he did not speak as he drew his sword.

With my heart throbbing everywhere but in my chest, I descended the steps, each creaking beneath my feet. There was no other sound in the square but my own breath, my own footsteps. Chin raised, sword lifted high, I approached my father.

CHAPTER EIGHTEEN

A S SOON AS I WAS within range, the king arced his blade in one smooth motion toward my neck. I barely had time to parry, and the force of his strike made me stagger backward. My opponent lost no time in taking advantage of my weakness. He began an onslaught of strikes, sweeping down toward my legs, my midsection, and my sword arm. I matched each with a swift block or dodge, bracing my arms and feet for each strike as steel clanged on steel.

Against my will, I heard Avrik's voice echoing in my head: *Block, block! Don't let your opponent overwhelm you with sheer force. He might be stronger than you, but you are faster and more agile. Let him revel in his strength, but don't let him sweep you off your feet before you can show off your own skills. Wait and let him grow overconfident…but don't wait too long.*

I dodged and parried, letting the king get near but never near enough to end the fight. He swung with heavy, skilled strokes, each swipe of his blade crashing against mine with jarring force. He had decades of experience against me; I had sheer strength of will, dexterity, and speed. My pulse pounded in my ears, sweat slithered down my back, and my arm ached, yet I was still faster than the king. Adrenaline sent newfound strength through my body and I was light on my feet, my steps smooth and graceful, my eyes alert for every movement of my father's. I twisted, leapt, sidestepped, and spun—anything to keep him moving, to wear him down, or to take him by surprise.

Taunt him. Tease him. He'll grow frustrated thinking that a little girl that shouldn't know how to fight is escaping his reach. Let the anger muddle his mind.

Create an advantage for yourself.

Again, the king swung his sword and I side-stepped. Despite his attempts to conceal his emotions, I could see the angry fire growing in his eyes.

"You do not know how to wield a sword," he protested.

I smirked. "I haven't lived with you for four years. You do not know what I can and cannot do."

He stabbed at my stomach, but I swung my sword faster and brought it down hard toward his hand. It bit deep into his flesh. He grunted, exchanging hands and glancing in disbelief at his bleeding wrist.

"You have no hope," he said. But for once, his voice shook and sweat dribbled down his temples. Framed in red, his eyes held a look so foreign to him I didn't recognize it immediately.

He was afraid.

I had him.

He launched another series of attacks and forced me backward. I dodged and leapt away until he drove his blade toward my foot. At the last moment I jumped away, but I lost my footing when I landed, stumbled, and fell. One second I felt the elation of victory, the next I was lying in the dirt.

The king lifted his blade for the kill strike.

Before he could react, I clutched the flat edge of my sword close to my chest and rolled away. I jumped to my feet and pointed my weapon back at him.

We stood motionless, facing each other, trying to determine one another's weaknesses.

I tried to play on his fear. "I've already won. If you could not kill me before, what makes you think you can now? And even if you did, what makes you believe you could stop the truth? The people have already heard it. Who do you think they believe: the king who sent them to war and executed their people, or the one protected by the Giver of Life himself?" I raised my voice, letting my words echo around us.

"Whether I live or die, I have already won."

"What do you want me to do? Surrender here before you, so you can publicly execute me and claim the throne?" The king swept a hand toward the Royal Guard. "My men still outnumber yours."

"I am not here for the throne—that belongs to neither you nor me."

He sneered. "Do you think your cousin is man enough to steal the throne from me? He never wanted it anyway."

He lunged, driving his sword straight at my heart.

I blocked and used my momentum to shove his sword downward. It grazed my leg and I stumbled backward. The king took advantage of the moment and swung again and again, his onslaught intensifying until I was only capable of defense and retreat.

My arms shook and my breath came in ragged gasps. Despite the strength the Life-Giver had lent me, I was too weary for a long fight, and my father was stronger and more experienced than I. My footwork grew sloppy and the blade felt too heavy in my hand. Sweat stung my eyes and my movements became more and more sluggish; I was losing my speed and agility, my advantages.

The king swung high, toward my throat, and I realized he was too fast for me. I would not be able to block in time; I—

His blade struck steel.

"Back away from the princess," Jennah snarled, her sword holding Zarev's at bay. Her skin shone in the sunlight, the white scar tracing her face making her look even fiercer.

Gare, Benor, and Layk gathered at my sides with Jennah, pointing their swords toward the king with me. But Narek and his guards were equally fast, gathering about the king and raising their blades against my band of rebels.

"What chance does a ragged group of rebels have against a king that controls armies?" my father spat. "An alliance with the princess ends in death."

"Everyone witnessed how the Giver of Life saved her. What makes you think you could kill her again?" Gare demanded.

The light in the king's eyes flared. "She still bleeds." His eyes darted toward Narek. "Kill them all."

I braced myself as the Royal Guard surged forward, expertly positioning themselves to create a barrier around their sovereign even as they moved in offense. Steel clanged as the rebels leapt forward to meet the guards' attack and defend me. They created their own wall, shoving me behind them so that I was hemmed in, trapped and only able to watch the fight unfold.

No, let me fight! I sprang toward a guard just as Layk cut the man down with one swift stroke. "Back down!" he yelled. "We need you alive."

I opened my mouth to protest, but the words died on my lips when I caught sight of Narek at the king's side. Narek's eyes bored into mine, his mouth a hard line while he stood barring the way to the king. Gritting my teeth, I grasped my sword hilt tighter and resolve hardened my heart.

Casting Layk's order aside, I charged forward, dashing around Layk and Jennah, who were locked in battle with three guards, and ducking to avoid the swinging blade of a fourth. Arrows darted through the air, but I didn't stop, didn't hesitate.

Another guard drove his blade in a sweeping arc toward my neck and I almost didn't have time to react. I dove forward, dropping my sword and somersaulting on the ground. Panting, I leapt back to my feet and stumbled toward my sword.

When I grasped its hilt, I paused long enough to assess the battle waging around me. Cries filled the air as the king's men and rebels fell around me, staining the dirt red and leaving bodies for the living to fight around, trip over, and collapse upon. I lifted my eyes toward the king, still surrounded by his men and shouting orders, and then landed on his captain. He wasn't charging into the fray, but standing guard before the king, blocking the rebels' path to him.

My mind flitted back to a cold night years ago when my life had turned upside down. Because of my father, and because of Narek. I still had strength left in me for this. I could do it.

But I only made it two more steps before my pace faltered.

Narek spun away from me, turning from the battle to face my father. The king opened his mouth to speak, but Narek was already moving, his blade flashing through the air, plunging into the king's chest. He drove it deep, burying it to the hilt. Blood leaked from the wound, staining the king's silver tunic, spilling onto Narek's hand. The king's eyes went wide and his face turned pale as the snow at his feet. Every wrinkle stood out starkly on his forehead while the light in his eyes turned cold.

Narek leaned forward, dipping his head close to my father's ear to deliver a message lost in the clamor around us. Then he ripped his sword from Zarev's chest, letting the blood splatter across his own breastplate and taint Vehgar's silver stars.

As the king crumpled to his knees, his glassy eyes found mine. I stared back, and I found there was no triumph, anger, or relief in my heart: I felt nothing. Blood bubbled from Zarev's mouth and dribbled down his lips—and then he collapsed, a crumpled form surrounded by his own men.

Wiping the king's blood from his cheek, Narek turned to his Royal Guard. "The king is dead!" he shouted, raising his sword over his head. "King Zarev is dead!"

The fighting faltered as guards, rebels, and citizens alike stared at the king's corpse, letting the meaning of Narek's words wash over them. Some of the guards charged forward, raising their weapons at Narek, who fended them off with easy strikes, but most, loyal to their captain, rallied to defend him.

The rebels and citizens looked dazed, uncertain whether to join the combat amongst the guards or raise their fists and rejoice. In moments, others took up Narek's cry, and deafening cheers erupted throughout the square and thundered in my chest until I felt as if the mere noise could knock me to the ground.

"King Zarev is dead! We are free!"

The words became a chant that inspired the people to riot. Citizens still gathered in the streets darted back into the square, rushed past us to the stand, and began to tear it down with their bare hands. Others, armed with whatever weapons they managed to lay their hands on, joined those already locked in battle and began to charge the guards. It was sheer chaos; a fevered push for revenge against a dead man.

As the king's loyal guards made a desperate attempt to push back the overwhelming flood of citizens, the rebels rejoined the fight to protect the mobs and overpower the king's men.

A guard slashed toward my neck and I lifted my sword to block him when Gare stepped in, stabbing the man in the back. "We need to retreat! We must empty the castle of Zarev's men and get you to safety," he said.

Drawing a deep breath, I nodded. He was right: I would do far more for my kingdom by keeping myself alive and undoing the king's damage than dying in battle now.

Nearby, Narek drove his sword into another guard and stepped forward. "I'll accompany you. I can ensure the guards know who you are."

Hesitant, I studied him. The look on his face, in his eyes, was unfathomable. His face and clothes were still stained with my father's blood; his sword dripped with it. He could slay me with as little hesitation—had already tried to do so. Suspicion squirmed inside my heart; one word from me and Gare could have his carcass sprawled at my feet. One motion from me and I could slay him myself, striking before he could anticipate my move and block it.

But he had killed the king.

Jennah darted to my side. "Gare and I have your back."

I glanced toward Narek, who stood motionless, waiting. "Very well," I said, letting him read my unspoken threat in my eyes: *One wrong move and you die.*

He nodded a silent assent and led the way from the main square. We raced through the streets, slamming into citizens as we went. Everywhere guards, rebels, and citizens were engaged in the fight while the people kept up the cries: "We are free! The king is dead!"

I darted straight into a burly man and toppled backward into the dirt.

"Watch where you're going, girl," he growled.

I blinked dazedly as Jennah offered me her hand. Staggering to my feet, I raised my head, letting the hair fall out of my face, and the man realized who I was. His eyes widened and he cleared his throat. "I—I'm sorry, princess," he choked out. He bowed his head and saluted.

"Come," Gare urged, tugging on Jennah's arm.

All around us, the people roared and swarmed like a pack of dogs on the hunt. Men and women alike charged the guards patrolling the streets. Most were too surprised to fight back, and the few who did were overwhelmed. Some fled while others fell beneath a flurry of fists and were trampled ruthlessly underfoot. Mothers cried out as they shielded their children from the rioting and scrambled to shepherd them toward the safety of nearby shops and inns.

Everywhere citizens and guards alike were falling, bleeding... Screams mingled with the shouts of victory. How many innocents would die today, even after the king was gone? I felt sick at the thought. There was so much bloodshed.

"Come!" Gare bellowed from his position ahead of us, beside Narek. Somehow in the madness he had grasped the reins of a passing horse. Its rider had fallen from the saddle or perished. "You and Jennah will ride! We will find another."

Before I could move forward to mount, he lifted me and threw me into the saddle and deposited Jennah behind me. I leaned forward, dropping the reins to sink my fingers into the horse's mane and slamming my legs into its sides.

Trotting through the streets was much like winding through a maze. Most of the people dove out of the way, but others were trapped by the crowds or oblivious to our approach, so I had to pick a wayward path to dodge them all. Mounted guards used their steeds to trample citizens and a few attempted to charge toward us, but Jennah's sword and the congested streets kept them at bay. Oncoming wagons and carriages stopped dead in their tracks at the sight of the rioting and fighting. Some turned around, while citizens spilled out of others and joined the fray, abandoning their wagons.

After a few minutes, though it felt like endless hours, the castle loomed ahead of us, stark black against a pale sky. My body was heavy with exhaustion, and I let my steed slow to a walk.

"Almost there," Jennah murmured in my ear.

I could not tell if she meant them as words of comfort or warning. Glancing over my shoulder, I saw Gare and Narek on mounts, riding close behind, so I nudged my horse forward.

We ascended the path up the cliff, halting at the top to peer into the castle grounds. They were eerily empty and quiet. We crept forward slowly, scanning for guards, for servants, for any sign of anyone at all. The gates to the main courtyard were still open, the doors to the castle heavily barred as usual and guarded by only two men.

Jennah held her sword out in front of her warily. "I don't like this."

As we neared the gateway, horse hooves thudded on the earth and Gare and Narek pulled up behind us.

"Who goes there?" one of the guards shouted, drawing a bow from his back and nocking at arrow to the string. One tug and his arrow would pierce my skull. I dared a glance at the other guard and saw he was aiming behind me, at one of the men.

"Narek, Captain of the Guard!" Narek shouted. "King Zarev is dead! Lower your arms and pay your respects to his daughter, Princess Halia!"

The men hesitated for one instant before they recognized their captain and lowered their weapons. Narek charged his horse ahead of us, its hooves pounding the courtyard cobblestones. The sound echoed loudly in my ears.

What game was Narek playing at?

"The king is dead!" he cried out, his voice bouncing off the high walls enclosing us. "Come pledge your allegiance to the princess!"

I waited breathlessly. Gare rode up beside me and we waited motionless on our steeds as Narek circled the courtyard, continuing his refrain.

Then the castle doors swung open. A row of guards poured through the doors and dropped their swords at my feet.

The guard at their head kneeled low before me, peering up with a steely expression. His posture spoke of humility, but his eyes held defiance and anger in their slanted gaze. Royalty or not, I was his king's enemy. My heart throbbed uneasily.

"Princess Halia. We surrender and offer you our arms," he said. He continued to hold my stare as he raised his fist to his chest in a salute. "In the wake of the death of King Zarev, your father, and in Prince Gillen's absence, we recognize you as our leader and pledge our allegiance...and plead for mercy from your hand."

He paused and there was a breathless silence. The men behind him stood solemnly holding their salutes and gazing at Narek, as if they were awaiting his next move rather than mine. Suspicion gnawed at my mind.

They were trapped with few options left but to surrender to me, but that did not mean I could trust any of them. Least of all Narek.

Narek turned his gaze toward me. There was a hint of a smile twisting his lips, a gleam in his onyx eyes. There was something happening here. Something wasn't right…

"I accept your surrender," I said, looking down to meet the man's gaze unflinchingly. I would not let him see my fear and doubt. "But as for your allegiance…or mercy…" I let the word drift on the breeze, waited for the men still standing to shift on their feet uncomfortably, for even Narek's stare to falter a little with uncertainty. "We will see."

I could feel Jennah's eyes boring into the back of my head, almost hear her asking, *What are you thinking?* As much as they outnumbered us, the men could lift their swords and cut us down in mere moments.

But they were loyal to their captain. Whatever Narek's intentions, he had an entire host of men at his call and he had not ordered them to kill me.

The guard's eyes narrowed. "Thank you," he said, though his expression said otherwise. He rose to his feet and joined the men behind him.

"Let us into the castle," I ordered.

The guards swung open the doors and we all entered together to find the servants collected in the entryway. They stared, unsure whether to be relieved or frightened, and bowed their heads, saluting and trembling.

I drew myself up to my full height and studied them all. "It is true that my father is dead. Gillen is the true king, but until he returns, you will be taking my orders." No one moved; every eye was fixed upon me. "Anyone still loyal to my father can leave now, no questions asked." Jennah gave me a sidelong glance. "All others can lock every one of these guards in the dungeons." I turned back toward Narek. "Except for him."

Narek's eyebrows lifted in the slightest display of surprise.

"For now," I snapped.

The servants scurried forward, dragging the guards away. If I had been in any other mood, I would have found the sight amusing: the muscled Royal Guard meekly submitted to even the smallest of the servants, unwilling to resist them and disobey their captain's orders.

I turned on the captain. "Where is my aunt?" I asked.

"Your father imprisoned her shortly after Gillen left."

My heart plummeted to my stomach. "Release her! Now!"

Without a word, the Captain of the Guard nodded and led the way. I dashed after Narek as he swept toward the prison with his long, easy strides. As we descended the steps and the familiar blackness enclosed about me once more, I heard footsteps trail after us. Narek paused to pull a torch, still burning, from the wall and hold it aloft to light our path, making the passageways flicker. He pulled a ring of keys off his belt and shuffled toward a nearby cell. Seeing the form huddled inside, I held my breath.

She leaned weakly against the far wall, lifting a hand to her face to shield her eyes from the torchlight.

"Lady Velaire," I said, watching hopefully as she stirred. "Aunt…Aunt Velaire?"

Narek stepped toward the door and unlocked it, swinging it open so I could stand in the entryway.

"Halia?" Her voice sounded hoarse. Slowly, she lowered her hand and blinked against the light. I watched as her dark blue eyes focused on me and widened in surprise. "How…?"

I rushed forward to embrace her, trying to ignore how frail and weak she felt in my arms. "I'm here. I've returned."

She gasped and her body sagged against me. Her eyes rolled back in her head and she went limp. My knees almost buckled under the weight. "H-help," I choked out, and Jennah and a servant girl were by my side in an instant.

"We will carry her to her chambers. She needs food and water—and rest. I'm sure she will be fine," Jennah reassured me.

As we exited the cell, I glared at Narek. "Now that my aunt is free, *this* will be your cell."

The male servant standing behind him took Narek's key ring and shoved him forward unceremoniously. Silent, the captain watched as the servant locked his cell.

With a flourish, I gave Narek a mock salute. "Thank you for your assistance."

He responded with a grin of his own, one I chose to ignore.

I turned back to the servants, already bearing my aunt away. "Take care of her!"

As I left the prison, another servant joined Jennah and me to escort me toward my own bedchambers, which looked much as they had years ago. As if they had sat untouched but for the diligent servants' cleaning efforts all this time. The sight was almost too eerie for me, but before I could protest a servant was pouring a hot bath in the washroom and another was putting fresh sheets on the bed. Jennah ushered me toward the bath.

"There is no time for this now," I said.

Jennah smiled. "Your aunt will be fine. The guards are in prison and the others will be here soon. The castle is secure."

"But…" I stammered.

"You were *dead!*" Jennah exclaimed.

The servants stopped their work and stared at us.

"Almost," I said feebly.

"You should not be alive. There is no explanation, but I won't pester you with questions now. You must rest, or you will be useless for the work ahead of you."

At Jennah's words, I felt my exhaustion rush over me. Every muscle ached and the weariness ran so deeply it felt like it had settled in my bones.

"Only for a moment," I murmured.

At my insistence, they left me alone to strip the ragged clothes from my body and scrub the filth and blood away. My emotions were a tangled mass I didn't dare study too closely, though I couldn't avoid the fresh waves of shock that poured over me each time I closed my eyes and saw my mother's lifeless form or my father spurting blood. A million concerns chased each other in my mind, wrestling for my attention. Were there enough rebels to overrun my father's loyalists? How many of my father's men would pledge allegiances to me I could not trust? Who *could* I trust with absolute certainty, even among the rebels? Ellok had been quick to betray us. How could I even begin to undo all of my father's wrongs? And what about Gillen…? I was sure that despite my exhaustion, I would not be able to sleep.

But when I pulled on the clean night shift laid out on my bed for me, curled up, and closed my eyes, I dozed.

I woke from a dream of riots and battles, blood and death. Shaking, I yanked my aching body from bed and crept to the window. The clouds had broken slightly, allowing for the smallest sliver of blue sky to peek through. Although it felt like ages could have passed in my dreams, the sun was high in the afternoon sky. Only a few hours had passed. The city was quiet, my room was empty, and the castle was still.

A knock sounded at my door, pulling me away from the window.

I tried to stand a little straighter to mask my weariness. "You may enter."

Jennah opened the door. Her eyes sparkled and her whole manner was light and free, as if she had just visited Evren Garden and couldn't wait to share her experience. I envied her. My entire body was like a weight dragging me down, and I was sure I would never feel light again.

"Kam and my daughters escaped to another rebel hideout." Her smile widened. "And Marke has returned safely; I found him there as well. I brought him here because he said he wanted to speak to you. He's waiting outside."

My heart leapt to my throat in a mixture of joy for Jennah, and then anticipation and fear for the news Marke brought. Did he have information about Rev and Lyanna? Kyrin…or Avrik?

Jennah waited as I hurriedly pulled on one of Velaire's dresses a servant must have hung in my wardrobe while I'd slept. Stepping back into my filthy boots, I followed Jennah through the halls and into the main courtyard. Marke stood beside the empty fountain, his face shrouded in the hood of his grey, fur-lined cloak. When he saw me, he saluted. "My lady."

"Do you have word from Evren?"

Marke nodded. "Lyanna and Rev were grieved at your disappearance.

As soon as Jennah told me you were here, I wanted to speak to you. But other than their concern for you, they are well. The sedwa have claimed no other victims."

I drew a deep breath, releasing some of the tension knotted inside.

"They also spread your news about Kyrin, and he was arrested. The people sentenced him to death."

My jaw clenched as I thought of Avrik and how he must have reacted. *And how is he?* I could not bring myself to ask Marke, was not sure I wanted to know.

"I brought you this," Marke said softly. Reaching into the inside pocket of his cloak, he drew out a paper, unwrapped it, and dropped something into my palm. I glanced down at the dried sprigs of lavender, tied together with twine in the way Lyanna always gathered and saved the flowers. I sighed. Still heavy with fragrance, it was a simple reminder of home. "Before I departed, Lyanna and Rev met with me, begging me that if I encountered you on my travels I would give you this and ensure you were safe." He hesitated. "I know you were also friends with Avrik. I asked him, before I left for the port at Kelwed, if he had anything to say to you, if I found you. He…" He shook his head. "I have no word from him."

Squeezing the lavender in my fist, I felt my anger and pain rise with renewed vigor. I knew Avrik was hurting, but this information felt like one last way he could spite me, as if he blamed me for his father's actions. Lavender buds dropped from my fist and spotted the snow. The last shreds of my hopes fell away with them: Avrik would not come to me, and he did not want me to go to him.

"I—I'm sorry, my lady," Marke stammered, clearly at a loss for words.

"It's not your fault." I closed my eyes for a moment, as if that could shut out the hurt.

Saluting, he turned back to his wife, who wasted no time in flinging her arms about his neck. "The Giver of Blessings heard my prayers," she murmured against his neck. "You are safe; the girls are safe. We are all safe."

Leaving Jennah and Marke to reconnect, I strode back toward the castle, walking the familiar hallways, listening to the overwhelming silence in the wake of the earlier tumult. Somewhere in the castle, the servants had laid my mother's body to rest; in other quarters, Gillen's chambers sat empty and still, awaiting his return; in the dungeons below, dozens of members of the Royal Guard paced their cells in anticipation of their sentences, but I did not want to think about that now. I stopped before the door to my aunt's chambers and knocked gently, receiving no answer. Slowly, I pushed the door open and found my aunt lying in bed.

I blinked back tears as I studied her, looking so small it seemed that her bed could swallow her. The wrinkles at the corners of her eyes told stories of past laughter, but the dark circles beneath them betrayed her present pain. Her auburn hair, tangled and dull with dirt, tumbled wildly about her face. Never in my life had I seen my beautiful and graceful aunt look so ragged. How long had she been in prison? I was afraid to guess.

At my approach, Velaire stirred. I stopped beside her bed and we gazed at one another for several silent moments. It seemed too wonderful to be together again; too awful to be reunited under such circumstances.

"I can hardly believe you are alive. You've grown so much…and you look like Ryn…"

I swallowed, pain and bitterness surging in my heart all at once.

She sat up and grasped my hand. "He sent Gillen away." Her voice cracked and her lips trembled. "I tried to stop him… He's destroyed…everything."

"He's dead," I whispered. "It's over. You are free, and we can end this war. He cannot hurt us anymore."

Velaire sighed with relief. "Gillen can come home?"

"Gillen can come home."

I climbed into bed beside her and lay my head on her shoulder. She cried, her shoulder shaking beneath me, and I embraced her. The recovery—for the city, for us—would be slow and painful. But with my aunt beside me, I could feel relief and comfort settle in my heart. Lyanna and Rev were far from danger. Velaire was safe and my cousin could come home from the battlefront.

I'd never known that I could feel this broken and whole at once.

When I sank back into my own bed that night, the vision came to me without warning, enveloping me as vividly as if I had left the castle and the city far behind.

Snowflakes swirled around the figure, blanketing the Evren countryside with a fresh powder that covered the old, dirty snow. Overhead the velvet sky was masked with grey clouds that kept all but a few dim stars hidden.

The form was treading its way along the path into town, a solitary traveler in a cold, black night. When the person entered town and passed by the windows of Wanderer's Rest, the light pooling into the street made the figure's face clear and I recognized Avrik. His breath misted around him while he shivered and rubbed his hands up and down his arms to warm himself. For one instant he stared longingly through the windows, and then he turned back toward the night.

When he drew up before the old stone building that enclosed Evren's dungeons, my heart ached. An Evren guard, his hood drawn closely about his face against the cold, lifted a lantern to peer into Avrik's face. Avrik's hair stuck up at every angle and dark circles traced his eyes. Pale and solemn, he looked worn and hollowed-out, as if all the light had been stolen from him.

"What do you want?" the man demanded gruffly.

"To see the prisoner." Avrik's voice was raspy.

The guard stared at him for a moment before turning to unlock the heavily barred door and shove it open. It creaked on its hinges and pushed inward to reveal a dim interior flickering with a single torch. Snow drifted in with Avrik. There were two barred doors on the left and two on the right, but the footsteps echoing along the stones came from the first door on the left.

Avrik approached the door and peered in through the grate to see Kyrin.

"Son," Kyrin said, his voice almost a whisper. His hair was as disheveled as his son's and his countenance looked paler than I had ever seen it. A smile spread across his face as he studied his son.

Avrik's expression remained solemn while his eyes bored into his father's. "Tell me you didn't do it." His voice sounded low, bitter. "Tell me Elena is a liar." My name had never been so rough on his tongue, as if it hurt to speak it. "Tell me how the people's rumors about you are founded in falsehood, because they don't like us."

Kyrin dropped his smile to match Avrik's stern face. "I didn't do it."

Avrik cringed like his father had struck him. "You lie. I can see it in your eyes."

"I told you what you wanted me to say. You know I only want you to be happy, safe..." He reached toward the bars, but Avrik pulled back. "The king's royal guard met with me, after we heard news of the war with Alrenor."

Avrik's hands clenched into fists at the reminder.

"He offered me a mission in the king's name. For every beast I slew, for every set of fangs I brought to Misroth City for the king, I would receive a greater sum of money than I could make from anything else I've ever sold. But far more importantly, I could guarantee that you would never be called to war. Your life would never be in danger."

"But I was in danger. You endangered countless lives," Avrik whispered. If possible, his face looked even whiter. "The people of Evren could have been hunted and killed, and I *was* attacked. My *friends* were attacked."

Kyrin shook his head. "I was there in the woods to find you and ensure you were safe. Everything I did was for you, to provide for you and build you a better life than a soldier's life or a pathetic existence in this miserable town. I've earned the king's favor, ensured you will never be sent to Argelon or Alrenor, and amassed a small fortune. We can leave Evren behind for a new life, a better one..."

Avrik clenched his jaw, but his voice quavered. "The people have sentenced you to death."

Kyrin's face was dark. "If only your friend Elena hadn't kept so many secrets of her own."

"She's gone, and I'm glad to be rid of her," Avrik snapped.

Kyrin didn't seem surprised at the anger in Avrik's tone. "We could send word to the capital to inform the king of my imprisonment. There is still hope for us." He stared at his son and stepped even closer to the bars, trying to cross the distance between them. "And if not for me, then for you. There is more for you than this."

Avrik's eyes looked almost black in the dungeons. "I didn't want more. I wanted a father."

His face set as hard as stone, he walked out into the night.

Though the vision had left me exhausted and aching hours earlier, I was still wide awake. The sound of the waves crashing outside my window could no longer lull me to sleep as it had when I was a child. Curled in bed, I listened to the wind and sea and imagined the storm brewing beyond my drawn curtains. Once, my mother would have soothed my childhood fears with her soft singing voice; my cousin Gillen would have stayed up late into the night with me, telling me stories almost as good as his father's or pretending we were on a quest together as we stole about the castle.

No one would come to comfort me tonight. Now only phantoms visited, memories of people and times that brought more pain than comfort. My mother was dead and my cousin was risking his life in a needless war. All of the servants I'd grown up with had been released from service or killed under my father's reign, and my aunt was still frail and sick.

My head ached. I rolled over in bed and sought the sprigs of lavender lying on my nightstand. I held them under my nose and inhaled their comforting scent. If I closed my eyes and tried to shut out the sound of the sea, I could picture myself back home, with Rev snoring softly in the next room and Lyanna rising before dawn to start a fire and prepare breakfast. Sometimes she'd rouse me to help; other times she would let me sleep to recover from an evening of sword practice with Avrik, even if she thought our fun was frivolous.

Avrik. His name pierced me like an arrow. I could still see his pale face in my mind's eye, and my heart filled with pain and fury all at once. Perhaps I could hurt for him and even forgive him, understanding what it was like to lose parents to deceit, but that did not remove the sting of his betrayal. It didn't change the fact that he had chosen to be angry with me, to leave me because I had shared the truth.

With a sigh, I slipped out of bed. I fumbled for the candlestick and matches on my nightstand and slipped into a robe. Leaving my bedchamber, I tiptoed through the halls and past dozens of silent, empty rooms until I stood before the dungeon entrance at last. Drawing a deep breath, I yanked open the door and descended the stone steps, letting the darkness swallow me whole.

When I opened the second door, my candle sent shadows skittering along the corridors. Most of the cells were quiet, but as I passed others, I could hear their occupants moving about and occasionally muttering words I did not hear. At last I halted before a cell and peered through the grate at the top of the door.

Inside, Narek slouched against the far wall, his hood pulled low over his face. When my light flickered within his cell, he stirred and stared at me.

"I need to know why you killed my father, and I need information about Gillen," I demanded.

Slowly, Narek stood to his full height and approached the door. He eyed my robe. "Princess Halia cannot sleep? What sorts of nightmares haunt the new ruler of Misroth?"

I clenched my fists. "Gillen is the rightful king."

"But Gillen isn't here." Though I couldn't see all of Narek's face, I could see the curve of his lips as he smiled. "Have you come to interrogate me personally, my lady? I am honored." He saluted.

Anger bit at my heart. "Enough nonsense!" I slammed my palm against the door, rattling it in its frame and ignoring the pain that shot through my hand. "I am not here to play at my father's games. Or yours."

Narek pushed back his hood and cocked an eyebrow at me. The light reflected in his black eyes like stars on a moonless night. "How brave the little girl has grown." There was no gentleness in his expression. I wanted to snap back, to remind him he was still a youth himself, but I held my tongue. "Ask me your questions, but know I was not privy to all of your beloved father's secrets."

"Then why did you kill him? Why change your allegiance now, after trying to kill me?"

Narek crossed his arms and studied me thoughtfully. "Your father and I had an agreement. He chose not to honor it."

I leaned forward until my cheeks brushed against the steel bars. "What agreement?"

"I told you to ask your questions; I didn't tell you I would answer them all."

Stepping back, I sucked in a deep breath and forced my impatience to melt away. "Then I won't ask questions anymore. Tell me where in Alrenor Gillen's regiment is located."

To my surprise, Narek threw back his head and chuckled. "So you do have your father's strength! Admirable. But you speak as if you know the forbidden lands beyond Misroth, my lady."

I frowned. "I studied their geography for years. I know—"

"That is not what I mean. There are dangers that lurk there—things that even your nightmares cannot conjure up." Narek ran a hand along his chin, where stubble had sprouted. "But that is for another time, I suppose. You want to know where Gillen is? You ask all the wrong questions."

I swallowed back my anger and frustration. "Then what are the right ones?" I asked through gritted teeth.

Narek's face grew solemn. "Halia, I confess you have proven yourself. You're not the cowering, obedient girl your father made you out to be, not anymore. You escaped your first execution, evaded my forces, survived your second execution, and overthrew a throne in a day. In my world, that means you are worthy of respect, and I reward those I respect with honesty."

I drew a deep breath, trying to maintain my patience. "Then tell me about Gillen and the war."

Narek smiled slowly. "There is no war."

"What? If you're lying to me—"

"The war was contrived with false evidence your father planted. He blackmailed and bought men to sell the lie or plant false evidence on poor wretches he framed and executed as Alrenian spies. Your father sought any reason to dissolve the King's Council and exert more power over the people, to encourage them to depend on him. Then your cousin came of age and your father did not want to yield the throne, yet didn't want to risk arousing suspicion by killing another member of the royal family. He told Gillen that Alrenor was hostile and sent him away to Toryn on a diplomatic mission to build an alliance. Zarev then announced we were at war, using fabricated evidence to convince the council and the people, and explained that Gillen had already led a regiment into Alrenor. He knew the boy would never return from the dangers awaiting him outside our kingdom. It's doubtful he is still alive. Your cousin was sent to his execution months ago."

My head pounded. "No," I said. "He would survive."

"Where do you think the sedwa of Evren came from? They exist nowhere in Misroth, save for in a town bordered by the mountains that cross into Toryn. And the sedwa are not the worst nightmare that stalks the lands outside of Misroth." Something dark lurked in his eyes, like the shadow of a memory passing through his mind. "Toryn is overrun with enemies that thrive on carnage and death, that exist only to torment and destroy."

I saw Gillen in my vision again, sprawled in the grass as he attempted to hide in the shadows from an unseen enemy. Except this time, the vision was different: blood soaked the ground around him and pooled in the swamp, and he was alone.

The dark look hadn't quite faded from his eyes, but Narek smiled anyway, his expression patronizing as he saluted. "You are the last surviving blood member of the royal family, my dear. Perhaps not yet of age, not yet crowned, but such trifles of the law hardly matter now. You are Queen of Misroth."

"No! Gillen is alive, and I'll save him." I backed away, desperate to leave this prison and find fresh air.

Narek laughed. "I'd like to see you try."

The shadows danced tauntingly around us; my pulse pounded everywhere, like war drums closing in.

I turned to the captain sharply. "Then that is what you will do. If you know so much about Toryn and where Gillen is, then you will lead me to him."

Spinning on my heel, I stormed from the prison, but its shadows followed me all the way back to my chambers.

TO BE CONTINUED

Thank you for reading *Silent Kingdom*! If you have a moment, please leave an honest review on Amazon.

ACKNOWLEDGMENTS

The list of people I could thank is countless, and I fear I'll leave someone out.

Two of the people I want to thank the most will never read these words, but I like to think they know of and share in my accomplishments in other ways. Thanks, Mom and Dad, for always being two of my biggest cheerleaders, encouraging me to follow my dreams and believing in me. You introduced me to some of my favorite literature and to the power of the written word, and I fell in love forever. Your love, light, strength, and inspiration continue to keep the path before me lit, and I can only pray everything good in you will somehow live on in my brothers and me. May I be worthy of the torch you passed on to me.

Thank you to Sheree Whitelock, my amazing bookworm/English major friend who has been by my side—figuratively, at least—throughout this long, occasionally grueling, and most definitely tedious process. Good thing we are both defiant, obstinate, and a tad obnoxious. ;) You've made this book so much better with your feedback, and helped me believe in myself when I encountered self-doubt. Thank you for helping make my dream a reality.

A huge shout out and thank you also goes to YA author David Estes (Web: www.davidestesbooks.com, Facebook: David Estes, Twitter and Instagram: @davidestesbooks), who offered invaluable help, suggestions, advice, encouragement, etc., by essentially mentoring and coaching me through the revision and publishing preparation process. Just because he wanted to! Thank you SO much for being there and believing in me.

Thanks to my friends Julienne Calhoun, Gretchen Fogle, and Chelsea Foos for their feedback and support. Lara Ferari also deserves a shout-out for all of her encouragement and her extremely helpful insight; I am incredibly grateful for your help and for reminding so many to reach for their dreams with courage and strength each day.

My beta reading team also deserves a huge round of applause: Jenny

Dickerson, Kimberly Fisher, Kayli Hinckley, Seliah Jimenez, Mary Parianos, Asma Qaiyum, Vanessa Stock, and Annie Vaughan. You offered loads of helpful feedback, which contributed significantly to the final version of this book, and for that I am immeasurably grateful.

Thank You to the One who gave me my ability to write and my passion for all things books, the Author of new beginnings. Thank You for opportunities to rebuild and restore; to share our voices and be heard; to experience life and renewal even in a world full of death and difficulty.

Finally, thank you to anyone who has picked up this book. I can't thank you enough for that!

ABOUT THE AUTHOR

Rachel L. Schade was born on the first day of summer in a small town in Michigan. She attended The Ohio State University to learn how to write obnoxiously long papers, cite people who use big words, and discuss her passion: books. She has a great love for the color blue, sunshine, chocolate, and not folding her laundry. Currently she lives with her husband and fur babies, and surrounds herself with books and coffee on a regular basis.

You can email Rachel at rachelschade@gmail.com, or find her on Facebook and Goodreads: Rachel L. Schade, and on Instagram and TikTok: @rachelschadeauthor.

www.rachelschadeauthor.com

9 781736 485682